# ANGEL
# IN CHAINS

# ANGEL IN CHAINS

## CYNTHIA EDEN

KENSINGTON PUBLISHING CORP.
www.kensingtonbooks.com

BRAVA BOOKS are published by

Kensington Publishing Corp.
119 West 40th Street
New York, NY 10018

All Kensington titles, imprints, and distributed lines are available at special quantity discounts for bulk purchases for sales promotions, premiums, fund-raising, educational, or institutional use.

Special book excerpts or customized printings can also be created to fit specific needs. For details, write or phone the office of the Kensington special sales manager: Kensington Publishing Corp., 119 West 40th Street, New York, NY 10018, attn: Special Sales Department; phone: 1-800-221-2647.

Brava and the B logo are Reg. U.S. Pat. & TM Off.

ISBN-13: 978-0-7582-6763-4
ISBN-10: 0-7582-6763-0

First Kensington Trade Paperback Printing: December 2012

10 9 8 7 6 5 4 3 2 1

Printed in the United States of America

*Thank you so much to all my fantastic readers!*
*Thank you for the support that you have given to*
*my Fallen series.*
*And I hope you enjoy Az's story!*

# CHAPTER ONE

Living in hell sucked.

Azrael, once the most powerful Angel of Death to grace the golden floors of heaven, hunched his shoulders against the sharp wind that blew off the Mississippi River and funneled into the twisting streets of New Orleans.

He'd fallen six months ago—fallen and *burned*—and he still hadn't gotten used to the stench that could fill the alleyways. Especially during Mardi Gras.

Why did humans worry so about dying and facing the devil in hell? This mortal realm was hell to him. With the voices, always crying out, the bodies, always too much, the sins—

*Everywhere.* No matter how hard he tried, there was no escape from the mortal sins that surrounded him.

More than enough sin to tempt an angel whose wings had burned away when he fell.

*"Help me!"*

The scream broke through the night, close, and Az's head whipped to the left. Over the odor of rotten garbage, stale cigarettes and old booze, he caught the scent of . . . fear.

And animal. Not just one beast, either.

*"Stay away from me!"* The voice again, a woman's, and now he could hear the fear mixing with rage in her screamed words.

Even as hard, biting laughter floated to his ears, Az found himself heading toward the mouth of another alley. Heading toward the sound of her screams.

As he rounded the tight corner, Az saw the men first. Three of them. Big, hulking guys who'd closed in on their prey. Az couldn't even see the woman, but he knew she had to be in the middle of the half-circle of men. A brick wall waited behind them, trapping her. There was no place for her to flee.

Az entered the alley and waited.

The cold whisper of Death hadn't come to this place. Not yet. If it had, Az would have felt the presence of another Death Angel. He always could sense his own kind, even if he wasn't ruling the cold bastards anymore.

But Death wasn't there. So the woman wasn't about to die, at least not yet.

Just then, the woman shoved through her attackers, and he saw her face. Wide, desperate green eyes, pale skin, dark red lips and—

"*Help me!*" She yelled the words at him.

Az didn't move. For thousands of years, his job had been to watch those who were dying. To wait until the last moment—and only then had he been allowed to touch. As a Death Angel, his touch killed. It took the soul straight from the body, and he carried that precious burden to the realm that waited beyond this world.

His job . . .

*No longer.*

He'd watched innocents die. Seen them slaughtered in times of war and peace. Seen murderers walk the earth, killing over and over, and he—

"*Asshole,* help me!" She snarled at Az, and he blinked. "Don't just *stand* there staring," the woman snapped. "Help—"

A guy with black hair and a leather jacket grabbed her

around the stomach and hauled her back against him. "He knows better than to go gettin' involved, Jade." A heavy drawl coated his words. "Knows that if he tries playin' white knight . . ." The guy looked up with a crooked grin that flashed too-sharp teeth, "he'll get himself killed."

That was when Az noticed the claws that had risen to wrap around the woman's throat. Not normal human fingernails. Instead, two-inch long, razor sharp claws sprang from the man's hand.

So not just regular mortal jerks. "Shifters," Az muttered as he rolled his shoulders. Interesting. Perhaps the night had just picked up for him.

All three guys were sporting claws and toothy grins. But the woman—no, no sign of claws or fangs from her, and she smelled . . .

Like strawberries.

He frowned. He'd recently developed a taste for the sweet fruit, and even ten feet away, he could catch the female's heady fragrance.

His body tensed.

"Back away!" Another man snarled. This one had a dark, tribal tattoo that snaked up his arm and the side of his neck. "Back away or start bleeding."

Az didn't back away. He kept his hands at his sides. Finally, a challenge. And here he'd been bored for days. "Let the woman go." His voice rang out, calm but strong.

The tattooed shifter laughed, then he charged right at Az. Az held onto his control—*careful, careful*—and when the shifter swiped out with his claws, Az tossed a ball of fire right at the fool.

The jerk howled in pain and dropped to the ground, rolling as he tried to put out the flames.

Fried shifter.

The woman stared at Az with eyes gone even wider as her lips parted in stunned surprise. He almost smiled. Poor little human. The humans never realized just how dangerous their mortal world was.

They truly were lambs out walking blindly with wolves. Or shifters.

"Duncan, *fuck!*" The shifter still holding the woman stared in shock at his burning friend and then glared at Az. "You just asked for death."

Az didn't stop his smile from spreading this time. "No, you did."

The shifter threw the woman against the nearby wall, and Az heard the sickening thud as her head hit the bricks. Then the leader and his backup dog both charged at Az. Az thought about playing with more fire, but he opted to get his hands dirty this time. He punched out, striking so fast he knew the shifters wouldn't even be able to see the movements of his hands and body, and in seconds, they were on the ground, bleeding and broken.

He dusted off his hands. Hmmm . . . He hadn't even gotten blood on his knuckles. Perhaps he was getting better at this business of physical fighting.

When he was sure they weren't about to rise, he stepped over their prone bodies and stalked toward the woman.

He hadn't just watched this time. The knowledge sank into him as he approached her. An innocent hadn't died while he looked on. Az reached for her. A faint line of blood trickled from the corner of her mouth. Gently, because he could show gentleness, he wiped the blood away and gazed down at her.

Humans were too weak. They could be broken and killed far too easily. He knew. He'd killed thousands of them in his time.

He lifted her into his arms and her head rolled back against his shoulder. The scent of strawberries was stronger, and a strange ache burned in his chest even as a rough tightness filled his body.

Her lashes cast dark shadows on her cheeks, and the flickering glow of a streetlight fell through the alley and hit the black curtain of her hair.

Holding her carefully, he turned toward the alley's entrance. Police sirens screamed in the distance, and, though it was already nearing dawn, he could still hear the drunken laughter that floated on the breeze.

During Mardi Gras, no one ever slept in this city.

"D-dumb . . . bastard . . ." It was the shifter who'd held the woman moments before. He spat blood on the ground and tried to rise. Failed. Since Az had broken both of his legs, the guy would need to shift in order to heal. Az figured he had a few more moments before the man had enough strength to shift.

Before any of them did.

And he and his human would be long gone by then. Tightening his arms around her, he stepped over the broken bodies once more and ignored the growled curses that filled the air.

As he left the alley, he tossed one last stare back at the shifters. "Come after me, and you'll only find death." He felt it was only fair to warn them. If they chose to ignore his helpful warning . . .

Then they could meet death.

The rage in their already glowing eyes had another smile lifting his lips. *You'll come for me.* So be it. He turned and stalked into the waning night with his human.

She was soft in his arms, a lightweight. Did she know how lucky she'd been? Probably not. In his experience, most humans were completely oblivious to the dangers that surrounded them.

The majority of humans roaming the earth didn't even know about the existence of the *Other,* all of the paranormal creatures that often walked right beside mortals. Demons, vampires, djinn—all of the so-called monsters were real.

Humans just didn't realize that fact.

The woman he held was a human who'd survived a pack shifter attack. He figured the odds of that survival were usually about a million to one.

Of course, those odds changed considerably when a Fallen became involved.

Few creatures on this earth were stronger than he was.

He snaked through the streets, turning left, right, and no one he passed so much as blinked in surprise at the sight of an unconscious, bloody woman in his arms.

*Mardi Gras.*

He'd just reached the steps of his apartment in the Quarter when an animal's roar reached him. The loud, ferocious cry of a big cat.

Az stilled. The men had shifted faster than he expected.

He hurried inside his apartment and kicked the door closed behind him. Then he carried her to the couch. The woman's eyes were still closed when he placed her on the cushions and a faint moan slipped from her lips as he eased her out of his arms.

Az stepped back and stared down at her. Pretty, he supposed. She had delicate, almost innocent features that were belied by the plump fullness of her mouth. His gaze tracked down her body. Humans were obsessed with sex. He'd always known that, so he supposed human males would be pleased with the woman's curving body and long, long legs. He was—

*Pleased as well.*

Az blinked. What the—

Her eyes opened. *No innocence.* Big, dark green and so deep Az took one look into her eyes and thought of tangled sheets, naked flesh, and the pleasures that humans took in the dark.

*I want pleasure.*

Her brow furrowed as she stared up at him. Then he saw

understanding come flooding back to her in an instant. She jumped up and let out an ear-splitting shriek.

When she went to run by him, Az just stepped out of her way. If she wanted to race right back to the pack . . . "It will just be your funeral," he said, shrugging. He'd done his good deed for the century.

His bored tone stopped her. She glanced back over her shoulder at him and blinked.

"They're probably hunting you now." He walked away from her and headed toward the window that looked out over the street. "Hunting *us*," he added quietly and realized he was anticipating the fight. When had he come to crave the fury? When had the bloodlust grown so within him?

She stood as still as a statue before his door. Her hand was up, hovering above the doorknob, and he could almost feel the fear rolling off her in waves.

But then she took a deep breath, and he saw her small shoulders straighten. She shoved back the heavy tangle of her hair and turned to face him. "How did you get us away from them?"

Az shrugged once more.

She took a step toward him. "You . . . you know what they are, right?"

Amusement flared in him. "I did notice the claws." Rather hard to miss those.

She blinked, and her eyes narrowed as she studied him. He'd never seen quite that shade of green before. She crept closer, bringing that light scent of strawberries to him. When she stopped, she was less than a foot away from him. It would be so easy to touch her.

Though he knew well just how dangerous a touch could be.

Yet she stood close enough to kiss. But angels weren't supposed to kiss mortals . . .

*You're not an angel anymore.* The whisper came from deep

inside of him. The same tempting whisper that he'd been fighting since his fall.

*You're not an angel. Do what you want.*

*You're not an angel. Take what you want.*

He was discovering that he could want many things.

The top of the woman's head barely reached his shoulders. She tilted her head and stared up at him. Then her gaze swept down his body.

Az stiffened even before she whispered, "What *are* you?"

Rather insulting question. "I'm the man who saved your life." Did she need to know more? He didn't think so.

Her hand lifted and pressed against her mouth. A small trace of blood still rested near her lips. "There were three of them, and, you're big and all, but there's still just one of you."

She might just be one of the most ungrateful humans he'd ever encountered. Stifling a sigh, Az inclined his head. "You're welcome."

She stared in surprise for a moment. Then she laughed. A soft, strangely lyrical sound spilled from her lips, and her wide smile lit up her face.

*Not just pretty.*

Az tensed as the wave of need hit him. Not lust for blood or death. This time . . . the lust was just for her.

*You're not an angel anymore. Take what you want.*

"Yeah," she said, as her laughter faded but the smile still lingered on her lips, "thanks for saving my ass." Then she held out her hand to him. "My name's Jade. Jade Pierce."

He stared at her hand. She wiggled her fingers at him. Slowly, Az lifted his own hand and caught those wiggling fingers. *Soft.* "I am Azrael." He dropped her hand. He hadn't used the name Azrael in centuries. "Most just call me Az."

"Well, Az, it's a pleasure to meet you." Her gaze slid over his body again. "But I'm gonna have to ask, once more, just what are—"

The door crashed in behind her. She didn't scream this time, but maybe Az just didn't give her a chance to scream.

Because as the three black panthers—fully shifted panthers—leapt into the room, jumping over the broken door, Az grabbed Jade and threw her toward the couch.

Then he ran right for the snarling beasts.

He should have known better than to let down his guard. Shifters and their damn acute senses. They'd caught his scent, her scent, and followed them right through the Quarter.

"I warned you," Az snapped and leapt at the nearest panther. He caught the beast's front paws and shoved the giant cat back. "You should have listened." There would be no more warnings now. Only death.

With a twist of his hands, Az broke both paws and tossed the cat back through the door.

*Ruined my door.* That panther had—

Claws dug into his back, driving deep into muscle and scraping bone. Hissing against the pain, Az snapped his teeth together and whirled around in a blur. He reached out as fury slammed through him and Jade's horrified yell rang in his ears.

*Attack. Destroy. Kill.*

He touched the panther, and the animal stiffened beneath his fingers. The beast's blazing gold eyes locked on him. Az's breath heaved as he demanded, "Ready for hell?"

The scent of flowers swept into the room, blowing in on the breeze from outside. It came right into his home and seemed to surround the shifter.

Az knew well what that scent meant. *An Angel of Death was close.* Despite what humans may have thought, Death didn't smell like rot. Death was sweet. The better to tempt and lead away the souls.

Az lifted his hand. The panther fell to the ground. The fur melted away, and he stared down at the tattooed body of the man who'd chosen to seek death. "I warned you."

A whimper had Az's head rising. The other panther crouched, and its head swung back and forth between Az and the body on the floor. Az lifted his hand, palm up, toward the beast. "Want to join him?"

The panther spun away and leapt through the window. Glass shattered, and Az bit back a snarl of his own. *Something else to fix, dammit.*

He rushed to the door. Both the surviving panthers were racing away. His brother Sammael would say they were hauling ass.

Finally. They'd realized they should fear him. And it had only taken the little matter of death to drive that point home.

"*Oh my God!*" The wild cry came from his elderly neighbor. He glanced over just in time to see Ms. Hattie McRae duck back inside her apartment. Great. A frantic call to the cops was probably being made.

Looked like he wouldn't be repairing the place after all. Time to clear out. Again.

Whenever humans found a dead body, they tended to ask endless and useless questions. When they asked those long and boring questions, he'd discovered the cops didn't like it when he told them to fuck off.

"You . . . killed him." Whispered from behind him.

Az straightened slowly. His back burned and his shirt stuck to the blood coating his flesh.

"How?" Jade asked. The floor creaked as she came closer to him.

His wounds would heal, but for the moment, the pain had his teeth grinding together. Now wasn't really the time for explanations. Not that he felt like offering any to her.

With a wave of the hand that had killed, he motioned toward the busted doorway. "Flee while you can." Another warning. Hopefully, she'd be smart enough to actually listen to him and get the hell out of there.

He'd do the same. Leave this place. Find another dwelling.

"Flee?" She repeated, voice rising a notch.

Sucking in a deep breath as he turned, Az nodded. "Yes, before the police arrive and find—" He gestured to the body. "Him." Because it didn't look like he'd killed a panther. No, now it looked like he'd just murdered a man. At the moment of death, shifters always returned to their human forms.

She knelt near the body. "There aren't any wounds on him."

No. He didn't have to wound in order to kill.

Jade fell back onto her butt and stared up at him. "How'd you do it?"

*With a touch.* That was what the Angel of Death did. He touched, and he killed, and the rest of the world feared.

That was his life. Or, it had been.

*Take anything you want.*

She licked her lips and the eyes that made him think too much of pleasure and human sins met his.

*Temptation.*

It was staring right at him. Sometimes, the most dangerous temptations were the ones that were right in front of you.

Then he saw the fear that slipped over her face. "*What* are you?" Of course, she'd ask that annoying question again.

It was the question he hated because the answer was—*an abomination.*

So Az didn't respond. He'd saved her. Warned her to flee. That meant he'd more than done his part. What happened next would be up to her.

He turned from her and slipped into the rising light of dawn. He blurred his body, moving quickly, and he knew that, to her, it would look as if he vanished.

If only he could.

But just disappearing from the world would be far too easy, and Az knew he wasn't meant for the easy path.

He was meant to suffer.

Her hero left her with a dead body. Jade stared down at the panther. "Austin, you jackass, I hope you're somewhere really, *really* hot." After the hell he'd put her through over the last few years, he deserved to burn.

The screech of sirens reached her ears. It figured the cops would be fast this one time, when she needed them to be slow. Jade jumped to her feet. *"Az!"*

She shoved through the broken door. The wood scraped her arm. Perfect. Of course she'd leave DNA evidence behind at a murder scene. But, hopefully, once they examined the body, the wise folks at the NOPD would realize they weren't dealing with a normal stiff, and they'd make this murder victim just . . . vanish.

*Other* deaths had a way of disappearing in the Big Easy. Mostly because there were so many *Other* hiding in the city. When supernaturals looked to blend in with the human population, they flocked to the big cities. It was easier for them to hide in plain sight there. Of course, in New Orleans, the city made for voodoo and magic . . . hiding in plain sight took on a whole new meaning for the paranormals.

She glanced to the left, then to the right. Where the hell was her savior? Big, blond, and way too gorgeous had vanished on her.

Freaking literally vanished. Come on, she did *not* need this right now. Her savior should have stayed put, and well, done more saving.

*You're not getting away from me that easily.*

Her gaze scanned the old cement sidewalk. Looking, looking . . .

*Blood drops.*

She locked onto those red drops and raced along the spattered trail. Austin had cut her hero too deeply. With that kind of wound, it was amazing that Az could walk at all. She'd been sure Austin had severed his spine—or come real close—but Az had acted like the wound had barely troubled him. An attack that brutal would have crippled her.

*Az had killed with a touch. He'd been super strong. And he had amazing endurance.*

Oh, yeah, he was the man she'd been dreaming of for years—the man who could finally help her.

*Not. Getting. Away.* When a girl had been waiting as long as she had for her hero to show up, she didn't let the guy fly away.

Police cruisers whipped by her. Jade hunched her shoulders and rushed forward even faster. The blood twisted down an alley. Great. Another alley that reeked of piss. Why couldn't just one ever smell like roses?

Her speed slowed way down as she entered the alley. Not rushing anymore, but more like creeping now as she carefully followed the blood trail. As far as she could tell, there was no way out of this dead-end alley. Red bricks stared back at her and her throbbing forehead reminded her that she'd already gotten up close and personal with the hard edge of bricks once and—

An arm snaked around her and hauled Jade up against a very big, very, *very* strong male body. There was no chance to scream—not that she'd been planning to scream—because a heavy hand covered her mouth.

"I told you to flee." *His* low, rumbling voice.

But then she'd known Az's touch instantly. There was no mistaking that deadly strength.

"You should have listened to me." His breath blew over her ear, and she felt the lightest touch of his lips against her lobe. Jade couldn't help it, she shivered. Her ear had always been a weak spot.

Besides, if Az wasn't the type of man to make a woman shiver, no one was. Tall, strong, with a face sculpted to perfection, the guy was walking, talking sex appeal. And danger.

Why, *why* did she always have to want the dangerous ones? She should have learned her lesson by now. Should have fallen for a quiet accountant somewhere.

But if she had, the quiet accountant would have ended up dead—*thanks to me.*

Better to stick to the ass-kicking type of man.

She opened her mouth to talk and realized, yep, his hand was still over her mouth. More sirens wailed in the distance. Jade tensed, hoping none of those cops felt the urge to search the area, or, oh, follow the trail of blood that led straight to them.

When Az eased his grip, she took a deep breath, and her tongue snaked out just a little and licked his palm.

Maybe that move hadn't exactly been accidental on her part.

*Seduce. Use. Betray.*

Some days, it was just her motto. If she'd been a good girl, she would have been dead long ago. Jade had learned that the bad girls lived longer.

Az sucked in a sharp breath at the sensual touch, and Jade felt the unmistakable response of his body behind her. Now that was interest—

He spun her around—spun *them* around—and pinned her against the bricks. He glared at her, those sky blue eyes of his so bright in the growing dawn. Too bright.

"You don't want to play with me." His voice probably would have frightened small children.

Good thing she wasn't a kid. And, um, who said she was playing? "Y-you saved me." He had. So impressive. "A-and you were hurt." She didn't even have to fake the tremble in her voice. Running from the cops often made her voice all trembly. It was that wild fear/adrenaline combo.

He glared down at her. "I heal fast."

*Wonderful.* Extra bonus for them. She licked her lips, and his gaze flickered down at the movement of her tongue. *Even better.* This morning—minus the mild concussion and near dismemberment—was rocking for her. "Yeah, well, while you're healing, you're also leaving a trail of blood all over town."

His brows pulled together as he tossed a glance at the blood that littered the ground near them.

"And cops are probably raiding your place right now," she continued, talking too fast. But they needed to *move.* "So why don't you let me take you someplace safe? You can finish healing, clean up the blood . . ."

His gaze searched hers. "You want to . . . help me?"

Not exactly. "Yes." She smiled at him. Jade hoped the smile looked innocent. She'd been told before that she could fake innocent pretty well. Okay, except for the eyes. Her eyes always screwed things up for her, so she carefully lowered her gaze. "You saved me. Now let me return the favor."

He didn't speak.

So she took his hand. Jade carefully laced her fingers with his. The guy's hand swallowed hers. His touch also made her heart beat way too fast.

"You shouldn't touch me." His words came out sounding gruff.

Now she forced herself to meet his eyes. "I'm not afraid of you. You saved me." If it hadn't been for him, she would have been on her way back to hell.

"You should fear me." He tried to pull his hand away.

She tightened her grip. "And you should learn to trust other people."

The wail of a siren drifted in the air. Jade tensed. The chitchat was fun, but . . . "We need to get out of here."

His bright gaze raked her once more. But, after the briefest of hesitations, he nodded.

*Yes.*

"I've got a car waiting," she told Az as she pulled him behind her. Good thing she'd stashed her ride close by, *before* the crazy shifter attack. She and Az could hop into the car and head out. Then he could just bleed in the vehicle and stop that dripping trail of blood. "In ten minutes, we'll be safe."

Well, as safe as they could be with one very angry pack of panther shifters after them.

Normally, panthers were a solitary breed. But if they got a strong alpha to lead them—a sick fuck who knew all about control—then they'd band together and make life hell for everyone else.

These particular panther shifters had been after her for years. Always hunting. Destroying everything and everyone in their path.

Some guys just had a real hard time letting go . . .

So you had to kill them in order for the message to sink in.

"Come on," she whispered. "Let's get the hell out of here."

Before another hunt began.

"Austin's dead."

Brandt Dupre glanced up at the announcement. The swamp waited behind him, bloody with the fire of the rising sun. He cocked a brow as he studied the panther shifter before him. Riley was practically vibrating with rage, probably because the blood and bruises on his body indicated the guy had just gotten his ass seriously kicked.

"Jade?" Brandt asked softly. Oh, but even after all these years, she could still surprise him. Taking out one of his most trusted panther assassins. He'd have to punish her for that, of course, but . . .

"It wasn't her." Riley spat on the ground. Blood dripped from his lips. "It was that big, blond bastard who—"

Brandt lunged at the shifter. His claws burst from his fingertips as he grabbed Riley by the throat. "A man was with Jade?" With *his* Jade?

Riley nodded as Brandt's claws sliced his throat. Riley didn't even flinch when the blood slid down his neck.

Rage burned in Brandt's body. Jade should have learned by now. She should *know* better.

This was their war. She didn't get to bring others into their battle. She sure as hell didn't get to *fuck* others.

How many dead bodies would he have to leave before she figured that fact out? Did she *want* him to keep killing those foolish enough to go to her aid?

She must.

He tossed Riley back a few feet. The shifter fell onto the dark earth. Brandt turned to face the swamp as he fought to control his temper. "He's dead." An order. And what the alpha wanted . . .

He got.

Why couldn't Jade understand that?

"He may not be so easy to kill."

Brandt stiffened at Riley's muttered words. Then he glanced over his shoulder.

Riley had risen to his feet. The shifter ignored his bleeding neck but brushed off his hands. "The guy's not human." Riley swallowed and his Adam's apple bobbed. "I'm not even sure what the fuck he is."

Interesting. "But you're sure that he was with my Jade?" *Mine.* She belonged to him, body and soul.

"Damn white knight." Riley's twisted sneer showed his growing canines. "The dude came rushing up out of nowhere, trying to *save* her."

His words calmed the beast inside of Brandt. If the stranger had rushed up and joined the fight, then the fool could have just been a good Samaritan. And perhaps the bastard wasn't fucking Jade.

But whoever he was, he'd still killed a shifter.

"Find him," Brandt ordered. "Bring him to me." He smiled. "Then I'll rip him open." He deserved his fun, and the panthers deserved their revenge.

After all, he'd rather liked Austin.

Perhaps he'd even let Jade watch while he slaughtered her knight.

Another death. More blood. When her knight died, maybe then she'd finally realize there was no escape.

She belonged to him. Forever.

# CHAPTER TWO

"You should strip."

Her big blond badass turned and frowned at her.

Jade offered him one of her innocent smiles. "Your clothes are soaked with blood. Give them to me, and I'll go wash them for you." Didn't that sound friendly? Helpful? "And you can, um, go shower." She waved her hand to indicate the small bathroom that waited just down the hallway.

Her temporary place—'cause, yeah, all of her places were temporary these days—wasn't much. A small apartment nestled on the edge of the Quarter. She was on the top floor and an abandoned antique shop waited below her.

She'd painted the walls. Covered them with murals of the city. She had a . . . thing about painting. It was the one talent she'd always had. Well, painting and killing. But the killing talent had come to her later in life.

So while the furniture in the place might look like shit, she thought the décor was pretty stellar.

Jade held out her hand. "Ahem. The clothes."

He turned to fully face her, and the guy showed no signs of being in the mood to strip. A real pity.

How was she supposed to seduce him if he was going to be so difficult? She barely smothered her sigh.

But then his hands reached for the bottom of his shirt. His

eyes were on her. She offered an encouraging smile. *Come on, big guy, take it all off for me.*

He yanked off the shirt. Tossed it to her with a casual wave of his hand.

She didn't let her jaw drop. But, wow, damn, Az was built. Talk about some extremely lickable abs.

"I'll . . . take care of this." She stepped closer to him and cleared her throat. "Now let me see your back. I want to make sure—"

But he stiffened.

She put her hand on his arm. Oh, he was nice and warm. "I know, you said you're a super healer. But just let me check those wounds out, okay?"

A muscle jerked in his jaw. "My back doesn't hurt."

Right. The tough guy didn't feel pain. "I need to see how badly you're injured." She stared up at him and waited.

His nostrils flared, just a bit. "Why do you," he inhaled again, "smell like . . . strawberries?"

Ah, okay. Not the question she'd expected. But maybe this was a good sign. He was showing actual interest in her. Or, at least, interest in her scent. "It's the soap I use." She inclined her head toward the bathroom. "Pretty soon you'll be smelling the same way."

His eyes narrowed. "I don't wish to smell like strawberries."

"Don't knock it." It was better than smelling like blood and a piss-filled alley. She shook her head and pushed him toward the bathroom. As he turned—*ha*, she got him—her gaze slipped over his back, and she couldn't control the gasp that broke from her lips.

"I told you I'd heal," he tossed back as he stepped into the bathroom.

And he was right. The deep gashes from the shifter's claws were gone. Blood stained his back, but the wounds were completely healed.

But it wasn't his super healing that had caused her gasp.

No, the shock had come from the sight of the angry, thick, and still very fresh scars that lined his upper back. Those scars perfectly traced the path of his shoulder blades. *Perfectly.*

He'd healed without so much as a scratch remaining from a shifter's attack on his spine. So what the hell had gotten hold of him and left those deep scars on Az's flesh?

He kicked off his boots. While she was trying to figure out what paranormal creature had cut him, Az ditched his jeans.

Of course, her gaze had to drop to his ass.

*Nice.* Actually, much, much better than nice.

Then he stepped into the shower and the rush of water filled the room.

Jade remembered to take a breath then. Okay, step one of her plan had just worked. She had the guy in her apartment. Actually, *naked* and in her apartment.

She grabbed his jeans and snuck out of the bathroom. Her hands dove into his pockets for a quick and dirty search. A search that proved totally useless. Dammit, no ID! Who went around New Orleans without so much as a wallet?

Az—Azrael. Did the guy only have one name? She needed more info from him. *About* him.

She shoved the clothes into the washing machine and hurried back toward the driving rush of running water in her bathroom. Steam filled the room, and she could see the hard outline of Az's body behind the thin shower curtain.

It had been a while since she'd had a lover. Actually, it had been seventeen months, fourteen days, and six hours. Not that she was counting.

Okay, so she was.

But she couldn't erase the memory of her last lover's screams from her head. No matter how hard she tried, Jade couldn't forget them. *My fault.*

The image of his death was burned in her memory, and she wouldn't be forgetting it, or him, anytime soon. Johnny had been another painful lesson for her. Most humans weren't strong enough to survive the battle that she found herself in. And falling for a human guy—one who couldn't fight the shifters coming for her—that was a plan sure to guarantee death.

Her gaze lingered on Az. He wasn't human, she knew that. But what was he? How strong would he really be? If she pushed him, if she got close to him, would he wind up the same way Johnny had? Bleeding? Broken? With her name on his lips?

*But he took out a shifter. Killed him with just a touch.*

She wanted to believe Az was strong enough to defeat anything or anyone that would come his way.

Only . . . *something had ripped his back apart.* He'd been attacked by a being so strong that he still bore the scars.

She reached for a towel. Placed it near the shower. Until she found out just who—*what*—Az was, she couldn't risk sleeping with him. She'd just have to go back to counting the days.

Seduction would have to wait.

She couldn't have another man's blood on her hands. Not again.

When Az stepped out of the shower, he half expected to find Jade waiting on him. Maybe he'd been *hoping* that she'd be there with her bedroom eyes locked on him.

But the room was empty. He grabbed a towel, dried off with a rough scrub, then secured the cotton cloth around his hips as he went to look for her. The blood had washed away, turning the water red as it slid down the drain. He'd healed and now . . .

*He wanted.*

Angels weren't supposed to feel emotions. Not desires. But since he'd fallen, he'd gotten slammed with every sensation that humans experienced. All the needs. All the wants. All the endless hungers.

And, right then, his body was hard and heavy with desire.

Because Jade had looked at him with hunger in her eyes. He'd seen the heat in her stare when she'd gazed at his naked body. She'd liked what she'd seen.

Only fair really. When he looked at her, he could certainly appreciate the view.

He opened the door. A quick glance revealed that Jade wasn't in the small bedroom that waited to the right. He eased out of the bathroom and turned left in the hallway.

And he found her crouched down, painting an image of a street performer on her wall.

She hesitated, then glanced back at him. A faint streak of blue paint lined her cheek. "Your clothes aren't ready yet."

Fine. He stalked closer to her. Took the brush from her hand. Let his fingers linger on her skin.

But she shook her head. "You don't want to do . . . this."

"This?" He asked, though he knew exactly what she meant.

She nodded. "It's not safe to want me. I thought . . ." Jade took a deep breath and licked her lips. He was discovering that he loved to watch the slick movements of her lips and tongue. "When your clothes are done," she said, "you should leave and forget that you ever met me."

He'd forgotten many humans. Remembered the screams of others. He put the paintbrush down on the small bucket of paint. Then his fingers slid up her arms. Curled over her shoulders. "I think forgetting you may not be an easy task."

"You don't get it." She didn't jerk away but held herself perfectly still as she told him, "Men who want me have an unfortunate history of death."

If she only knew . . .

Her smile was sad as she rose—and pulled away. "So for once, I'm going to do something right." But her gaze dropped down his chest. "Dammit."

He lifted a brow and stood beside her.

"Thanks for saving my ass today," Jade said as she took a few steps away from him. "But once you have your clothes, you really need to just get the hell away from me."

Not quite what he'd expected. Before he'd entered the shower, Az had thought the human female was trying her hand at seducing him.

Others had tried. Tempted him.

But he hadn't wanted them, not the way he wanted her.

He wanted Jade on the big bed in her bedroom. Wanted her open to him, her arms around him. Screaming for him.

He wanted to taste the pleasure that humans enjoyed so much. With her.

Every angel was tempted at some point . . .

"I know it's none of my business. . . ." Her words had a husky edge that he found . . . sexy. "But," she continued in that voice that seemed to stroke right over his flesh, "what happened to your back?"

"I fell." Flat. The truth.

Her dark brows lifted. "You fell." Jade gave a slight shake of her head and whistled lightly. "That must have been some fall."

"It was." He wanted to touch her again. Touch had been denied to him for centuries, and he hadn't realized just how pleasurable it was to feel a woman's skin against his.

So he stalked forward and let his fingers skate down her cheek.

*Soft.*

"You shouldn't . . ." Her voice was like a whisper during sex.

"I should." What else did he have to lose? His gaze locked

on her mouth. Red, plump lips. "I want to know what you taste like."

He caught the hitch of her breathing, but she shook her head. "I told you—"

Now he laughed. "I'm not scared of death."

Her lips parted in surprise.

Az didn't wait any longer. His lips took hers. Not a gentle, seeking kiss. He wasn't much for gentleness these days. His tongue thrust into her mouth. Drove inside and *took*.

She tasted sweeter than strawberries. So sweet. His tongue tasted her and his hands curled around her as he pulled her body closer to his.

Her body was small, her breasts lush, and he wanted *more*.

His cock shoved against the towel, thickening and stretching toward her. He couldn't pull away from her. Didn't want to. Her lips sucked over his tongue and his whole body tightened.

He stumbled forward with her. Caged her against the wall and—enjoyed her.

*Mouth. Tongue. Flesh.*

The towel was in the way. He wanted skin to skin. He wanted to see the pink folds of her sex. Wanted to be *in* her.

Wanted, as he'd never wanted another.

Her hands curled around his shoulders. Her nails dug into his skin, and he liked the rough sting.

A growl built in his throat.

His mouth tore from hers, and he began to taste her throat. She trembled against him. Ah, she enjoyed that. Right there, on the curve of her neck and shoulder and—

"No!"

His head snapped up, and he stared down at her. Her breasts were tight, hard peaks, pushing against his chest. Her hips had arched hungrily against him, and her eyes—there was no missing the lust in her stare. The same lust that heated his own body.

But the human was telling him no.

*"Why?"* Grated from him. Was it because he wasn't . . . like her? He wasn't less than human, no, he was—

She trembled against him as her fingers slid down his arms. "I told you," Jade said again, "I'm dangerous. You don't want to be with me."

He did. He wanted to be fucking her right then.

"The best thing that you can do is to get away from me." Her hands flatted on his chest and she pushed against him.

Az eased back a step. Just one.

She stared up at him with those green eyes that he suspected had probably broken mortal men. "That panther pack will be coming after me again. Coming after me and anyone who stands with me. So trust me on this, you don't want to get caught in this war."

Then she eased around him. Her body brushed his, a soft glide of feminine flesh.

"I'm going to shower," she said. "You should—you should be gone when I come out."

If that was the way the little mortal wanted things . . .

She headed for the bathroom. Didn't look back at him. Why did that fact anger him? And why did he feel like he had to ask, "Why do the panthers want you?"

She paused with one hand on the door frame. "I guess I did something to make them angry."

It would seem so.

"Now, they aren't going to stop. Not until they kill me."

A human against a pack of panthers. Hardly seemed like fair odds to him. A human against just one shifter wasn't a fair fight.

"But this isn't your battle." She still didn't look back. *Why not?* "You should leave while you have the chance. And don't just leave my apartment. Get out of New Orleans. If you don't, they'll pick up your scent. They'll hunt you down. They'll rip you apart."

Highly doubtful. "I'd like to see them try."

She swung around in an instant. "I wouldn't." Soft. Wait, were those tears glittering in her eyes?

A mortal, crying over *him?*

"You helped me. You didn't know me. But you . . . you saved my life." She gave a fast, negative shake of her head. "Now let me save yours. Az, *get the hell out of here, and don't ever come back.*"

She sounded like she meant those words.

Jade spun around and slammed the door behind her. A few seconds later, the water flooded on with a roar of sound.

Az stared at the closed door. After a moment, he waved his hand and instantly clothed his body in fresh clothes. He hadn't needed her to wash the others. Working magic was easy for him. Always had been. Magic was one of his gifts.

The water continued to pour in the bathroom.

The mortal wanted him to leave her alone . . .

But sometimes, mortals didn't always get what they wanted. Especially not when they tempted him so much.

*He'd left.*

As she tiptoed out of the bathroom, Jade's hands tightened around the towel that covered her body. It was good that he'd left.

So why did her chest ache?

She took a deep breath. For once, she'd done the right thing. She hadn't dragged Az into her hell.

She could handle this nightmare, and he—he'd be much better off the farther away he got from her. For his sake, Jade hoped the guy hightailed it far and fast.

Besides, she was used to being on her own. It was the way she wanted to be. Az would have just complicated things for her. Distracted her.

And . . . and she could still taste him on her lips.

*Dammit.*

* ★ *

Az waited until the sun fell, then he sought out his brother Sammael at the Fallen's favorite club.

*Brother.* He and Sammael—or, rather, Sam, since his brother preferred that version of his name—weren't exactly close, especially since Az had spent an inordinate amount of time attempting to kill Sam over the centuries.

But, well, *bygones.* That was all in the past. He hoped. As long as Sam didn't come looking for some payback anytime soon.

A long line of humans waited outside the doors of Sunrise. Humans were always trying to play on the dark side. Maybe they sensed that the club catered to a wilder clientele. Maybe they wanted the rush that came from risking death.

Fools.

He shoved past the paranormal bouncer and headed inside. Sam was at the bar, looking bored as he talked to one of his demons. Sam spent too much time with the demons. And with hellhounds. But, luckily, Sam's hound wasn't in Sunrise right then. Perhaps later the beast would make his appearance.

Sam gave an exaggerated sigh when he caught sight of Az in the bar's mirror. He spun on the stool to face him. "Visiting again?" Sam waved toward the stage. "And the entertainment hasn't even started yet. My, you are out prowling the streets early tonight."

Az's back teeth ground together. "I want to talk to Seline."

Sam raised a brow. "Now what would you want with *my* Seline?" Possessive steel had entered his voice.

Because Seline was his. A woman who'd traded heaven to live with Sam in this hell. Az still didn't get quite why she'd made that particular choice. For love, or so she said.

"Ah . . ." Sam nodded and his gaze sharpened as he

snapped his fingers. "You want to grill her on how to get back upstairs, right? Because that's always what you fucking want to do . . . go back. *Go back.* Sometimes, Az, you can be such a whiny bitch." He grabbed a shot glass and drained the contents in a quick gulp. "You screwed up, you got tossed here, now deal with it."

But he didn't want to deal with it. Az was tired of the emotions that were growing stronger every day. *Ripping me apart.* And since he'd met Jade, the lust inside had been growing—*all day.* He couldn't stop thinking about her. Couldn't stop wanting her.

He could still smell the scent of strawberries.

Az exhaled on a heavy breath. "This world isn't for me." He'd ruled over an army of angels, and now he was reduced to fighting shifters in a dirty alley in order to get his kicks. "I'm going back."

"Not unless you get redemption," a soft, feminine voice told him.

*Seline.*

He glanced into the mirror and saw that Sam's mate stood just behind him. Seline's warm, brown gaze met his in the mirror. "If you really hate it here so much," she continued, shrugging her slender shoulders and sending her blond hair sliding back, "then prove that you should get the free pass back upstairs."

*Upstairs.* Where there were no pesky emotions to plague him. No feelings to tie him into knots. No needs that made him ache. Only duty and death.

"*If* that's what you want . . ." Sam interrupted, voice taunting as he offered his hand to Seline. She stepped toward him and their fingers locked. "But something tells me that the longer you're down here," Sam said, amusement flickering in his eyes, "the more you're gonna like it."

Az's gaze drifted around the bar. Couples were dancing, their bodies too close together. Nearly screwing right there in public. Drinks poured and were guzzled instantly. Magic drifted in the air.

Booze. Alcohol. Sex.

*Jade.*

He blinked, wondering for a moment if he'd imagined her. But, no, this wasn't another fantasy.

She was there. Standing just inside the doorway with her eyes narrowed as she scanned the bar.

"See something you like?" Sam taunted. "Because I sure think you must."

Az realized his whole body had stiffened. He'd even taken a step toward her without realizing it.

Sam's left hand slapped onto Az's shoulder, and it felt like a burning poker had been laid against his skin. Probably because Sam was still pissed at him and wanted the touch to hurt. Sam was as powerful as Az, and the other Fallen knew how to control fire and magic just as easily—if not *more* easily—than Az did.

"Go ahead," Sam told him. "Go find a human. Screw yourself silly. *Live a little.*"

But with every moment that he spent on earth, Az felt like he slipped farther away from his past. From his real life.

*Not meant for earth. Too much pain.* It ate at him here.

"Redemption," Seline said softly as she pressed against Sam's side. "It's your only way."

It was his only way. Because if he stayed here, well, a very long, long time ago, a certain powerful prophet had predicted that Az might just bring about the end of the world . . . when he killed his own brother.

He'd had the chance to kill Sam before. He'd passed. End of the world apocalypse averted.

For the moment. But every day, Az could feel a darkness stirring inside him. If the emotions just kept growing stronger, what would happen?

Could he keep holding on to his control?

Or what if that old prediction finally came true? If the darkness inside of him grew too strong, Az wasn't sure what would happen or what he might do.

His gaze returned to Jade. He could barely see the top of her dark hair now. She'd slipped to the side, moving almost stealthily as she turned toward the hallway that led to the darker part of Sunrise.

The part humans weren't meant to see.

She was a human. Lost. Alone. Hunted by the *Other.* Weak.

Sam began to laugh behind him.

Humans were weak, but they were also favored.

"You're going to regret so many things," Sam murmured to Az as he pulled Seline closer. "So many . . ."

Az turned his head and offered a tight smile to his brother, the only angel who'd ever been able to equal him in power. The angel who'd fallen when he'd slaughtered dozens of humans. "Fuck off," Az told him.

But Sam's grin didn't fade. It only stretched wider as he said, "Now that's the spirit, brother."

Az left him. Intent on finding Jade, he pushed his way through the crowd. She shouldn't be there. It was far too dangerous for her to be in that wild crowd.

*Redemption.*

He pushed back two demons who'd blocked his path. Demons . . . they looked just like humans, unless you were powerful enough to see through the glamour that they used. Usually, only other demons could read past the illusion. A demon's true gaze was pitch black. Darker than the worst night in hell.

The demons didn't bother with glamour when they glared at him. Az shoved a burst of his power at them and sent the demons stumbling back. In this town, he was used to enemies being near. He was used to enemies being everywhere.

The dark corridor on the left snaked away from the main bar. A few more steps down that corridor, and Az found himself in front of a barred door. A seven-foot-tall bear shifter blocked his way—and there was no sign of Jade.

"Where is she?" Az demanded.

The shifter smiled.

Fine. Az grabbed him and slammed the shifter's head against the door. Once. Twice. The third slam broke the door.

He tossed the shifter aside and peered through the shattered remains of the door. Another hallway waited.

But voices reached his ears. Men. Probably more demons or shifters. And then, he heard her.

Az entered a cavernous room and, even with the cluster of bodies, he caught the scent of strawberries. He focused on that scent. Followed it.

There she was. Jade was leaning over an old wooden table. Two demons sat at the table, with their eyes too intent on her body. She slapped a wad of cash down on the table's scarred surface. "Here's the money, now *do it.*"

One demon jumped up. Grabbed her. And put a knife to her throat.

In that instant, the dumb-ass demon begged for death.

And Death heard his plea.

# CHAPTER THREE

The blade slipped down her throat, slicing the skin—then the demon was yanked away and tossed across the room.

What the hell?

Jade covered her throat even as she scrambled for the knife that had fallen to the floor. She needed that knife, she needed—

*"Get out of here."* Oh, hell. She knew that deep, rumbling voice. Az was there. He grabbed her before her searching fingers could close over the knife's handle. "Run," he told her. "I'll take care of them."

Run? *No, thank you.* Her throat stung, but, luckily, the blade hadn't sliced her too deeply. "What are you doing here?" Had the guy totally not listened to her at all? She'd tried to do the right thing, but, no, here he was, looking all tall, strong, and avenging, and—

And he'd been the one to toss the demon across the room.

*So screwing up my plan.*

"Go." Az pushed her toward the door. Jade guessed that he didn't realize the door was now blocked by two really pissed-off looking demons. "I'll handle them."

She didn't go.

The demon he'd hurled across the room had now risen to

his feet. His eyes—no longer a warm green but instead a cold, pitch black—locked on her. "You set me up, bitch."

Well, no, she hadn't. She'd come in, intending to do this deal right. Couldn't a girl hire a paranormal hit squad anymore without issues coming up? No deal was ever simple these days.

"I didn't set you up," she told the demon. William. A hard-hitter with a reputation for taking care of business. She'd worked for weeks arranging this meeting. Jade tried to step around Az. He glared at her and blocked her path. *Wrong time, hero.* "There's just a—a misunderstanding going on here."

She needed these demons. If they went after the panthers, they could take out the whole pack.

"He had a *knife* at your throat," Az snarled. "You're bleeding because of him."

"The lady wanted a close look at my silver blade." William shrugged and offered a smile that was icy. "She wanted to see how I'd killed the last two shifters who were dumb enough to cross my path."

No matter what the stories said, silver didn't just work on werewolves. It was an all-purpose weapon against most shifters.

But in order to take down Brandt and his panther buddies, they'd need a whole lot more than just a few silver tricks.

*Been there, done that.*

Az turned his head, and she saw his gaze searching the room. Scanning all the demons who now wore kick-ass expressions.

Her master plan was so screwed. "We can still make this work," Jade said, fighting to keep her voice calm, but the desperation she felt wanted to leak into her words "You can take the money, take the hit—"

"Oh, I'll be taking the money." William snapped his fingers, and one of his freaking minions swiped up the money in an instant. "As far as the hit goes . . ."

*Take it. Take out Brandt. Do it.*

He flashed her a grin. "I'm afraid you're not the first one to come at me with a deal, honey."

Crap.

"Your boyfriend came to me first. And he paid more."

Now Jade took a step back and wished, *really, really wished,* that she'd run as soon as Az appeared. But when you couldn't run—

*You fought as hard as you could.*

"He's put a price on your pretty head." William smirked at her as he sidled closer. With the back of his hand, he swiped away the blood that trickled from his busted lip. Az had made the demon bleed nicely when he'd tossed his sorry assassin butt across the room.

"He wants me dead?" Jade asked, but she wasn't really surprised. It had only been a matter of time before Brandt grew tired of the game and decided killing her was the best option.

"No, he wants you very much alive." William's gaze darted to Azrael. "But he didn't say a fucking thing about me not getting to kill any assholes who were with you."

Az straightened his shoulders and he just—smiled. The smile made him look all the more gorgeous, but, um, did the guy get that he was surrounded by some cutthroat supernatural killers?

Az's gaze raked over the demon. "You don't know who I am, do you?"

"A dick who's about to die?"

The other demons snickered.

Jade saw the glint of the knife. It had fallen under the table. Not too far away. If she moved fast enough, she might be able to grab it.

"I guess I don't come in here often enough for folks to

know me," Az said slowly, speaking in a thoughtful tone. He paused, "But I bet you know my brother."

William lifted his hands, and a ball of fire appeared between his palms. Demons and fire. Such a deadly mix. "Do I look like I give a shit whose brother you are?"

Az didn't look particularly scared of those flames. "Since you're in his bar, you should."

For some reason, that statement made some of the demons blanch. And she caught the whisper of . . . *"Fuck, Sammael!"*

Then Az just walked toward that demon and his ball of fire. "Tell you what," Az said, "to be fair, I'll even let you take the first shot."

What? *"No!"* Jade screamed, but it was too late. William had already thrown his ball of fire right at Az.

She dove for the knife. Her fingers wrapped tightly around the hilt. Jade leapt up. *Don't burn, don't!* She spun as fast as she could—and buried the knife into William's side. *"Get away from him!"*

The demon shuddered and stumbled back.

"Az?" She barely breathed his name. Her gaze swept over his chest, but—but there was no sign of any burns. Not even a wisp of smoke.

His eyes were on the demon. "My turn."

Then he reached out and pressed his hand against William's chest.

The demon's eyes widened. His lips opened as if he were trying to speak, but then his body tumbled back, and he hit the floor with a hard thud.

*Dead.*

Jade glanced down at him. Then she looked back up at Az. "What did you do?" Her voice was hushed. But . . . this was just like in the alley. He'd touched, and he'd killed.

His gaze met hers. Az didn't speak.

"What are you?" Her stark whisper. She had to know.

Now his lips turned up in a smile that chilled her. "I'm Death."

Like he was the first man to tell her that line.

*"I'm death."* Brandt's yell echoed in her ears. *"Wherever you go, whoever you turn to—I'll know. And I'll fucking kill them all."*

She bent down and yanked the knife from William's body. Then she held up the knife because it was the only weapon she had. "Stay away from me."

A line edged between Az's blond brows. "I helped you."

Where was the demon who'd taken her cash? She'd be needing that back. But it looked like those guys had scrambled. They probably had been racing out of that place even as William's body hit the floor. "Did you follow me here?" Her heart pounded so fast that Jade was worried it might break right out of her chest.

Az shook his head. "I was already at Sunrise when you came in."

Lie or truth? But, wait, he'd said his brother owned the place. Maybe his words were true.

Maybe not.

She began to back away from him. Jade kept the bloody knife up. She wasn't dumb enough to drop her guard with him, not when she knew how easily he could kill. "Just stay there, okay?" Stay where she could see him as she fled.

"You're afraid of me."

Yeah, because she wasn't an idiot. Men who could kill with a touch—any sane person would fear those guys. "Keep your hands to yourself, big guy, and we won't be having a problem."

"I thought you liked it when I touched you."

Five feet separated them. Not nearly enough space. And now he was getting all personal and sexual on her? *Now?*

She cleared her throat. "That was—"

"Your nipples were hard against me. Your hips pressed up

against my cock like you were hungry for me." Why did his words sound almost clinical? Cold words, but his gaze looked hot enough to burn.

She was feeling scorched. "Okay, look, there's a dead demon on the floor. How about we just talk about this other stuff later?" Because she had another demon to catch. A demon who thought he was getting away with her cash. As if she'd just kiss that dough good-bye.

Her gaze darted to the distance between her and Az. Alright. That looked like enough space between them. Well, enough for a good head start anyway. Jade spun away from Az and raced for the door.

He caught her. Just *appeared* right in front of her. She screamed in surprise and then again in real fear when his hands closed around her.

"Don't kill me!"

But his mouth pressed against hers. Stole the words. His tongue thrust into her mouth.

She had the knife in her hand. She could use it on him. Could shove it right under his ribs and twist for optimum pain.

She'd done that to a man before.

But Az hadn't *hurt* her. He'd killed twice, both times to protect her. He could destroy with a touch, but right then, his hands were light upon her skin and his mouth was almost caressing hers.

So she didn't shove the knife into his ribs. Instead Jade lowered the weapon.

"Good choice." He growled the words against her mouth as his lips lifted. "You don't kill me, and I won't kill you."

Fair plan. Then his mouth came back to hers. Just the touch of his lips, and dammit, she *wanted*. She'd tried to play it safe with him, tried the whole do-the-freaking-right-thing routine, but—

But Az seemed to want her just as much as she wanted

him. So Jade's mouth widened. Her tongue met his. She tasted. She took. She craved so much more.

His hands were on her ass now. Pulling her up against him. There was no missing the hard length of his arousal. Death and desire.

Some men fed on that dangerous combination.

So did some women.

Jade pushed her left hand against his chest. *The demon.* Her mouth broke from his. "I have to . . ." She shook her head, then just twisted away from him.

He watched her with an unblinking stare.

"The demon's got my money," she said, breath rasping. "I'm not letting him get away." Luckily, she'd become pretty good at tracking over the years. Good for a human, anyway.

She eased around him. Az didn't stop her, though she expected him to.

Wanted him to?

Jade rushed forward—and nearly slammed into the chest of a tall, smiling god.

Big, dark. Features so perfect it had to be a sin.

"Is that a dead demon in my bar?" He asked, voice almost . . . amused.

His bar?

But before Jade could answer, the guy shook his head. "Really, Az, I'm beginning to think you enjoy playing down here."

Playing?

Then the man's eyes locked on her. His blue eyes were just like Az's. Only one glance into this man's eyes and her heart felt chilled.

"And what have we here?" He drawled, lifting a hand toward her. "Something tempting . . ."

*"Don't touch her."* Az's snarled order. Then he was there. Moving in that too-fast way of his that still freaked her out. He put his body between her and—

"Sammael, don't ever fucking touch her."

But this *Sammael* just laughed. "Language, language . . ." he chided. "Each day you just seem to grow more and more like the whole *fucking* rest of us."

She peeked around Az's shoulder and saw Sammael's gaze rake him.

Sammael asked, "I guess you're not so perfect anymore, are you, brother?"

Az lunged forward and grabbed Sammael. Okay. Right. Family thing. Whatever. She had her own business to take care of. So Jade took that moment to dive for the door.

There was a demon out there someplace, with her last wad of cash. She should have known five grand was too low a price to pay for death, but she'd been desperate.

Once she got hold of that thieving demon, he'd be the desperate one.

Surprisingly, Sam didn't fight. Az shoved his brother to the ground and expected to feel a bolt of lightning hit his chest.

But Sam was too busy laughing. "I knew," Sam threw out, "I *knew* the longer you were down here, the more tempted you'd become."

Sam was right. Damn him. The feelings and needs and wants were pressing on him all the time. Constantly tempting him.

No wonder humans were so drawn to sin. If Sam hadn't interrupted, Az would have taken Jade *right there.*

"She's gone, you know," Sam said as his laughter slowly faded, and he rose to his feet. "Ran away like a frightened rabbit." He frowned. "You know, on second thought, perhaps you should go in easy. A human truly isn't the best choice for your first lover."

First. Because angels didn't need sex. They didn't hunger for the pleasure and the—

*I hunger for her.*

"We can get a bit . . . rough." Sam continued as he shrugged his shoulders. "You'd better start off with a shifter, or maybe a vamp. Someone who can handle our excess power. Once you get more control, then you can work up to bedding a human."

Az ground his back together. "I don't want another." That was part of the problem. Other women had come to tempt him, trying to sway him, but his body had never burned with hunger as it did for Jade. One kiss—and he craved her.

*Must. Have. More.*

He wanted to see why humans were willing to die for their pleasure. Was the sex truly that good?

It couldn't be.

Could it?

Sam's brows shot up. "If you don't want anyone else, then why'd you let her rush out of here?" His gaze swept to the dead demon in the corner. "They're hitters, you know. Pay 'em enough money, they kill whoever you want."

*"He's put a price on your pretty head . . ."* The demon's words drifted through Az's mind and his hands fisted. "You know that they do—yet you still allowed them in your bar?"

"Well, I *was* planning to kill them all tonight." Sam seemed completely unconcerned. "But then you just had to jump in and play hero before I could take out the trash."

Az's eyes narrowed to a slit at that.

"Now the other assholes are out running loose." Sam tapped his chin. "And the little human you were so intent on guarding is out there all alone."

Snarling, Az shoved past his brother.

"Careful," Sam's voice hardened, and Az glanced back at him. "They really aren't as weak as you might think," Sam warned.

But Sam was wrong.

Nothing was weaker than a human.

Az headed after Jade.

"You'll learn." Sam's taunt followed him. "Soon enough."

The demons had run, fast. They'd hauled ass and gotten out of the bar at near light speed.

Jade stood outside of Sunrise, ignoring the crowd. Her gaze searched the street. If she had a shifter's nose, she'd just be able to smell the demons and follow their scent.

She didn't have that talent.

She didn't have claws. No magic. No super strength.

But she was smart, dammit. She could figure this out without any paranormal mumbo jumbo.

Her gaze followed the dips and turns of the street. If she were running, she would have kept to the shadows. She would have gone away from the crowd. Tried to disappear into the darkness.

Jade marched for that darkness. Her fingers still curled around the knife, but she had the weapon lowered and hidden near the side of her hip. Its weight reassured her as she walked through the night.

One step. Another.

The bar faded away behind her. Her steps came faster. Faster. More running than walking.

She heard the whisper of laughter on the wind. The growl of an engine.

Jade rounded the corner. Oh, hell, *no*. She recognized the demon currently shoving *her* cash into the saddlebag on a black motorcycle.

Pushing herself as hard as she could, Jade lunged forward. She whipped up the knife and wrapped her arm around the demon. Her stomach pressed into his back and the tip of the blade slipped over his throat. "You've got something of mine."

He stilled.

Then he laughed. "Figured you'd be coming after me."

"You figured right." Did he want some kind of bonus points? "Now *give me back my money!*" A girl had to live. and she had to possess enough money to keep the devil off her back.

He yanked up the saddlebag and tossed it to her. She let the blade of the knife slide deeper into his skin.

"You're gonna die," he told her, his voice a snarl.

Now it was her turn to laugh. Like a little death threat would bother her. It wasn't the first time she'd gotten one— or even the fifth time. "You'll be the one to see hell first. How do you think Brandt's going to react when he finds out that you had me, but you just let me walk away?"

Brandt didn't exactly take well to failure.

She felt the sudden tension in the demon's body. She brought her mouth close to his ear. "Get ready to have some of that skin clawed right off your body. Brandt enjoys taking his pound of flesh." Very true.

But she didn't. Jade jumped back, taking the knife and saddlebag. The demon could use that bike and get the hell out of town. If he was smart, that was exactly what he'd do.

The motorcycle growled behind her.

*"Fucking bitch . . ."*

And she knew the demon wasn't going to be playing it smart. Pity. That would have made things easier. She'd tried to give him an out. No dice.

Jade started to run.

The motorcycle's engine stopped growling and started to roar. Sparing a fast look over her shoulder, she saw that the demon had spun his bike around. He was coming right at her.

Some guys just had a death wish.

She zagged to the left. Felt the breath of the bike behind her.

So close now. *So close.*

She dove over a pile of garbage. Slammed into the cement. The motorcycle missed her right foot by about two inches.

Then the demon circled back around.

The beam from the headlight cut through the darkness. "No human bitch is getting away from me!" the demon yelled.

Jade rose to her feet. The motorcycle had braked about ten feet away. She walked forward, dodged the garbage, and stood in the middle of the street.

She'd left the saddlebag full of money behind the garbage. Her hands were down, half hidden behind her jeans. She lowered her head, offering a pose of submission.

Weakness.

All *Other* knew just how weak humans were.

*Wait for him. Wait . . .*

The motorcycle roared once more. He came racing toward her.

Jade tilted back her head and met his stare. She smiled. In that instant before impact, she leapt to the side, then struck out with her knife. His scream filled her ears even as metal screeched and the motorcycle slammed into the road.

Her shoulders hunched as she stared down at the body. The knife was in his chest. The back of his head had smacked right into the pavement, and his leg was twisted beneath him.

The motorcycle had rolled twice. Now it lay in a wreck just a few feet away.

"Bitch . . ." Not a snarl this time. Only a whisper.

Jade licked her lips. "You should have just walked away." Didn't he understand? Brandt wanted her back for a reason.

*Because I'm as screwed up as he is.*

Killing had come too easily for her. All she'd needed was a little guidance. Brandt had been so willing to guide her.

As she turned away from the demon, Jade could have almost sworn that the light scent of flowers teased her nose.

She paused and glanced back. The demon's eyes were still open. Still on her.

"I didn't want to kill you," she said and sadness made her words heavy, "but I'm not ready to die."

The flowery scent seemed to deepen. She grabbed the money. Left the knife in his chest.

And walked away.

Brandt found the demon's body. Tossed like garbage in the street. He bent and studied the knife that was still buried hilt-deep in the demon's chest.

Jade had been shopping. The woman always liked her silver. He touched the handle, being careful to keep his hands away from that burning silver blade.

The demon gasped.

*Still alive.*

Brandt smiled. "You called. You told me that you had my Jade." He made a point of glancing around the empty street. No partying here. No celebrating. Just death. "But I don't see her."

The demon tried to talk. Blood gurgled from his lips.

"Why don't I see her?" Brandt asked and gave a little shake of his head. "I paid you money—very good money at that—to keep her for me." He didn't trust his pack anymore. Not with her. They kept screwing up, every damn time. So he'd branched out. Hired muscle.

And Jade had driven a silver knife into the guy's chest.

Oh, but he fucking loved her.

"Now where the hell is William?" He demanded. William was the demon in charge of this group of killers. The big boss demon. "If he doesn't have her . . ."

But he'd seen the demon's lashes twitch. Brandt stilled. *"Where's William."* Not a question. A demand this time.

"D-dead . . ." A gurgle of sound.

"By Jade's hand?" Impressive. She was gaining new skills.

He'd suspected she always liked the blood, but two demon kills in one night was just taking her game up to a whole new level.

"B-bastard . . . with . . . her . . ."

No, no, that was damn well *not* what he wanted to hear. Brandt drove that knife down as hard as he could. It ripped past bone and flesh and sank into the pavement beneath the demon's body.

No more gurgles. No more whispers. Just wide open eyes and a demon that was looking at hell. Brandt sure hoped the guy enjoyed the view.

Riley paced behind him. "You think it's the same man?"

Brandt surged to his feet. *Fuck yes.*

And was the man screwing her? He was sure killing for her. Twice now. And why else would he kill, why else would he get involved? The unknown asshole *had* to be fucking her. "Find him," it was hard to speak as a man when the beast inside was snarling so loudly. "Get every hunter we have in this city—and *find him.*"

"You want him dead or alive?" Riley asked quietly as he backed up a space.

Dead or alive—the same question that had been asked about Jade.

"Alive." Because he'd be the one to kill the bastard. Jade would watch.

Just as she'd watched before.

*She likes the blood, too.*

Revelers still packed the streets of New Orleans. The parades had ended hours ago, but as Jade shoved her way through the streets, she knew the folks celebrating on Bourbon Street didn't really care that the beads weren't flying anymore.

Laughter floated in the air on an alcohol breeze. Women hung off balconies, flashing for the crowd below.

She hadn't gone back to her place. At this point, Jade just wasn't sure if the small apartment was still safe. First the pack had come for her, and then she'd learned about the demons.

Her temporary anonymity in this city had definitely been blown to hell.

Jade was afraid that if she went back to that apartment, she'd find another hunter waiting for her.

The city wasn't a haven for her. Not anymore.

"Hey, baby." A big, smiling guy jostled into her. "Can I buy you a drink?"

"No, thanks." She pushed away from him. The last thing she wanted was to get chummy with some frat boy looking for a good time.

"But, baby!" Now he sounded hurt. "I've got—"

The crowd around her cheered. The women on the balcony to the right had flashed. Again.

"You've got the wrong woman," she told him. "Go try your luck with someone else." Maybe one of the Ms. Flashies.

His eyes narrowed on her, and she realized that, unfortunately, he wasn't as drunk as she'd thought. "Holy shit, is that blood on you?" frat guy demanded, now with a note of shock in his voice.

And, yes, yes, it was. Demon blood could be a bitch to get out of a girl's shirt, too. No matter how many washes, that thick stuff just stayed.

This time when she yanked away from the frat boy, he let her go. Actually, he all but shoved her in his haste to get away. Hmm. Future reference note. *Show a little blood and the guys will vanish fast.*

She pushed through the crowds as she wound her way up to the nearest open apartment that she could find. Lucky for her, some folks invited the world in to their homes for a Mardi Gras party.

A good, nonstop party was going on right at the end of

the street. She slipped inside the open doors. Found a bedroom. Two couples were making out on the bed. She ignored them, they ignored her, and she grabbed a clean shirt from the closet.

Jade ditched her bloody clothes and dressed quickly. The top was a little tight across the breasts, but she wasn't about to be complaining.

Not even close.

She eased up the stairs and then out onto the balcony. Her gaze swept the crowd below. She saw a large, rippling mass of bodies. Laughter. Drinking. Kisses.

Then . . .

Az.

He stood in the middle of the crowd, silent, strong, and he was staring right up at her.

Her heart seemed to stop. His stare was so hot, even across that stream of bodies. It almost seemed like she could feel the burn of his gaze and the heat from his touch.

Fear? Yeah, she feared him. How could she not, after everything that had happened? But, she wanted him, too. In that instant, Jade realized that she wanted Az far more than she feared him. Dangerous, but . . .

She wasn't exactly the type to play things safe. Her reckless side was part of her problem.

*He's the key. Use him. They can't hurt him.*

But . . .

But her gaze darted over Az's shoulder, and she saw two familiar figures moving toward him through the wild crush of the crowd. The figures were steadily closing in on their prey. Az was focused on her. He didn't even know that danger was *right there.*

Riley and Anton, two of Brandt's vicious packmates, were stalking toward him. Their gazes were *on* him. Even far away, she could see the flash of their claws.

"No!" Jade shouted as she gripped the wrought-iron balcony railing.

But the crowd below her just cheered. Az didn't move.

He'd touched and killed, but what would happen when he didn't have the chance to strike first?

Jade didn't want to find out. "Riley, Anton!" She screamed their names. "Here I am, bastards!"

More roars from the crowd. They would yell at anything. But she knew the shifters heard her because their gazes ripped away from Az and locked right on her.

"Leave him alone." She knew her words would be lost to the madness of the crowd, but those shifters with their enhanced senses, if they couldn't hear her actual words, then they'd still be able to read her lips.

Riley smiled at her, and shook his head. Then he brought his claws up to his throat and mimicked slicing across his neck.

Bastard.

Az was *not* going to die while she watched.

# Chapter Four

The crowd's roar drowned out her screams. Az began walking toward her. The shifters kept stalking behind him.

*No, no, no.*

"Behind you!" Jade yelled as loudly as she could. "They are right *behind you!*"

Az didn't glance back. This was not working. Her gaze darted below her. Okay, that was just a one story drop. She'd survive that fall, right? Maybe with a few broken bones, maybe just with some bruises. She could do this.

She *had* to do this.

Drawing in a shaky breath, Jade climbed over the railing. The crowd cheered louder. *Louder.*

She jumped.

And was caught by three guys. *What the hell?* They swung her around, cheering.

Crazy assholes. But they had just saved her some hurt. So she placed a fast kiss on the nearest cheek and leapt out of those cradling arms. Then Jade started running for Az. "They're after you, they're—"

A gunshot ripped through the crowd. The blast of the gunshot finally—*finally*—brought silence.

Silence that lasted for only a moment's time because then another shot thundered in the air.

Jade's eyes were on Az so she saw the jerk of his body as the bullet tore into him.

Then the screaming started, as the shock melted away from the revelers. The humans scrambled, running, shrieking, dropping their drinks and their beads as they rushed away from the gunfire.

Desperate to get to Az's side, Jade shoved her way through them. *My fault.* This was what happened to men who tried to play her white knight.

They wound up stained with blood.

Her side ached as she rushed toward him. He was slowly turning around now, finally facing the bastards who were after him. Too late.

Another crack of gunfire. She was close enough to hear the thud as the second bullet sank into Az's flesh.

His body trembled.

"Stop!" Jade screamed at Riley because he was the jerkoff with the gun. "Leave him alone!"

She grabbed Az's arm and pulled him close. Blood poured from a wound near his shoulder, and she knew he had at one bullet in his back. "We have to get you out of here!"

She could already hear sirens. The cops were responding fast this time. No big surprise. No one wanted a slaughter during Mardi Gras. That was bad for business.

Her gaze flew to the left, the right. There wasn't any nearby cover for them, and Riley still had his gun up. Only it wasn't aimed at Az any longer. It was aimed right at her.

Riley smiled.

But she knew bullshit when she saw it. "You can't kill me," she snarled at him, not even a little bit afraid of what he might do. "Because the minute you do, you're dead."

She understood how this game worked. Riley wasn't an alpha. He was a good little soldier shifter who did exactly as he was told.

A muscle jerked in Riley's jaw as he stalked closer.

"Maybe I can't kill you . . ." Rage beat beneath the rumbling words. She knew that, oh, yeah, he *wanted* to murder her, but if he did, then Brandt would rip the skin from his body. "But I can still make you bleed."

The gun wasn't pointed at her head anymore. He'd dropped it, and taken aim at her leg.

She saw his sharpening canines when he smiled. "Let's see how fast you can run with a bullet in—"

He didn't get to finish his threat. A ball of *freaking* fire rolled toward him.

Riley and Anton leapt back.

The crowd shrieked even louder because, sure, bullets and fire would flip most people the hell out.

She pulled Az's arm around her shoulder. Then she tucked her body close to his. Before the shifters regrouped, she had to get him away from there.

And she had to dodge the cops. There was a little matter of a few dead bodies from her past that she didn't exactly have time to deal with right then.

Those explanations could wait for another day.

"Come on," she whispered. Wow. The guy was heavy.

He didn't speak, but his hand tightened around her shoulder, and Az let her lead him through the crowd. Luckily, after a few stumbling steps, she and Az soon blended with the fleeing throng.

Two streets over, she found a car. An older, black BMW that sat alone beneath a broken street lamp. Leaving that ride alone in that spot was a bad mistake.

The driver's loss.

She lifted up with her right foot and smashed in the back window. An alarm immediately blasted. Easing away from Az, she unlocked the door, hopped around inside the vehicle, and two seconds later, she was under the dash. It barely took a breath for her to stop the alarm and get the engine flaring to life.

She might just be human, but she had some serious skills. *Thanks to Brandt.*

Damn him.

Jade helped Az into the BMW. Well, helped, shoved, same thing. The guy still wasn't talking. With the bullets in him, maybe he was just in too much pain to talk right then. *The shifters had been playing with him.*

Those sadistic jerks had just wanted to hurt Az. No doubt on Brandt's order. Because if they'd wanted him dead . . .

Riley was a good shot. If he'd wanted Az on a morgue slab someplace, he would have simply blasted a bullet in his brain.

*While I watched.*

Those sick shifters had to be stopped.

"Just hold on," she told Az as she yanked the gearshift back and spared a fast glance in the rearview mirror. "I'll get you someplace safe and dig those bullets out." Worried, Jade glanced at him.

He wasn't slumping in the seat. He was looking right at her, with a faint frown pulling his brows low.

Crap. "Are you in shock?" Great, the last thing that—

He reached into the gaping hole on his shoulder and yanked out the bullet. When his fingers dug into the torn flesh, the contact made a sucking sound that raised goose bumps all along her body. After just a moment of searching, he had the bloody bullet gripped in his fingers.

Jade swallowed. "I'm guessing that means you aren't in shock."

He rolled down his window and tossed out the bullet.

"Okay then . . ." Now wasn't the moment to gripe at the guy for littering. Blood prioritized right then. She turned her attention to the road. Sirens were screeching on the next block, and there had to be some folks from that crowd who would be sober enough to provide descriptions of the shooters—and of Az. Her foot pressed down on the accelerator. *Nice and slow.* All of the glass had busted out of the back side window, so if anyone looked at it, they'd just think the window was rolled down. They wouldn't realize she'd done a smash-and-grab.

As long as she played it cool, she had this.

Then *he* appeared.

Brandt walked out of the darkness. Tall. Muscled. A walking, talking fantasy. *No.* Not a fantasy, a nightmare.

How could someone so handsome be so fucking crazy?

He crossed his arms over his chest. Stood in the middle of the road.

Waited.

She slammed on the brakes.

"Who is he?"

Ah, now, *finally,* Az spoke. Jade's fingers whitened around the steering wheel. "A dead man." She shoved her foot down on the accelerator as far as it would go. *Dead.*

The BMW lurched forward. The scent of burning rubber filled her nose. Fast, faster . . .

The motor snarled.

Brandt cocked his head and grinned at her.

Did he think she was playing chicken? After the hell he'd put her through? She wasn't going to swerve away from him.

The collision wouldn't kill him. The guy was too strong for that. But she wanted him to *hurt.*

Wait. Dammit. Was she really becoming just like him?

*No. Won't be. Can't be.*

Brandt leapt away just as she swerved.

Her heart slammed in her ears, and the rough drumming was so wild that it shook her chest. She spun around the approaching curve too fast, and the car lurched on two tires.

Swearing, Jade jerked the steering wheel and barely managed to keep the car steady. Risking a quick glance back, she saw that Brandt had picked himself off the pavement. He was staring after her.

And the tough shifter wasn't smiling anymore.

The accelerator was already flat on the floor. Time to get the hell out of that city.

Good thing she'd already scoped out the area and come up with a backup plan. She did that whenever she was in a new city. For those instances—*like this one*—when she needed to run fast and seek cover.

Az reached for her hand. His blood coated her fingertips. *"Who was he?"* Anger—no, more like rage—thickened beneath his words.

But she'd put a target on the guy's back, so he deserved the truth and his rage. "Brandt Dupre." A brief pause. "He runs the most powerful panther shifter pack in the Southeast." Hell, probably the whole U.S. "He's vicious, smart, and he loves to make his prey suffer."

Az didn't let her go, and she could feel the weight of his stare on her.

They swept past the tall tombs of the cemetery. The heavy monuments rose over the old wall, dark, cold.

"Who is he . . ." Az asked, then pushed, *"to you?"*

"He's the man who took my life away." Everything she'd had. Everything she'd been. "And he's the asshole who's hunting me now. Brandt isn't ever going to stop. He's going to keep coming, keep attacking until I'm dead—"

"Or until he is." Flat, final words.

Her gaze flew to him.

Az's skin wasn't even pale. He'd taken bullets, lost a ton of blood, and he sat there, eyes glittering with intensity and dark determination carved onto his face.

"This isn't your fight," she told him, her voice quiet but firm. "You can't understand . . . you have no idea what they're like." He might *think* he knew about the paranormals out there, but Brandt's pack was different. Savage. She'd never encountered anyone else like them.

Her gaze darted back to the road. The interstate was deserted. Perfect. *Run, run.*

She'd spent the last ten years running.

"They shot me. They made it my fight." Now his fingers fell away from hers. "They're the ones who asked for death."

Her stomach felt like it was twisted into knots.

"So they are the ones who will get him."

His words sounded like a promise.


"The bullets didn't even slow that joker down," Riley muttered as the gray SUV hurtled through the city.

Brandt stared straight ahead. "Those bullets can slow down anything." He'd made sure of it. He'd fucking traded more than a pound of flesh for them.

That particular batch of bullets had sent vampires to the ground and caused demons to scream in agony.

They could damn well take out the bastard with Jade.

"I put two of 'em in him," Riley said as he yanked the steering wheel to the left and took the sharp turn. "He didn't even stumble. He just spun around and sent a ball of *fire* at us."

Interesting. Brandt rubbed his chin. "What the hell is he?"

"Not human, that's for sure." Riley exhaled on a rough sigh. "He's not gonna be easy to kill."

The good prey never was.

"Jade was desperate to get to him." Riley's fingers tapped on the steering wheel. "She jumped off that balcony and ran to him, screaming his name."

Brandt's jaw clenched. He didn't particularly enjoy this news.

"I'm tellin' you . . ." Riley hesitated and Brandt caught the tremble of what could have been fear in the shifter's voice when he said, "we need to find out just *what* that bastard is before we do anything else."

Brandt remembered the look in Jade's eyes as she'd driven toward him. Rage. So much rage. But . . .

*You veered away, baby. Can't kill me, can you?*

Just as he couldn't kill her.

"I'll tell you what he is," Brandt smiled as his fingers slid down to stroke the edge of his chin. "He's fucking dead."

Let the hunt begin.

The three-story cabin sat nestled on a lake, its large glass windows gleaming in the early sunlight. Jade braked near the edge of the long, winding drive and jumped out of the car. Vaguely curious, Az watched as she ran from the vehicle. But she didn't go far. A few seconds later, she was back—and tossing a FOR SALE sign into the back of the BMW.

"I figure we can stay here for a night, maybe two." She slanted him a concerned glance as she drove the car up the drive. "We can crash here long enough to get you patched up."

But he was already healing. At least, his shoulder was. His back ached and burned where the bullet still lodged near his spine.

Pain was an unusual sensation. Since falling, he'd realized there were so many different ways to feel pain. Fast cuts, slices with a knife that opened the flesh in an instant. Deep, burning pain that tore beneath the skin when a bullet lodged in muscle and—

"You're not going to pass out on me, are you?" Worry had roughed her voice.

Jade braked the car, and Az realized she was staring at him with wide eyes.

He lifted a brow. "Hardly." Her suggestion was fairly insulting. As if he couldn't handle a few bullet wounds.

"Good." Her breath expelled in a fast rush. He watched her hurry out of the car and race around to his side. She opened his door and reached for him. "Come on. Just lean on me."

How . . . interesting. She was trying to help him again.

Once out of the car, he leaned. Az didn't need to, of course, but he liked the feel of her body against his. She took his left arm and draped it over her shoulders. Her body angled toward his, and the lush fullness of her breasts pressed into his chest.

*So soft.*

Her scent teased his nose. Those strawberries again. He needed a taste of them. Of her.

His head tilted toward her as she maneuvered them along the stone path that led to the dwelling. It was odd, but her body—small, slender—seemed to fit just right beside his.

When they got to the front door, a rectangular lock box waited for them. Jade yanked on it. Nothing happened. She yanked again, swearing—

Az grabbed it for her and ripped it loose. A key popped free. Jade caught the key in midair and gave him a sunny smile.

The smile stopped him. She had a dimple in her right cheek. He hadn't noticed that before, but there it was. Small, almost hidden. And her lips looked even fuller than before.

*Taste.* He'd gotten to sample her mouth, but he wanted it again. Wanted so much more from her.

She opened the door. Az barely glanced at the cabin as he entered. He couldn't take his eyes off her.

Jade was biting her lower lip. She wasn't looking at the cabin's interior, either. Instead, she stared at him with eyes that were too big and dark.

Those eyes that made him think far too much of sin.

Az reached for his shirt. He yanked it over his head.

Dropped it on the floor. There was no missing the hitch in her breathing.

Her mouth dropped open in surprise. "Your-your shoulder . . ."

He knew that wound had already closed. Az turned his back on her. "I can't reach the second bullet." This was the area that bothered him.

Silence.

Then the wooden floor creaked as she walked toward him. When her silken hand touched his shoulder, Az tensed.

"I don't . . . I don't want to hurt you."

Glancing back over his shoulder, he said, "You won't."

Her gaze held his. "You don't know that." Her gaze fell to his back. He saw the faint flare of her eyes as she took in the damage. After a moment, she gave a grudging nod. "But we have to get that bullet out." She bit her lip. "We should get you to a doctor. It's so close to your spine—"

"I don't need a doctor."

"Uh, yeah, trust me, you do—"

"A human doctor can't work on me." Not unless they wanted the doc to freak and call in the cops.

She sighed as she eased away from him. "There's a bedroom through there." She pointed to the doorway. "I—"

"You've been here before." Not a suspicion. A certainty.

Her smile seemed sad. "It helps to have a backup plan in place."

He wasn't sure what those words really meant.

Jade headed toward the kitchen area. She said, "I'll see if I can sterilize—"

"No need." He rolled his shoulders and felt the pull of the bullet. "I'll heal from any infection almost immediately."

Jade wasn't looking at him as she said, "Those aren't . . . normal bullets."

He'd already figured that out. Weapons of man couldn't

hurt his kind. A normal bullet would have been nothing to him. This—it had ripped and torn, and inside, it *burned*.

She washed her hands. "Go get on the bed," she said again. "I'll be right there."

He turned away from her and stalked to the bedroom. The bed was big, easily wide enough for him and Jade, and he could picture her there. Naked. Waiting for him.

*Focus on the pain.*

Because he didn't need to be thinking about sex with her. Not again.

There was a job to do. Jade needed him, and if he played this game just right, she might wind up helping him.

A human, hunted by *Other.* Saving her would be noble. The right thing to do.

A task that might even earn him . . . redemption.

He'd looked at this all wrong before. The fall wasn't about living in hell. Instead, it was about showing that you belonged in heaven. If he did the job right, if he helped her . . .

*I might get to go back.*

Az lay facedown on the bed. The creaking hardwood told him when Jade entered the room. A few moments later, the bed dipped beneath her weight.

"Have you removed a bullet before?" Az asked. Not that it mattered. The bullet *had* to come out. By an expert or novice hand.

Her hands pressed against his back. "Do you want me to lie and say yes?"

Az almost smiled.

He felt her breath blow over his skin. "It's so close to your spine . . ." She'd said that before, but this time, heavy worry weighted the words. Then she lifted her hands. "I don't think I can do this."

He turned, caught her hand. "You have to." His jaw locked, and Az said, "It burns, Jade. Like it's eating away at me from the inside."

She licked her lips. "It . . . it is. Brandt got those bullets from some witch. I don't even know that the hell they are made of, but Brandt's pack uses them to take out the paranormals who get in their way." Her lips turned down as sadness flickered over her features. "For up close kills, they always use their claws, but from a distance . . . nothing stops their guns."

"Magic bullets." Az shook his head. So the shifters had stepped up their game. "Guess I'm just lucky the bastard was a poor shot." It took a whole lot to kill a Fallen, but maybe—

"You weren't lucky." Her hands were on him again, and her slightly cool touch soothed his overheated flesh. "They didn't want you dead. They wanted you incapacitated. They were—"

She stopped.

But Az knew what Jade had been planning to say next. "They wanted to make me easier prey?"

"The better to torture later," she said quietly. He felt the press of metal on his back. She must have found some kind of tool in the kitchen. "Don't move." Her nervous whisper. "*Please* don't move."

He felt pressure on his back. More pain as the burning deepened.

"Almost got it," Jade told him. She moved her body, straddling his legs and ass. "Almost—*there*!"

The pain receded instantly. The muscles and tissues began to heal with a faint tightness that stretched across his back.

"Un . . . freaking . . . believable." Jade's hushed voice. "Your back—I can actually *see* the wound closing."

And he could feel the warmth of her body all along his.

But then she was scrambling away from him. Climbing off his back and onto the bed beside him. In her hand, she held the bullet.

Az turned and pushed up beside her. He took the bullet,

staring down at it. Gold in color, the bullet had a surprisingly heavy weight, and it *burned*. The heat singed his fingertips. The bullet he'd taken from his shoulder had burned, too, and that was why he'd ditched it at the first opportunity.

Now that he knew just how powerful this bullet was, he'd be holding onto it.

Curious, Az glanced at her. "Did it hurt you to touch it?"

"No." Jade shook her head. She slipped away and headed toward the bathroom to wash the blood from her hands.

*The bullets didn't burn humans.* Interesting. He put the bullet on the nearby nightstand. He'd have to find out just what special hell was in that bullet.

Huh. Maybe it *was* hell. Literally. It seemed to him that the supernaturals had gotten particularly vicious and inventive with their attacks lately. Even going so far as to use Angel's Dust against each other.

*Angel's Dust.* The *Other* weren't talking about a drug when they named this weapon. They were referring to the actual dust that was left behind when an angel's wings burned away. A few enterprising paranormals had managed to catch or find some of the stuff, and they'd been using it—with deadly consequences.

The magic from an angel's wings could be very, very potent.

So now, angels appeared to be the main course on the menu—because everyone wanted that special kick of power. Like there needed to be another reason for the *Other* to go after his kind.

Az looked up and found Jade's intense stare on him. "Tell me what you are, Az. I need to know." She stood near the edge of the bed.

She'd asked before. He hadn't answered. This time, he wouldn't lie to her. In fact, he couldn't. Angels weren't allowed to lie.

But he wasn't exactly an angel, not anymore.

"Those marks on your back, the ones that cut across your shoulders . . ." She leaned forward and traced a fingertip over the left scar—a scar that marked where his wing had once been.

When she touched his scar, a shock of pleasure stole through his body. The pleasure was so intense that he shuddered.

"Az?"

Her fingers were lightly caressing the scar.

The wings were always the most sensitive part of an angel's body, and even the scars still maintained that enhanced sensitivity. So when she touched him, he just thought—*want more.*

"Keep touching me," he gritted. The fire in his body didn't come from his wound any longer. It was pure, hot need. Desire.

Lust.

Humans lusted. They needed. They took their pleasure.

*I want the pleasure.*

Her hands feathered over his back. "What happened to you?"

"I fell." Truth.

Now both of her hands were on him, stroking over the scars that lined his shoulders and sending pleasure pulsing through his body.

That sweet scent of strawberries filled his nose as she leaned in even closer. Then—

He felt her lips on the scar that cut across his right shoulder blade. "I'm sorry you hurt," she whispered and kissed the scar.

A dull roar seemed to fill Az's head. Raw lust and need flooded his body. He spun, locked his arms around her, and pulled Jade close. His mouth found hers and his tongue drove deep.

Her fingers were on his scars, sliding gently over them even as her tongue stroked back against his.

Az's cock jerked toward her, so full and thick that he ached. *Pleasure.*

He shifted their bodies to better bring her beneath him. Az kissed his way down her throat. He liked the way she gasped his name. Liked the lush feel of her breasts against his chest.

*Liked her.*

He yanked up her shirt. Her breasts spilled against the black cups of her bra. *Taste.*

With a hand that wasn't quite steady, Az pushed the thin bra straps down her shoulders. Her breasts pressed toward him. Her small nipples were tight and dark pink. He lowered his head, and his tongue slipped over the edge of her nipple.

"*Az.*"

She tasted better than strawberries.

He licked her again. Again. His mouth closed over her breast, and he began to suck her flesh.

No wonder humans enjoyed sex. So far, it seemed pretty damn fantastic.

Her hands were on him. Her hips arching toward him. Her body was silk and sin and he wanted more.

But . . .

*Angels didn't need sex. Angels didn't crave.*

He craved her. Az's hands were on her jeans. He yanked the button loose. Eased down the zipper.

*Temptation.*

He should fight the temptation. He should—

*A thin scrap of lace.*

Az shoved down her jeans. His fingers slipped under the edge of her lacy panties.

*Touch her. Take her.*

So much temptation.

"I want you," her voice, whispering to him. His head lifted. Her lips were red. Full. He kissed her again. Drank her in and wanted more. His cock was so heavy with arousal that he felt like he'd explode any minute.

*In her.*

But her hand caught his. "I want you, but Brandt destroys everything—*everyone*—I want." The memory of pain darkened her words.

Az grabbed onto his control and held tight. *Take. Touch.*

Jade shook her head. "This isn't a good idea. They're already after you because of me." Now she pushed against him. "Let me go, Az."

He didn't want to let her go. Not then, not—

*What am I doing?* Az yanked his hands away from her and rolled to the other side of the bed. He stared at the ceiling as he sucked in deep, heaving breaths.

Jade didn't leave the bed. She stayed there, just inches away. "He killed the last man that I slept with—Brandt *killed* him right in front of me."

Bastard. Az turned his head and gazed at her. Jade's eyes were on him.

"They're gunning for you now, because you helped me that first night," she told him. "Brandt . . ." She swallowed and her eyes were sad. "He likes to play with his prey."

He didn't really gave a damn about Brandt right then. Not while his body was hard and tight with need for her.

She sat up and climbed from the bed. *Her body* . . . perfect. "Having sex with me will just make him want to hurt you more."

He watched her walk away, and the rage exploded.

In an instant, Az was across the room, in front of her. Reaching for her arms and hauling her up against him. *All that sweet flesh.* "Do you think I care at all about what some panther bastard thinks he can do to me?"

Her eyes widened. "Um, no?"

"I am a Fallen. I fear no one or nothing on this earth."

"A-a Fallen?"

"I've seen heaven. I've seen hell. I've been the hand of death."

She swallowed.

"The panther can hunt me, but in the end, *I* will be the one to kill him." As he'd killed so many others. Thousands of souls—taken.

*What's one more?*

Her pink tongue snaked across her lower lip. The lip he'd kissed. He could still taste her.

"The scars on your back . . ." she whispered.

*Tell her all.* "My wings burned away when I fell."

Jade's eyes widened as she slowly shook her head. "No, no, that's not possible. You're saying that you're—"

He released her. Stepped back. "I don't lie."

Her chest rose and fell with her rapid breaths. Rose and fell . . . and her breasts were still tight with arousal. Just as his body still yearned for her.

"I'm a Fallen angel, and you—" His voice roughened with both his rage and his lust, "You're my temptation."

# CHAPTER FIVE

An angel.

Jade stood in the shower, letting the rough blast of water slide over her skin. The shower was supposed to cool her off, but, um, *no*.

Because she kept picturing Az. His intense gaze. His wide, muscled chest, those *lick me* abs. She could feel his hands on her skin. His mouth on her breast and—

*A Fallen angel.*

Her eyes squeezed shut as she put her face under the water.

Sure, she'd heard tales about angels. When she'd been seventeen, she'd had a brutal awakening to the supernatural world around her. Since then, she'd seen just about everything out there—demons, vamps, even a djinn once—and he'd scared the hell out of her.

But—an angel? Oh, damn, if he knew all the things she'd done . . .

She was covered in blood and sin.

The shower curtain was yanked to the side and the sudden rush of cold air had her eyes flying open as she spun around.

Az stood there. His gaze swept slowly over her.

Should she pretend a modesty that she didn't feel? His stare was scorching and—

"Someone's outside," he said.

Aw, crap. This wasn't about wild sex.

And, ah, so much for a safe place.

She jumped out of the shower. He didn't move back. Her body brushed against his as she yanked for a towel.

"You're afraid of me," Az charged with his voice flat and cold.

But, no, she wasn't. "Should I be?" Jade asked as she secured the towel between her breasts.

She expected an instant denial. He'd been the one saving her ass for the past few days. He was the hero. The *angel* for goodness sake. But—

"Yes."

Then she heard the pounding at the door. What had to be a fist thudding into the wood. Somebody sure wanted inside the cabin awful badly. Not a good sign.

"Get dressed," he told her as he backed up. Finally. She could breathe. "I'll take care of our visitor."

Wait, take care of—how exactly?

But he was gone and she rushed to pull on her jeans even as she heard a voice call out . . .

"This is the police. Open the door!"

No, no, *no!* "Don't, Az!" Jade yelled back and she lurched forward. She'd managed to put on her jeans—no underwear—and her bra.

Az turned to stare at her.

"You can't let the cops in," she told him, her voice hushed. No one could be allowed to get in. They had to run.

He frowned at her.

Oh, jeez. *Angels.*

The front door thudded again. "*Open up!*"

She jerked a fresh white T-shirt over her head. "We *stole* a car," she reminded Az and grabbed his hand. *A car that had probably been equipped with some kind of anti-theft tracking device.* Dammit, she hadn't even checked for that. Beginner's mistake, but she'd been in a rush. "He probably tracked us." It had been three hours since they'd made it to the cabin. Three too-fast hours.

Plenty of time for a cop to hunt them down.

"We've got to get out of here."

He just stared at her.

Okay, maybe she needed to break this down for him. "He'll throw us in jail."

Az offered her a crooked smile. "No, he won't."

She blinked.

"Because he's not really a cop."

Then Az pulled away from her. He stalked to the front door. She could all but see the tension that coiled his body with fierce energy.

Wait—had he said . . . *not really a cop?*

The door shook again. Even harder this time.

Az yanked the door open. She caught a fast glimpse of a police officer's uniform. A badge. A gun that was aimed at Az—

And then Az snatched the gun right out of the guy's hands. In an instant, the gun was flying across the room, and Az had the cop by the throat.

*Um, he sure looks like a cop to me.* Over the years, she'd sure encountered her share of those uniformed men and women, too.

Jade rushed across the room. "Az! Put him down, you can't—"

Then she saw the cop's teeth. The too-sharp canines that hung behind his lips. The man's claws were out and currently digging into Az's arms.

Despite the attack, Az wasn't letting go of him.

"I could smell him," Az said, lifting the fellow even higher into the air. "Shifter. Same scent those other jerks carried."

But she didn't recognize this guy, and she'd thought that she knew every panther shifter in Brandt's pack.

She rose onto her toes and peered over Az's shoulder. Was this maybe-cop another hunter Brandt had hired?

"Call him . . . off . . ." The guy grunted. "I'm not . . . gonna hurt you."

Like she hadn't heard that one before. Jade scrambled back and found the discarded weapon. She checked to make sure it was loaded—oh yes—and then rushed around Az to aim the weapon at the cop. "Step back, Az."

After a moment's hesitation, he did.

The shifter fell to the floor, gasping. Az had a killer grip.

"Who are you?" Jade demanded as her hold on the gun tightened. "And why the hell are you dressed like a cop?"

His palms flattened on the wooden floor. "Because I *am* a cop." He looked up at her, revealing a hard, chiseled face—and a wicked smile that flashed his sharp canines. "And a shifter."

"Are you working for Brandt?" Because Az had said the guy smelled like the others.

"I'm working to take Dupre down." He said those words with vehemence. "That twisted bastard is destroying the panthers in Louisiana." Now the stranger rose to his feet. "We're not all psychotic fucks, despite what you may think."

"You mean despite what I've seen." She wasn't lowering the weapon. Jade didn't trust this guy. Sure, cops were supposed to be all good and safe, but the only man she felt safe with was—

*Az.*

Az's gaze darted between her and the cop.

The shifter grunted. "Look, my name's Tanner. Tanner Chance. And I want to stop Dupre just as much as you do."

"Doubtful." Highly.

Az spread his feet a bit and straightened his shoulders, a slight movement that held an aura of menace. "How did you find us?" Az wanted to know.

"You stole a car." The cop shifter shrugged. "There's an APB out for you. I was just the lucky bastard who found you first."

"I don't believe in luck," Jade said. Especially since she'd only seemed to have *bad* luck in the last few years.

The gun was a steady weight in her hand. She was a good shot, but even if she hadn't been, it would be hard to miss her target at a range this close.

"Fine. Don't believe in it." The guy called Tanner exhaled heavily. "Believe in a GPS locator and a cop who hauled ass to get to you before anyone else could."

She could buy that bit.

Tanner's gaze slid to Az. "Who's the muscle?"

Az crossed his arms over his chest and stared steadily back at the cop.

"Caught my scent, huh?" Tanner frowned at him. "So you've got an enhanced sense of smell, and you're too damn strong to be a human."

"I'm her guardian," Az said. "Azrael."

Her gaze slipped to him. As in . . . guardian angel? Seriously? Of course, it totally figured that her guardian angel would have fallen from grace.

Tanner's gaze narrowed. "You're also the asshole that managed to piss off the pack of panthers in New Orleans."

Az smiled.

Her heart did a crazy jump in her chest. Why did she like his smile so much?

"I do what I can," Az allowed. He hadn't relaxed his body, not yet.

But then, she wasn't about to drop her weapon either. Jade had met far too many boys in blue that she didn't trust.

The cop raised his hands, probably trying to show that he was harmless. The fact that he was sporting two-inch long claws didn't help his harmless act any. "Look, you don't have much time," Tanner said. "Brandt has a bounty on your head, and, if they aren't already, then every supernatural in the area will be gunning for you."

Jade laughed at that. "He's been hunting me for years."

"No. Not you. Not this time." His dark head inclined toward Az. "Your guardian." Tanner's green gaze slid back to catch hers. "You know panthers don't share well." She saw the slight flex of his nostrils.

*Damn shifter senses.*

"Your scent's all over him, and even your shower can't hide the fact that he's been all over *you*."

Az punched him. The shifter stumbled back and fell against the wall.

Jade grabbed Az's arm. "Wait!" His muscles were rock hard beneath her touch. He started to shake her off. She just held him tighter. *"Wait, Az."* Because the battle wasn't just about her anymore.

*I can't let Brandt get Az.*

"I want to hear what he has to say," she told Az.

His jaw clenched and she knew he'd just prefer to beat the crap out of the guy. Tempting, but they needed to try another option first.

"Please," she said, easing her hold so that she was stroking the tense muscles of Az's arm. "Give him just a minute. If we don't like what he says . . ."

Az inclined his head. "Then I'll make him wish he'd never spoken."

Sounded good to her. Jade glanced back at Tanner.

The shifter swallowed. "Brandt doesn't realize you've been fucking yet," he said as he pushed away from the wall, and Jade caught the hardening of Az's jaw.

*We haven't, yet.*

Temptation.

"But when he does, you know what Brandt will do."

*Brandt liked to play with his prey.*

The cop's head cocked to the side. "How much torture do you think you can stand?" He asked Az.

And Az smiled. "More than you can imagine."

Tanner lifted up his shirt to reveal flesh that had been savaged. Long, twisting scars covered his stomach and swiped around to his back. With deep, old scars like that, he would've been injured long ago. Before his first change as a shifter.

He would have been just a child.

"Trust me, I can imagine a hell of a lot." Tanner's voice was a growl.

Unfortunately, she'd seen marks like that before. Brandt bore scars just like them. "You're in Brandt's pack."

"No." Tanner shook his head. "I *was* in the pack, until I was twelve years old, and I managed to get the hell away from Brandt and his old man."

Because Brandt's father had been the one to give Brandt the scars he carried. *To prove I can handle any pain.* Brandt's voice whispered through her mind. He'd told her those words, the first time she'd seen the scars that marked his body.

Brandt's bastard of a father had enjoyed torturing, and he'd passed that love on to his son.

"You understand," Tanner said, staring at her with eyes that saw too much. "You know why I had to get away from them. I wasn't gonna end up like those assholes."

Twisted. Broken.

Killers.

Jade lowered her gun.

Az frowned. "Just because he left, it doesn't mean this guy isn't like them."

"*I'm not.* I got away from them," Tanner said, anger roughening his voice. "And I stayed away. But then they came to *my* town—"

"Looking for me," she finished. Brandt and his pack were

based in northern Louisiana, but they'd headed down south to track her.

Tanner nodded. The badge on his uniform gleamed. "I almost had you in the Quarter. I was there when those bastards started firing at your . . . *guardian*." His jaw tightened. "But I had to help the humans. I had to take care of them."

"We didn't need your help," Az said. Right. Because he'd taken the bullets and kept on standing—and tossing around fire.

But Jade didn't have the luxury of super strength. "What do you want?" She asked Tanner.

"I told you, I want to stop Dupre."

But what was a cop's definition of "stop"? "A cage isn't going to hold him." She tried to put it as delicately as she could. "You're not going to be able to arrest the guy and—"

Tanner glanced down at his badge. Then, slowly, he shook his head. "I'm not looking to arrest him." A pause. "I'm looking to kill Brandt Dupre, and any who follow him. The only way they're gonna stop is if they can't draw breath."

A truth she knew too well.

"And you can help me," he said. "We can work together, and we *can* kill the bastard."

*Been there, tried that.* "He's not exactly easy to kill."

Az sent her a fast glance. "Anyone can die."

Maybe. Maybe not.

"Look, we don't have a lot of time to keep talking now." Tanner swiped a hand down his face. The shifter was sweating. "About a dozen cops will be closing in on this place soon."

*"What?"* She lunged forward but, surprisingly, it was Az who caught her shoulders and held her back before she could grab Tanner.

"Easy," Az told her.

Screw that. She wasn't feeling *easy* then. Not if cops were about to storm the place.

Tanner grimaced. "Witnesses saw you nearly plow down a civilian in New Orleans—"

"Oh, come on," Jade exploded, "that was just Brandt—a hit from the car barely would have slowed him down." Just given him some bumps and bruises and made him feel some of the pain that she felt.

"They *saw* you, so now the cops are after you." Tanner cocked his head to the right as he studied her. "I've arranged for a motorcycle to be waiting for you. If you cut through the swamp, it's about three miles northwest of here. After I traced you I got a buddy to leave the bike there for me."

Az asked, "And we're supposed to trust you?"

"Yeah, you are."

Jade wasn't the trusting sort. She didn't think Az was, either.

"And you need to start hauling ass," Tanner continued. "I only had about a ten minute head start on the rest of the police crew, and now I'd say you're down to—"

"Five minutes," Az finished.

Fabulous.

"Yeah." Tanner nodded. "So get the hell out of here, take that motorcycle, then meet me tonight in New Orleans—"

"You want us to go back into the city?" Jade demanded. Really dumb plan. "With Brandt hunting there?" Maybe she could stop to paint a big bull's-eye on her back, too. She yanked away from Az.

Or rather, Az let her go. Mostly because he was now studying the shifter with assessing eyes. "He wants to use you as bait."

She'd figured that out on her own. Bait to dangle right in front of the big, obsessed psycho. Lovely.

"Tonight, I just want to talk." Tanner's words were gritted. "Meet me at the St. Louis Cemetery. Midnight."

Even better. Because she wanted to hang out in the

dark, in a cemetery, and wait for a panther that she didn't trust.

Tanner took a step toward her. "I can make this all end. I can give you back your life, Jade."

What life?

Then she heard the faintest screech of a siren. It looked like the cops weren't coming in quietly.

Tanner's gaze didn't leave her face. "We're out of time. *Trust me.*"

No.

He dug into his pocket and pulled out a set of keys. Tanner tossed them and Az caught the keys easily in his fist.

"Now you're gonna have to take me out before they arrive." Tanner inclined his head toward Az. "It has to look like you overpowered me so no one thinks—"

"That a cop is helping a criminal," Jade said. Right. She got it. "Fine, I think we can—"

Az swung out with his fist. He slammed the punch right into the shifter's jaw with a rough crunch of sound. Tanner went down, eyes closing, and the guy's slack body hit the floor.

"Or *you* can handle it," she muttered and cleared her throat. Well, Az *had* saved her knuckles some bruising.

Az glanced at her. She was pretty sure he'd enjoyed delivering that punch. The guy was fighting a grin.

Bad angel.

*I like 'em that way.*

"You up for a run through the swamp?" Jade asked as she pulled him away toward the back of the cabin. Judging by those sirens, the cops were getting way too close.

"We shouldn't trust him," Az said, moving slowly and slowing *her* down.

"Of course not. We shouldn't trust anyone." But she trusted Az. How could you not trust an angel? "One thing

we know . . . the cops *are* coming. Those sirens are screaming louder every second, and we need to get our butts out
of here."

Jails sucked. She'd spent some unfortunate time in one before. Back when . . .

No. Jade slammed the door shut on that memory. She
would *not* think about them. Not now.

As a general rule, she never let herself think about *them*.
It hurt too much.

She realized that she was holding Az's hand, her fingers
intertwined with his. Jade stared at his hand. Strong. Warm.

*Temptation.* The whisper burned through her.

She pulled away from him. Did Az even know how much
he'd hurt her with that one word? She was already another
man's curse.

Couldn't she ever be more?

"Give me the keys, and I'll get the hell out of here on my
own." She lifted her chin. "You can go the opposite way.
The cops probably don't even know about you. You can
leave, we can split, and both just get on with our lives."

He opened his palm. Jade tried to swipe the keys, but he
snatched them away from her.

*What?* Jerk.

"We go together."

Her gaze held his. "Sure that won't be too much *temptation* for you?" Oh, yeah, she said it.

But then the guy surprised her when he said, "Will it be
too much for you?"

Her jaw dropped. *Maybe.*

Screw this. Jade rushed for the back door. They could
play coy and settle the tension between them later. Now was
the time for running.

Her feet thudded down the wooden steps, and Az rushed
right behind her. They hit the edge of the swamp at a run,

ducking and dodging fallen trees and branches. The heat beat down on them, and Jade didn't even want to *think* about the snakes that were probably lying in wait.

She hated snakes.

The thick scent of vegetation surrounded them. A line of dark green water, covered by algae, waited to the left. A log—*no, not a log, a gator*—drifted lazily in the sludge.

Her heart shoved into her ribs. Faster, faster, she zipped through the swamp. *Northwest.* Three miles wasn't so much.

Except it seemed like a whole hell of a lot when you were running through a damn creature-infested *swamp*.

Then Az grabbed her wrist and jerked her against him.

"What—" she began, panting.

He covered her mouth with his hand.

*"Someone's following us."* His whisper.

And she heard the thud of pounding feet—coming quickly toward them.

A shifter would be able to pick up their scent and follow them perfectly in the swamp. But if it were just humans . . . humans wouldn't be able to track them even half as well.

Her hand pressed against Az's chest. His gaze held hers. They waited.

Humans . . . or shifters?

Az pulled her deeper into the shadows of some swaying trees. His hand slipped away from her mouth. They stood close, bodies brushing. Neither dared speak.

"Dammit!" A man's angry shout seemed to echo through the swamp. "I saw them run out here!"

"Now I don't see a fuckin' thing," came another voice. Also male. Also pissed.

The sound of her breath seemed far too loud to Jade. And those voices were too close. She rose up on her tiptoes, and, over Az's shoulder, she caught sight of the men.

Uniforms. "Cops," she whispered. Cops who were heading in their direction.

She felt the tension in Az's body. His head bent toward hers. "I can take care of them." Barely a breath of sound.

No doubt he could. But, if possible, she'd really like to avoid adding the assault of two police officers to her already extensive résumé. So Jade pulled Az closer and tried not to make a sound.

*Go away. Head back in the other direction.*

"Shit, they could be anyplace by now," one of the cops snarled.

Not just anyplace. She'd gone northwest. She'd scouted before she picked this house as a retreat spot. She knew how to mark the directions. And this way—it led to the old dirt road that cut around and looped through the back of the swamp.

The cops kept talking, but the sound of their voices grew softer. *They were moving away.* Going back to the house. Muttering about not getting paid enough to dodge snakes.

She waited until those voices faded away completely. Then she took a deep breath. Jade glanced up and found Az's eyes on her—well, on her mouth.

Her hand was still on his chest. Right over his pounding heart. She cleared her throat. "I . . . uh, think it's safe now." Though the cops could return with reinforcements anytime.

He nodded and stepped back.

*Get a grip, girl.*

She turned away and headed straight ahead, away from those sheltering trees.

"You sure that you know where we're going?" He asked.

Glancing back, she tossed him a real smile. "I'm good with escape plans."

His eyes narrowed on her.

She shook her head. "Come on, angel, let's get moving."

They didn't speak again, not until they'd cleared the swamp. The motorcycle waited under a weeping willow, just where Tanner had promised.

*This is too easy. Has to be a setup.*

After years of running and struggling to survive on her own, now she suddenly had an angel *and* a cop who wanted to help her?

No way. Fate wouldn't smile on her like that.

Az climbed onto the motorcycle. Of course, he looked good—better than good—on it. Hot sex on a summer day better.

But she knew just how dangerous a sexy man could be.

The weight of the gun she'd taken from Tanner pressed into her lower back. Had Az seen her grab the gun and slip it out of the cabin? Maybe. Maybe not. Either way, she wasn't exactly defenseless anymore.

Jade cocked a brow. "I get that you're the big, tough supernatural and all." She lifted up the keys. "But I'm the one who knows the area, so I'll be the one doing the driving."

He blinked at her.

Jade grinned. "Move on back, angel."

She slipped in front of him. Started the engine and enjoyed the purr of the motorcycle.

Az's thighs pressed around her. His arm slid around her stomach.

"Hold on," she told him and shot away from the tree. A cloud of dust followed in her wake. "Things are going to get rough."

Just the way she liked them.

# Chapter Six

Ten minutes until midnight.

Az stared up at the tombs as they rose over the heavy, brick wall that surrounded the cemetery. The scent of flowers teased his nose, but he knew that scent wasn't coming from some floral tokens left on the graves by mourners.

*You can always catch the scent when Death is close.*

A tell-tale sign that an angel was nearby. Death Angels were at their strongest when they were about to take a soul. In those few moments, humans could catch the sweet scent of flowers.

*A death scent.*

Death didn't really smell like decay and rot. That smell just came to the bodies after the souls were gone.

Tonight, death was close. Following him.

His eyes narrowed as he scanned the darkness. Who'd be dying tonight?

"Okay, this is as far as you go." Jade crossed her arms over her chest and stared at him. Her eyes seemed to shine under the light of the moon and stars. "Now you take the motorcycle and go someplace safe."

His lips twitched. How . . . charming. She thought to protect him once more. She kept doing that, despite what she knew of him. "Trying to get rid of me again?"

She shook her head. "Look, I don't even understand . . . why do you *want* to help me? I'm nothing to you!"

Anger stirred within him as the mild amusement vanished. She was hardly nothing.

"I appreciate the white knight routine, believe me, I do, but *why?*" A faint line appeared between her brows. She stood just a few feet away, on the cracked sidewalk, and asked, "Why do you want to help me? Why are you risking your life for me?"

And the truth came from him. "Because I think you can give *my* life back to me."

Her eyes widened. "What?"

He shoved down the kickstand and climbed from the motorcycle so he could close in on her. His gaze tracked to that line of stark tombs that rose over the steep walls. "I've been here before."

"Yeah, well, you, me, and every tourist who wants an up-close look at the cities of the dead—"

"I fell here."

She didn't say anything in response to that. Interesting. He'd found that Jade often had plenty to say. Not this time.

Her mouth actually hung open a bit.

He brushed by her and headed for the heavy gates that led into the cemetery. Dark shadows stretched from the entrance. And he remembered . . .

*Crashing. Agony. Pain.*

"I didn't know who I was." Not at first. The descent had been so intense, the fire so hot, that his memories had been wiped from him.

Az crossed the threshold into the cemetery. His gaze swept around, and then he was snaking through the old graves. Left. Right. Moving more by instinct than anything else.

She followed closely behind him. "Az . . ."

"After the fall, no one ever remembers, not at first." It had been good, too, not knowing. Living in ignorance of the lives he'd taken. The sins he'd committed.

Another turn. Another.

He heard her gasp behind him. Before them, an old crypt had been smashed, and wide cracks spread out from the broken tomb's middle like spiderwebs. Beside the remains, a broken stone angel looked mournfully at the wreckage.

It only seemed fitting that she'd lost a wing, too.

He stared at that crypt. "Do you know what it's like to wake up in hell?"

"Yes."

Frowning, Az glanced back at her.

Her gaze was on him, not the crypt. "We all have our own hell." Her hand touched his shoulder. "I-I'm not sure what you're exactly expecting. I can't give you back heaven."

Maybe not.

But maybe . . .

"A witch found me." He turned to better face her, and Jade's brows lifted at his admission. "She cleaned me up, gave me food, then, just when I was growing stronger, she turned around and sold me out to a bunch of bastards who got off on torturing *Other*."

Jade swallowed. "What happened to them?"

She needed to see him for what he was. "I killed them all." Well, those Sam hadn't gotten to first, anyway.

She held his stare. "And the witch?"

"Her time will come." She wouldn't escape him unscathed. Az planned to make certain of that.

Jade stared up at him in confusion. "You're standing here telling me that you're some heartless badass, but you're *helping me* so I—"

"I'm helping myself." The words fell heavily. "You're a human. Favored. Weak."

Deceptively so. Humans were gifted with the rush of emotions. With pleasures. Pains.

He could seek vengeance on those who'd wronged him. Vengeance was his by right. But to give her protection, to aid one weaker . . . now that just might be enough to earn some *redemption*.

"So I'm just the lucky human you saw about to get an ass-kicking? Who I am doesn't matter? You would risk your life to save any of us?"

He nodded. "Yes." He would do what was necessary. *Protect the weak*. Fight and claw his way back to heaven.

Her sigh held a sad edge. "Not all humans need protecting." A pause. "Not all humans *want* protecting." Then she turned away from him. "We also don't all enjoy being called a 'temptation' by some lost Fallen with some intimacy issues."

He blinked and stared after her. *Intimacy issues?* He'd never been intimate with another. Angels weren't allowed the luxury of intimacy. "You don't understand what the world is like, for me." So much noise. The feelings. The emotions. They were all ripping him apart.

Except . . . except it hadn't been so bad in the last few days. Not since he'd been with her.

Jade didn't look back at him. "Was it really that much better up there?"

He didn't answer.

At his silence, Jade glanced over her shoulder at him. "I mean, it's not all sunshine and rainbows down here, but we're alive. That has to count for something, right?"

Something.

"Instead of trying so hard to get back upstairs," she told him, "maybe you should consider that you're exactly where you're supposed to be."

With her.

But then she shook her head and looked away from him. "I think that cop stood us up. And being in a cemetery, at midnight, is *not* my idea of a good time."

But even as she spoke, Az heard the rustle of footsteps. Sliding away—or coming closer?

Either way, he took a step toward Jade.

"Muggers hide out here," she told him, voice quieter now as she scanned the shadows around them. "But they're not even the start of what we need to fear."

He knew all about the vampires who liked to stalk the cities of the dead. They'd hide in the dark, waiting for victims who were curious—and even willing—and then they'd strike.

Those victims would die.

But it wasn't a vampire who stepped from the shadows. It was the shifter.

Az didn't relax his guard, and he could tell by the stiffness of Jade's shoulders that she wasn't relaxing hers, either.

"You pack one hell of a punch," Tanner said as he studied Az. The full moon fell onto them and sent their shadows chasing across the crypts.

Az shrugged. He'd actually gone easy on the guy. If he'd wanted, he could have broken the cop's jaw with that punch.

Tanner whistled softly. "There's a very high price on your head, man. You gonna be up for the hunters coming your way?"

He couldn't wait to face them. A battle would drain some of the growing tension from his body. Tension that increased every time Jade touched his skin.

*Want her.* He'd stroked her flesh. Tasted her.

And learned why mortals killed for pleasure.

Az shoved those memories aside. "I'm ready." Fear was the only emotion he'd yet to feel on earth. What was there to fear? What was there left to lose? *Nothing.*

"He doesn't have to be ready." Jade's voice. Flat. Calm. "This isn't his fight. I'm the one going after Brandt." She turned to Az and put her hand on his chest, right over his heart. Her voice lowered as she said, "I'm not your salvation. Helping me isn't gonna give you some free pass into heaven."

Her scent slipped around him. His body hungered for hers. Needed.

"And I'm not going to be your temptation, either." Now a thread of anger slipped into her voice. Anger. Hurt? "I've already been there and done that for another. Dammit, *I'm more.*"

Pain was reflected in her eyes.

She tried to turn away then. He grabbed her hand and held tight. *Won't let go.* "You need me." He didn't bother lowering his voice. He wanted the shifter to hear this. If they were going into a fight, they'd need his strength to win.

Jade would need *him.* He didn't know why it was so important for her to admit that.

It simply was.

"Look," Tanner growled, "you two can have your lovers' spat later, but right now, we need to go figure out our plan of attack."

Az felt the shifter's eyes on him then. Seeing too much. His hold on Jade tightened as he looked up and regarded the shifter with deeper suspicion. *Just because you were a cop, it didn't mean you should be trusted.*

He sure didn't trust the jerk.

*Just because you were an angel, it didn't mean you were good.*

He knew that better than others.

"You didn't come alone," Az said, certain.

"Because I'm not so trusting, either." He shrugged. "And because I know you're no *guardian.*"

No, but he *was* guarding Jade. While angels couldn't lie outright, they knew how to twist the truth to conceal their secrets.

"So who's watching us?" Jade wanted to know. With her free hand, she pointed to the shadows.

"My backup plan." Tanner didn't look away from them.

"Now are we going to stand out here all night, wasting time, or are we ready to get down to business?"

"Business?" Az repeated.

"Brandt's death. It's what we both want."

It was what Jade seemed to need.

"He's not exactly an easy guy to destroy," Jade said softly. "In case you haven't noticed."

Tanner laughed, but the grating sound held no humor. "I noticed alright. I also know that *everything* can die. You just have to get close enough to make the kill." Tanner stalked toward them. "Getting close isn't exactly a problem for you, is it, Jade?"

She didn't answer. Az narrowed his eyes on the shifter.

"But there's close . . ." Tanner murmured, "and then there's *killing close.*"

Jade sucked in a deep breath. "Do you have a plan?" she demanded. "Or are you just out here to spout bullshit?"

Az smiled. He liked the woman's fire. She seemed to have more fury in her than most humans.

So hot, you could almost feel the burn.

Tanner smiled at her, too, and that grin flashed his sharp canines. "I thought a human would be more afraid."

"I am scared. Scared every single moment." That wasn't sarcasm coming from her, either.

Her confession gave Az pause. He hadn't realized . . .

"I just want the nightmare over," she continued, "and I want to be able to live like everyone else. So if you've got some great plan, then share it, and let's cut the crap."

Az listened carefully, not to Jade and the shifter, but to the whisper of sounds that surrounded them.

Another rustle. A brush of fabric against stone. The softest of breaths.

*There.*

Az moved in an instant, rushing toward the watcher, and moving so quickly that he knew he'd appear to be a blur.

He caught the watcher in his grasp even as he heard Tanner call out a warning.

*Too late.*

He stared at the person in his hands—a person very familiar to him.

Wide eyes. Close-cropped blond hair. Small. Deceptively delicate.

*Witch.*

The same witch who'd sold him out months before. In that instant, Az knew they'd walked into a trap.

"You're dying," he told her. She'd traded his life. Now he'd take hers.

*"No!"* Tanner's shout, cutting through the night. "Fuck, *no, don't hurt her!"*

It wouldn't hurt. He could be compassionate. Death could be as gentle as a whisper.

*Vengeance is mine.*

"Az . . ." Jade's voice, drifting on the wind to him.

The scent of flowers teased his nose again. A Death Angel was close.

Az looked back. Tanner had his claws at Jade's throat. In turn, she had a gun pointed right at his heart.

"I think we all need to take a minute and calm the hell down," the shifter called out.

Az felt amazingly calm. The witch barely seemed to breathe.

"We need each other," Tanner growled. "Brandt and his pack are too powerful for us to face alone."

Doubtful.

Az stared back at the witch. A faint smile lifted her lips. "Still think you're the strongest force on earth, do you, angel?"

"I think I'm looking at a dead woman," he said.

But she laughed. "Not yet, you aren't.

Why was he hesitating? "You sold me out once already."

"And I'll do it again." Sounded like a promise. "That's why you need me."

Footsteps raced toward them. Jade and Tanner. Not taking aim at one another any longer. Instead—

"Don't hurt her," Tanner ordered. "That witch is our ticket into the pack."

"Witch?" Jade staggered to a stop beside them. Az's focus shifted to Jade even as he kept his grip on the witch.

Jade's gaze flew between Az and the woman. "No one mentioned anything about a witch—"

"I told you that every *Other* in the city would be after your guardian." Sweat trickled down Tanner's temple. "Well, Heather here has a certain . . . reputation."

"For selling out everyone she meets?" Az demanded. He hadn't let the witch go yet, but he hadn't killed her, either.

He thought he was showing pretty good restraint.

"Almost everyone," the witch said.

"Heather . . ." A warning tone entered Tanner's voice.

But Heather didn't heed that warning. "I was trying to do the world a favor." She held Az's gaze. "Some *Other* are too dangerous to live."

"Wait a minute!" Jade grabbed Az's arm and hauled him away from the witch. Only because Az let her haul him. "You're the one who found Az?" She asked the other woman.

Heather's lips curved. "The world is smaller than we like to think."

Jade nodded. "Right. Okay. I'll take that as a yes." Then she drove her fist right at the witch. Heather took the hit in the jaw and tumbled back. "You freaking sold out an *angel*, you crazy bitch!"

Heather blinked, then rubbed her jaw. "My, my, aren't you the feisty human."

Az rather thought she was. She'd just . . . fought for him. Or at least punched for him. No one had ever—

"We're out of here, Az." Now Jade was yanking his arm. "Whatever game this shifter is working, we *don't* want to be a part of it."

Not if the witch was involved.

But he wasn't ready to walk just yet. *Vengeance.* Right there, so close.

*"Will you be strong enough to kill him . . ."* The witch's voice was different now. Heavy with power and magic. Az looked at her and saw that the bright gold of her eyes had faded as she continued, *"when the time comes?"*

Her faded gaze wasn't on him. It was on Jade.

*"Will you sacrifice?"* Heather continued, and a light breeze blew against Az's flesh. *"Will you make the choice to save the others and face death?"*

The witch was pushing his self-control and seriously getting on his nerves.

"What in the hell are you talking about?" Jade wanted to know. She didn't sound shaken or worried, just pissed.

*"Love has a price."* That same, weird rumble that wasn't a human's voice. Not quite. *"Sacrifice is the payment. The choice of life or death. You have to kill what you love."*

Jade's eyes narrowed. "Let's be clear, here, alright, witchy woman? I don't love Brandt. I hate him. He has taken *everything* away from me. My home. My family." Her chin lifted. "So when the time comes, oh yeah, I'll do what I have to do. If the choice is my life or his, then he'll be the one dying."

Heather's eyes brightened once more as the fog seemed to fade from her gaze. She smiled at Jade. "You're going to be tested soon."

"Why are we still here?" Jade muttered, tugging on Az. "Let's—"

But Tanner stepped forward. "The pack won't welcome me back. Not unless I bring them . . ." His gaze fell on Az. "Something."

"You mean someone," Jade charged. "You want to take Az to them? Are you—"

"Actually, I want to take *you* to Brandt. If I bring back his lost mate, there's no way he will turn me away."

*Mate.* Why did that one word have Az tensing as a white-hot fury rose within him? "She's not his mate." Shifters and their mates. So possessive. So territorial.

*Not. His.*

Tanner held up his hands. "Easy there, big guy. This is just about what Brandt thinks, not about what actually is. Didn't mean to step into any . . . uh, personal business there."

"Tanner takes the human," Heather came to stand by the shifter's side. "And I take you in," she told Az.

Because she was so good at selling people out.

"They'll believe I'm there for the bounty on your head. They'll let me in, and they'll take us both right to Brandt," Heather finished with a little smirk.

"No," Jade said immediately, and that smirk slipped a bit. "This isn't going to work, it—"

"Seems you pissed off the pack alpha." Tanner rubbed his jaw as he studied Az. "And he wants you brought in alive."

"Only so he can take his time cutting Az apart." Jade shook her head. "No way. We're done here. Your plan is crap. If we follow it, we'll all die."

Not all.

"Can't you kill him?" Heather asked Az, crossing her arms. "I mean, you're the Angel of Death. All you need to do is touch him, right?"

He saw Jade's jaw drop. "Angel of Death? As in *the*—"

"Not anymore." His growl. He would have told her that part, eventually.

"But you can do it," Tanner snapped. "You're the only one who can. Brandt is stronger than most paranormals. He's got magic on his side, and he's not afraid to use it. If we want him taken out, we need your help."

Jade's lips trembled as she stared into Az's eyes. "I already told you, this isn't your—"

"You want to use me as bait." Az wanted to be clear on the rules. "The witch takes me in—"

"And collects the bounty," Heather added quickly.

"Of course." Figured she'd take her cut. Not like she'd do this out of the goodness of her heart. From what he'd seen, the witch didn't have a heart. "Then I get my turn to eliminate Brandt." And to save Jade. To start his journey back upstairs.

Jade's body practically vibrated with fury. "This is *stupid*—"

"I'll be there for backup." Tanner rocked forward on the balls of his feet. "Together, we'll take out that whole pack."

Az didn't really need his help. But if the shifter wanted some revenge of his own . . .

"You can't do this." Jade gripped both of his hands now and shook him. "This is crazy. You don't want to just walk right up to Brandt."

"No?" Now Tanner's anger had broken past his control. "What's your big plan then? You want to keep running from him? Hiding? While others die?"

She flinched. "I'll go to him. I'll end this myself."

"You don't have that power." Tanner was certain.

So was Az.

Her gaze held his.

"Please," she whispered. "I don't want you to get hurt because of me."

And the choice was made. A life for a life. Sacrifice. He pointed at the witch. "Betray me again, and I'll make certain you feel the full fury of hell."

"Been there," she muttered.

"And you will be again." A promise.

She swallowed and glanced away from him, and he knew she understood the consequences. Fair enough.

*Angels never lied.*
The deal had been set.

Angels were idiots. They had to be. As Jade followed Az through the winding hallway located at the back of a voodoo shop, she wondered what the hell she was doing.

Trusting her life to a shifter cop and a witch? Oh, no, not a good idea.

They were the two she should probably trust the least except . . .

Except Tanner had helped her get out of that swamp. He could have turned her in to the authorities or handed her over to Brandt then.

"Trust me," Az's words. Az's hand around hers. And she did trust him. How could you not trust an angel? That was probably some kind of rule someplace. *Must trust angels.*

Everything she'd ever heard about them said they were the good guys, if anyone was ever really good. They protected humans, just as Az was trying to protect her.

Now the deep scars on his shoulders made sense. *Wings.* His wings must have burned away when he fell.

But why had Az fallen?

"I'll arrange the meeting," Heather said as she opened another door. The thick scent of incense filled the air. This room was filled with old books, glass vials, and some stuff that Jade didn't want to stare at for too long. A heavy mirror sat on the table to the left. And, yes, it looked like blood stained its surface.

She guessed that answered the question of good witch/ bad witch.

Jade didn't have tons of experience with witches, but she'd heard whispered stories. Some witches could scry with mirrors to see the future. But whenever they looked into that future, they had to use the darker magic.

Jade didn't want any part of that kind of magic. As it was,

she had more than enough darkness to deal with on her own.

"So here's the deal." Tanner pulled out a chair, flipped it around and straddled it. "We'll make the exchange at dawn."

She still wasn't loving this plan. But Jade could admit it was better than nothing. "So Az and I just stroll in as your big, fat bait? What guarantee do we have that you won't just leave us there for them?"

Before Tanner could answer, Az spoke. "It doesn't matter," he said. "Once I get close enough to Brandt, I can take out him and his men." He stood next to that bloody mirror. She saw his gaze drop to the glass.

Right. Big, tough, immortal badass *angel*. She could count on him.

Tanner cleared his throat. "And you don't know me from Adam . . ."

Az snorted at that.

"But believe me, I want to stop Brandt. I want to stop them all."

Her gaze dropped to his chest. His shirt covered the scars, but she wouldn't be forgetting them anytime soon. So much pain.

Enough to fill a man with fury.

Her breath exhaled on a rough sigh. It looked like whether she wanted to or not, she was in as bait.

But it was time for Jade to issue a warning. "If you screw us, I'll make sure that you pay." Tanner and the witch probably thought she was just making some tough threat without any substance. They were wrong.

Brandt had just thought she was bullshitting, too. Until he walked into his home and found the trail of blood that she'd left for him.

*Don't think about that now. Don't.*

It had taken hours to wash the blood away from her hands and body.

"Don't worry," Tanner said, rolling his broad shoulders. "If this plan goes to shit, Brandt will be the one who takes his pound of flesh from me."

He'd take more than a pound of flesh. Brandt would kill him. Slowly.

She glanced back at Az. His gaze was still on the mirror. And the witch had sidled closer to him.

Jade's back teeth clenched. That skinny chick was just pissing her off. She might have to trust Tanner, but that woman—no way, Jade wouldn't trust her for half a minute.

"Want to know what the future holds for you?" Heather asked Az softly. "All you have to do is bleed for me."

Oh, seriously, hell *no,* the woman hadn't just said that.

Az kept staring at that glass as if he were hypnotized. Not good. "You can't see my future," he finally said, voice rumbling.

"Because of what you are?" Heather asked, and then she laughed.

Jade hated that grating sound. The woman laughed like a hyena.

"Don't fool yourself into thinking you're the only angel I've met." Her hand brushed down his arm.

He was the only angel that Jade had ever met. And the witch was standing too close to him. The witch also needed to stop that touching bit. *Now.*

"I told you why I turned you over to those men before."

Being in the dark sucked. Jade wished she knew more about what had happened between Az and Heather. *Hello, jealousy.* She recognized the feeling for exactly what it was.

"Poor Azrael. You think your job is to save the world." Heather's lips twisted as she turned her focus on Jade. "When you're really just here to destroy it. Bit by slow bit."

Bull. Az had done nothing but help since—

"Isn't that what the legend says about you?" Heather taunted. "You and your brother Sammael—the two who fell from grace so they could wreck the world."

Az lifted his brows. "That's not *exactly* the way the story goes."

"Close enough," she murmured.

Eyes narrowed, Jade began to stalk toward the witch.

"The legend says that one day, a brother will be slain by another. When that day arrives, hell will come to claim the earth."

Wasn't that just a lovely tale to share? "Most legends are no more than lies," Jade said, shrugging. "Good to scare kids and fun to entertain bored bitches—I mean, witches. Witches who don't have enough power to see what will really be coming in the days ahead."

"I already know his future." Now Heather was talking to her, not Az, and her cheeks flushed red. "I saw it when he fell. I took his blood, and I saw what could be."

Jade noted the phrasing. "There's a big difference between what will be and what *could* be." She *could* yank that clawlike hand off Az. Or she *could* be a lady for a few more minutes.

The witch inclined her head. "Angels are harder to read, they take a whole lot of power, but humans, ah, humans I get right every time." And her hand fell away from Az.

Good move, but . . . "I'm not bleeding for you." They were wasting time with this talk. She'd come to the voodoo shop for one reason—weapons. Tanner had promised Jade that he could give her what she needed.

*No way am I going into an ambush without power.*

But Tanner wasn't speaking, and Az—well, at least he'd managed to look away from the mirror.

"Sooner or later, you will bleed." Heather seemed absolutely confident. The red had begun to fade from her cheeks so the woman must have been getting her control back.

The crazy witch could be as confident as she wanted to be. But Jade was getting out of there. The incense in the place was driving her crazy and making her temples pound.

"Give us the weapons," Jade said, "and then we'll get out of here."

"You don't need to leave." Tanner frowned at her. "This place is safe. You can stay here until our meeting at dawn."

Jade didn't want to stay there, but Az was nodding. What? Since when was he game-on for trusting these two?

"There's a room you can use upstairs," Heather said with an airy wave of her hand. "Get some rest, and we'll make sure that you stay safe."

She'd make sure, huh? "Why doesn't that reassure me?" Jade muttered.

"Because you expect everyone to betray you." Heather's instant answer. "Most of the time, you're right. This time, you're wrong."

Doubtful. "You already betrayed Az."

"To save others."

So she said. Because he was the *evil angel*.

"This is personal." The witch's voice had softened. "Brandt took away something very precious to me." Her hands fisted. "Now I want to take everything away from him."

*Join the club.* "I'm not here to trade sob stories with you, lady."

Heather stiffened.

"I want weapons." That had been the deal. Az might be able to kill with a touch—*still scary*—but she didn't have that super skill, and regular bullets just weren't going to cut it for her.

"Of course." Heather strolled toward a heavy, wooden cabinet. She swung open the doors.

Wow.

Dozens of weapons gleamed back at Jade. Knives. Guns. Bullets. Even what looked like an old broadsword.

"Will you feel better if you're armed with silver?" Heather's voice held only mild curiosity.

"Yeah, I will." Lots better.

"But we'd feel even better," Az said, finally speaking, "if we have more of these." Then Az pulled out a bullet from his pocket. Because of its color, she recognized it instantly. It was the same bullet that Jade had dug out of his back.

She hadn't even realized he'd retrieved it from the nightstand back at the cabin. Tricky angel.

The witch glanced at the bullet, and Jade saw the slight widening of her eyes. Such a faint movement, and Heather recovered quickly.

The witch reached for the bullet. She lifted it toward the light. Tested its weight. "This isn't like any bullet I've seen before." She brought it close to her nose and inhaled. "Brimstone."

Now Jade was the one to stare in surprise. "As in hell and brimstone?"

A nod. Heather's fingers curled around the bullet. "Let me keep it. I'll see what I can find and—"

In an instant, Az had the bullet back in his own hand. Sometimes, Jade loved that super speed of his.

"Or not," Heather finished softly. She smiled. "I'd imagine a bullet like that would be very handy. It could probably take down just about anything."

*Even an angel?* If the bullet had hit Az in the heart, would it have killed him?

Enough of this. Jade pushed by the witch and reached for the silver bullets that were calling to her. She loaded them into her gun. Then decided to grab an extra weapon, just in case.

A girl could never be too careful.

"Now go rest," Tanner said. "Take the room at the top of the stairs. We'll set up the meeting."

Her gaze met Az's.

Trust.

Hell, no, she didn't have it to give. But Jade nodded and followed Az from the room.

Someone would be dying come dawn. That someone just wouldn't be her.

# CHAPTER SEVEN

A z shoved the old wooden door closed, then twisted the
lock. The thing was so flimsy that he doubted it would
keep anyone out. But then, if anyone came in, he'd be ready
for them.

"We can't trust those two." Jade paced back and forth near
the lone window in the room. "After what she did to you—
no way can we trust them."

He'd barely managed to chain back his rage as he talked
to the witch. "We can use them." That was the plan. No
trust. He didn't trust anyone.

Except—

"They're using us. That witch will get a big payout when
she turns us over to Brandt." She rubbed her arms. "But I
guess when you're stuck between hell and a hard place, you
don't really get to choose your allies, do you?"

No.

She dropped her hands. Stared at him. "You can take
Brandt out." Not a question. "I've seen what you can do
with my own eyes. I know how strong you are."

He stalked toward her. Slowly. She didn't back away, not
even when he lifted his hand and cupped her cheek. "I can
kill him as easily as I can kiss you."

Her breath whispered out. "An angel assassin. Az, you're
the last thing I expected to find in that dirty alley."

And she was the last thing he'd ever expected.

Her fingers rose and curled around his hand. "Kiss me."

His heart beat faster.

"This is the end right?" Her words tumbled out. "In a few hours, we have our big standoff. We use our secret weapon—you—and take out the bad guy."

That was the plan. It wasn't about trusting the cop and the witch. It was about using *them* in order to get an up-close audience with the panther shifter he'd be sending to hell.

"I'm protected," Jade told him. "There's no risk of pregnancy or—or, um—" She broke off, flushing a bit.

Az lifted a brow. "I have no diseases or illnesses. Angels can't get them."

Her breath sighed out. "Good to . . . know." Yes, it was.

"Kiss me," Jade told him again. "I don't want to spend the next few hours worrying and being afraid of what will come with dawn."

He wanted her mouth. More, he wanted *her.*

Jade brought her body closer to his. "I'm your temptation, right?"

He hadn't meant—

"Then let me tempt you." She was. "After dawn, after we face what's coming, we'll go our separate ways."

Redemption.

"But let's be together now." She stood on her toes and her lips brushed over the line of his jaw. "I need this. I need to be with you."

She knew the power he held, but Jade wasn't afraid. He didn't think she'd ever been afraid of him. Not his touch. Not the fire he controlled.

Should she fear the lust he felt for her? Because it could rage out of control.

Az caught her hands. "I'm not like other men."

Her gaze held his. "Good."

She didn't understand. "I'm not . . . safe."

She stared back at him. The desire he saw in her stare made his cock harden even more.

He tried to warn her. "If I lose control, it could be dangerous for you."

But she just laughed. "You're an angel, you can't—"

Jade didn't understand, and the lust rising in him would soon push him too far. "I'm *Fallen*."

She kissed him. On her toes, so she could better reach him, but Az still lowered his head and her mouth pressed against his. Sweet, soft lips. Stroking tongue.

Her hand snaked down between their bodies. Found the snap of his jeans. Unhooked it. The hiss of his zipper filled his ears even as her fingers slipped inside and curled around his cock.

*Yes.*

She licked his lips and her stroking fist pumped his aroused flesh.

"Tonight," Jade's whisper was against his lips, "it's just us. Give me this much."

Right then, he would've given her anything.

He took over the kiss. Thrust his tongue into her mouth. Tasted her. Savored, and loved the light flavor of her.

This time, he wouldn't stop. He'd take the pleasures humans felt. He'd take her.

*One night.*

Didn't he deserve that much?

Her hand lifted from his straining flesh, and he immediately missed her touch. Az hooked his hands under her hips and picked her up. Jade gasped against his mouth. He liked that little sound. He spun around, and pressed her against the nearest wall.

Her legs wrapped around his hips. His cock strained toward her. *Pleasure.*

Though the lust pounded at him, Az knew that he had to make the sex good for her. She'd need the pleasure, too.

His head rose and Az's eyes locked on hers. She stared right at him, not seeming to see the monster that had to gaze so hungrily back at her.

Why couldn't she see him? Why wasn't she running?

*I won't let her run.*

He kissed her neck. Scored her flesh with his teeth. Sucked the skin. Licked her.

"Az . . ." His name was a whisper of need that spilled from her lips. Her nails dug into his arms. "You don't have to go easy with me."

Good. Because he didn't want easy or gentle. He needed hot and hard and wild.

His hands pushed between her legs. He wanted the clothes gone. Wanted flesh to flesh.

Her nails sank deeper into his flesh, marking him, as she arched her hips against him. "I don't want to wait . . . not the first time."

He yanked off her shirt. Threw it and her bra. Az kept her pinned with his body and stared down at her flesh. Pretty little pink nipples. Full breasts that would fill his hands. Perfect.

He lifted her higher, holding her easily, and took her nipple into his mouth.

She moaned. He licked her. Sucked her. His cock shoved up from his open jeans, hungry, eager.

*For her.*

Holding her tight, he whirled away from the wall. Five steps, and he had her on the narrow bed. Two seconds, and he had her completely naked. She waited for him on the bed, arms on either side of her head, eyes on him.

He'd never taken a woman before. Angels didn't need—

*I need her.* "What if I hurt you?" He didn't want Jade to

feel pain. Only pleasure. It was so important that she wanted him as much as he wanted her.

And Az wanted her more than he wanted his next breath. She had to feel the same.

"Don't worry, I've already left scratches on you." She smiled at him, and her dimple flashed. "You won't break me."

She still didn't understand how dangerous he could be.

But he couldn't warn her any longer. The need to take was too strong.

Az ditched his clothes and climbed onto the bed. She touched him, sliding her hands over his flesh even as she rose up to lick his nipple. The wet touch of her tongue sent desire knifing through him.

His cock strained toward her. Her thumb stroked the heavy tip of his arousal, and then she brought her thumb up to her mouth and tasted—

Tasted *him*.

Az put his fingers between her spread legs. She was wet, warm. Ready for him.

He couldn't wait any longer for her. It felt as if he'd waited too long already.

Centuries.

He caged her under his body. Pushed his hips between her legs. The head of his cock brushed against her slick sex. His eyes held hers as he began to thrust.

*Tight. So tight and hot—*

Sweat beaded his brow. He couldn't look away from her gaze. He knew she would see too much in his stare, but he couldn't look away.

He wanted to pound into her and race toward the promised release, but she seemed so small beneath him. Fragile. Human.

Her nails scratched down the base of his back. Her hips slammed up to meet his.

Az's control broke. He thrust into her as deep as he could

go. She gripped him, her delicate, inner muscles straining around his cock, and the pleasure lashed through him.

His hands slapped onto the mattress beside her. He lifted up his hips. Withdrew. Drove deep.

Again and again and again.

She shuddered beneath him as her breath panted out. Her legs curled around his hips and her neck arched as Jade choked out his name.

*Thrust. Thrust.* He couldn't get deep enough.

Her body was perfect. Her sex a fist-tight glove. The back of his spine tingled. His thrusts became harder. Deeper. He kissed her. Drove his tongue into her mouth even as he took her body.

He kissed her, became even wilder for her. His lips tore from hers and he pressed his mouth to her throat.

Then she screamed, and he knew that high cry was only from pleasure. Her climax rippled around him as her sex contracted. And he drove deeper into her. Az never wanted to let her go.

Couldn't.

*Thrust. Th—*

His release ripped through him and seemed to consume him as the blasts of pleasure shook his body. And in that moment, he held on to Jade tighter than he'd ever held on to anyone or anything in his very long life.

Sex. Lust.

Pleasure.

The world seemed to splinter as he focused only on her.

Now he understood . . . now . . .

*Need more. Must have her.*

Temptation.

How was he supposed to resist?

Tanner walked slowly through the halls of the empty magic shop. Customers, even curious tourists, rarely came inside this place. Maybe they could feel its darkness, and it kept them away.

When he entered the weapons room, he found Heather staring into her mirror. That dark mirror always made him nervous.

"The trade's set," she said. "We meet the panthers in the swamp at dawn."

He'd finally get his justice. He'd claw the flesh from Brandt's body, make the bastard beg, and then send him to hell.

Tanner inhaled. The thick scent of incense was gone. Incense—and magic. "Did you really think that was wise?"

Heather looked up slowly. Her face seemed paler. "I don't know what you mean." Her voice was perfectly expressionless. She did that when she lied. Let all the emotion drain away until nothing was left.

He tapped his nose. "Shifter senses, remember? When we came in, I noticed you'd added something extra to your usual incense mix."

Her lips curled in a faint smile. "It was just a light spell. Harmless, really."

Did he look stupid? "What did it do?"

She shrugged. Her hands were on the mirror, as if she were trying to shove images back inside of it. "The spell I cast simply lowers inhibitions. It makes us more likely to take the things that we want."

His eyes rose toward the ceiling. He had no doubt what Azrael wanted. "Brandt will smell him on her." He looked back at Heather.

"Yes." Her smile held an icy edge. "And it will make him furious."

Furious was probably way too mild of a word. "Brandt killed her last lover." When he'd first started digging into Jade's life, he'd learned details that made even him shudder.

She hadn't been given an easy time of it, no thanks to Brandt Dupre.

Heather lifted her hands from the mirror. "But we're counting on him not being able to kill Az, right? That is our master plan."

Not *our*. "Did you scry? What did the mirror tell you?"

Her smile faded. "Someone will find death at dawn."

"Brandt." About damn time. Satisfaction had his body tensing.

"His heart stops."

Tanner suspected his grin was savage. Working with Heather had been a risky business, but he'd known the witch held just as much of a grudge as he did.

Brandt had a way of leaving hell in his wake. He'd nearly broken Heather. Promised her eternity, a love that wouldn't die . . .

But then he'd met Jade, and he'd tried to destroy the witch he didn't want any longer.

Heather rubbed her right shoulder. Tanner knew her fingers pressed against the edge of scars that began at her shoulder and ended at her heart. Scars made by a shifter's claws.

"Brandt can be a jealous bastard," she said quietly. "That jealousy will make him weak. He'll be so enraged that he won't stop to think. He'll just attack."

Blind rage could be a weakness. For a shifter, it could also be a deadly power. Rage gave the beast within strength.

He sure hoped this gamble paid off. Because if it didn't, there'd be no escape for any of them.

Tanner turned away from her.

"Wait!"

Shoulders stiff, he turned back. She was frowning at him. "The magic . . . it didn't affect you?"

No, it had. He wanted. Heather was a beautiful woman, but he knew just how deadly she could be. Brandt hadn't only left scars on her body, he'd twisted her soul. *Use her, don't trust her.*

So he was holding on to his control. The witch wouldn't get any more power over him.

"What will you do when Brandt's dead?" He asked her instead of answering the question. As long as he'd known her—and he'd first found her years ago, nearly dead and covered in blood as she tried to crawl out of the swamp—she'd never talked about her own future. Others, yeah, she talked about what would come for them all the time.

Had she ever scryed to see what her own life would be like?

Her brows lowered. She shook her head. "I don't—"

He sighed. Tanner knew fear when he saw it. "Maybe you should figure it out."

She bit her lip and didn't look quite so all-powerful.

"You're not evil," he told her. Twisted, just like he was, but at her core, Heather wasn't without a soul. "Maybe, maybe you can find the girl that you used to be."

Her hand slipped to her heart. Pressed over the soft fabric that covered her. "She's lost." Sadness hunched her shoulders and made her eyes look lost. "Sometimes, I think she's dead."

"No." His answer was instant. "Brandt's the one who's dead. The bastard just doesn't know it yet."

Az thrust into Jade's sex, filling her, stretching her inner muscles, and she gasped at the delicious friction.

She sat astride his hips, her knees digging into the mattress, as she stared down at Az. His eyes were so blue, burning bright, and his face was locked in lines of heavy need and raw lust.

Her nails raked down his chest. He thrust harder, arching her off the bed. The first climax had barely ended for them both when he'd started to thrust again.

And again.

Her angel was insatiable, and she loved it. Her core trembled with aftershocks of pleasure. Every move of his body had her tensing and wanting more.

She'd thought to deny him? Deny them both? *Why?* Hell could come at dawn. She'd take this time, take him, and never look back.

Her head lowered. She pressed her lips against his. Tasted him, even as his fingers slid between their bodies and his thumb pressed over her clit. *Yes . . .* The man knew how to use that touch of his just right.

She tightened her sex around him, squeezing with the surge of pleasure. Then she nibbled on his lower lip. When his breath panted out, she stole it, and gave him her own before indulging in a deep kiss.

Her head lifted slowly as she stared at him.

"I . . . understand now . . ." Az gritted out the words.

His hands were on her hips. Holding so tightly that she might bruise, but Jade didn't care. She rose onto her knees, then pushed down.

"Humans and sex . . . the *need* . . ." His voice was raw and rough with passion.

And he'd better not be about to call her a temptation again.

"You'd . . . kill . . . for the pleasure."

Some had. Some would again. With Az, the pleasure was so intense it seemed to rip her apart. Would she kill for this? For him?

He rose up, positioning his body so that he faced her and his arms were tight around her. Her hands slid over his back. Touched the thick ridge of those scars.

She saw his control break at her caress. His pupils flared wider, seeming to swallow all of the blue in his eyes. Az growled, an animalistic sound as he thrust faster, harder. They wrecked the bed as they rolled and fought for their release.

He caged her beneath him. Lifted her legs so that he could thrust as deeply into her as possible. The pleasure wasn't a wave this time. It was an explosion. One that rocked through her and made the whole world go dark for an instant.

His name slipped from her lips.

He erupted in her.

Pleasure worth dying for.

Oh, yes . . . *more, please.*

"They arrive at dawn." Riley strode to stand beside Brandt as the alpha peered out over the old dock and at the murky water. "The witch will be bringing them. Her and that stray we threw out years before."

Brandt's back teeth clenched as rage hit him.

Riley continued, "Who would've thought those two would be the ones to bring in the bounty? That piece of shit shifter couldn't—"

Brandt spun and, in one fast and brutal move, he drove his claws into Riley's chest. Blood spurted onto him as Riley's words ended in a strangled gurgle.

"Careful," Brandt admonished as he took his friend's heart with a yank of his claws. "That's my *brother* you're talking about."

And, finally, *finally,* his brother was showing that he had what it took to carry the Dupre name. Bringing back Jade. Offering her protector's body. No one else in the pack had been able to bring in the prey he wanted.

Only Tanner. The little brother who'd run from them one dark night.

The little brother who was coming home again.

Brandt jerked his hand from Riley's body. The man who'd been at his side for the last ten years shuddered, then fell to his knees. His eyes were wide open, his heart gone.

But he still lived. Some shifters just took one hell of a long time to die. Brandt smiled at him before he lifted his boot and kicked Riley as hard as he could. Riley tumbled to the side, fell off the rickety dock, and sank into the murky green water.

In the distance, Brandt saw two gators slide off the bank and begin to cut a fast path through the water. A path that would lead straight to Riley.

Gators were good at following a blood trail. Not as good as panthers, but still . . .

Pretty damn good.

"Good-bye, Riley." His friend's death was overdue. Had been, from the moment Brandt realized that Riley didn't want to catch Jade. The bastard wanted to *kill* her.

No one hurt Jade. No fucking one.

And no one screwed with his family.

The gators swam closer. "Don't worry," he promised them. "There will be more blood coming." There always was.

# CHAPTER EIGHT

"Remember the plan," Tanner said as he braked the car at the end of the old dirt road. The thick, sloping trees of the swamp surrounded them and nearly blocked out dawn's light. "I take in Azrael, and you . . ." He pointed to Heather, "You take in Jade."

Jade's heart slammed into her chest. She had the gun tucked into the back of her jeans, and she'd taken the liberty of strapping a knife to her right ankle. Az hadn't taken any weapons.

*Too confident.*

And his hands were currently cuffed. Just for show, of course, because even though the cuffs were supposed to be some sort of *Other*-proof trinket that Heather had pulled out of her box of tricks, Az had snapped free of them earlier in about two seconds.

A test breakaway. To make sure he'd be able to ditch the cuffs when the real action came. And the real action was coming, soon.

"Wait until he comes toward you," Tanner told Az with a hard glare. "Don't go charging up to him. Brandt can move faster than any other shifter I've ever seen. If we attack first, the game is gonna be over for us all."

Because the plan was for Az to wait until Brandt came to him. When Brandt was close enough to touch . . .

Az would do his thing and the nightmare would end.

So they hoped.

"We all know the plan," Heather muttered. "We've gone over it enough times by now."

Yeah, they had.

Tanner exhaled. "Alright. Let's do this." Jade wondered if he knew that his voice trembled. The cop was scared. You didn't need a shifter's senses to smell his fear.

Tanner and Heather climbed from the car. Hesitating, Jade glanced at Az. After the fury of sex and pleasure, she wasn't sure what to say. Except . . . "Please be careful." A hollow ache filled her gut. She'd never planned on Az. Wasn't even sure *what* she felt for him, but she knew that she didn't want to lose him. "Brandt is very smart and very dangerous."

Az cocked his head and studied her. Then he lifted his cuffed hands. Touched her cheek. "You were my first."

She blinked at that. "First?" First what? First human who'd dragged him into a hell of a mess with her psychotic ex?

"I watched death and suffering for centuries," he said as his eyes searched hers. "I never stepped in. Never stopped it, until you."

Oh, wait, that was . . . um, not sweet, exactly. Something more.

"It seems only fitting that my first taste of real pleasure came from you."

She hadn't meant for last night to happen. She'd stared at him, needed, and her self-control had vanished. So much for holding back and keeping him—

*Whoa. Wait.* His words sank in. Was he saying . . . *first*? She was pretty sure she lost her breath right then. "You should have told me." Things could have been different, she could have—

He kissed her. Her lips were open, and his mouth just

seemed to fit hers so perfectly in that moment. No danger. No fear.

Just him.

She squeezed her eyes shut and pressed against his chest. Her tongue met his, and she realized how very much she loved his taste. Jade didn't break the kiss, just enjoyed it. As she enjoyed him.

When he slowly pulled away, she had to whisper, "Where were you ten years ago?"

He didn't speak. Jade opened her eyes and forced herself to smile. "I guess you were upstairs, looking down on us mortals."

His eyes narrowed.

*I wish I'd met you first. Wish I'd known you before Brandt.*

Life could have been different. Her family would have been alive. She wouldn't have been a murderer.

Tanner cleared his throat and knocked on the window. "Let's do this."

Because it was time to face her own personal devil. She pulled away from Az and opened her car door. He exited on his side, and they met in front of the vehicle car.

Heather was moving nervously from her left foot to her right, then back, over and over. Tanner stood with his arms crossed and stared into the darkness.

Jade's heart was racing, and the fear swirling in her gut had her whole body tensing up. Because of last night, she knew Az's scent was all over her. Just as her scent marked him. That scent would infuriate Brandt. Before they went into this battle, she needed Az to understand. "I'm not going to watch him kill you."

If something went wrong, if the plan didn't go the way they'd figured . . .

He lifted a brow. Gave her a faint smile. "You won't have to," he said. "You can just watch me kill him."

So confident.

Why was she so afraid?

They stared at the trees and the fog that drifted from the swamp. Insects chirped and called out. The heavy odor of vegetation filled the air.

Heather approached Jade. The witch pulled out a gun and pushed it into Jade's back. *It had better still be unloaded.* She'd checked the gun right before they parked. No bullets. At least, there hadn't been any in the chamber *then.*

"Move," Heather told her, but the word broke with nervousness.

Jade exhaled heavily and started walking. Az was beside her, being "pushed" forward by Tanner. They went straight ahead, going deep, deeper into the swamp. As they walked, the calls of the insects began to die away even as the fog thickened around them.

Maybe the insects sensed the predators in their midst.

Shadows began to move in the fog. Big, menacing. Growls reached her ears. Those were the same growls that she heard in her nightmares.

A pond waited up ahead. The water lapped lightly against the shore.

Laughter drifted in the air. Cold, cruel. The sound made her spine snap even straighter.

Then Brandt stalked toward them, seeming to just appear in the heavy layer of fog. He was smiling and his eyes were on her. "I missed you, baby," he said. The words were those of a lover. The claws that ripped from his fingertips were the weapons of a beast.

The barrel of Heather's gun shoved harder into her back. "I want my money!" The witch's frantic call. Heather should really try playing this thing cooler.

Slowly, Brandt's gaze trekked from Jade's face to the witch. He took another step toward them. One more. His eyes narrowed on Heather. "I suppose it's a good thing you lived. You have proven useful over the years."

Okay, now that gun was jabbing Jade so hard that it hurt.

"I guess we were both more than just pieces of trash to be thrown away." Now this came from Tanner. Az wasn't speaking. He was just glaring at Brandt as if he were marking the panther for death, which he probably was.

Brandt smiled at Tanner. "Welcome back, brother."

Jade's gaze flew to the cop. His claws were out and at Az's throat.

Then Brandt clapped his hands together. A guy with a big, black bag came running toward them. "Payment," Brandt said with a wide smile, "for a job well done." He pointed at Jade. "You led me on a nice chase, but the hunt's over now."

He shouldn't be so calm. Jade clenched her hands and refused to show fear. Brandt should have caught the mixed scents by now. He should be enraged. Not mocking and controlled.

Brandt tossed the duffel bag through the air. It landed in front of Jade's feet. The barrel of the gun was immediately removed from her back. Heather scrambled around and grabbed the bag. She jerked it open.

Nothing was inside.

Heather's head whipped back. "What the hell are you trying to do?" Her gun lifted and pointed at him. The barrel shook.

"Since when does a witch need to use a human weapon?" Brandt asked, voice flat. "Why not just use a spell to knock out your captives?"

Because they hadn't been willing to play that way. Heather had sure wanted to use her magic mojo, but Jade hadn't been willing to run the risk. The witch could just kill them while they were out. *No, thank you.*

"Because *he* can't be knocked out," it was Tanner's snarl that answered Brandt.

Jade slipped back a step. Her right hand began to rise slowly. Not time to pull her own weapon, not yet.

"You know he's not human." Tanner's claws had drawn blood. The red drops slid down Az's throat. "He can resist Heather's magic."

Brandt's nostrils flared as he studied Az. "Who are you? Why the hell are you in this fight?"

Because she'd pulled him into it. Because—

"I'm the man who made Jade scream last night."

Oh, ahem, yeah, but she'd made him shout, too.

Brandt's claws lengthened. She saw a muscle jerk along his jaw. Finally, his control was showing signs of cracking. "I *will* make you wish for death." A promise he'd carried out before, to others.

Even when she'd begged him to stop.

Begged and fought, but Jade hadn't been strong enough to help.

This time, things would be different.

"You're not doing this to me again!" Heather threw the bag back at him. "I did my part. I brought them here, now I want my money!" Power, magic, seemed to vibrate in the air around her.

"Walk away, Heather," Brandt told her softly. "While you have the chance, just turn and walk out of here."

Yeah, it was time for the witch to head for safety.

"What about *my* pay?" Tanner demanded. "I was promised money, too. Are you just going to double-cross me, too?"

*Brothers.* Jade had known that, though, from the first moment she'd seen Tanner's scars.

The only other pack member with scars like that was Brandt—and Brandt's bastard of a father had been the one to slice his flesh. His flesh—and his brother's.

"You brought me the thing I want the most in this

world." Brandt's body was held painfully still. He'd never been one for restraint, so where the hell was his self-control coming from now? If their attack was going to work, he had to move within striking distance of Az. "For that," Brandt said, "you can come back. You can be pack again."

Silence.

Then Heather drew a deep, shuddering breath. "You almost killed me once." She still had her gun. The useless gun?

Now Brandt did take a step, but it was toward Heather and not to Az.

"You slashed me, drove your claws into me," Heather's voice grew louder as wind began to whip through the area. A furious wind fueled by the witch's magic. "Then you left me to die."

Brandt shrugged. "You betrayed me. What else did you think I'd do?"

"I never—"

Another gliding step toward her. "You took my blood, witch, I know you did. You used it to scry. To see what future we'd have. You looked *when I fucking told you never to see!*"

"I saw *nothing! Only darkness with you because*—"

Then he had her. One lunge, and he'd ripped the gun out of her hand. He tossed it into the bushes and his fingers closed around her neck. He lifted her up and her feet dangled in the air.

No, no, this was *not* the way the deal was supposed to go down.

"This time," Brandt told Heather, "I'll make sure you die."

*"No!"* Jade screamed and she brought up her gun. But she didn't have a clear shot at Brandt. Heather's body blocked him. "Let her go!"

Brandt laughed. "Now how did I know that you weren't

the defenseless little prisoner brought in by the big, bad witch?"

Then he tossed Heather's body, slinging her through the air. Her head slammed into a tree, and she crumpled on the ground like a broken doll.

Brandt brushed his hands as if he were wiping away dirt. He glanced at Jade's gun, then back up at her. "Come on, baby, we both know that you won't—"

She fired at him. Fired again and again until the gun just clicked because all of the bullets were gone.

But . . . Brandt didn't fall down. Blood poured from his chest, and his eyes narrowed on her. "That *hurt,* Jade."

"It was fucking supposed to, Brandt!" But, dammit, how had she missed his heart? How was he standing? Silver bullets in the heart should kill a shifter but—

*I missed?*

Brandt shook his head. "I'm gonna have to punish you for that . . ."

"No, you're not." And just like that, Az stood in front of her. Big, strong, the cuffs broken and his hands free. "You're not touching her ever again."

"Neither are you." Brandt's voice had roughened into a snarl. "Neither the hell are you!"

Jade's head swung to the left. Four panthers had sprung from the shadows, and they had launched at Tanner. He was fighting, swiping with his claws, but the guy was weak against them because he was still in his human form. No time to change, not for him. If he stopped to shift, the panthers would slaughter him during those vulnerable moments.

Heather wasn't moving.

Jade's gun was empty.

*Screwed.*

Jade tossed the weapon and put her hands on Az's back,

right over his shoulders and those thick scars. "Kill him," she whispered.

Her angel assassin.

Then Jade stumbled back so she wouldn't get in Az's way.

Brandt raced forward, finally coming at Az with his claws up and ready to attack. Jade couldn't breathe. She stood there, watching, waiting for death to come. *I hope you like hell, Brandt.*

Az caught Brandt's hands. Held those claws just inches from his body. Yes, *yes,* Az was touching him. Brandt would hit the ground, immobile, any moment. In the meantime . . .

Jade yanked her silver knife from her boot and ran for the swarm that was attacking Tanner. She wasn't about to let those panther bastards slaughter him. She drove her knife into the back of the nearest panther. Roaring in agony, he swung around and tried to swipe out at her. Ducking low, she avoided the slice and raked her knife down his stomach.

The panther rolled away, bleeding, breath heaving. Tanner tossed another panther a good ten feet then turned to drive his claws into the back of his next attacker.

A vicious fighter. She liked that. It would help—

Brandt's laughter froze her. A dead man shouldn't be laughing. She glanced over her shoulder. Brandt stood over Az . . . *why was Az kneeling on the ground?*

Brandt's fingers dripped blood.

She started running then. Jade barely felt the sting of claws as they raked down her back. *"Az!"* Her scream.

He turned his head slowly to look at her. His eyes were puzzled, and she could see the pain on his face.

"Know your enemy, fool," Brandt taunted him. "And know when you're up against someone who doesn't give a shit about your Death Touch."

His claws shoved into Az's chest. "I know who the fuck you are, Azrael," Brandt taunted. "And I'm not scared of you."

*"Stop!"* A few more feet. She just had to get—

"You can't kill me," Brandt said as he yanked out his claws. Blood dripped from Az's lips and poured from the giant hole in his chest. "But I can slice you apart while she watches."

*Not going to watch.* Az had tried to help her. When he'd needed her, she'd turned away. Raced to fight others.

*I shouldn't have left him. Shouldn't have—*

Jade threw her body against Brandt. Using all of her strength, she drove the silver knife into his side. Then she jerked it as hard as she could to the left. His bellow hurt her ears even as . . . as the scent of flowers drifted in the air around them.

Flowers? In hell?

Brandt caught her arms and yanked her closer against him. "You fight for that bastard?"

"He's not the bastard." Brandt never seemed to realize just how screwed up he truly was. "You are."

He shook her, sending her head whipping back. "After all I've done for you, after I—"

Her slick hands found the handle of the knife. The weapon was still embedded in his side. She caught it and twisted.

And he kissed her. His lips crushed down on hers, and she could taste his rage and lust.

*"No!"* She shoved against Brandt even as she was ripped from his arms.

Az. Holding her tightly. On his feet again. Bleeding, but strong.

"So like me," Brandt whispered. His gaze found hers. "Dark and dangerous . . . killer instinct, it's right there."

"I'm nothing like you!" She didn't want to be like him.

Az pushed her behind him. "What are you?" He threw the words at Brandt.

Brandt yanked the knife from his side and tossed it to the ground. "I'm the man who's gonna kill you, angel."

Jade eased to the left and saw Brandt lift his claws. "So get ready for an ass kicking."

The two men lunged at each other. Fire crackled in the air around them. Thick, hot flames that forced Jade back. Brandt cut with his claws while Az pounded the shifter with powerful fists. Over and over. The crunch of bones and the thud of flesh filled the air.

Jade rushed forward, but the fire pushed her back. The flames circled around the men. Caging them, and keeping all others away.

Az. Damn him. He'd put up the fire. To keep her out. To protect her.

But he was bleeding. Stumbling.

Her gaze darted around the area. Tanner was fighting the last two panthers. Heather—Heather was trying to rise to her feet. Jade ran to her side. "We have to help him!"

Blood dripped down the side of Heather's face. She stared at the line of fire. At the two men locked in brutal combat.

Heather nodded quickly. "We have to . . . we have to distract him," Heather whispered as she yanked a knife from a sheath on her thigh.

A hidden weapon. Huh. Maybe they were more alike than Jade had thought. But . . . "We're going to need a lot more than silver to stop Brandt."

But just then Brandt let out a long, screaming cry of agony. Jade's gaze flew to the men. Az had broken Brandt's wrist and just plunged the shifter's own claws into Brandt's chest. Brutal.

Smart.

But Brandt head-butted Az and sent her angel sliding back.

"Az has lost too much blood . . . the panther weakens him . . ." Heather's voice pulled her attention back to the witch. Jade saw the woman's fingers tighten around the knife. "Brandt is . . . more than a beast. I should have *seen* it before."

Screw this. "Send out some magic! Help Az!"

"We need to weaken Brandt . . ." Heather's voice was so soft. She weaved a bit as she stepped forward. "Have to take his heart . . ."

Then she raised her knife and plunged it toward Jade's chest.

Jade tried to jump away, but she didn't move fast enough. The knife drove into her chest. A white-hot slice of pain cut through her and stole Jade's breath. The blade sank to the hilt, and then Heather yanked the knife out.

"You'll know what it feels like, Brandt!" Heather yelled and laughed and thrust the knife at Jade again. "You'll know what it feels like to lose what you love!"

The witch was strong. But this time, Jade was ready for her. A roar filled the air behind her. Heather's golden eyes burned so bright. Too bright. When that blade came at her again, Jade caught Heather's hand and held the weapon away.

The witch shuddered, and her eyes just burned brighter. "I'm taking his heart," Heather said, almost growling the words. "I have to make him weak."

Jade's blood soaked her shirt. She kicked out at the witch and caught the other woman in the knee. Jade heard something pop, and the sound filled her with vicious pleasure.

Heather fell back. Jade fell, too, even as her hand rose to her chest and tried to stop the blood. Crazy bitch . . .

A blur of black fur flew past her. A panther. Brandt. He'd shifted. Gotten out of the flames.

He went for Heather's throat. The witch never even had time to scream. His teeth sank deep, killing her, nearly severing her head from her shoulders.

"Jade?" Az's voice. Az's hands on her as he turned her to

face him. She felt cold right then, but her body shook as if she had a fever.

"Stay away from her," Az ordered fiercely. *"Stay away."* And she saw that he was staring over her shoulder. Wait, who was behind her? Not Brandt. He was busy a few feet away, killing Heather.

The panther's snarl raised the hair on her neck.

"You're not taking her," Az said, still staring behind her. "So stand the fuck back."

She tried to push up into his arms. She'd been stabbed, but she wasn't out. She'd survive this but—

But Brandt, in full panther form, was charging at Az's back. She saw him over Az's shoulder, running fast with his mouth open, his teeth bloody from his recent kill. He rushed forward—

*"No!"* She screamed and shoved Az to the side.

Brandt's claws struck out. He was too close. *Too close.*

His paws sank into her chest. The pain lanced her, tore through flesh, muscle, and bone.

*Killed* her.

Az leapt up and grabbed the panther. With a roar, he tossed Brandt back. Even as the panther flew through the air, the fur melted from his body. Bones began to snap and bend—

*I'm dying.*

Jade couldn't look at her chest. She didn't want to see what he'd done to her. She'd wanted to kill him, but instead, death was coming for her.

"No!" Az was the one shouting the denial. "You're *not* taking her! I won't let you!" His hands were on her, pulling her up, but her head wanted to sag and her eyes were trying to close.

He shook her. "Stay with me." No plea. An order.

She wanted to stay. But . . . but it seemed like she . . .

*"Stay."*

"Jade!" Brandt's anguished bellow.

Everything was growing darker, but she saw Az's head jerk in the panther's direction. "You're dead." Az had never sounded so cold. So brutal.

Then a blast of fire shot from Az's fingertips. One ball. Another. Another. The flames lit up the darkness around her as they popped like fireworks. The fire flew at Brandt. Melted his flesh.

Then the ground began to shake. Dips and turns. The earth cracked open. A long, wide crevice split and raced toward Brandt. He tried to jump out of the way, but that crevice just seemed to chase him.

Then it swallowed him. Screaming, Brandt sank into the hole. Az laughed and lightning flew from his fingertips. The powerful lightning bolts hit the ground and seared the air with sulfur. And the lightning . . . it sealed the earth, locking Brandt inside.

Then Az glanced back at her. His eyes glowed with a brightness that matched the lightning. His face was twisted and so dark. Enraged.

Her angel looked like the devil.

"You won't die," he vowed.

Even an angel couldn't stop death. Jade tried to speak but couldn't. The scent of flowers was so strong now that the fragrance drowned out the death and blood. And . . . there was a woman standing beside Az. Jade strained to see her better. A woman with long, blond hair. Pale blue eyes.

And—wings?

Az stiffened. His head jerked to the left. "Marna, don't even think of touching her."

But Marna's hand was already out. Just inches away. Jade's chest burned so much. She could feel her heart struggling to beat. So weak. So—

Az wrapped his arms around Jade and seemed to fly ten feet. It hurt to be held so tightly against him and a moan broke from Jade.

"Don't touch her!" He yelled again. "Marna, I swear, if you come near her again . . ." More lightning lit the area. Lightning that seemed to come from Az. "I'll fight you."

Then Az was racing away, with her held in his arms. Moving so quickly that everything was a blur. When the world stopped spinning, Jade found herself in the backseat of the car they'd used just moments before.

"Drive!" Az ordered. Jade managed to turn her head, and she saw that Tanner was in the front seat. How had he gotten there? He'd been . . . fighting panthers.

Hadn't he?

It was getting so hard to think now. Even harder to breathe.

Tanner spun the car around with a squeal of tires. Jade would have fallen onto the floorboard, but Az held her tight in hands that trembled.

"You took the blow for me." He pressed his lips against her cheek. She tried to touch his face, but her hands wouldn't lift.

She couldn't take in a full breath. When she tried, she choked on her own blood.

*Dead.*

"A human isn't supposed to save an angel," Az said, voice rough. "We're stronger. We protect. We—"

She couldn't keep her eyes open any longer. Her last sight would be of Az and the fear and rage that twisted his perfect face. She wished she could talk to him, but she just hurt too much. Everything hurt. There was no way to say . . .

*Good-bye.*

Brandt burst from the earth with a scream on his lips that was Jade's name. Dirt flew around him, spewing from his mouth and eyes. The fucking bastard had tried to bury him alive.

"I'll rip you—"

The angel was gone. Jade was gone. All that remained where she'd been was a pool of blood.

*I hurt her.* The beast within clawed and roared. *Jade. I . . . hurt . . . her.*

But only because that angel had shoved Jade forward. Yes, yes, that was what the coward had done. He'd yanked Jade up and forced Brandt to hurt her.

*Don't be dead, baby. Please . . .*

He needed her too much.

A moan had his head snapping to the left. The witch still lay near the moss-filled cypress tree. Blood had turned the ground red beneath her. She stared up—up at the woman who stood above her. A woman with long blond hair and black wings.

The woman wasn't even glancing his way. She had to know he was there, but the winged woman just stared down at Heather. As he watched, she slowly lifted a hand to touch the bleeding witch.

*I know what you are.* Just like Azrael. Rage broke through him as Brandt rushed for the blonde. His claws swiped out and tore right through her wings.

She screamed, the sound high and keening, and the woman turned toward him in shock. Tears swam in her blue eyes.

He smiled at her. *"Hello, angel."* He'd seen wings like hers before. Long, long ago.

She stumbled back, slipped over Heather's prone body, and fell.

"You're about to get those wings clipped."

Her head shook frantically. "You can't—you can't see me!"

He sliced her arm open. "Oh, I see you just fine." He pulled back and aimed to take another swipe at her.

She flew by him, a wild rush that tossed his hair and brushed across his skin. But his claws were out when she tried to race past, and he knew he caught her.

Her blood rained down on him even as the little angel tried desperately to make her way back to heaven.

But it would be hard to fly with broken wings.

A rasp rattled from Heather's chest. Slowly, his gaze dropped back to her. Despite the gaping wound in her neck, she still lived.

Because the angel hadn't touched her. *Son of a bitch,* all of those fucking stories had been true.

When his packmates had first come back to him with intel they'd gathered in New Orleans, he hadn't really believed their news. Jade's new watchdog was an angel? Bull.

But . . . but one of his panthers had bribed a demon who worked at a club called Sunrise. That demon had been ready to spill secrets, for a price.

According to the story, Azrael was a Fallen Angel who'd gotten his ass kicked out of heaven. And angels, well, they were hard SOBs to kill. In fact, no mortal weapon could kill them.

He glanced at his hands and the claws that still burst from his fingertips. Good thing he didn't have to use any mortal weapon when he attacked.

Since this wasn't his first time to meet an angel, he'd already known Azrael's weakness, and he'd attacked with a vengeance.

Heather's breath rattled in her chest once more. A death rattle. The sound should have meant she was seconds from dying. If he hadn't just sent her Death Angel fleeing, the witch *would* be dying.

*Now you . . . you aren't.*

He knelt beside Heather. Her eyes were open and tears trickled down her cheek. "Easy," he whispered and smiled at her. "I'm going to take care of you." He'd see to it that she lived, because Heather would be useful to him. "And you're going to help me find what you fucking nearly *took* from me."

She tried to crawl away. He laughed. "Don't worry, once I have Jade back, I'll let death take you." After he'd had his fun.

After.

But first . . .

*Jade, be alive.* Because if she wasn't, he'd rip his way through hell to get her back.

# CHAPTER *N*INE

"She's dying." The pronouncement came from Tanner as he threw a fast glance into the backseat. "This shit wasn't supposed to happen, and *she's dying.*"

Jade's blood stained Az's fingertips. No matter how many times he tried to stroke her flesh and share his warmth with her, Jade's skin remained ice cold. Colder than death. He knew that touch too well.

"Death isn't here yet." Because he'd left Marna behind. Scared the angel. Angels weren't supposed to feel fear. But Marna had always been weak. Too curious about humans. Too slow to take the dying.

If there was one angel he could push around, it was her.

So if she came back, he'd make certain he pushed again. "We just have to get the bleeding stopped," Az said and his gaze locked on Jade's still face.

Tanner muttered, "I think we have to do more than that."

"Just get her to a doctor." If she'd been *Other,* she could have already been healing instead of growing colder with each moment that passed.

"The city's at least forty-five minutes away."

Because they'd driven deep into the swamps of Louisiana to find a prey that was stronger than Az had ever anticipated. *My touch should have killed him.*

Had Jade known what he was up against? He'd find out,

once she *lived*. "I don't think she's got forty-five minutes," Tanner said as he jerked the car and it flew to the left with a screech of its tires. "But I know a doctor who's closer. He's got a clinic in the bayou—"

"Get us to him."

The car was jumping and hurtling down the dirt road. "I will, but, fuck, man, don't expect a miracle."

Why not? Others had gotten them. Why couldn't he?

"She could die any—"

"I won't let her die." Az was adamant. Her death wasn't an option for him. "Just take us to the doctor. Get us there, and I'll take care of Death."

On his watch, no angel would get to her. And if an angel couldn't claim Jade's soul . . .

Then she couldn't die.

Az held her tighter as the car whipped along the old, dirt road through the twisting trees. Jade's eyes weren't open. Blood soaked her chest, but her heart still beat. His hand was over her heart, so he felt those precious, struggling beats.

"Stay with me," he whispered to her.

No one had ever come between him and death before. No one had ever sacrificed for him.

Until now.

The car screeched to a jarring stop moments later. Tanner flew from the front seat. The cop yanked open the back door and tried to take Jade. Az just held her tighter. If an angel came, he had to be close to her.

With her still in his arms, Az carefully climbed from the car. Her head sagged back against his shoulder. Dark shadows lined her closed eyes.

Tanner ran toward the shack that rested near the woods. His fist pounded onto the door. "Cody! Dammit, Cody, open the door!" But then he didn't give Cody a chance to answer his summons. With not even a second's hesitation, Tanner kicked the door open.

And he was immediately shoved back through the air. "What the hell are you thinking, Tanner?" a hard voice snarled. "You don't bring your arrogant panther ass down here and ram in my door."

Tanner shoved to his feet. "We need your help." He pointed toward Az and Jade. "She's hurt."

Cody's dark head turned and his eyes—dark eyes, demon eyes—locked on Jade. "She's dead."

Az thought about incinerating him. But, no, they needed the guy. For now. "Demon, are you a doctor?"

Cody stiffened. "I'm no demon."

Az strode toward him. "Tell that to someone who can't see you for what you really are." He knew demon eyes when he stared into them. No magic glamour could fool him.

Cody's hands lifted as if to ward him off. "Don't bring a dead girl to my door. There's nothing I can do for her."

"She's *not* dead." But the doctor could be, very soon.

"Brandt attacked her." Tanner ran a shaking hand through his hair. "Those were his claws that tore open her chest."

"Fuck." Cody rocked back on his heels. "Our psycho of a brother won't ever stop, will he?"

"That's *Jade*." Intensity fueled Tanner's voice.

Cody's brows climbed and his arms dropped. "Brandt's Jade?"

Hell, no. "*My* Jade." Az stepped toe-to-toe with the demon. "And if you want to keep living, then you'll make sure she does, too. You have to stitch her up. Close those wounds. *Help her.*" An order when it should probably have been a plea. But he'd never had to plea for anything before. Even when he'd been cast out of heaven, he hadn't begged. He'd raged. Cursed. Fought.

Cody swallowed and nodded. "I–I'll do what I can."

Not good enough. "You'll do everything." He strode through the entrance and was surprised to see that the place was actually much bigger inside than he'd realized. It snaked back, dipping low and twisting around.

Cody hurried around him. "This way. I have a small clinic set up for—"

"For emergencies like these," Tanner finished quietly.

The demon doctor shoved open another door. The room inside was small, but packed with medical equipment.

"Put her on the table." He grabbed a pair of gloves. "We need to cut off that shirt so I can see what kind of damage we're dealing with."

Az lowered her onto the thin table. Her head rolled to the right. Carefully, he pulled away her shirt, ripping it when it stuck to the drying blood because he didn't want to jar her. The slashes were deep into her chest. Thick, gaping. He ached when he saw them.

And he wanted to tear Brandt apart. *Death will make you scream.*

"Sadistic bastard." Rage thickened Cody's voice. "I thought she was supposed to be the one that he loved."

Tanner shook his head. "You know he can't really love anything. He can only destroy. He can—"

"He meant to kill me." Az brushed back her hair. "She . . . got in his way."

"You mean she took the attack for you." Tanner was by his side. "Brandt has killed too many people that Jade loved. I wasn't there back then, but I know the stories. She wasn't just going to let you die, too."

Az frowned down at her. "Jade doesn't love me." She needed him. She . . . wanted him.

But *love*?

The cop didn't respond.

The one called Cody stared down at Jade's savaged body. "I can close the wounds . . ." He licked his lips. "But I'll tell you now, she's lost too much blood to survive."

Tanner's head snapped up. Az saw the shifter's nostril's

flare. "Flowers," Tanner mumbled. "That scent, I smelled it before . . ."

*Found us.* Az spun away from the table. "Close her wounds and get her ready for a transfusion—"

"I don't have any blood here." Cody cut through his words instantly. "I can't—"

*"Get her ready!"* He yelled back at him. Az followed that floral scent out of the house. If he hadn't been so intent on Jade, if the smell of her blood hadn't filled his nostrils, then he would have already *known.*

Death stalked them.

Time for him to send Death running.

He shoved through the broken door and stood on the slanting porch with his legs braced apart and his arms loose at his sides. "Marna, I told you what would happen if I saw you again!"

An angel appeared in front of him. The angel's long, black wings stretched toward the sky. But this wasn't the delicate Marna. This . . . This was Bastion, an ancient Death Angel. An angel who'd been second only to Az.

"Where is she?" Bastion demanded as his wings lowered. His eyes, golden as the streets of heaven, penned Az.

Az didn't move. "You're not getting to her."

Bastion's eyes narrowed. Interesting. The angel had never shown any emotion before. Or . . . perhaps Az just hadn't noticed the signs when he'd been in heaven. Maybe he hadn't wanted to see them.

*Because that would have meant that we were all weak.*

"Your human should have left this world already," Bastion said flatly. "Her name is in the book."

The damn book. It had once belonged only to Azrael. Immense, magical, it contained the names of all the dying. Once a name appeared in the precious book, the soul would be collected within forty days.

There'd only been one soul to ever escape the collection. Only one. A vampiress.

But if one could escape, then the rules could be broken. "Jade is not going with you."

Bastion shook his head. "You don't want to fight with me."

"Yes, I do." And he tossed a ball of fire right at Bastion's chest. Unprepared, the angel took the blast and flew back through the air.

Fire couldn't kill an angel. The angels could control that element too well, but it could take them by surprise.

Bastion rose to his feet in an instant. "You would war with me?"

That wasn't the option he'd prefer, but, yes. "It's one soul." There were thousands more to take. Millions. "You can stand to lose her, just this once."

"You know that's not how it works." The flames lingering on Bastion's skin vanished with a wave of his hand. "And you can't stop me. You're not an angel any longer. You're not the one in charge upstairs. You can't—"

"I'm Fallen." Az jumped off the porch and reached in his back pocket for the bullet that he'd dug out of his own skin. He'd taken Jade's gun earlier and tucked it into the back of his jeans. As he strode toward Bastion, Az loaded that single bullet into the weapon. "Being Fallen means I don't have to play by the *good* rules any longer."

Bastion smirked at the weapon. *Smirked?* The angel was playing with all kinds of emotions. Did he realize how dangerous that was? Did he even care?

"Bullets won't hurt me. Have you lived with the humans too long? No weapon of man can kill an angel." Bastion shook his head. "And your death touch won't work on your own kind."

Footsteps thudded behind him. "Az!" Tanner's shout. "We need that blood, now! She's—she's—"

Bastion inhaled a deep breath. "Her heart is stopping. The doctor can't help her."

*"Now!"* Tanner yelled.

Tanner wouldn't see the angel. Only those with angel's blood in them could ever see the angels. Those with the blood . . . or those near death. When it came time for Death to take you, the dying could always see the angels at their sides.

"I can help her." Az lifted the gun. His finger curled around the trigger. "Get out of here, Bastion. You're not taking her tonight."

"Uh . . . Az?" Tanner's confused voice.

Bastion didn't move. "And you're not in charge anymore."

"No, but I'm the man holding the bullet made of brimstone—and I'm the one who'll shoot you with it if you don't fly your ass out of here."

Bastion blinked. "B-brimstone?"

Az knew fear when he heard it.

"It's not a weapon of man. More a weapon of the devil." The gun didn't waver. "I can personally attest, these bullets *burn*. And when they're fired into an angel's heart, I'm laying odds that they will kill." He lifted a brow. "Shall we find out?"

Bastion backed up a step. "I want Marna."

"Then go and find her. Just stay away from Jade. She's not dying for me."

Bastion's wings unfurled. He stared hard at Az, then glanced up at the sky. One moment passed, two . . .

*"Az . . ."* Tanner grabbed his shoulder. "Stop talking to your damn self and—"

"She's not the innocent you think." Bastion took another step back. *Retreating.* "You think you're saving a weak human, but she's not what you believe her to be."

"She's exactly what I believe her to be."

"A killer?"

Az didn't let his surprise show.

"Because she has killed, and not just once." Bastion raised his arms before him. "Would you really battle with your own kind in order to protect the soul of a killer?"

*She took the blow meant for me.* "You don't want to test me right now, Bastion."

But the angel wasn't backing down. "You've already failed every test. That's why your wings burned to ash."

Bastard. "And it's why you're about to have a heart full of brimstone."

*"I hope to God you're really talking to someone,"* Tanner snapped. "Because I just can't deal with another crazy asshole right now."

Bastion's eyes narrowed. *"She dies now!"*

No, she didn't.

Az shot him. Not the heart. He didn't want to kill Bastion. But the bullet thudded deep into the angel's stomach.

Bastion doubled over and howled in agony.

"That's pain," Az told him. "It's what it feels like when angels *hurt.*"

Bastion glanced up at him, eyes stunned.

"Get out of here," Az told him. "And *stay away from Jade.*"

The angel's fingers were stained with blood. "You . . . you'll regret this . . ."

Az stared back at him. "You'll need to dig the bullet out. The longer it stays in you, the more it will hurt and burn."

Bastion's wings began to flap as the angel rose. "I'll . . . be back for her."

But not right away. The angel would need to heal. That would buy them some time.

"You . . . you've just asked for a war."

He'd asked for a life.

A muscle flexed along Bastion's jaw. "The punishment angels will come for you."

Like he was supposed to be afraid of them? Not likely. "Are you forgetting?" He asked. "I've already fought one punishment angel. And Rogziel was the one who wound up in hell, not me." *Enough of this.* Jade needed him. "Want to join the bastard?"

Bastion's eyes narrowed as he fought the pain. "Death always finds a way," Bastion snapped. "You know that." Air rushed against Az's skin as Bastion took to the sky. Despite his injury, the Death Angel soared quickly, hurtling upward and vanishing almost instantly.

Gone. For now.

"The scent . . ." Tanner inhaled. "Okay, want to tell me what the hell is going on?"

Az shoved the gun into the back of his jeans. "Not now." He hurried inside and left the shifter on the porch. The smell of blood was stronger, and when he entered the back room, he saw Cody bent over Jade's prone form. Tubes ran from her arm. The doc held one piece of tubing and a big-ass needle in his hands.

"This isn't the way we're supposed to do this . . ." Cody began.

Az stalked forward. It was the way they'd have to do it.

"A transfusion like this is too risky." Sweat covered the doctor's forehead. "The risk of infection, disease—"

"I don't have any disease." The guy could knock that worry off the list.

The doc didn't look reassured. "What if your blood type doesn't match hers?"

"Consider me a universal donor." He knew his smile was bitter as Az ripped open his own vein and got to work connecting the tubing. Angel blood was supposed to be all-powerful. And his blood was Jade's only chance. He'd either save her or—

*Or I will keep fighting death as long as I must.*

Cody rushed around the table and began the work of adjusting the tubes and monitoring the beeping array of machinery that he'd set up. Blood flowed from Az, dark red, as it filled the tube and slid its way to Jade's body.

Az realized he was barely breathing. Waiting. Watching. *Fight, Jade. Fight.*

The blood in the tube reached her. Fed into her body.

One second. Two. Az's own heart had nearly stopped. *Jade . . . stay with me.*

Jade's eyes flew open. Her eyes weren't the dark green that reminded him of lush fields he'd once seen in Ireland. Instead, the green was brighter than he'd ever seen it before.

Relief had his shoulders sagging. She'd be alright. She'd be—

Jade screamed. Again and again. Her long, horrified screams filled the air. Her eyes were on him. Full of terror.

And her screams wouldn't stop.

Marna didn't return to heaven. Bastion paced the Great Hall, unease rippling through him. She should have flown back to their realm by now.

He wasn't afraid. He couldn't feel fear. But a tightness constricted his chest as he remembered Azrael. Az—a Fallen who'd been ready to kill to protect a human.

Marna had been the one sent to claim the woman's soul. Had she faced Az's fury as well? Except . . . perhaps Az hadn't just *threatened* to kill her.

Bastion's wings spread as he launched from the Hall. Clouds raced by him, one after the other. He knew *where* Jade Pierce had been scheduled to die. At the edge of a Louisiana swamp, right under a cypress tree that swayed near a gator-infested pond. She should have died there, with Azrael at her side.

Marna had foreseen the human's death days before. She'd

come to him and told him because she'd been startled that Azrael had been in her vision.

Marna wasn't like the others. He'd tried to protect her over the centuries and attempted to make sure that no one saw her weaknesses.

Or her fears.

She'd been afraid of Azrael. Most beings were, though. But Bastion knew that when Marna had gone out on that last mission, she'd been afraid to take someone that belonged to the Fallen. She'd feared how he might retaliate.

Perhaps she'd been right to be fearful.

The ground was a sea of green beneath him as he flew over the trees. Marna couldn't just vanish.

His feet slammed down into the earth just yards from the swaying cypress tree. He stared at the signs of battle. Blood on the ground. The battered earth.

So much blood . . .

His nostrils flared as he strode forward. There was blood, but . . . more.

His heart began to pound faster in his chest. So fast that the deep beating startled him. He'd never been worried before. Never been afraid.

But this time . . .

Black feathers—*wings*—were on the ground, smeared with blood. His hand shook as he reached for the wings. An angel didn't just lose her wings. It was nearly impossible to cut them. They could burn off in a fiery fall from heaven.

Or . . . or they could slip away when an angel died.

The drumming of his heart grew even louder. Marna was a good angel. Only wanting to help others. She should never have been a Death Angel. Carrying souls actually seemed to wound her. She should have been a guardian. She should have—

A scream ripped from him. Fury. Pain.

There were more black, bloody feathers. So many more. And the scent of blood that coated the feathers—it was angel blood.

Azrael had made sure that his mortal's life was spared, and in exchange, he'd known just how to balance the scales of death to give Jade Pierce more of a fighting chance.

*A life for a life.*

If Bastion checked the Book of Death, Jade's name probably wouldn't even be listed anymore. A soul had been taken. Death had been satisfied for that instant in time.

Because Azrael had sacrificed an angel to let a human live.

Bastion's heart burned in his chest. A Death Angel shouldn't want vengeance. Punishment angels would be the ones to deliver fury and wrath.

*But Azrael has already killed a punishment angel.*

After his fall, Azrael had battled a rogue punishment angel named Rogziel. Rogziel hadn't been given the lighter sentence of banishment from heaven for his crimes. Instead, Azrael had been the instrument of his destruction.

Would the other punishment angels go after Azrael for this offense?

Or would they fear him too much?

Azrael had introduced fear into the hearts of many angels.

The feathers fluttered in the breeze. There was no sign of Marna's body. Only the broken remnants of her wings.

Bastion forced himself to rise. Slowly, his fingers released the black feathers that they clutched.

If the punishment angels would not do their job, then he would seek vengeance.

Azrael wouldn't get to keep his human. He wouldn't get to cheat death.

*Because Death is coming for you, Az.*

This time, Azrael would be the one to fear—and to die.

*Marna, I am sorry, but you will be avenged.*

★ ★ ★

"I've done all that I can." The demon doc tossed his bloody gloves in the trash. He shook his head and stared down at Jade with tired eyes. "Now we just have to wait and see if your blood can help her."

Jade hadn't stopped screaming, not until Cody had pumped her full of sedatives that had knocked her out. Az had tried to get close to her, to comfort her, but as soon as he'd advanced, her screams had become even more frantic.

She'd looked at him, but seemed to see a monster.

*Now she's really seeing me.*

"How long will she be out?"

"At least till dusk. Hell . . ." Cody rubbed his forehead. "With all those tranqs I gave her, an elephant would be out until sunset."

Az stood by her side. He couldn't move away. Her color seemed better. No lines of pain ravaged her face anymore. A sheet covered her chest and lower body. Beneath the sheet, bandages hid her injuries.

There was no way a human wouldn't scar from those wounds. But then, a human shouldn't live with them, either.

"You know that she'll be . . . *more* when she wakes." Cody's voice was hesitant.

Az frowned and glanced at the demon.

Cody still gazed at Jade with a faint furrow between his brows. "Human before," he murmured, "but, now, with your blood . . ."

"She'll be the same as she was."

Cody lifted a brow and turned his too dark stare on Az. "Do you really believe that? Or are you just trying to make yourself think that it's true?" Cody exhaled on a rough sigh. "When the first angels fell and mated with humans, their blood mixed—"

"And demons were born." He didn't need a history lesson. He'd been *there* for that history. He'd witnessed the temptations. Cleaned up the chaos left in the wake of so much recklessness.

"Even vampires can go wild when they ingest an angel's blood." Cody lifted Jade's wrist and checked her pulse. "I've heard vamps say they can actually drink an angel's power through the blood." He put her hand back down and stared at her still form. "I can't help but wonder . . . did you think about the risks to her? Or did you just not care?"

"I wasn't letting her die," Az growled.

"But you weren't going to let her stay human, either, were you?"

"She still is human! She won't change."

The doctor turned away. "She already has. Didn't you hear her screams?"

Az brushed back her hair. He let his hand linger on her cheek. "She was delusional. Out of her mind from the pain and the attack—"

"No." The demon stared out of the small window. "She just opened her eyes and saw monsters all around her. She saw monsters when she'd only seen men before."

Az's body tensed.

"She saw my black eyes," the doctor continued as he turned to slowly face Az once more, "and I'm curious to know, what do you think she saw when she looked at you? Because whatever it was, that sight made her scream the loudest."

# CHAPTER TEN

It was the beeping that woke her. A slow, steady beep of sound that gradually penetrated Jade's consciousness. She opened her eyes, then immediately squinted against the light.

"You're back."

She stiffened at the deep voice.

"Don't worry." A warm hand covered hers. "You're safe here."

Jade turned her head and met Tanner's worried stare. She licked her lips, swallowed back what tasted like ash on her tongue, and managed to ask, "Where am I?" Her voice came out cool and . . . normal. Why had she thought that she'd be hoarse? Why did the memory of screams whisper through her mind?

"Ah . . ." He exhaled. "Okay, don't freak on me, but we're at my brother's place."

In an instant, she yanked her hand away from him and snapped upright. Something sharp yanked on her arm. Quickly, she glanced at her right arm. What was that? A needle? An IV? She *hated* needles. Jade ripped it out and tossed it away from her. "You sold me out!"

"Easy." He lifted both of his hands in one of those *I'm-harmless* gestures that people did. "I'm not talking about that brother, okay? Not the insane, psychotic prick who wants us both dead." He jerked his thumb behind him, to the wall of bandages and medicine and what looked like hospital equipment. "My brother Cody is a doctor, and after you were injured—"

"You mean after you and that bitch witch friend of yours tried to kill me—"

"You weren't going to make it back to the city alive."

Okay, that stopped her. "I knew I was dying." Crazy, but, she'd almost felt death touching her.

"Your angel wasn't real keen to let you go."

*Angel.*

Her gaze flew back to his.

"Yeah, I know what he is. This isn't my first ball game, lady. And when we got here and he started talking to people that I couldn't see and my nose"—he tapped said nose—"kept catching the scent of flowers, I knew Death was standing close by."

Now Tanner had lost her. "Flowers? What are you even talking about?"

"An old legend. At least, some folks think it's legend. When an angel's close by, if you pay attention, you'll catch the smell of flowers in the air."

"Az doesn't smell like flowers." Man. Power. Not petunias.

"That's because he's not *exactly* an angel anymore, now is he?"

She swallowed. "No, he isn't." The bandages on her chest were pulling on her skin. She didn't want to look down and see the mess that had been made of her flesh. She could still feel Brandt's claws, sinking into her chest.

Jade took a deep breath and forced her head to lift. Tanner's gaze was full of sympathy and that just made her feel vulnerable. And a little sad. "How am I still alive?"

"You're alive because your veins are pumping with that not-quite angel blood."

Shock froze her for a moment.

"We rushed you here," he said. "My brother got you on his table, did his best to patch you up, and then Az gave you the dirtiest blood transfusion that I've ever seen."

"Blood transfusion?" Goose bumps rose on her flesh.

"Um . . ." He inclined his head toward her. "I thought you were dead, but that ex-angel of yours brought you right back to life."

She didn't remember any transfusion. She didn't remember a doctor. Only . . .

Black wings, rising above her. A monster with eyes darker than night.

Jade licked her lips. "Where is Az?"

Tanner glanced toward the shut door. "When we saw that you were starting to wake up, we figured it might be best if you didn't see him or Cody first thing."

"Cody?"

"My brother."

Brandt had never mentioned him. But then again, he hadn't told her about Tanner, either.

Jade rolled her shoulders. The doctor must have given her some fabulous drugs. She didn't hurt at all. Actually, she felt stronger than she'd ever been before.

But . . . "Why would it be best for me not to see them?" That part didn't make any sense.

"Because the last time you saw the two of them, you screamed so loud and long that we had to knock you out."

Shaking her head, she said, "No, no, I didn't—"

"I was outside, running in the woods, and your screams damn near deafened me."

He didn't look like he was bullshitting her.

"We wanted to make sure you woke up feeling calm and safe."

A shifter was supposed to make her feel safe? She

would've felt much safer with Az. Jade glanced around the room as she pushed up into a better sitting position. She was in a bed, a small, twin bed that had been pushed against the far right wall. Faint sunlight trickled through the thin white curtains. "How long was I out?"

"About ten hours."

So long?

A light knock rapped at the door.

Tanner didn't take his gaze off her. "You ready for this?"

She gave a light laugh that just came out sounding lost. "I don't know what you're talking about."

"You will. 'Cause you aren't the same anymore." He squared his shoulders. "Just remember that you're safe. I'll be right beside you."

She wanted Az beside her.

"Come in!" Tanner called out.

The door opened. A man's dark head appeared. Not Az.

The guy came in. His broad shoulders pushed past the doorway. His head was down, his long hair brushing over his cheeks. "Glad you're awake." His voice was a deep rumble of sound. "You were starting to worry us." His head lifted and his eyes met hers.

*Black eyes.* Completely black eyes. Even the sclera. Every single part of his eyes were black.

Jade didn't make a sound.

She'd heard stories, of course. She knew about the demons who walked the earth. Some demons possessed enormous power, enough to level a city block. Others were barely more than human. But, according to the stories, they all had the same eyes. Eyes as black as the night. They used glamour to change the color of their eyes and fool humans so they wouldn't realize what monsters stood beside them.

This guy wasn't using any glamour. He was showing her his real eyes.

He reached for her wrist. She managed—barely—not to yank her hand back from him. *Brandt's brother, and a demon. Talk about having two strikes against you.*

"I'm not going to hurt you." Two fingers pressed against her inner wrist as he checked her pulse. "I'm not like Brandt."

She couldn't look away from his gaze.

"You see me for what I am, don't you?"

"I-is there a particular reason you aren't bothering with the glamour magic?" Maybe he felt safe in his home. Maybe . . .

"I *am* using it. You can just see right through it." He released her wrist. "You saw me the moment his blood filled your veins."

So now she was seeing demons? Great. What she needed to see was an angel. "I want Az."

"You sure about that?" Tanner had moved to the foot of the bed. He was watching her with that half-worried, half-sympathetic gaze that was making her feel increasingly antsy.

"You seemed to . . . want to be away from him when you saw him last." Now that bit came from the demon doctor.

"I was out of my head then." The doctor reached for the bandages that began near her shoulder. "I want Az," Jade said again.

His fingers brushed the tip of the bandages. "Lay back down and let me check your wounds. Once I'm sure you're healing well, I'll call him in."

Tanner offered her a faint half-smile. "Cody's afraid you're gonna freak out again and mess up all his fine handiwork."

She slid back down on the bed. "Check me out, then get me Az." She needed him.

When Cody got to work slowly pulling back the bandages, she stared up at the ceiling. Faint cracks crisscrossed the white paint above her, and she focused her gaze on them. The sick feeling in her gut told her that she'd have scars on her chest that looked just like those cracks. Long, jagged.

A light touch of air hit her skin when the demon pulled back the bandages.

"How . . ." Surprise roughed the word even as the doctor leaned closer to her. *"I'll be damned."*

She'd been avoiding looking at her wounds but now . . . Jade risked a fast glance down, but only saw the doctor reaching for scissors. Tweezers.

Her gaze immediately jumped back to the ceiling.

After a moment, she felt a light tugging on her chest. Then he pulled something out—stitches? She had to look like Frankenstein's monster, and she knew it was weak, but Jade didn't want to see those wounds right then. Give her a few more hours, and she'd woman-up and do the deed but right then . . .

"You're healed."

*Lie.* But . . . her eyes darted down to the ravaged flesh that she hadn't wanted to see. Only it wasn't marred. Not so much as scratched. Pale as ever, smooth. No sign of the deep cuts that had torn through flesh and muscle.

*"Az!"* She screamed his name because in that moment, she was terrified of what she'd become.

The door flew open and slammed back against the wall. Az stood in the entranceway, filling the space. His hands were clenched. His eyes blazing. "Get away from her!" He roared. And in the next second, he'd leapt across the room. Az grabbed the demon by the back of the neck and hurtled him against the wall.

Jade realized she was naked from the waist down. She yanked up the sheet and ended the peep show.

"Easy!" Tanner lifted his hands when Az rounded on him. "We weren't hurting her."

"I was . . . just . . ." The demon rose and winced. "I was merely checking her out."

"I saw that." A lethal edge underscored Az's words. He spun to face the doctor, giving Jade his back, and that was when she actually paid attention enough to notice his wings.

Not real wings. More like shadows. Thick, black, they rose from his bare shoulders and extended high above him.

They were dark and so beautiful.

"She was scared," Az snarled as he closed in on the demon. "I heard her fear." His hands were clenched into powerful fists.

Uh, oh. Jade kept a hold on her sheet as she hopped out of bed. Her knees didn't so much as jiggle when her feet touched down on the wooden floor. That angel blood sure packed a powerful punch.

"Because she realized—we *both* realized—" Cody spoke quickly now as he pressed his back against the wall in an attempt to put more distance between him and Az. "We realized that she's healed."

Jade crept up behind Az. Tanner didn't move. She reached out and her fingers skimmed over those shadowy wings. She could almost feel them against her skin. Like silk.

Az stiffened. He'd loved it when she stroked his scars before. What effect would it have on him when she touched these shadowy remnants of his wings?

"Jade . . ." Her name was a rasp, heavy with need, lust.

She stroked the shadows once more.

This time, he shuddered.

"She's healed," Cody said again. "And—"

Az turned to face her. His jaw was locked, and his eyes still burned hot enough to scorch her. And the man looked like he could eat her.

Oh, my.

"I think it's time for us to get out of here." Tanner hurried over and grabbed Cody's arm. "They need to . . . talk."

"Talk? I don't think talking is what—"

Tanner knocked his brother's head into the wall then hustled him out of the room.

The shifter made sure to slam the door closed behind him.

Az's wings were out of her reach now, but she wanted to touch them again. "I can see them," she whispered.

He shook his head. "Nothing's there. The wings burned away when I fell."

Maybe. But those shadows were still there. She stepped closer to him. Jade kept one hand on the sheet that she'd hurriedly wrapped around her body while her left hand lifted and touched those shadows. "What does it feel like when I touch them?" Jade whispered.

"They *aren't* there."

Something was. Her fingers went right through the silken remnants.

He stepped back and put enough distance between them so that she couldn't touch his wings. Then he caught her hand and held tight. "You're seeing what was," he gritted. "My blood's in you. Only those with an angel's blood can—"

"Thank you," her soft words cut him off.

He blinked. Shook his head.

"You saved me." That she knew with certainty.

His fingers tightened on hers. "I was afraid I was too late."

No. Leave it to an angel to know just how to cheat death.

"Are you afraid of me?" Az asked as his eyes searched hers.

She let the sheet drop. It pooled on the floor between them. "No." Jade moved closer to him.

His head lowered toward hers. "You're sure . . . ?" Only inches separated their mouths as he asked, "You're certain you aren't still hurt?"

She smiled up at him even as her heart raced in her chest. "The demon said I didn't even have a scratch."

He still didn't kiss her. "You scared me."

The big, tough angel?

"Don't ever do that again," he ordered, then, *finally*, his mouth took hers.

It was as if an inferno ignited inside of her. With the touch of his lips against hers, lust seemed to fuel her blood. She opened her mouth. Her tongue met his.

He tasted even better than she remembered.

Since his chest was bare, her breasts pressed against his skin. His flesh seemed hot, so strong, and rippling with muscles.

His hands were tight around her—tight, but not hurting. Az knew his own power too well.

Her hips pushed against him. The thick length of his arousal was impossible to miss. Her fingers unsnapped the button at the top of his jeans. With a low hiss, his zipper slid down.

His cock sprang forward, heavy, straining, and she stroked the tip.

Az pulled his mouth from hers. "Should go slower . . ." His breath rasped out. "Should take care . . ."

"Yes." She licked his neck. Bit lightly with her teeth. "You should definitely take care of this need I have." Only for him. She'd never wanted anyone so quickly, so much. "Show me that I'm still alive, Az. *Show me.*"

He lifted her up. Held her as if she weighed nothing. To him, she probably did. Two steps, and he had her on the edge of the bed. Her legs wrapped around his hips. His cock pushed between her legs.

No foreplay. No soft words. No fake promises.

Sex. Lust. Need.

Life.

He thrust into her. Filled every inch of her, stretched her so full she ached.

Then his fingers pressed against her clit and that ache

changed into a delicious curl of pleasure. Her sex clamped tight around him. She loved the thickness of his flesh in her body.

Az stood between her spread legs. He leaned over her as he thrust into her. When he pulled back, his flesh slid over her sensitive core. Then he thrust balls-deep into her body.

Their eyes held. Her heart thundered in her chest. The bed was soft beneath her. He was hard *in* her.

The rush of pleasure was consuming. She arched up again, but his hands clamped around her hips, stilling her. His eyes seemed to burn her. She'd never had anyone stare at her with such raw lust before.

Brandt had acted as if he owned her. Az . . . he acted as if he'd die without her.

His cock filled her completely. Since he held her locked against him, she couldn't force him to thrust with the arch of her hips. But . . . Jade tightened her flesh around him and squeezed his cock with her inner muscles.

His pupils flared wide.

Then he began to thrust and withdraw again, but, this time, it was different.

The consuming hunger was still there, held barely in check. He moved a little slower. Softer.

Sweat beaded his upper brow. His hands, though lethally strong, were lighter on her flesh.

Gentleness. She'd only expected heat and hunger.

"I won't break," Jade told him.

"I'll never let you." A vow.

He kept the easier motions. Lighter, but still just where she wanted him. Now she could arch her hips against him, and every drive of his body rubbed against her clit. The sensation was a pure stroke of pleasure that vibrated through her body.

"I won't lose you," he said, the words a growl but his hands still gentle on her body.

She wrapped her legs around his hips. Her body was tightening and preparing for the release that was just moments away. She could feel it building inside her. Az leaned close to her, and Jade bit the curve of his shoulder.

He shuddered, but the control he'd grabbed didn't break. He thrust slow. So slow. Forcing the pleasure on her with each movement of his body.

No, not forcing pleasure. Giving it to her.

She wanted to give to him.

"You make me want more than any other." His hands rose. Found hers. His fingers threaded through hers and held them locked to the mattress. "How?"

She could only shake her head. "Az . . ." Jade trembled beneath him. *"Harder."*

But he wasn't giving her harder. He was controlled. Measured. And she was about to go out of her mind.

"Az!"

He drove into her. Again. Again. He bent and his tongue swirled over her breast. Her sex contracted greedily around him.

"This time, we take it slow." His jaw clenched as he gritted the words. "I almost . . . lost—"

She spread her legs wider, lifted her hips, and he sank in deeper.

Her head tipped back at the hard stab of pleasure. Good, but . . .

He lifted her arms above her head. Caged her wrists with one hand. Then Az let his right hand stroke between their bodies. His broad fingers pushed down between her legs. Found the center of her need.

"I want to see . . . you . . ." Voice rougher, his touch became more demanding. He thrust—

She came on a long, hot explosion of pleasure.

His control broke. *Yes.* The small bed rammed into the

wall with the force of his thrusts. He plunged into her, so deep she cried out. Not in pain. Oh, no, not pain.

The orgasm continued to rip through her. His thrusts seemed to double the pleasure, making the climax stretch longer on a wave that never seemed to end.

Az stiffened against her and called out her name. Not a gentle whisper. More of a roar as he came inside her.

His shadow wings rose above them. His blue eyes darkened so much they appeared black. And he held her so tightly she wondered if he would ever let go.

In that one instant, she actually thought he never would.

"You're not dying." Brandt grabbed Heather's chin and jerked her face toward him. "The bleeding's stopped, and you're all stitched up."

The witch's eyelashes fluttered, then her eyes opened, just a crack. Dried blood had hardened on her face and neck. Brandt dropped her chin and crossed his arms as he looked down at her. "I'm not quite as talented with a needle as my brother is, but you won't be bleeding to death anytime soon." Well, at least not until he was finished with her.

Her pale hand lifted and, with trembling fingers, she traced the twisting path of stitches that cut across her chest and neck. Heather blanched.

He smiled. "Now, unless you want me to start slicing you back open . . ." Brandt let his claws burst out of one hand. "You'll answer my questions."

Heather's too plump lips trembled. "I-is that why I'm . . . alive?" Her voice was a broken rasp. Probably from all that screaming she'd been doing when he stitched her up. Eventually, she'd passed out.

Eventually.

"I let you live because you *were* the one to bring Jade back to me."

Now she tried to smile.

"Her and that *fucking bastard* that you led straight into my camp." He lunged forward and sliced open the two stitches across her collarbone.

Heather screamed. Good, now her smile was gone. The witch wasn't gonna play him. In this game, he was the one with the power. Time for her to recognize that fact.

"Don't fuck with me," he told her. "I went to a lot of trouble to save you." He'd never saved anyone before. It had just felt . . . wrong. Heather had screwed him over. She'd attacked Jade. The witch had deserved her punishment.

Yet he'd saved her.

Brandt exhaled and rolled his shoulders. Tension was making his whole body ache. "If you aren't going to be useful, I'll just rip open your throat and hunt them down myself."

Her ragged breathing seemed too loud in the small room. She kept her wide eyes on him.

Brandt lifted a brow. He could almost see the gears rolling in her head as she schemed. "Trying to pull together enough magic to work against me, huh?"

"As soon . . . as I'm . . . stronger . . ."

"Blah the fuck blah." She was never going to be stronger. He'd seen to that. The witch didn't even know what he'd done. She would. Soon enough. He sat on the small bed next to her and rather enjoyed the way she flinched away from him. As if she hadn't begged him to touch her so many times in the past. "Tell me everything you know about Azrael."

She blinked. "Who?"

Fine. If she wanted more pain . . . He lifted his claws over her neck. "Az-ra-fucking-el."

A tear leaked from her eye. "Oh, him."

Right. Him. "I've got some demons in New Orleans who

tell me that that bastard is supposed to be pretty damn strong." He paused. "But then, angels are, aren't they?"

She nodded and his claws scraped over her chin.

Good. She wasn't going to deny what the guy was. "How'd you find him?" He pulled his claws away from her throat.

A laugh spilled from her lips. Sad. Angry. "I found him naked in a cemetery. He'd just fallen, and I went to help him."

Brandt didn't let his expression alter even though his heart was suddenly pounding far too fast. "You're not exactly the helping sort." One of the things that had always kept him on edge—Heather could be as brutal and cold as he was.

That was why she'd be dying soon. But first . . . He leaned forward and brushed back the hair that had gotten stuck in the blood on her cheek. Heather watched him with wide eyes. Eyes that had always seen too much.

"Just where had this Azrael fallen from?" He asked, testing her.

She swallowed. "Where the hell do you think?"

Brandt didn't hurt her. Not this time. "Once upon a time, you told me that you had a vision that an angel would kill you. That he'd destroy the whole world." Heather and her visions. She'd looked into the dark so many times. At first she'd scryed because he'd wanted to see what the future held. But later, Heather had done it because she'd grown addicted to that wild rush of power.

He knew how tempting darkness was.

When a witch scryed, she looked past life and death. She looked into the very darkness that waited for man and for the *Other.*

The death and darkness looked back at her. Sometimes, they even struck out at her. Heather had the scars on her body to prove that.

She'd first come to him, young and scared, because of that initial death vision. She'd wanted to find someone to keep her safe from the angel who would be her doom.

She'd turned to the wrong man.

She'd gone back to look in her mirrors, over and over, but her death vision had never changed.

An angel would slay her. An angel who walked the earth without wings. An angel who only knew death.

Cocking his head to the side, Brandt asked, "Has your future changed?"

A ragged breath, then, "Some things can't . . . be changed."

"No, they can't be." Some people couldn't change. But he was surprised because . . . "If Azrael is the one who is supposed to kill you, then why is he still breathing? Why didn't you send him to hell on your own?"

"Because you can't kill Death."

Maybe the witch had finally gone crazy. Too much darkness could do that to a weak spirit. Brandt shrugged. "He bled easily enough for me."

She glanced away. Ah . . . hiding something. No matter. He'd get to that truth soon enough. Right now, he wanted to know . . . "Why is he with Jade?"

"Because he's fucking her."

Inside, the panther snarled, even as the man shoved his claws into the nearest wall. A wall mere inches from Heather's head.

"I made sure of it," she whispered and she stared right into his eyes as she confessed, "I even . . . helped them along."

With a yank, his claws came free and chunks of drywall littered the bed. "Your damn spells."

Her smile had once been beautiful. Now it was just cold. "I simply gave Jade the courage to take what she wanted." She tried to shrug, but the motion stopped when she winced in pain. "It would have happened . . . eventually. I saw the way she looked at him. The way . . . he looked at her."

Heather wasn't a stupid woman. Things would have been easier if she had been. "You know that he dies now." But that was what she wanted.

"I know he's starting to want her just as desperately as you do."

His back teeth ground together. "You *want* me to kill him." To make sure that her vision never came true. If this Azrael really was the angel from her vision, the one that she'd feared for so long . . .

"I wasn't certain that . . . you could," she said. "But . . . perhaps . . ."

"You're sure he's an angel?" Brandt asked because in this world, he knew beings were not always as they seemed. There could be no surprises when they faced off again. Only death.

"I'm sure he'd never known temptation, not until Jade crossed his path. He'd never known sin, not until her."

That was a load of shit. He'd stared into Azrael's eyes. That was a man well acquainted with sin.

After all, Brandt knew that look too well—it was the same look that his own gaze possessed.

"He won't let you have her." Heather's breath panted out as blood seeped through her stitches. Perhaps he should have done more than just close the skin. Maybe he should have worked on the internal wounds? Oh, well. Too late now. "He's . . . guard . . ."

A guardian? From what he'd heard, those angels weren't big threats.

But perhaps a guardian who'd fallen would be more of a challenge. "If he bleeds, then he can die." His claws had sliced right through Azrael's skin easily enough. "Just tell me where he is, and I'll kill him." One fast scry and she'd have the guy's location.

But Heather shook her head. "Too . . . weak."

Sighing, Brandt climbed to his feet. "Right. You should rest. Get your strength back."

She nodded.

He turned away. Paced to the nearby table and let his fingers curl around the dark mirror he'd sent a packmate to retrieve.

In an instant, he sprang back to the bed. His claws ripped open her arm and Heather's blood flew onto the glass.

She screamed.

"Heather, do I look like I give a shit how weak you feel?"

Now the witch whimpered. Yes, she should have known better. "My asshole brother is out there with this angel. Jade *betrayed* me. Tanner betrayed me *again*. I want all of them, and I want them *now*." He caught the back of her neck. "Before you go to hell, stare into the darkness and fucking find out where that angel is hiding."

She stared into the darkness. As her eyes began to haze over, he knew the darkness stared back. He shoved her face toward the mirror.

*I'm coming, Jade. And I'm going to kill everyone close to you.*

It was an old and familiar promise. One she knew too well.

One he'd fulfill, once again.

# CHAPTER ELEVEN

"Why didn't you tell me about him?" Az's hand stroked over the curve of Jade's back. She sat on the edge of the small bed, and, at his question, she glanced over her shoulder at him.

Her cheeks were still flushed, her lips red and plump from his mouth.

She was so beautiful to him. Even now, he ached for her, but . . .

*But she set me up.*

With an effort, Az kept his voice calm as he asked, "Was there a reason you didn't tell me the truth about Brandt?" *Did you want him to kill me?*

She blinked those fuck-me eyes of hers. "I . . . told you. He's a psychotic shifter. Super strong, super crazy, and—"

"And he's got a whole lot of angel blood flowing through him." Now the rage did break past the ice in his words. "Didn't you think it was important that I knew that little fact? The death touch won't work on someone like me." One of the little safety clauses that the big boss had put in place. Angels weren't supposed to kill each other.

But Jade was shaking her head. "He's no angel. You saw his claws—hell, I've seen him shift! He's a panther. He's *not* like you."

Az just stared at her as his mind whirled. He'd broken so

many rules for her. He'd thought she could offer him re-demption, but the chance to get his life back had never been farther from him.

Now they didn't just have to deal with her bastard of an ex, they also had to deal with Death Angels who'd be on their trail.

"Every *Other* can recognize their own kind," he said. It was a rule of nature. Shifters could catch the scents that would identify others of their ilk. Witches could feel the magical pull from those with powers like their own, and as for Death Angels . . . "My touch would have killed a nor-mal shifter." He lifted his fingers off her skin. The possibili-ties ran through his mind, then the strongest one clicked in his head. "My guess is the guy's a hybrid."

She rose from the bed and turned to face him. The woman didn't even seem aware of her nudity. That was fine. He was plenty aware of it for them both.

"A hybrid?" She repeated with a little line deepening be-tween her brows. "You mean, like, his dad was a shifter and his mom—"

"Probably was an angel."

Her eyes narrowed. "He never talked to me about his mother." She searched the room. Found her shirt. Frowned at it when she realized it had been sliced to pieces.

"So you truly didn't know?" He rose slowly, stretching. Her scent was on his skin. Az rather liked that. What he didn't like was the idea that she'd deliberately set him up. While his touch hadn't been able to kill Brandt, that guy's claws had done a thorough job of slicing him to pieces.

Shifter claws weren't a weapon forged of man, so, yes, they'd do the trick when it came to killing an angel.

*Is that how Brandt's mother had died?*

Her hands clenched in the torn fabric of her shirt. "You actually think I set you up? To die?"

He stared back at her, waiting.

She threw the shirt at him. "No, jerk, I didn't!" Then she whirled around and started yanking open closets and drawers. Jade growled when she didn't find any clothing, then she spun back around with blazing eyes.

Red stained her cheeks, but he didn't think that glow was from passion anymore. More like fury. "*I'm* the one that took the claws to the chest in order to protect you. Remember that sweet little moment? Because I sure do. It's kinda etched in my memory."

He'd never be able to forget that moment. In that instant, he'd decided—

"So, no, I didn't think it would be a fun game of shits and giggles for me to set you up so that my ex—*who has made my life nothing but hell and blood for the last ten years*—could slaughter you. I was really rather hoping that the all-powerful, badass angel would be the one to take *him* out." Her chest rose and fell with her fast breaths.

She was strangely beautiful when enraged.

Her gaze dropped to his cock. Narrowed. "Don't even think it right now, got me? You just accused me of using you as some kind of kill toy for Brandt. That's not how I work, and you, angel, well, you need to think again." She stomped away from him.

He should let it go. Let her go. But . . .

"Who did you kill?" Az asked her.

She froze with her fingers inches from the doorknob.

With a wave of his hands, he conjured clothes for himself—and for her. She might be pissed, but he wasn't letting her waltz out of the room naked, not with the others just a few feet away.

In an instant, soft jeans and a white T-shirt appeared on her body. She didn't acknowledge the clothing, though she started in surprise. *Still not looking at me.* He'd *make* her see him. After what he'd traded for her, she damn well owed him the truth.

"Did Brandt tell you that I'm a killer?" Her voice was soft. "You know you really shouldn't trust him. He's a pathological liar."

"It wasn't Brandt. It was an angel I've known for centuries." A guy who *couldn't* lie. Unlike Brandt, the guy wasn't a hybrid. Pureblood angels only spoke the truth.

Since the words had come from Bastion, he knew they weren't a trick. He'd thought she was innocent. In need of protection. But she'd been lying to him all along.

Not so innocent. Not even close.

*Why do I still want her so much?*

She still didn't look at him. Her fingers reached for the doorknob. "Then I guess you know the truth."

Jade opened the door. *No.* He grabbed her. Slammed that door shut, and in an instant, he had her caged between his arms. "Who was it?"

A faint sheen of tears filled her eyes. "Go to hell."

He stepped back, shocked more by the tears than by her words.

"Don't stand there and judge me. You're a *Death Angel*. Not some gentle guardian. Death is all you know. How many lives have you taken, huh? Hundreds? Thousands? You don't know what *my* life has been like, and you sure don't understand what I've had to do in order to survive."

*Kill.*

"Humans adapt, right? That's our strength?" Her lips curved in the hardest smile he'd ever seen her give. A smile that didn't match the trace of moisture in her eyes. "Let's just say I'm a pro at adapting. Now do me a favor and *step back*."

He stared down at her and didn't move an inch. "Do you know what I traded for you?"

"Considering I was ready to trade my life for you, right now, I don't really care." She didn't wait for him to move. Jade shoved him—shoved, and Az flew back five feet.

Her jaw dropped open. "How did I—" She broke off, staring at her hand. "I'm sorry. I-I didn't mean . . ."

He rose from the floor. *The blood*. He'd have to tell her what to expect, but . . . he didn't *know* what to expect.

Jade whirled around and yanked open the door. She rushed out even as Az called her name. She didn't get far though. A few steps, and she slammed right into Tanner.

The shifter caught her arms and held her in place. "We've got a problem." A muscle jerked along his jaw.

She pulled away from him. "*A* problem?" Her laugh held a ragged edge. "Trust me, I think we've got a whole lot more than just one problem to deal with here."

Tanner glanced over her shoulder at Az. "He's hunting us."

Az just nodded. He'd figured that Brandt would come after him sooner rather than later.

"We maybe have an hour, probably less than that, before he tracks us here."

"How do you know that?" Jade demanded as she ran a hand through her hair. "How can you possibly?"

"'Cause I've got one friend still in that pack, and he just called to tell me that we need to get the hell out of this place." He huffed out a rough breath. "Heather's still alive. Brandt forced her to scry, and she told him exactly where we are."

So the bastard was coming for him. Fine. "Let him hunt."

Tanner lifted a brow. "You're that eager for another ass-kicking? 'Cause I'm not."

Az crossed the room in an instant. His power might not work on Brandt, but Tanner was one hundred percent shifter. "You *knew* what he was."

Jade hadn't. He got that, now. But Tanner . . .

"Yeah, I knew."

And with a wave of his hand, Az tossed the bastard

through the nearest window. Glass shattered as Tanner sailed toward the dock.

"Az!" Jade spared him a shocked glare before she rushed outside after the now-groaning shifter. "Jeez, a punch would have sufficed," she yelled back at him. "The slam through the window was a little much."

Not really. He figured he owed Tanner more.

He conjured a ball of flame and followed her out of the house and onto the rickety dock. Tanner had just risen. He took a look at the flames hovering above Az's hands and his claws immediately sprang out.

But then Jade jumped between them.

Az held back his fire.

"Is there a reason you didn't tell us about Brandt's little, um, side powers?" Jade demanded, voice hot enough to burn like the fire in Az's hands.

"I thought you knew," came Tanner's instant answer. "Hell, I thought there wasn't anything you didn't know about Brandt. And if you believed this guy—" He pointed a claw at Az. "Could take him out, then I believed it, too."

Until the moment Brandt had sunk his claws into Az's chest. Then they'd all stopped believing. "Here's some angel trivia for you." Az let the fire die. He could always conjure it again easily enough. "It takes more than the Death Touch to kill our own kind. Angels, even half-breed ones, can't be killed with mortal weapons." Give 'em a few more runs through the blood chain, a few more generations to dilute that powerful blood, then you could have a being that would die with a touch. But full-blood and half-blood angels were too strong.

Their magic fought Death.

"So if you can't kill him, then what are we supposed to do about Brandt?" Tanner wanted to know as he began to pace the length of the dock. "What? Are we just gonna wait around here, let him come and kill us all?"

"That's not a good plan," Jade snapped.

No, it wasn't. "He has the witch."

Tanner stopped and nodded.

"We need her." He didn't like Heather. Didn't trust her—especially after what she'd done to Jade—but if they were going to take out Brandt, they'd have to save her. "She knew about that brimstone bullet. She might have even—"

"She's the one who made him the bullets," Tanner admitted, stopping Az's words. "She found a wounded hellhound a long while back. She ground up its claws to make the bullets."

A hellhound, huh?

"Wait!" Jade held up her hand. "He told me that he got those bullets from a witch in Vegas."

"Yeah, that's because he originally hooked up with Heather in Sin City."

"Hooked . . . up?" Jade asked. Then she shook her head. "You don't mean they—"

"Right. They were hot and heavy, until Brandt met a certain human who got under his skin. Heather told me that once he met you, he left her—for fucking dead, by the way."

Her hands clenched into fists. "Sounds like Brandt."

"You knew all of this about her " Az strode along the old dock as he closed in on Tanner, "And you still trusted her? You sent us in with her and—"

"He cut her up and tossed her into the swamp!" Tanner stood toe-to-toe with him. "It's not like she was mooning after him. The woman wanted vengeance! I thought she'd help us."

"She wanted vengeance alright." Jade's angry voice had Az's gaze sliding to her. She rubbed her chest. "She was willing to kill me in order to get it."

"I never thought she'd attack you," Tanner said. "I swear, okay? I figured she'd want to kill Brandt, not you."

But Az understood. "She *was* attacking Brandt when she went after Jade."

Jade nodded. "She told me that she was taking his heart."

By killing her.

"Bitch," Jade mumbled as she rubbed her arms, as if chilled.

"I'm sorry." The gritted words were Tanner's. "If I'd thought for a moment that she would try to kill you, Jade, I never would have taken her with us."

It was a mistake Az would make sure they didn't repeat.

But Jade's assessing stare was studying Az now. "Well, whatever else we say about her, the witch knows her weapons. Those bullets she made worked on you."

"So they'll work on him, too." Wound Brandt. Kill him. "We just need Heather to give us a new batch." Then they'd be on equal battling ground. Claws versus brimstone.

Maybe not equal.

And maybe Brandt would be dead.

Az smiled. "Let him hunt us. While he comes after us, we'll be heading right back into his camp." *And taking the witch.*

A sharp bark of laughter escaped Tanner. "You're crazy, aren't you?"

Perhaps. A Fall could send some angels into raving insanity. Create killers, monsters.

*Nightmares that walked the earth.*

"But that's a pretty fucking smart plan," Tanner continued. "One Brandt won't see coming. We'll need to move fast though." His head jerked to the left as his nostrils flared. "What in the hell?"

Az followed his gaze into the twisting darkness of the trees.

"Has he already found us?" Jade's hushed voice asked.

Tanner strode past her. "Someone's hurt out there. I can smell the blood."

Shifter senses.

"Not human," he added, almost as an afterthought.

Jade frowned at him. "Who is these days?"

Az let his gaze search the trees. This could be a trap. Brandt was a wily hunter. He could've put out weak bait to lure them in.

Az had seen killers use this move dozens of time over the centuries. "You got a lock on the scent, Tanner?"

The shifter nodded. "A mile to the left. Whoever it is, they're moving real slow." He glanced back at Az. "Could be close to dying."

The dock squeaked. Az glanced back and saw Cody advancing on them. Now their little group was all together.

Worry showed on the demon's face. "We can't leave someone to die out there."

Jade stiffened when she saw the doctor, and she took a quick step toward Az.

"We don't have a lot of time to waste," Tanner growled. "Brandt's hauling ass over here. We can't defeat him and his whole pack right now. We need to be gone."

"We need the witch," Az said. He had to get those bullets and Heather was the one who could provide him with that perfect weapon.

There was no way he'd forget or forgive what she'd done to Jade. Or to him. But he would be using the witch. "She's the one who can give us the weapon we need."

"Is she really our only option?" Jade's delicate jaw clenched as she moved closer to Az. "Sorry, guess I'm just a little hesitant because of the whole *trying to kill me* bit."

His fingers brushed over her cheek. "She's not going to hurt you again."

"No," Jade was definite, "she won't. I'm not going to give her the chance."

Tanner cleared his throat. "We're all pissed. We all want our pound of flesh." He sighed. "But if we want to use her, then we have to hurry up and go get her."

"Not yet."

They all turned at Cody's hard snap. The demon stood his ground. "We're not leaving yet."

Like the doc was going to stop him.

But Cody pointed to the woods. "I can smell the blood, too," he said. "Someone's out there, hurt. Are we really just going to leave 'em?"

No, they weren't. Az inclined his head, and Tanner took off running. He cleared the dock and headed toward the left. They all fell in behind him, racing through the thicket of trees. The shifter didn't hesitate as he tracked through those woods. When it came to hunting, nothing beat a shifter's nose.

And Tanner made short work of cutting through the swamp and finding his prey. The others followed him, and Az made sure he kept Jade close to his side. Until he found out all the effects his blood would have on her, Az didn't want Jade out of his sight.

Tanner stopped. Inhaled. Pointed to the side. "The scent of blood and flowers is coming from that way."

Blood . . . and flowers? Az's heart began to beat faster.

Tanner cocked his head as he studied Az with a growing understanding in his eyes. Jade and Cody huffed out breaths as they paused.

"You sure you want to play hero again?" Tanner asked. "Maybe this isn't someone you want to save. Maybe it's someone that you already gave one ass kicking to."

Maybe. *Blood and flowers.* He wouldn't know for sure, not until he actually saw the prey.

They started moving again. Faster now because Tanner was closing in on that scent. Jade was moving too fast for a human, and she didn't even seem to realize that fact. He didn't know how long the blood would keep impacting her. The fact that she'd seen his wings—

*She wasn't afraid.*

The trees seemed to blow past them as limbs reached out and scratched at his flesh.

"Tanner!" For an instant, he lost sight of the shifter.

Then Az rounded a bend, leapt over a fallen tree, and found Tanner crouched on the ground.

A blond woman lay in his arms. Skin pale and blood-stained. Marna.

*No.*

In an instant, he was at Marna's side. She was on her back, with her eyes closed. He lifted her up carefully. Her clothes were torn but the skin of her stomach and chest were fully healed. Angels could heal so fast, even from a panther's claws.

But as he lifted Marna higher into his arms, he realized that some wounds just couldn't be healed.

Her wings had been sliced off. The flesh of her back was still mending, crossed with thick, red slashes, and her wings were—*gone.*

"Az?" Now Jade's voice held fear.

*The angel who came to take your soul.* Did Jade remember her? He couldn't look at her then. The guilt was too much. Marna's injuries were his fault. He'd interfered. Altered fate.

An angel couldn't fly to the gateway and enter heaven without her wings.

"I know that handiwork." Tanner's low, rumbling words. Az glanced at him and saw that Tanner's face was twisted in fury. "Looks like Brandt got hold of her."

Marna's eyes weren't opening.

Jade touched Az on the shoulder. "You know her."

He nodded. "Her name . . . She's Marna."

"Another angel?" She whispered. "This—this probably sounds crazy, but I think I've seen her before."

"You have seen her." An angel's power came from her wings. Without the wings, it would take Marna weeks to build up her strength. The others could see her now because her wings were gone. Marna's *life* was gone. "When it was time for you to die, she's the one who came to take your soul."

Jade sank to her knees beside him. "Then why is she the one broken on the ground?"

*Because of me.*

Cody bent to press his hands against Marna's back. "I can stitch her up. We need to get her back to my place. I'll clean the wounds, bandage her—"

"And then Brandt will appear and finish slicing her up," Tanner finished. "Sorry, but hell, no. This woman's best chance for surviving is to get out of here."

He was right. Az stood, with Marna cradled in his arms. His gaze met Cody's. "I'm trusting you with her life. If anything happens to her, you don't even want to know the fury that's gonna rain down on all of us."

Cody nodded and reached for her. "I'll treat her, I'll—"

"You and Tanner will get her out of here. You run as fast as you can, and don't look back." Because when Brandt came hunting, he'd follow Jade's scent, not Marna's. Jade's and Az's. They had to split up from the others if Marna was going to survive.

Az held the demon's gaze. "When she wakes, whatever you do, don't let her touch you."

The doc's eyes widened. "Why would—"

"She's going to be furious, and you'll be the demon within striking distance. One touch, and you'll be dead."

Cody swallowed. "Guess I'll be strapping her down." His hold tightened on the unconscious woman.

"If you want to keep living, you will."

A nod from the demon.

Jade was silent beside him.

"How will you find us?" Tanner demanded. "Once you get the witch, what's the big plan? You going after Brandt on your own?"

Perhaps. "Head back to New Orleans. Be at a bar called Sunrise tomorrow night, right at midnight."

"And you'll be there?" The shifter pressed.

Lying wasn't an option, so it was a good thing that Jade said, "Yes" before Azrael had to reply.

"Go!" He told the other two, because tension already held his body tight. Minutes were trickling by. Brandt would be coming closer.

Tanner and Cody vanished into the trees. They'd protect Marna. Az just hoped she didn't wind up killing them for their trouble.

"We need to make sure that Brandt has a scent to follow," he said. "You're the one he wants, so he'll ignore everyone else and focus just on your trail."

Jade nodded, then turned and started running deeper into the woods. He stayed right on her trail. Running with her, keeping close, but not trying to mask her scent in any way.

Then they broke through the bush. She stood gasping at the edge of the thick, green bayou water. "Now . . . what?"

They'd run far enough to lead Brandt on a nice chase. Az caught her hand. Pulled her close. He'd never tried this with another person. "Do you trust me?"

"Yes." No hesitation.

"Then hold on." He tightened his arms around her.

And they vanished.

When Jade opened her eyes, the whole world was spinning. She stumbled away from Az and nearly fell to the ground. The guy's reflexes were superfast though, and he caught her right before she could slam into the earth.

"Easy," he whispered against her ear. "It'll take your body a few minutes to adjust."

Adjust to what? Nausea welled in her stomach, and she had to crouch, putting her head between her knees. "What just . . . happened?"

"We moved very, very fast."

Blinking, she glanced back up. The bayou was gone. They stood just a few feet from an arching cypress tree. Not just any cypress. She remembered staring up at this tree as she struggled to live.

Azrael paced away from her. He bent and studied the ground. She saw his shoulders tense.

The ground seemed to shake beneath her feet.

Jade sucked in a deep breath. Then another. She followed him on shaky legs, and saw the bloody black feathers on the earth. The feathers were far too big to belong to a bird.

*Come with me, Jade. It's time for you to rest.* She remembered the words, whispering through her mind, though she hadn't told Az about them. She remembered the words and the angel who'd appeared.

Marna.

But Marna had never touched her. If the angel had, Jade knew she wouldn't be there.

"Where's his camp?" Az asked as he kept gazing at those feathers. "Where's the hole that the bastard retreated to after he sliced her apart?"

Az glanced up then and she went very still. His eyes weren't blue now. They were demon black.

And the rage in them stole her breath.

"Where would he go?" Az stalked toward her. "You know him. Know how he thinks. Where would the bastard set up his base?"

Close by. Jade stiffened her shaky knees as she pointed. "Probably across the water." She knew this area. Now that the fog was gone, she recognized the place because she'd visited it in her youth. "They could have gone over on motorboats. From what I remember, there used to be a campsite over there. Lots of abandoned buildings."

Az straightened and strode to the twisting pier. Gators slowly glided in the water.

She could just make out the old campsite. "He won't have left the place undefended," she told him. "He's too smart for that. He's hunting, but he'll have left a trap behind. Left men behind."

"I was counting on that."

The deadly promise in his voice made chills rise on her arms. This Az . . . he was different. From the moment he'd found Marna in those woods, a coldness had crept over him.

"Let's see how fast they die," he whispered even as he snagged her wrist. There was no warning this time. Just the wild rush of wind. The feel of a thousand skeletal hands on her body, and in the next instant, they were across the water. On the shore.

And she knew Az was about to hunt.

They'd appeared right in the middle of the area, less than two feet from a lounging shifter. When he saw them, the guy let out a startled grunt and jumped toward them with his claws up. Az wrapped his hand around the guy's throat and lifted him into the air. "I want the witch," Az ordered.

The shifter swiped out with his claws. Blood poured from Az's shoulder.

Az just smiled.

That smile chilled her. This wasn't the Az she'd come to know. This guy—he was something altogether different.

With his left hand, he broke the shifter's wrist. Shattered bones.

"You're dying," Az told him. "It's just a question of . . . how painful do you want that death to be?"

A faint glow appeared beneath Az's hand as it gripped the shifter's throat. Smoke began to rise from the panther's skin as he convulsed.

"You can burn," Az told him, "from the inside out."

And he was.

"Az . . ." Jade lifted her own hand, then hesitated when the shifter started to speak.

"T-to the left. Th-third building. Witch's—th-there . . ." The words ended in a choked gurgle as the shifter fell to the ground. His body was still smoking, but his eyes were open, and staring at nothing.

Jade turned away and glanced to the left. She saw the shadowy bodies of two more shifters coming toward her. Only they weren't attacking as men. They were rushing forward on the silent paws of panthers. She opened her mouth to cry out a warning.

There was no chance to warn Az. No chance, and no need. A ball of fire flew from his fingertips and headed for the pouncing panthers. One cried out, a high, keening sound, and flew to the right. The flames slammed into the second beast. He fell to the ground and immediately began rolling as he fought to put out the flames. His fur vanished as he lost the body of the beast, and the man's flesh burned as he transformed.

The other panther rose. Faced Az.

Az began to stalk toward him.

Okay, fine, so he had this. She'd take care of the witch. Maybe she'd even get some payback herself because it wasn't like she'd ever forget that woman shoving the knife into her chest.

Jade raced behind Az. Counted the buildings. One. Two. Thr—

She kicked in the door. "Okay, witch, I'm—"

Heather was tied to the bed. Blood pooled all around her. The witch's face had been sliced. Her body clawed. There was blood. *So much blood.* Yet she still lived.

How?

Jade swallowed back the bile that rose in her throat. Heather's head had turned when the door flew open, and her dazed eyes locked on Jade.

"H-help me . . ." The witch whispered.

Pity tore through Jade even as she remembered . . . *The*

*knife shoved into her chest. "I'm taking his heart . . ."* Only Heather hadn't taken Brandt's heart.

*She tried to take mine.*

Jade eased into the room. Her gaze searched each corner, all the shadows. No panthers waited.

"Please . . ." Heather's strangled cry. "Need . . ." She tried to lift her hand, but the rope on the old bedpost wouldn't allow her wrist to rise.

Jade crouched near the bed. Damn. Those slices were deep. And all that blood . . . "You're going to be okay now." No, she wasn't. Not unless Az could get in there and help her.

*His blood.* That angel blood of his might be strong enough to save Heather.

"You're going to be okay," she told Heather again, meaning it this time. *"Az!"* Jade screamed his name.

The witch had suffered. So much torture. Jade didn't forgive the woman for what she'd done, but dying like this . . .

No one deserved to die like this.

Jade yanked at the thick ropes around Heather's wrists and managed to get the witch's left hand free.

*"Az!"* She yelled again. She needed him, now. Dammit, if he wasn't coming in, she'd have to go drag the angel off those panthers.

Jade turned from the bed, but Heather's free hand flew out and wrapped around her wrist. "Sorry . . . so sor . . . ry."

Shaking her head, Jade said, "Forget that now. You can beg forgiveness, I can kick your ass—later. We'll do that whole bit after—"

"Had to hurt you . . . to get . . . to him . . ." Heather's breath heaved out. "Only way . . ." Blood trickled past her lips.

Yeah, well, it had been a shitty way, but they'd deal with that after they stopped Heather from dying.

"You make . . . him weak."

"Nothing makes Brandt weak." Heather should have realized that. "He doesn't really love me. He can't love anyone." He was a sociopath. Incapable of actual love. She'd learned that long ago. He'd said the right things at first. Done the right things. But the man was broken inside.

"I'll be right back," Jade promised her. "I'll get Az. He can help you."

But Heather wasn't letting go of her wrist. "You . . . kill him."

The witch's nails dug into her flesh.

"Have to . . ." More blood bubbled from Heather's lips. "He'll . . . destroy everything."

"If you want me to stop Brandt, then *you* have to help me." Jade tried to keep the fear out of her voice. The witch didn't look like she had much life left in her. "We need those brimstone bullets that you made for Brandt. Az thinks they can take him out."

She moved her head in the smallest of negative shakes. "No . . . more."

Well, hell.

"*You* kill . . ."

A rush of air shoved back Jade's hair. She blinked and found Az kneeling beside the bed.

When she saw him, Heather cried out and tried to back away. There was no place for her to go. "*Don't!* Don't touch—"

"Where are the bullets?" He demanded.

Heather started gasping.

Jade grabbed his shoulder. "She doesn't have any more bullets. Just . . . shit, *help her.*"

He turned his head slowly to meet Jade's stare. "She drove a knife into your chest. And she laughed while you bled."

Um, she didn't exactly remember that whole laughing part.

Then Heather started to laugh again and the trickle of an icy memory flowed through Jade's mind.

"Knew . . . knew it would be you . . ." Heather whispered. "Always . . ." Her eyelids started to sag closed.

Az shook her. "You're not dying yet."

"I'm . . . already dead." She didn't open her eyes. "You know . . . how it works. Should have taken me before . . . can't stop death."

The chill just roughened Jade's skin all the more. "Are there more brimstone bullets at your shop?"

"Go to . . . hell . . . to get them . . ." Heather's breath seemed to choke out. Her chest barely rose. "Maybe . . . maybe I'll find some when I get there." Her pale, blood-stained lips curled.

"Do something, Az!" Just watching the witch die was tearing her apart.

But then the room seemed to grow very, very dark. As if something were sucking all the light away.

A thick shadow appeared near the bed. A shadow with the form of a man. He hovered over Heather. Reached for her.

Even as Az reached out at the same instant. Az's hand pressed on top of that shadowy hand. Heather stiffened. Her mouth parted in a soundless cry. Her chest stopped rising.

Jade whirled away. Shoving open the door, she fled outside. Two shifters lay sprawled on the ground. Motionless. Were they dead, too?

She was so tired of death. Jade ran toward the woods. Maybe she should have felt relief that Heather was dead. One less crazy bitch out there who wanted her dead. But . . .

But she wasn't relieved. Heather shouldn't have ended up that way. No one should suffer that much.

Jade slammed into a strong chest. Powerful arms reached for her. Held her tight. Jade's head whipped up. Her eyes were caught by a golden stare. One that seemed ice cold.

"I've been waiting for you," the man said, and his hands tightened around her. "Time to come with me."

Jade kicked him in the groin. Startled, he let her go. His hair blew in the breeze.

"Keep waiting, asshole," she told him as she backed up a few precious steps. "I'm not going anyplace with you!"

A line of fire appeared, separating her from the grabby stranger. "Stay away from her, Bastion!" Az roared. "Don't touch her!"

Too late. He'd touched. And the guy—Bastion—just leapt right through that wall of flame and grabbed her again. Grabbed her—and she finally saw the wings that sprouted from his back. Oh, damn.

He lifted her up, holding her effortlessly. His face—handsome, strong, *too hard*—came close to hers as he stared into her eyes.

Those wings of his seemed to block out the light. Not shadows like Az's, but full, real, thick wings. Black wings.

Bastion's eyes froze her. "You should be dead."

*Same song.* "I've been getting that a lot," she whispered.

"Bastion!" Az bellowed, and then he slammed into the other angel. At that shuddering collision, they all hit the ground. Jade grunted at the impact and rolled away. She sprang up and found Az and Bastion circling each other.

"Going to shoot me again?" Bastion taunted. "Going to keep turning on your own kind in order to protect the human?"

What? "Az . . ." He'd shot this guy?

Az immediately leapt toward her, half-positioning his body in front of hers.

Bastion laughed at the move, but the sound held no humor. Just more ice. "Trying to play the hero? What? Does your little mortal mistakenly think that you're the good guy in this story?"

Then the wind rustled around her. No, not the wind.

Bastion. He'd moved in a flash, coming to stand right beside Jade. "You're a fool," he told her. "Azrael was cast out for a reason."

Her hand reached for Az's. Her fingers locked with his.

Bastion's gaze dropped to their entwined hands. He blinked, as if confused, then his eyes slowly lifted once more. This time, his stare met Az's. "You'll destroy her. You know that. We destroy everything that we touch."

"Not this time." Az's words sounded like a vow.

But Bastion shook his head. "She should be dead. One touch, *and she should be dead.* Don't you realize what you've done?"

Az wrapped his arm around her and pulled her closer to his chest.

"You've *already* destroyed her," Bastion said, voice softer. "You just don't even realize it." Then he lifted his hands. He stirred fire, just as she'd seen Az do many times. Bright, red and gold flames. Dancing. Spinning in a circle. Spinning— and flying right at her.

Jade screamed as the fire swelled even higher. She felt the scorch of the heat on her skin. But then Az was there. Wrapping her in his arms. Shielding her and taking the blistering fire right into his flesh.

Taking it, then sending it back at the other angel. Bastion screamed. The scent of burning flesh filled the air.

Bastion vanished.

At first, Jade didn't breathe. Her gaze swept the clearing. Left to right. The ground around them had blackened with the blaze. "Is he . . ." She sucked in a deep breath, cleared her throat, and asked, "gone?"

Az didn't let her go. "No."

Great.

"But he won't attack again, not yet. Not until he's sure he can take me out."

That wasn't the reassuring news she'd been hoping to

hear. Az needed to work on that whole building team morality bit. "Then let's get the hell out of here, okay? Do that superfast move of yours and get us someplace safe." Even if it made her feel nauseous. Being sick was better than being dead.

She had no doubt that Bastion wanted her dead.

"There is no safe place from Bastion. He will be able to follow us, anyplace we go."

Again with the whole not-what-she-wanted-to-hear response. But before she could speak, Az lifted her into his arms. She wrapped her hands around his neck. Held onto him as tightly as she could.

When the world spun around her, she wasn't even afraid.

Okay, maybe she was. Because as she glanced back over Az's shoulder and saw the twisting trees begin to fade as he raced away, she glimpsed the hulking shadow of powerful black wings.

Bastion. Chasing right after them.

*You've already destroyed her.*

# CHAPTER TWELVE

"Jade." Az held her easily against his chest. She felt right in his arms. Her body soft, curved.

*Mine.*

No, no, a human couldn't belong to an angel. That path had been tried before, by others. Those angels had fallen for their lust. They'd suffered.

*I've already fallen.*

Her eyes were closed, casting dark shadows onto her cheeks. She seemed too pale in the waning light. She'd wanted protection. Instead, she now had a vengeful angel after her.

He bent his head. His lips brushed over her hair even as he inhaled her scent. After the hell she'd been through, how did she still smell of strawberries?

Her arm hung limply around his neck. Halfway through the journey, she'd fallen unconscious. A human's body, even one fueled by angel blood, simply couldn't withstand the speed he'd used.

He strode forward into the cabin. A bed waited just a few feet away. For now, this place would be their temporary shelter.

Their time together would come to an end all too soon.

*I don't want to let her go.*

Why couldn't he keep something of his own, just this once? Would it be so wrong?

Her lashes began to flutter. Clenching his teeth, he lowered her onto the bed. His hands wanted to linger, but he forced himself to step back.

Her eyes opened and seemed to find his instantly. "Az?" She breathed his name, her voice the same husky purr that it was during sex.

His hands clenched. "You're safe, Jade."

She glanced around the cabin. "Where are we?"

"Where angels fear to tread." The smart ones, anyway. Sam had been the one to tell him about this place. "Unhallowed ground." At least that's what his brother had called it. More like cursed ground. Ground that had once been soaked by the blood of vampires and demons in an epic battle. Sam had actually witnessed that battle as he'd gone to collect the dead.

The power had been great here. The whispers of magic still floated in the air. Magic . . . and evil.

Witches had used many spells here over the centuries. Spells to hurt. To kill. The taint of dark magic was in the air, and it pressed down on him like hands shoving upon his back.

As long as he could keep the darkness at bay, they'd be safe there.

As long . . .

*He's not the good guy.* Bastion had taunted him, but . . . angels couldn't lie.

"He was . . . following us." A faint line appeared between her brows. "I saw him. Flying after us with those great, black wings." She pushed up onto her elbows. Studied him. "Is that what your wings were like?"

"Yes."

"That Bastion . . ." She licked her lips. "He's an Angel of Death."

*Tell her.* Az paced to the window. He wasn't even sure who'd built this cabin, but Sam had used it when he needed to lick his wounds after battles. His brother had been through plenty of battles.

"Az?"

He forced himself to turn back to her. Jade was sitting up, and her hair was a wild tangle around her face. She looked tired. Pale.

*Still beautiful.*

Why were mortals so weak? So breakable?

He saw her gaze dart over his shoulder. Curious, he asked, "Can you still see my wings?"

She nodded. "Yes."

Then his blood was still fueling her. Perhaps she wasn't as weak as he feared.

A lone howl echoed in the distance. Jade shivered. "This place kind of creeps me out."

It was supposed to. Humans could feel the vestiges of magic in the air—magic that had been used to keep them away. Without his blood, she probably wouldn't have been able to set foot on the land.

"You can't leave my sight," he told her, deliberately keeping his distance. Going to her then wasn't a good idea. The magical power was pressing on him. Pushing against the darkness he'd kept chained inside for so long. "It's far too dangerous now."

"Because of Brandt?" She exhaled and rose. The jeans he'd conjured hung low on her hips and he caught a flash of her smooth belly. "So we're out of bullets. We can come up with a backup plan."

He was working on one. He could try ripping off the panther's claws and using them to slice the bastard's head from his shoulders. That would work. No, it *should* work. But he suspected that the hybrid had been using magic to amp up his power.

No wonder Brandt had taken the witch as a lover . . . what better way to get up-close access to magic?

In order to take Brandt down, to be *certain* that he'd have the strength to defeat that bastard, Az knew he would have to increase his own power.

Though a magnification of that sort brought risks.

"What is it?" The old hardwood creaked beneath Jade's feet. "Something's wrong."

Everything was. He could kiss heaven good-bye now. There'd be no going back upstairs. No forgiving and forgetting for the things he'd done. Or for what he'd do.

The darkness shoved from inside his chest. He'd tried so hard to do the right thing. He'd chained the whispers inside, and done his best to defeat the dangerous needs that called to him. He'd fought them every moment that he'd been on earth.

*Until her.*

"Az?" The floor creaked again as she took a step toward him.

He held up his hand. "Stop." She couldn't touch him. Not now. "Bastion was right."

She stilled.

Time for his confession. "You haven't even asked why I fell."

"And you haven't asked how I wound up with a jerk like Brandt."

Surprised, his gaze flew to her face. She was watching him with an intent stare. Focused, but not afraid. When would she learn that she needed to fear him?

"I'm not perfect," Jade said quietly even as her chin notched up. "So I don't expect you to be."

But she also didn't expect him to be a monster. To bring hell to earth. The witch, she'd expected that of him. Promised him that he'd destroy everything and everyone. She'd warned that one day he'd break through the binds that contained the monster inside—and no man would be able to stop him.

"I killed Brandt's father." Jade tossed the words out so casually that Az blinked. "He was the big, bad alpha leader. The man who'd tortured his son for years. The man who thought he was going to torture me . . . but I killed him." Her laugh was bitter. "He didn't sense a threat from me. 'Cause I'm just human, right? Weak. Helpless. No danger to a tough guy like him."

She was dangerous. The ache in his chest grew. This place . . . it was pressing too deeply into him. Bastion would never venture here. He was too good to survive this place. As for Brandt, he wouldn't expect Az to ever bring Jade to such a dwelling.

*Evil.*

It was growing thicker in the air, as if enjoying her confession.

"I met Brandt when I was seventeen years old."

He didn't want to hear about her time with the panther. The drumming of Az's heartbeat began to pound louder in his ears.

*You ever need to recharge, go to Devil's Lake. Consider it a safe house, of sorts. The magic there will fire you up, but be careful, brother . . . it comes with a high price.*

Sam's warning. Az hadn't been afraid of paying, but . . . but now as the fury in his body built, he wondered just what he'd be sacrificing in exchange for the power coming his way.

*Why hunt out a witch when you can steal the power they left behind?* It had seemed faster, smarter, to come here and soak up the remnants of magic.

Sometimes, you had to fight the dark with—

"He seemed perfect when we met," Jade said. "Strong. Handsome."

*I don't want to hear this story.*

"I left my family to be with him. They told me to be careful, that I was too young, that I didn't really know him." She shook her head and stood there with her shoulders slumping a bit. "But I loved him, he loved me, and I knew we were supposed to be together."

*Loved him.*

He could almost feel the stretch of his phantom wings. "He wasn't for you to love." The fury inside roughened his voice, but he held onto his control. This place *wouldn't* break him. He'd take the power. Keep Jade safe. Destroy anyone who tried to take her away from him.

"At first, everything was perfect." She took another step toward him.

Az tensed. His cock was hard and swollen. His body tight with need. Whenever she was close, he craved her. But he didn't want to take her here. Not in this place.

*Not her.*

"Brandt can be charming. He can be seductive."

He could be a dead man with his head severed from his body.

"But I started to find . . . *more* in him." Jade's eyes held memories he didn't want to see. "My mom had always told me that the devil was a good-looking man, so perfect that you wouldn't see past his beauty until it was too late." Her lashes lowered and shielded those memories. "I saw too late."

Brandt raced back to his makeshift base. In the form of the panther, his powerful legs flew over the earth. A snarl broke from him even as the scent of blood filled his nose.

Two of the men he'd left behind turned at his approach. Still in human form. Their eyes were wide. Their hands up as if they'd calm him.

*Jade's scent.*

She'd been there. While he'd been out, searching so desperately for her, she'd been there . . . *with him*. The fucking Fallen.

Brandt launched into the air and took the throat of the first fool who should have captured Jade. Blood burst into his mouth, and he drank the guy's last breath.

The other shifter tried to run.

There was no place to run.

Brandt tackled him. Let his claws rip into the shifter's flesh. Severed his spine.

And more blood flowed. The beast always wanted more.

"I didn't even realize what he was, not at first."

She was coming too close to him. Az wanted to back away, but needed to be near her. Needed it more than humans needed their breath.

"Guess I couldn't see the monster hiding right there behind the man's smile. I didn't see it until it was too late."

Everyone had a monster inside. *Other.* Humans. A dark side that some fought. Some embraced.

Some kept imprisoned.

"It had been a month since I ran away with him. Love . . . it seems like the only thing that matters when you're seventeen." She blinked quickly, and he wondered if she realized he could see the tears on her lashes. "But I missed my mom. My dad. I missed them, and no matter how many times I called, I couldn't ever get them to answer the phone."

Az waited. He wanted to hold her, but he was afraid to touch her.

"So I slipped away one night. I stole a motorcycle—Brandt had been the one to teach me to hot-wire them—and I went back home." Now a teardrop slipped down her cheek. "They were dead. They'd been dead since the night I left. The-the neighbors told me it was some kind of wild animal attack. My parents had been killed, buried, and I didn't even know."

"An . . . animal attack?" His own words sounded like the rough growl of a beast.

Her eyes closed. "Even then, I still didn't realize the truth. Brandt found me. He comforted me at their graves. Told me that he'd make everything better for me. That our life together was just beginning."

A life bathed in blood.

"Then one night," she licked her lips, "this guy at a bar started flirting with me. Brandt got into a fight with him. I saw . . . his claws came out. He sliced the man, cut his chest right open. I tried to stop him, but I couldn't."

A human would be no match for a shifter.

"I ran from him. But Brandt found me, and he told me that I'd never get away. He said we were meant to be together, forever. That nothing or no one would ever come between us." She swiped away the tears on her cheeks. "And he told me . . . he admitted to killing my parents. He said they would have gotten in our way eventually, so he helped me, and he got rid of them."

Her voice had grown ragged with pain. "I didn't want them gone. I *loved* them. But they were dead, and I was left with a man who could turn into a monster." Jade's laughter was broken. "He thought I should appreciate what he'd done. I kept wondering when he'd kill me, and he kept saying how he'd proven his love for me."

Az couldn't stay away from her. The darkness was still there, pressing on him, but . . .

But she needed him. Az reached for Jade. He wrapped his arms around her even as she continued her tale. "He took me to the pack. We'd been staying on our own, in cheap hotels and cabins, but Brandt said that since I knew the truth, it was time to take me home."

Home to hell.

"There wasn't a chance to get away from him. He was always watching me."

Guarding her.

"Brandt—he had scars all over his body. Scars that I realized—too late—came from claw marks. He got them when he was a kid, long before he ever shifted for the first time."

She pulled back from him and stared up into his eyes. "His father is the one who marked him. He got off on hurting Brandt. On hurting anyone that he could. When Brandt went out on a hunt, he left me with that bastard. That night . . . they both made a serious mistake."

*I killed Brandt's father.* He searched her gaze. "How did you do it?" A human against an alpha panther?

"A silver knife to the heart. I'd been hiding the knife for days. Waiting for the right moment. I-I thought I'd use it on Brandt . . . but his father came at me. Hitting. Clawing . . ."

There was more. He could see it in her eyes. "Jade?"

She blinked and seemed to push back the past. "While he was trying to rape me, I shoved that knife into his heart. I twisted it, and I made *sure* he died."

The darkness swelled even higher within him as the rage burned. "Good." He pressed a kiss to her forehead. *You'd better be burning, bastard.*

"And then I left. I ran as fast and as far as I could. I never wanted to see Brandt or any of those other shifters again."

"But he kept hunting you."

Her smile was sad. "That's what he's good at . . ."


Brandt followed Jade's scent into the witch's room. He padded inside and sniffed the body. Heather had finally found her hell. She'd never understood . . . he'd only needed her power, not her.

Only one woman had ever been strong enough for him. Only one had ever battled *for* him.

Jade.

She'd fought the one thing he feared in this world. She'd given him freedom. Life.

All by dealing out a little death.

The panther inhaled the scents around him. His body tensed. Azrael. And . . . another.

He rushed outside. His pack—some still in the form of panthers, some standing back as men—tensed.

The beast swept past them. He ran. Ran, following the trail Jade had taken.

Then he stopped.

Because the trail had vanished. The panther tossed back his head and roared.

"I thought I'd be able to get away from him at first."

Lightning flashed outside, sweeping in with the growing darkness. A storm was coming in with night.

"I thought I could find a safe place to hide from him. That I could just start a new life, and he'd forget me." Her smile faded. "I'd have nightmares about him, but I would get my life back."

Az waited, his body tense.

"Months passed. Eventually, I stopped waking up, screaming. I got a job as a waitress at a diner in Arkansas. I even . . . I even met a man who didn't scare me."

She'd backed away, just a step, as if she sensed the dark energy that had come to surround him. But Az was fighting that darkness—fighting it, even as he drew the energy from the magic that stained the land like blood. When she'd backed away, his hands had fisted so he wouldn't touch her again.

The darkness had already touched her enough.

"Brandt killed Paul in front of me. Told me that I couldn't be with another. That I was his, forever."

*Not his.*

"I screamed and I begged, but Brandt sliced his throat right open. Paul's eyes were on mine when he died."

You could always see the life drain from a human's eyes at the moment of death. When the soul left, nothing remained.

"How did you escape from him that time?" Az wanted to know. Brandt would have been on guard then. Even more desperate to keep her at his side.

Thunder rumbled, echoing his words. He glanced toward the windows. The storm had rolled in so suddenly. Angry, rough . . .

And Az realized that his powers were slipping past his control. He was pulling in the storm even as he pulled in the latent energy from the unhallowed ground.

"Brandt actually thought I'd be glad to see him. He acted like he'd done some grand gesture for me." Her lips twisted. "He sent his men away. We were alone together. I don't think he ever even realized I had the knife. Not until I drove it into his chest."

Az blinked, surprised. Impressed.

She caught his stare and inclined her head. "Let's just say that at that time, I never went far without a silver knife. When it didn't kill him, I thought I must have missed his heart. I knew I wouldn't get another chance right then, so I ran like hell." Jade shrugged. "I think that's when he started to enjoy the hunt."

The fur melted from Brandt's body. Bones contorted, broke. His back paws turned into feet. Human fingers gripped the dank earth. He bowed his head a moment and sucked in deep breaths.

*Jade.*

Then he looked up and found his men assembled around him. They feared him, as they should. He'd earned the alpha title, slicing his way through all that came into his path.

Now, they waited. Ready for orders.

"We're hunting," he told them, voice calm despite the beast still clawing inside. But he was always calm on a hunt.

It was easier to track prey without emotion.

*Find. Hunt. Capture.*

But this time, his prey was different. Because this prey had stumbled right into his path. *You'll give me the power I need.*

"Jade?" Duncan demanded. Ah, Duncan. He'd just joined the pack when Jade had first escaped. He knew just how much Brandt valued her.

But Brandt shook his head. "Not this time." Not yet. Because before he could get to Jade, he'd have to take out her protectors.

Two. Two men not of this world.

"First, we're catching us some angels, and we're gonna show them just what hell on earth really means."

"For years after that, I was afraid to get close to anyone. But . . . I made a mistake." Her shoulders slumped. "Found another man who was so kind. Johnny . . . we'd barely even begun to date when . . . when Brandt found him."

And killed him. Yes, Az could figure out how that story ended.

"After Johnny, I knew the only way to truly stop Brandt was death. Either his . . . or mine."

Lightning flashed. Bare inches separated their flesh. *Don't touch.* "You're not dying."

Her laugh doubted him. "Then why do I have an Angel of Death after me?"

"I'm not—"

Her fingers pressed against his chest. His heart raced even faster. "Not you. The other one. Bastion."

"You weren't meant to see him." Had it not been for Az's blood, she never would've known about Bastion.

Her eyes seemed so deep as she stared up at him. "What did you do?"

Brandt had killed to keep her. And Az . . . he'd been ready to fight Death for her. His jaw clenched. "You shouldn't touch me."

Her hand pressed harder. "I don't think I'm supposed to be here, am I?"

Thunder rumbled.

"If an Angel of Death is pissed and on my trail . . ." She exhaled softly. "I'm guessing that means I should be dead."

*No.*

"It wasn't your time," he said. *I made sure of it.*

Her gaze searched his. "I don't want anyone else to die for me. I can't stand there again and watch—"

He broke. The cabin shook as the wind howled around them. Thunder rumbled so loudly it sounded like a drum. Az grabbed her. Lifted her up against him. "And I will be damned if I watch *you* die before me."

His lips crashed onto her. *Control, control*—a frantic shout in his head, but a shout he couldn't heed. His body was burning with need and lust and rage and . . . fear.

Fear, the darkest of all emotions.

*Won't lose her. Can't.*

She was the only thing he'd ever wanted more than heaven.

Jade didn't push against him. Her hands curled around his shoulders, and she opened her mouth wider for him.

Her taste just fueled his frenzy. A wave of his hand had her clothes falling off her body and dropping to the floor. Two steps, and he had her on the bed. Her hand went to his cock, to the aroused flesh that strained toward her, but this time, he needed more than just the wild rush of release.

He needed everything.

Az's hands wrapped around her thighs. Such smooth, supple skin. He parted her legs. Stared down at her pretty, pink sex.

Knew he had to take a taste.

His fingers stroked her first. Sliding lightly over the soft flesh, he found her wet and hot. A push of his index finger showed just how perfectly tight she was inside.

*Take.*

But first, he'd taste.

When he put his mouth on her, Jade's hips arched up against him. His tongue swept over her. *Sweeter than strawberries.* So much better. He licked. He kissed.

His fingers pushed into her even as his tongue stroked over her clit. Jade's fingers fisted in his hair, and she jerked when she came against his mouth.

The first time.

Because he wasn't done. Az was just getting started. His hands locked under her hips, and he forced her sex even closer to him. He held her, kept her trapped just where he wanted her, and he tasted every inch of Jade's sweet core.

Her breath panted, her body trembled, and she cried out his name as the climax hit her again.

He could taste the pleasure on his tongue.

His cock ached. The heavy flesh felt so big and swollen that he knew he'd come any moment. Az rose up. Licked his lips, and tasted her again.

Lightning flashed.

The rain beat down outside. A hard, driving rain that washed everything away.

Everything . . .

He positioned his cock at the entrance of her body. Kissed her as he thrust deep.

The rain fell.

Her legs wrapped around his. Held tight. His thrusts grew harder. Rougher.

The thunder was so loud it drowned out the squeaks of

the old bedsprings. Az kissed his way down Jade's neck. His teeth scored her flesh.

Her sex gripped him so tightly. Every move sent pleasure spiking through his body. Faster. Harder.

Her nipples were taut peaks against him. Perfect for his mouth. He tasted her there. Thrust harder.

She met him with her body and held on to him as fiercely as she could. Her right hand grabbed the sheet on the bed. Clenched it as she tossed back her head and squeezed her eyes shut.

More pleasure. More heat.

Temptation.

*"Jade."*

Her eyes flew open. Bright. Wild. Lost.

Did his look the same?

Her hand rose. Stroked over his shoulder and onto his upper back. Her caressing fingers traced the outline of his wings.

"So beautiful," she whispered. "My angel . . ."

Not an angel. Didn't she see? Couldn't she feel the darkness?

But her touch was all he needed. Az erupted inside of Jade on a hot, nerve-shattering explosion of release. The pleasure gutted him, ripping through his body and leaving him gasping for breath.

After a time, the thunder quieted and his heartbeat slowed.

Az rose onto his elbows and stared down at Jade. Her breath still panted out, as did his own. He brushed back her hair. "You shouldn't be with me," he said, even as his body began to thicken within hers once more. He just couldn't seem to get enough of her.

But she was already running from one monster. She didn't need to be in bed with another.

Jade's gaze seemed tender as she looked up at him. "There's no one else I want. Only you."

She didn't realize how dangerous the words were. Surely, she didn't. To offer them to a man who'd never had anyone *want* him before.

"You know all of me now," she told him, voice husky—sex and sin. "I'm not perfect. I've done . . . some pretty terrible things. Things I know I'll never earn forgiveness for."

But she wasn't asking to be forgiven.

She was fighting. Planning to destroy the man who'd taken her own life away.

"You know me," she whispered as her hands traced down his shoulders and skimmed over the thick scars that remained on his flesh. "So when do I get to know you?"

*He's not the good guy that you think . . .*

Fuck Bastion.

Az never wanted her to know the truth about him. He wanted her to keep looking at him like he was a hero. Like he was a protector. A man she could count on. A man she wanted.

Not a monster she feared.

"You know all that matters about me." He began to thrust again. Slow, easy movements. "The rest is just hell and death. It doesn't matter."

He wasn't the same as he'd been before. Jade made him want to be different.

For her, he would be.

She sighed softly, the sound so sweet and lush that he bent and caught it with his lips. This was need. This was pleasure. This was . . . life.

So very different from a world of death.

Her hands clasped his. He rose up and stared down at her perfect breasts. Not even a hint of scarring marred her flesh. He'd stopped Death's touch.

And he'd do it again.

Bastion wouldn't have her. Az had given up the witch to death. He'd let her go, but Jade—*no.*

His fingers tightened around hers. Jade wouldn't die. She wouldn't slip away.

Not when he'd just found her.

And if he had to fight all of the angels in heaven in order to keep her, then he damn well would.

# CHAPTER THIRTEEN

Sunlight streaked through the old window. Jade lifted her hand to shield her eyes. Dawn had finally come. The light should have made her feel safer.

It didn't.

Her gaze drifted to the right. Az slept beside her. She started to touch him, but hesitated.

Last night, she'd felt a darkness around him, filling the air. And his blue eyes had turned black.

Her breath exhaled slowly as she slipped from the bed. She'd talked to him and bared her soul in an effort to pull him back to her. Whatever rage burned inside him, she'd wanted to quench it.

But . . .

But she knew she hadn't.

The sex had been phenomenal, as she was pretty sure it always would be with him. Yet Az had been different. So intense. Like a fire was chained inside him. One that would erupt at any moment.

She reached for her clothes and dressed with barely a whisper of sound. Even at rest, his body, bare to the waist, appeared so strong and lethal.

*Not the good guy.*

But she wanted him to be.

Maybe he would have been, if it hadn't been for her. Because now she had him locked in a death battle with her ex, and from the sound of things, she'd managed to turn his own kind against him.

*Am I supposed to be dead?*

She couldn't think of another reason for a Death Angel to be on her trail. And Az couldn't fight both that Bastion guy and Brandt. Even he wasn't strong enough to face two powerful *Other* enemies.

She opened the door. The squeak had her tensing. *Crap.* But a fast glance over her shoulder showed Jade that Az still slept.

Okay. Good. She could do this. Last night, she'd peered out of the window and seen the gleam of metal near the edge of the woods.

*And if I was gonna stash a ride at this place . . .*

That sure would have been the spot she picked to hide her vehicle.

Jade rushed outside and headed toward the woods. Goose bumps rose on her flesh. Even in the daylight, this place just felt weird, and she could have sworn she heard the echo of old whispers floating in the air.

Five more steps, and she was at the edge of the woods. She saw the gleaming metal again, and realized someone had tried to use a green tarp to hide this prize. She grabbed that faded tarp and yanked. It flew away to reveal the heavy frame of a motorcycle.

Someone had left a backup plan behind. She started to smile.

A twig snapped behind her. Tensing, she glanced over her shoulder.

No Az. No other vengeful Death Angel coming at her, either. No—

"Going somewhere?" Az's deep voice demanded.

She jumped and lost her breath. Then she yanked her gaze back around, following the sound of his voice. He was in front of the bike, head cocked, arms folded over his chest.

Her breath came back, only to be expelled in a fast rush. "I just . . . I thought I saw this"—she waved her hand toward the motorcycle—"last night. And while you were sleeping, I figured I'd check it out." Her gaze held his and refused to drop, even when that too-intense stare searched hers.

"You're lying to me."

Okay, some shifters were supposed to be able to pick up on lies, maybe to even *smell* them, but did angels have some built-in lie detector, too? She didn't think so.

"No, I'm not." She'd bluff her way through this.

His smile held a cold edge. "After everything, were you going to just drive away and leave me?"

The darkness was even more intense in him today.

She reached for his hand. "No, I want us to both get the hell out of here." Unhallowed ground. Translation—ground they needed to fucking get away from. It was working some kind of bad mojo on Az, and she wanted her hero back.

She sure didn't want to deal with his bizarro dark side.

He glanced down at her hand. She followed his gaze. Her skin seemed so pale, while his was darker, golden.

"I dreamed about you."

She swallowed. Okay, dreams were good, they were—

"You died in my arms."

Dreams sucked. When his stare returned to her face, Jade tried to smile. "Good thing dreams don't come true, huh?"

"For angels, they do."

Her smile fell away.

"We see when our charges will take their last breath. We know of the moment that we must take them with our touch." He was holding her hand and stroking his fingers over the back of her knuckles. "I've taken thousands of lives. Never hesitated even once. Not like Keenan."

She had no idea who Keenan was. "Sorry, don't think I know him."

Faint lines appeared around his eyes. "Keenan was a powerful Death Angel. But when it came time for him to take his latest charge, he hesitated. He felt sympathy for the mortal, and he didn't want to take her soul."

Jade didn't know what to say, but that was okay because Az wasn't done talking.

He said, "Keenan lost his wings for her."

That was kind of sweet. "So they survived? Got to live happily ever after?" Great, now she sounded like a fairy tale. Maybe even a perky greeting-card-wannabe girl.

The goose bumps on her arms were getting worse. A cold wind seemed to surround her.

"Because Keenan didn't take her when he should have, his mortal was bitten by a vampire."

Jade tensed.

"Now Nicole St. James has to spend an eternity feeding off others."

So, not a happy ending.

"Keenan knew what he had to do," Az continued, voice a deep growl. "I told him, but he wouldn't give her up. He was ready to trade his life for hers."

She didn't like where this was going. "I don't want anyone to trade for me." She wouldn't be taking on that burden, thank you very much. "So if an Angel of Death is coming, he's coming for me. Not for anyone else."

The blackness deepened in Az's eyes. That was just creepy. Was her angel showing some demonic tendencies? He needed to stop. "Let's get out of here," she whispered. "Please, Az, let's just go."

He leaned over her. Seemed to surround her. "You want

me to stand back and let death take you?" Fury snapped through his words.

She didn't back down. "I want you to get your ass on that motorcycle and get us the hell out of here." Because she felt like Death was reaching out to grab her with his icy fingers right then.

*It's this place. We've got to leave.*

Locking his hands around her arms, Az grabbed her and lifted her onto her tiptoes. "I know how Keenan felt," Az muttered. "What I asked him to do . . . I *know* now."

Wonderful. Fabulous. They could—

"I told him to just kill her. To touch her, take her soul, and come back home. To forget about her."

Jade frowned up at him. That was some cold-blooded shit.

Az's mouth curled, but that was no grin on his face. "Bastion told you I wasn't the good guy. And you should know . . . angels can't lie."

Oh, hell. She tried to jerk away from him. He just held her tighter.

"I know how Keenan felt," Az grated. "Because if Bastion came to me and told me to kill you, I'd destroy him."

She froze.

"How?"

Now Jade was lost. How what?

"What did you do to me?" His hands tightened on her. "I never cared for a human, but I can't let anyone hurt you." The blue flashed back again in his eyes, as if he were fighting something. Someone. "Even myself."

In the next moment, Jade found herself on the back of the motorcycle. Az was in front of her, revving the engine.

"Hold on!"

She locked her arms around his stomach. Held as tight as she could. The motorcycle rocked forward with a blast of power that she didn't think was entirely natural.

But then, the unnatural was becoming more normal for her every day. Jade glanced back at the old cabin. The woods were so twisted around it now that the vines and vegetation appeared to swallow the place. And, for an instant, she could have sworn she saw thin, ghostly images walking near the woods.

Images that stared after her with fury.

Before vanishing in the light.

Jade turned her head away and pressed her face against Az's back. Whatever the hell that place had been, she *never* wanted to go back there again. She had more than enough darkness in her life.

Curses, spirits—they could just stay the hell away from her.

Az braked in front of an all too familiar looking dive in New Orleans. He killed the engine and shoved down the kickstand.

Jade glanced up at the entrance of Sunrise. Didn't almost dying in the place once mean that they should probably stay away? She thought that might be a good guide for them to follow.

And she realized that she was still clinging tightly to Az. Clearing her throat, she managed to unhand the guy and climb from the motorcycle. "Wanna tell me why we're walking down bad memory lane? I mean, we've got the whole city as a meeting place, did you have to tell Tanner to catch up with us here?" Only, they weren't meeting Tanner right then. It was a long way until midnight, and she sure didn't want to just kick the time away in that hole.

Az glanced at her. His blond hair shone in the sunlight. No helmets for them—none had been stashed with the bike. Yeah, they were all about dancing with death.

He studied her a moment. His eyes were back to being that bright blue that she loved—thank goodness. Hopefully, "bad Az" had been left behind at that hell-forsaken cabin in the woods.

"We need brimstone." He climbed off the motorcycle.

She sighed. "Yeah, well, unless you're planning to make a little pit stop into hell, getting brimstone might be a problem for us." Taking a field trip into hell wasn't her idea of a good time.

Az strolled past her and his fist pounded against the closed front doors of the bar. The place might be called Sunrise, but she knew it didn't open until well after sunset.

Jade glanced nervously up and down the street. Being out in the open wasn't such a stellar plan. She inched closer to Az. Her fingers slid down the side of his arm. "Maybe we should come back tonight." They could find a nice spot to lay low until then.

He shook his head. "It's better when no one's around." He stopped pounding, obviously getting the hint that the door wasn't going to be answered. Az waved his hand, and the entrance flew open. The doors banged against the interior walls.

Handy, having power like that.

"Come on." He took her hand, and they hurried inside. The doors slammed closed behind her. "Maybe it's here."

Um . . . *it*?

The club was dark, with sunlight barely trickling inside. Chairs had been stacked on top of the tables, and the curtains were closed on the small stage. The scent of a dozen perfumes lingered in the air. A heavy, golden cage hung from the ceiling above them. Yeah, that cage freaked her a bit.

They'd taken about ten steps inside when she heard the growl. The hair on her neck rose at the guttural sound. "Az . . ."

He stopped and turned to the left. A heavy, metal door

waited about twenty feet away. A door that had been pad-locked.

"Perfect," Az said, and actually sounded like he meant it. "I thought they might keep it here during the day."

Again with the "it" that made her so nervous.

"Stay here," he said.

Right. Like she wanted to go following him toward that creepy growl. *No, thanks.* She backed up a few steps, just to be on the safe side. Let the tough angel go investigate, she'd just—

Strong hands closed around her shoulders. Jade didn't waste breath screaming. *Brandt.* She spun around and struck out with her clenched fist.

And the guy caught her fist mid-punch.

*Not Brandt.* She recognized Sammael instantly. No mis-taking those eyes that looked like they'd spent way too much time gazing into hell.

*More monster than man.*

"Well, hello there," he murmured, his voice a silky threat. "I see my brother has taken to breaking into my place . . . and bringing violent friends to visit."

*Don't show fear, but . . .* "Tell me you aren't here to kill me."

He smiled.

"He's not." Az was at her side. Pushing the other guy back. "Sam owns Sunrise."

Now the breaking and entering bit made sense.

Sam lifted a dark brow as he studied her. "Well aren't you just something . . . different."

Jade shook her head. "Since when does being mortal make me different? You guys are the strange ones, not me." She couldn't go around touching people and making them drop dead. If only. Then she wouldn't be in this mess.

Sam took a step forward, sliding more into the light, and

she saw the ripple of shadowy wings stretching from behind his body. Wings that weren't there. Wings she shouldn't see.

Bastion's wings had seemed to break right through his clothes. But, since angels could conjure clothes, she figured it was really just some magical clothing fit over the wings. With Az and Sam, the same thing appeared to be happening with their shadow wings. The shadows just burst right through the back of their shirts.

They didn't even seem to realize it.

And she'd been staring at him too long. Flushing, Jade yanked her gaze back to meet his. Too late. Judging by the look on his face, he knew she'd been staring at wings she shouldn't see.

"Different," he murmured again. "A demon made, not born."

"What?" Her heart slammed into her ribs. "Did you just call me a demon?"

But now the guy wasn't even looking at her. His gaze drifted to Az. "You've been screwing with the wrong people, Azrael. Heaven wants you dead, and the bastards here on earth want to give you a one-way ticket to hell."

She noticed he didn't sound particularly concerned.

And Az shrugged, not looking like he really gave a damn either. Since when did life not matter to him?

"Where's the hound?" Az asked, and she saw his gaze sweep around the bar—and return to those locked metal doors.

Sam lifted one brow. "Why? You eager for that trip to hell? I suppose Beelzebub can drag you there. Though I would have thought you'd learned your lesson after that last round with a hound."

"Wait a second here." Jade held up her hands. Her head was starting to throb like a bitch. "Who's Beelzebub?"

"My mate's pet hellhound." Sam grinned. It was a terrifying sight. "And I'd wager he's getting pretty hungry about now."

Oh, no. No way. The guy had not just said—in a flash, Jade grabbed Az's arm and forced him to face her. "There's a hellhound here? A real, live, freaking hellhound?"

And what sane person would want to be around a beast like that?

"Before she fell, Sam's . . . mate . . . was a punishment angel." Az's gaze held hers. "Punishment angels are the only ones who can control the beasts."

"That's right." A woman's smooth voice floated in the air. Jade spun around and saw a gorgeous blonde stroll up next to Sam. Her eyes were dark and measuring as they swept over Jade. "Beelzebub isn't some attack dog that I loan out," the woman said and she sounded . . . offended. Definitely huffy. The blonde paused and added, "He's family."

Right. Because it was normal to have a hellhound as a pet. No, as family. Jade released Az and stood there, trying not to look as frightened as she felt.

"I just need his claws." Az turned toward the blonde. His hands were loose at his sides now. "It's not like they won't grow back."

Sam threw back his head and laughed. "You think a hellhound is gonna let you trim his nails? Not fucking likely, brother. More like he'll rip you open." The smirk remained on his face. "Though I do think you've got a bit of pain due your way."

The woman's stare was still on Jade. "She's . . . she's not human." Her voice was soft and husky.

Sam pressed his lips to the blonde's cheek. "Az has been a very, very bad Fallen. Seems he's gotten into the business of making demons."

A fist seemed to slam into Jade's stomach. That was the second time he'd mentioned her being a demon. She glanced over at Az. "What's he talking about?" You couldn't just make a demon. At least, she didn't think you could.

"Do you know what being is created," Sam asked in that rumbling voice of his, "when an angel and a human reproduce?"

She didn't really want a biology lesson, but she actually knew this. "A demon." She'd heard these legends. Stories said that modern demons were actually the descendants of the original Fallen. Those who'd left heaven because they were tempted by the humans.

*You're my temptation.*

She shoved away the memory of Az's angry words. The demons on this earth weren't minions of the devil—at least, she didn't think they were. Some were all powerful, able to wreck as much destruction as a hurricane. Others were barely more gifted than human psychics.

Either way, she wasn't a demon.

"You can see our wings," Sam said as the lady with him watched silently. "That means you have angel blood in you."

Jade straightened her shoulders. "Az saved my life. I was dying. He-he gave me the blood so I'd survive."

A frown pulled down Sam's dark brows. "How very un-Az-like." He shook his head even as he pointed at Az. "That would explain why the angels have a hard-on for you. I bet Uriel is eager to lay out some particularly painful punishment for you."

"He doesn't deserve punishment!" Now her voice was getting loud. Who cared? "Didn't you hear me? Az saved my life!"

"And changed fate." It was the woman again. The too-pretty lady with the eyes that saw too much. "Now, Az, how will you protect her when the Angels of Death come?"

"Making her a demon has only marked her more." Sam seemed regretful. "They'll say she's an abomination. Made, not born."

The woman flinched. Sam brushed his fingers over her cheek. He appeared regretful—had to be fake—as he said, "You've just put a bigger target on her back. As far as I know, a human has never *become* a demon before—"

Her control snapped. "I'm not a demon!" A hot blast of air seemed to whip through the room.

"Why didn't you tell her?" The woman asked Az. "Didn't you think she deserved to know the life she'd lived was over?"

No, no, that chick was *wrong.*

"Human blood." Sam sighed. "Mix it with angel blood. We've already said what type of being will be created . . ."

"Demon," Jade snapped out.

"You're a whole new breed," Sam continued and the guy studied her like she was some kind of science experiment. She was starting to feel like she was. "Wonder just how strong you'll be?" Then he moved with angel speed, instantly appearing right in front of her. He wrapped his hand around her neck and lifted her off her feet. "Or how weak?"

She couldn't breathe. Jade kicked him as hard as she could—

And Az tackled him.

Jade fell to the ground. Her hand automatically rose to her throat. The bar seemed to dip and sway and a giant crack raced across the top of the ceiling.

"Don't you ever try to hurt her again!" Az's bellow. He had his brother up against the wall and his fist was raised as he prepared to do some damage to Sam's face.

Sam wasn't fighting. Just laughing. Then he said, "You are so fucking lost. You can't get back upstairs if you're breaking rules and making new demons."

Sam's mate hadn't moved, but her body was tense and Jade saw her gaze dart toward the padlocked doors.

Uh, oh. Jade's gaze followed that crack in the ceiling once more. The bar had been shaking, but she didn't think that power burst had come from the two Fallen. That crack went to the left, following the path of the woman's gaze and heading toward those metal doors.

Just what was behind that lock?

*Hellhound.*

"Az . . ." She licked her lips. "I think . . . we . . . we should leave now." Dealing with a psychotic panther was bad enough. Facing a hellhound?

Not today, please.

But a growl was rumbling through the building. Az stared down at Sam. "He's still under orders to protect you, isn't he?" Az asked.

One of Sam's shoulders lifted, then fell, in an *almost* careless move. "What can I say? Seline likes to keep me safe."

Seline . . . that would be the woman who was hurrying back to Sam's side right then.

Hurrying, as Az backed away and turned toward those heavy doors. Jade rushed forward and blocked his path. "Bad plan. Okay? *Bad.* Let's just think of something else. There's got to be another way—"

"Another way to stop a shifter/angel hybrid?" Az demanded. "Then tell me what it is. Because his claws can slice right through me, but my Death Touch won't do a thing to him."

"Oh, man, you are screwed." Sam's voice was calm. "Guess it's time for you to try a few rounds with Beelzebub. When you lose a little more flesh, I think we'll finally call things even between us."

Even? That guy was insane.

Az ignored him and didn't look away from Jade. "We need these weapons," he reminded her. A reminder she didn't need. "If you want to be free, then you'll let me face him."

"He could kill you!" Seline cried out. "Don't you get that? The longer he stays in this realm, the stronger Beelzebub gets. And—and he has a taste for sin."

Jade's heartbeat drummed in her ears.

"Have you been staying lily-white?" Sam mocked. "Or have you really fallen now, Az?"

He'd fallen. Killed. Fucked.

"Beelzebub judges." Seline was trying to warn Az. Jade realized she was starting to like the blonde. "He can see what's in your heart. If he sees evil, he will attack."

Now Sam had come to Az's side. "Do you even know what's in your own heart?" He spared a glance for Jade. "Does she?"

Az gave a nod. He stepped forward and brushed a kiss over Jade's lips. "Don't worry."

She caught his hands. "Don't you die for this." *For me.* "There's another way. I know it."

But he shook his head. "This is the *best* way. We can get a supply of bullets. I can use them. *You* can use them."

"The hound won't just give up those claws." Sam tapped his chin. "You're gonna have to fight hard for them."

This plan sucked. "No," Jade said adamantly. "Forget it. Not going to—"

Az kissed her again. A brush of his lips. A slide of his tongue. Then . . . "Keep her safe, and don't let her follow me."

He vanished. No, didn't vanish. Just rushed by her because she felt the fast whip of wind as he passed. Jade turned to run after him, but Sam grabbed her hand.

"I can't let you do that," he murmured. "Sorry, demon, but . . ."

In a blink, he had her across the room. He'd tossed her up in that big, golden cage that dangled over the dance floor. A wave of his hand had the door locking, and a blast of fire from his fingertips melted the lock—effectively sealing the cage and trapping her inside. "But Az doesn't need you distracting him right now."

Growls reached her ears then. Snarls. Inhuman sounds. And the walls shook as the beast attacked.

She grabbed the golden bars. "Let me out of here!"

Sam was on the ground below her. He shook his head but didn't look particularly regretful. "Trust me on this, he deserves to have a pound or two of flesh ripped away. Your angel isn't exactly the prize you think."

"He's *exactly* what I think he is." And she was tired of everyone saying differently. "Now let me *out!*"

But he just turned away. "If he wants Beelzebub's claws, then Az will have to bleed for them."

"No!" Jade screamed. The bars wouldn't break. The cage swung back and forth from its heavy chain, and those growls just grew louder.

Az thundered down the old staircase in the back of Sunrise. He'd made short work of the metal doors and the padlocks upstairs. A wave of his hand and fire disintegrated the next set of padlocks that barred his path. A fast kick, and the reinforced steel door before him flew inward.

Az rushed inside, and the hound immediately attacked him.

The beast's breath, hot and reeking of hell's stench, blew into Az's face. Giant, yellowed teeth came at his throat even as the hound's claws swiped over Az's chest. He bellowed at the white-hot pain and kicked the beast off him.

The hound flew through the air, but landed easily on its feet. Thick, matted black fur covered the hulking body. Long, bloodstained claws raked across the floor.

The beast stared at him.

*He can see sin.*

And Beelzebub attacked again.

The hound drove Az back into the wall. Sheetrock fell around him, and Az was pretty sure that crunch was his ribs breaking. The hound's teeth sank into his shoulder.

Pain tore through him. A hellhound's teeth didn't just cut

and tear, they burned an angel. Clenching his teeth, Az grabbed the beast's head and yanked those razor-sharp teeth from his shoulder. He held the beast's head in his hands and gazed into the eyes lit by hellfire.

"You're not killing me today," he snarled. Sam had to find a better place to keep the beast. Sooner or later, it would start eating the Sunrise patrons.

The beast leapt back.

Az swiped his tongue over his lower lip and tasted blood. "And as much as I want to . . ." The beast circled around him, tossing back its ferocious head and howling loud enough to wake the dead. "I'm not going to kill you." He knew Sam and Seline were a little too fond of their monster pet.

The beast charged again. Az leapt out of the way. The hound's head slammed into the steel door.

"Won't kill you," Az said again as the hound rose, shaking its head, "but I will be taking those claws."

He could have sworn the hound smiled at him then. So many teeth. Then the beast lunged for him, and those claws sank into Az's stomach.

Sammael—Sam—was just going to stand there while Az died. And Seline sure didn't look like she was about to rush to Az's aid. "Why are you doing this?" Jade demanded. She'd yanked on every bar in the cage. No freaking give, not even near the lock since the guy had used his fire to solder the door shut.

Sam glanced up at her. "Az is the one who wanted to tangle with the beast. I just gave him what he wanted."

"Why do you hate him so much?" She couldn't get her heart to slow down. Her hands shook as fury filled her body. "I mean, I get it—he's your brother, so there's probably some sibling rivalry bullshit going on."

Sam's gaze iced.

"But he could *die* in there. Brandt almost killed him before. Az isn't as strong as you seem to think he is."

Laughter spilled from the Fallen. "And he's not as weak as you seem to think."

When his laughter faded away, silence filled the room. No more growls. The snarls had stopped.

The cage swung back and forth.

Her hands knotted around the bars.

"He'd better not have hurt my hound." Seline's mutter reached Jade's ears. "I owe your brother, so I let him in the ring with Beelzebub, but if Az hurt—"

Az shuffled into the room. A trail of blood followed him.

"Az!" Jade cried out.

His hands were on his stomach. Deep gashes covered his chest and arms. When he lifted his hands, Jade gasped at the sight of the deep wound that cut into his gut.

His gaze rose at the sound of her shocked breath. Blood trickled from his busted lip. "Don't worry." Despite his injuries, his voice was cool, even calm. "I got what we needed."

Then he put his hand in the mess that was his stomach. He pulled out one thick claw. Another. Another.

Her knees wanted to buckle so Jade just held tighter to the bars in order to stay upright.

"Your pet broke a few nails," Az told Seline as he dropped five heavy claws onto the floor.

Seline crept forward. "Did you—"

But she didn't get to finish. Because a great, hulking black beast burst from those metal doors and headed right for Az's back.

Jade yelled out a warning, but she knew it would come too late. The hellhound was a nightmare. Teeth barred, eyes burning like the fires of hell.

And there was nothing she could do. She was trapped. Az would die.

"*No!*" The scream seemed to break from her soul as her fury erupted. It burned hard and bright and washed right through her. As she fell to the floor of the cage, a ball of fire ripped out of her body and hurtled toward the beast. The fire slammed into the hound and stopped the monster just before it could reach Az.

Her breath heaved out. Oh, shit, had she just done that? *Demon.*

Jade pushed up onto her knees. A wild smile lifted her lips. The hound was down. Az was safe. She'd used magic and—

And the beast was getting bigger. Right before her eyes, he doubled in size.

Sam's brows lifted as he stared up at her. "Hellhounds like the fire, demon. You just made him stronger."

The hound rose to its feet and rushed toward Az.

# CHAPTER FOURTEEN

Jade was screaming his name. Fear tightened her beautiful face. She grabbed the cage's bars as tears slid down her cheeks.

Az didn't look away from her. Couldn't. He put his hand up behind him.

Beelzebub whined, then licked him. The beast's hot breath blew over Az's skin.

"What the hell?" Sam muttered even as Seline said—

"You tamed the beast." Her voice was dazed, but admiring.

"Not exactly a taming." He pushed his hand into that thick fur. "I guess he decided he didn't like the way I tasted, so he let me go." Now he seemed to have a four-legged friend that he couldn't shake.

And why was Jade up in a golden cage? Was she actually crying for him?

As he stared up at her, her hands slowly released the bars. She swiped at the tears on her face, and he saw the tremble in her fingertips.

"Beelzebub must have liked what he saw in your soul," Seline said as she walked around him. Az glanced back in time to watch her fingers sink into the hound's fur. "So no matter what you think about yourself, you really aren't a heartless bastard."

The hound pressed against her side. She bent and inspected the jagged remains of his claws. "Come with me, Beelzie," she told him, voice crooning, "I'll file those back into shape for you in no time."

The hellhound followed her like a doting pup.

Az winced as the torn muscles and ligaments in his body began to mend. The blood had finally stopped gushing out of him. A good sign.

"I told you that your woman was a demon." Sam sauntered toward him with his hands crossed over his chest. "And she's got more than a bit of power in her."

The cage swayed drunkenly above him. Az narrowed his eyes. "I don't remember telling you to lock her up."

"It was my way of keeping her safe." A pause. "You're welcome," Sam said grandly.

Az grunted. He shouldered by Sam, but his brother reached out in a deceptively slow move and clasped his shoulder. "Is there a hybrid angel on the hunt you need to warn me about?"

Az glanced back toward Jade. There were no more tears from her. No emotion at all showed on her face. But the fear and desperation had been there before, and they'd seared him.

"I'll take care of that guy." Az's words were a promise. "You don't have to worry about him."

"I worry any time there's a being out there that can kill me." Sam's hold tightened on his shoulder. "You sure you've got him?"

Az turned his head and met Sam's stare. "Get me a witch who can craft bullets out of those claws, and the shifter is as good as dead."

One brow lifted. "Oh. Is that all you need?"

He nodded.

"Then consider it done, but, you should know, Mateo doesn't work for free. There'll be a cost."

Ah, yes, Mateo. The magic man who had fought with Sam months before in Mexico. "There always is," Az said.

With a nod of his head, Sam sauntered away. The guy was even whistling as he dodged the bloody trail Az had left behind.

"Uh, yeah, this is a great family moment and all," Jade's tight voice snapped out, "but how about we get me out of this *cage*?"

He waved his hand. The cage door flew open.

Jade jumped down. He caught her and held her easily in his arms. Her gaze searched his face. The remnants of fear lit her gaze. "If you ever do that again . . ." She swallowed. "I'll find a way to kill you myself."

Frowning, Az put Jade on her feet. He hadn't expected that response.

Her hands clenched into fists at her sides and she said, "We're supposed to be partners here. When you have a partner, you don't run off facing the big, bad hellhound on your own."

"One swipe of his claws would have killed you." His own anger began to spike even as he felt the continued ache from his healing flesh. "You really wanted me to risk your life?"

"No, jerk, I didn't want you to risk yours!" Then she marched over to retrieve the bloody claws. "These!" She lifted them into the air. "They aren't worth your life."

"They're a weapon we need."

She shook her head. "I don't want to ever be trapped again when I can't do anything but wait for the screams to come as you die." Heat flushed her cheeks. "I've been there before. When Brandt came after . . ." She broke off and lifted her chin. "I won't be helpless while someone dies again!"

He crossed slowly to her. His steps seemed to echo in the cavernous bar. "I won't be dying."

Her lip trembled. "You'd damn well better not."

She cared. He could see that. She was the only woman who ever had.

His fingers, still bloody, brushed over her cheek. "You . . . you make me feel things that I shouldn't." The emotions seemed to rip him apart. The lust. The need.

But there was more.

He wanted to be by her side in the darkness. Wanted to hear her laugh. Jade didn't laugh enough. Didn't flash her real smile often enough to please him. How long had it been since he'd seen that wink of her dimple? *Too long.*

What would she look like when she was truly happy? Would her green eyes shine?

Would he ever find out?

"It's your lucky day, Az." Sam's mocking voice jerked his gaze off Jade.

He saw his brother stride toward him from the direction of the back offices. Sam held a thin piece of paper between his thumb and forefinger. "Mateo's in town."

Tension tightened his body. Mateo wasn't *just* a witch. He was a caller, the hybrid son of a crossroads spirit and a witch who'd wanted too much power. You had to be careful when you dealt with Mateo, because sometimes, the payment for his services was your life.

Az's gaze slid to Jade. The last thing he wanted was for her to get too close to Mateo. If Sam had been curious about her powers, then Mateo would sure as hell be fascinated. And having Mateo fascinated wasn't a good thing.

"Oh, no," Jade said as she pointed at him with a bloody claw. "Just stop thinking it. You aren't going to ditch me while you chase after this Mateo guy."

"You don't want to be on his radar," Az told her. "Stay here. Sam can keep you safe."

"So I'm baby demon sitting now?" Sam murmured. "How fun for me."

He didn't glance at his brother. He'd burned and bled for the guy back in Mexico, so he figured Sam still owed him.

"You aren't leaving me behind." Jade's eyes narrowed. "We're in this together, remember?"

But it was Sam who told her. "If you go with him, you'll pay a price."

"Fine." She barely spared Sam a glance. "Then I'm ready to pay. Az is in this mess because of me. Because he was trying to save *my* life."

One side of Sam's mouth hitched into a smile. "Isn't he the hero."

"Yeah, he is—to me."

Az blinked.

"And I'm staying by your side," Jade continued, voice and face determined. "So deal with it. If either one of you tries to toss me in that stripper cage again . . ."

"Don't knock it," Sam advised.

"We'll see just how much more fire I can throw."

Sam scratched his nose. "You sound so fierce."

Right. Like Sam would ever be afraid of a little fire. Or even a lot of fire. The guy had been willing to walk into hell in order to save his Seline. He'd actually begged to get into hell . . .

All for love.

Even Fallen Angels could be weakened.

"Go wash the blood away," Sam advised him. "You can use the apartment upstairs. Then you and your . . . ah . . . lady friend . . . can meet Mateo. But you'd better hurry. When the sun sets, he'll be gone, and the only way you'll find him then is to call him at the crossroads."

Not an option. Crossroads deals never worked out well for the fool who did the calling. Sure, the summoned spirit was duty-bound to grant the idiot's wish, but after that wish was granted, then the spirit started twisting. You wish for wealth, you get it—but only because your wife dies in an explosion and you get insurance money. You wish to live forever . . . you do, but only because you're lying comatose and can't move as machines keep you alive indefinitely.

Making a deal with a crossroads spirit was as bad as making a deal with the devil.

But it wasn't like they had a lot of options right then.

Az inclined his head. "Thank you."

Sam's eyes widened a bit.

Had he ever thanked his brother before? Thrown him out of heaven, yes, tried to kill him . . . *yes.*

But thanked him? *No.*

Az cleared his throat. "I owe you." Az wanted to make sure Sam understood this. "I will find a way to pay my debt."

A muscle flexed in Sam's jaw. "You fought to save my Seline. As far as I'm concerned, we're even."

No, they weren't.

Perhaps one day they would be.

Az took Jade's arm. They'd clean up and get back to hunting.

"Be careful." Sam's warning. Stilted.

Az looked over his shoulder to find that Sam's stare wasn't on him. It was on Jade.

"I was ready to burn to keep my mate with me." Sam's eyes flashed with the painful memory. "When I lost her, I lost my control."

It was too dangerous for a Fallen like Sam to lose control.

"A witch once told me that you'd destroy the world," Sam continued. "When she said that, I had to wonder . . . what could possibly push you so hard that you'd turn on everyone around you?"

Jade's hand was soft and delicate in his grip.

"Be careful," Sam warned him again. "Make sure you don't ever have to face the same darkness that I did."

Az nodded. Sam had been ready to destroy, to kill—but

Seline had come back to him before he'd crossed the point of no return.

What would have happened if she hadn't been there?

Az and Jade hurried up the old staircase. And as her body brushed his, an insidious whisper had him tensing. A whisper that came from within.

*What would I do without her?*

Bastion stood in the shadows, watching the mortals as they hurried down the New Orleans Street. No one saw him. They couldn't—no one there was due to meet death.

His gaze locked on the building across the road. Sunrise. He knew Sammael's bar well. The Fallen catered to humans and the *Other* there, flaunting their sins for all to see.

But Sammael had been sinning for centuries, ever since Az had banished him from heaven. One brother, turning on another.

An old prophecy.

But Az had been right to banish his brother. Sammael had broken the rules. He'd taken souls not his to claim. Az had been given no choice in his brother's punishment.

He had a choice now. He had a choice—and he'd chosen to attack other angels.

*Where was Marna?*

To sever her wings . . . Az had known what lost wings would cost Marna. Wings didn't just grow back. Angels could regenerate from most wounds, but not that. Never the wings.

She wouldn't be going home again.

Horns honked. Voices lifted and fell in a soft cadence. The scent of the river drifted in the air. He ignored all of that, too conscious of the sin Az had committed.

Az had taken away the one thing that Bastion cared for in this world.

His head tilted back as he saw the shadow of forms moving on the upper floor of Sunrise. Two people. A man. A woman. Right behind the curtains.

Az had taken something from him, and now he'd take everything from the Fallen.

*Everything.*

The water from the shower pounded down on Az's flesh. Jade stared at him through the thin pane of glass. She wasn't going to let the guy's sexiness distract her.

Az turned. Met her stare. Crooked his finger.

Sexy bastard.

*Don't distract. Don't . . .*

But a girl needed to get clean, right?

She yanked her shirt over her head. Tossed her bra. Kicked away her shoes, and had herself naked in about thirty seconds. Not as fast as Az's instant-clothes-disappearing technique, but still pretty darn good.

But she didn't just hop in the shower. She could do this right. Make him want as much as she did. Jade straightened her shoulders. Tossed back her hair, and let her gaze dip slowly down his body.

The water ran over those lick-me abs of his. Such sculpted flesh. His wounds were already healed. He was once more all fine-tuned muscle and golden skin. Of course, he was more than human.

Her gaze dropped a little lower. No missing that aroused flesh. Hungry, hard. For her.

As she stared at his erection, his cock swelled even more, and she licked her lips.

He put his hand on the pane of glass.

She lifted her hand and let it rest on the glass, placing it right over his. The glass was cool to the touch. Her hand seemed so much smaller than his. Weaker.

*I won't be weak again.*

His gaze held hers through the glass. Steam began to rise, slowly blurring his image.

He slid open the shower door. She stepped inside, being very careful not to touch him. Not yet. Her body slipped past his, barely an inch of space. She could feel him all around her.

But Az did that. He made her feel him, every moment. He had, from the beginning. She let the water hit her. Let it wash over her and slide down her flesh.

Az didn't touch her.

She still didn't touch him.

Jade turned beneath the shower and found his eyes on her. Hot. Hungry.

The water pounded down.

She smiled at him and crooked her finger.

In the next second, he had her against the tiled wall of the shower. His mouth was on hers. Open. Their lips met. His tongue swept into her mouth.

His hands held her hips against the wall and positioned her perfectly. Jade arched against him even as her hand slid between their bodies. She found his cock. Stroked him. Guided his flesh to the entrance of her body.

No foreplay.

No more seduction.

She just wanted him.

When he thrust into her, she wanted to freeze that moment. His strength around her. His mouth on hers. His body in hers. *Az.*

But you couldn't stop time. Couldn't hold it close no matter how much you might want to.

He pulled back. Drove deep even as he cushioned her back with his hands. His mouth became harder, more desperate. She couldn't even feel the water on her anymore.

Only him.

Her legs slid over his. Her hands held tight to his shoulders. The pleasure built inside of her, but she fought the climax.

*Not too soon. Not yet.*

Deeper. Deeper. He filled every inch of her eager sex.

Az's mouth lifted from hers. His eyes stared at her, nearly blind with pleasure. "Only . . . you." His growl. He thrust again. "Only . . . you . . . Jade. Only . . . want . . . *you.*"

And he was all that she needed. The past didn't matter to her. What he'd done, what he'd been. In that moment, he was hers.

The pleasure crested, pounding through her on a climax so intense that she cried out as she arched against him.

He held her tighter. Thrust again. Again. When he came, she felt the hot splash of his release inside of her and the wild rush of his heart against her.

And the water poured down into the shower.

He lowered her slowly. Her sex contracted, holding him close as the aftershocks of pleasure rippled through her. She knew she should say something to him then, but she was scared.

Az had come to mean too much to her. She'd made a mistake. A very dangerous one.

She'd fallen in love again.

The first time she'd loved, her parents had died for her mistake. Her lover had turned on her, changed from caring to obsessed in one wild one-eighty.

Az was different. She knew that. Az was different because . . .

Because she knew he didn't love her back. Couldn't.

She squeezed her eyes shut. He wasn't speaking either, but he was pulling away from her. It seemed like he always pulled away when the sex was done. *Take the pleasure, nothing more.*

She turned back into the blast of water.

*Nothing more.*
So why did it feel like he was everything?

Az used his power and conjured a fresh pair of clothes for them. Jeans and a T-shirt for him—a T-shirt that looked damn good as it stretched tightly across his powerful chest.

The jeans he gave her hugged her hips a little too close for comfort, but when she saw Az's eyes drop to her ass and flare a bit in appreciation, Jade decided she wouldn't complain—not about them or about the top that flashed a little too much cleavage.

Besides, she figured no matter what she wore, it was far better than the bloodstained duds she'd been sporting before.

When they reached the bottom of the stairs, there was no sign of Sam. It looked like he'd split with his lady love. Hopefully, they'd taken that hellhound with them.

"So . . ." Jade cleared her throat and tried to act cool when her heart was actually about to gallop out of her chest. "You think this Mateo will be able to help us?"

"I think Mateo is one dangerous SOB, and when we find him, I don't want you to leave my side."

She blinked. Um, okay. "I get the feeling you know him."

Az opened the back door of the club just a bit so he could gaze out. "I've dealt with him before. He owed Sam a blood oath, so he was bound to pay that debt." He glanced back at her. "Without an oath like that, Mateo doesn't have to do anything he doesn't want. For a job like this, he'll want us to pay."

She tensed. "Pay what?"

"Whatever we've got." He brushed the back of his hand over her cheek. "If you thought Heather was dangerous, sweetheart, you haven't seen anything yet."

In fact, she'd seen plenty. She might not be some centuries-old angel, but she'd seen more than her fair share of blood and death while walking the earth.

"He's not just a witch. He's got powers that are dark, and believe me, they come straight from hell."

She didn't flinch or back away. Brandt had taught her to never back down, not even when she was afraid. Especially then.

She'd learned that particular lesson well. "Then let's find him before he skips town." Find him, get the brimstone bullets, and take out Brandt.

Simple enough plan. So why was her gut knotting with worry? Why did she feel like danger was just waiting to descend?

Because it was.

Az opened the door fully. Sunlight spilled inside the bar. The motorcycle waited outside. Az could probably just use his magic to zip then wherever they needed to go, but that traveling mode wasn't exactly her preference. They had the motorcycle, so they could darn well use it—and she could avoid the aftereffects of feeling like she'd vomit after traveling.

So they hurried toward the motorcycle. Az had the engine growling in about two seconds. Three more seconds, and they were racing down the street.

Racing so fast that she almost missed the shadowy figure across the road. The tall, blond man who watched her and Az hurtle away.

The angel who'd come for her before. *Bastion.*

"Az!" She tried to shout out a warning to him, but the snarl of the motorcycle's engine just ripped her cry away. Jade glanced back, her hands tightening on Az, but Bastion was gone.

"Is she gonna make it?" Tanner demanded as he stared down at the pale form on the bed.

*A fucking angel.* Tears had dried on her cheeks long ago. Her lips, trembling, were no longer breaking with cries of pain.

Her wings were gone. Cody was good, but the guy wasn't a miracle worker. Her wings had been cut off, the skin on her back savaged. Cody had stitched her up, he'd drugged her so the pain would stop, but there wasn't much else he'd been able to do.

*Gone.*

Tanner had known for years that his brother was a sadistic bastard, but . . . doing this? To an angel?

She lay on her stomach, with her face turned toward him. Thick, white bandages covered her back. He brushed his hand down her arm. He'd been touching her almost constantly, wanting to comfort the little blonde who'd bled and begged.

This shouldn't have happened to her. This wasn't her war.

*It's mine.*

"She'll heal," Cody's voice was quiet. "But from all the tales I've heard, those wings won't be growing back."

An angel's skin could regenerate. Her torn muscles could mend. She'd recover from her blood loss. But, without her wings, she'd be trapped on earth.

"Az can give her his blood." They'd be seeing the Fallen in just a few hours. "With his blood, she can—"

"We both know the blood loss isn't going to kill her." Cody glanced up with his pitch-black stare. Cody never bothered with glamour when it was just the two of them. Why pretend? Tanner knew exactly what his brother was.

He knew what *both* of his brothers were.

"His blood won't make her wings grow back. Only a miracle can do that," Cody said.

She looked so small. So weak. Not like some all-powerful immortal being right then.

Cody pulled out a pair of handcuffs from a black bag.

Tanner tensed. "What the hell are you doing with those?"

But his brother just reached for her right hand. "When she wakes up and shakes those drugs out of her system, she's going to be pissed."

"We saved her life! She's not gonna be—"

"Our brother cut her wings off. He left her to die." Cody snapped one cuff around her wrist and stretched her arm to lock the other end around the thin bedpost. "If she's a Death Angel, all it will take is one touch to knock us both out of this world. You heard what Azrael said—we can't let her touch us."

Cody pulled out another set of cuffs.

"Since when do you carry around cuffs?" Tanner had a grip on her left hand, and he didn't want to let go.

"They're *Other*-proof, thanks to a sweet little voodoo queen I met in the bayou." Cody held the cuffs loosely in his hand. "They'll keep her hands off us until we can calm her down and help her to see reason."

"Reason?" Tanner exhaled on a rough sigh and eased back so that Cody could snap the cuffs in place. "Our brother cut off her wings. There's nothing reasonable in that."

"No, there isn't."

Tanner straightened his shoulders. "You ever wonder . . . I mean, we've got the same blood. What if we—"

"Become twisted fucks like him?"

He nodded.

"The day I do, that's the day I want you to take me out."

Tanner met Cody's coal-black stare. He'd always known there was a darkness inside Cody. Demons and darkness went hand in hand.

"Promise me," Cody said, voice thickening "and I'll do the same for you."

*Take me out.* "I promise." He knew that if the time ever came, he'd be the one to kill Cody.

Just as he'd be the one to kill Brandt. His gaze fell back to the broken angel.

*Sick bastard.*

Then, whispering through his mind . . . *I never want to be like him.*

But the fear was always there, hiding in his head. *Don't want to be, but what if I am?*

She expected Az to take her to some small shop in the Quarter. A place that promised magic and dreams with a dozen magic crystals and potions stocked in the windows.

But he drove past the Quarter and left the crowds of the city behind. Her gaze lit on the tossed beads as they headed out. Beads that dangled from lamp posts. Beads that had been shattered in the street.

Only a few more days of Mardi Gras madness were left. By the time the big party ended, what would her life be like?

Jade held tighter to Az as houses began to blur past them. Soon, the houses were gone, and she saw bigger buildings. Old warehouses. They crossed train tracks. Turned to the right. The left.

He braked the motorcycle. She glanced up. Another warehouse. All the windows on the lower floor had been boarded up, but the windows on the second floor shone in the sunlight.

Not exactly where she'd expected to find a witch, but nothing was really what she expected these days.

When she climbed off the bike, Az took her hand. "Remember what I said," he told her, voice soft. "Stay close. Mateo is very dangerous, very strong, and he doesn't exactly play by the rules."

There were rules? Why hadn't anyone told her about them?

Stopping in front of the double doors, Az raised his fist and pounded. The fierce knock seemed to echo inside. Jade glanced over her shoulder, half-expecting to see Bastion lurking behind her. But she didn't see anyone.

She looked back at Az. His body was tense, on alert, and she wondered just what—

The door opened with a groan. A tall, muscled guy in a black T-shirt and faded jeans cocked a brow at them. Tribal tattoos circled his shaved head. "I was wondering when you'd be on my doorstep, Fallen," he said, with just the faintest hint of a Spanish accent. "You and your . . . *querida.*" His dark stare locked on her.

Az's fingers tightened on her arm. Mateo's gaze dropped, noting the movement. A faint smile curved his lips. "It's like a sickness, isn't it?"

"What?" Az frowned at him.

"Emotions. Once you start to feel them, they get inside and tear you apart." The guy smiled. "They can slice deeper than anything, even a panther shifter's claws."

Chill bumps rose on Jade's arms. "You know about Brandt."

"There's very little in this world I don't know about." He stepped back and motioned them inside. Once they entered, she expected him to immediately close the doors behind them. Instead, he stepped to the threshold and gazed out with that faint smile still on his lips. After a few moments, he looked back at her. "You're a wanted woman."

This guy was creeping her out. "So I hear."

He bolted the doors and headed for a rickety staircase on the right. "Come."

Jade glanced at Az. He shrugged and started following Mateo.

"There will be a fee, of course," Mateo said without glancing back. The staircase squeaked as they headed upstairs. Nothing was on the bottom floor. Well, an old desk. Two chairs. Nothing else.

Mateo opened another door at the top of the stairs. This doorway led to an apartment, or at least what looked like an apartment. The whole place had been redone. Kitchen. Den. The room sported a giant flat-screen TV. Not what she'd expected. It just looked like any other guy's bachelor pad. Had witches gone mainstream?

But Mateo walked past all that. He headed down a hallway. Opened yet another door.

Ah . . . and this was where the magic happened. She saw the carvings on the wall. The black and red chalk that had been drawn carefully on the floor. A black table sat in the middle of the room, and she could see the gleaming surface of a mirror resting on the top of that table. A mirror, and a knife.

"Been scrying lately?" Az asked, voice flat.

So Heather wasn't the only one who liked to gaze into the future.

"Sometimes you need to know what's coming." Mateo stopped next to the table. His fingers were just inches from the knife. "You got to be prepared for the enemies who'll be at your door."

"We're not your enemies!" Jade said, the words bursting from her. She reached for the small black bag she'd knotted at her hip. "We just . . . we need your help."

"*Sí*, everyone needs something."

Az took the bag from her and tossed it to Mateo. The witch caught it with one hand. "Had to bleed for these, didn't you?" Mateo asked.

"It was a small price to pay."

Mateo laughed. "So different now, aren't you? Not like the angel I met before."

Jade glanced between them.

"She thinks she knows you," Mateo said to Az. "Thinks that she can trust you to be there for her in the end."

Yeah, *she* was in the room. "*She* does," Jade snapped.

Mateo's dark eyes found hers. "But does she know that what you want the most in this world . . . is to leave this place? That you want to get away from the needs and lusts and emotions that swamp humans?"

Jade wouldn't look away from Mateo. "I know I can count on Az." She could. No doubt. From the first moment, when he'd come charging in to save her . . . *no doubt.*

No one had ever tried to save her before Az.

"He ruled in heaven, now he kills for you on earth."

Wait, ruled?

"But death has always been his business," Mateo continued, voice rolling lightly. "It is what he does best."

Anger stirred inside of her. "He's more than death."

Mateo nodded. "And you . . . you are more than human."

And there they went again. Was more demon talk coming?

Mateo opened the bag and pulled out the claws. His fingers traced over the razor-sharp edges. "So you think you'll be able to take out the earthbound angel with these?"

Az stalked forward with a ripple of muscle and menace. "I think I'll be able to take out the psycho killer on our trail."

"Sammael's woman was earthbound, too. When one form ended, she was just born again."

Jade stepped to the edge of that table. The mirror's surface wasn't gleaming now. It was pitch black. "Brandt isn't an angel." More like a devil.

Mateo shook his head. "He has the blood. You need to know that killing his human form may just unleash something . . . else."

What? "You're saying we can't kill him?" Not the news she wanted. *I'll never be free.*

Mateo placed the claws on his mirror. "I'm saying you both might not survive the battle that comes."

She put her fingers on the mirror and was shocked by its icy feel. "Is that what you've seen?"

He slowly glanced up at her. "To know what I see, you have to pay a price."

Jade swallowed as fear trickled through her. His stare . . . how could dark eyes seem to blaze?

"I'll pay," Az said immediately.

"You can only see my future." Jade spoke quickly, too quickly. "You can't know about Az because he's—"

"I'm not some dime store witch." Power vibrated in Mateo's words and in the very air around her. "I can see beyond earth, beyond heaven and hell. When I call, the dead answer *me*."

Um, right. She slanted a glance at Az.

"But it's not his payment I want first." Mateo's voice was calmer now, a good thing, or good until he said, "It's yours."

"No." Az grabbed her hand and yanked it off the mirror. "I'm the one who'll pay. Tell me what you want. Tell me the price for those bullets and—"

"You have no wings to trade me. I won't be getting any Angel Dust from you." He shrugged. "It's a pity. An angel's wings contain such powerful magic. They can bind just about anyone."

This was the guy who was supposed to help them? No wonder Az had given her so many warnings about him. And, as she watched, the tattoos on his head seemed to alter, just a little. As if they'd just moved a few inches.

He smiled at her. "Now are you ready to pay my price?"

The claws waited on the mirror. "What do you want?"

"A debt."

Uh, huh. "You're gonna have to be a little more specific than that."

But he shook his head. "Not the way it works. I do this for you, and you promise that when I come to call on you in the future, you'll do what I want, no questions asked."

Did she look insane? She must if he thought she'd offer him anything.

"No deal," Az growled.

"Then I can't help you."

"You mean you won't." Now Az slapped his hand down on the mirror. "But what you don't understand is that I'm not leaving here without those bullets."

The mirror's surface began to swirl beneath Az's hand. "Az . . ." Jade began.

"I'll bleed for you," Az told him. "I'll give you a pound of flesh, if that's what you want. *I'll* agree to be in your debt, but you leave her out of this."

"Why?" Mateo seemed honestly confused. "*This* is all about her."

And it was. Her battle. Her fight. Her life. So why should Az be the one to sacrifice?

"But if you're truly willing to offer up all that you have," Mateo murmured to Az, "then I might be willing to—"

"No!" The denial burst from her. Shit, shit, shit . . . "This isn't gonna be you wanting my firstborn, is it? Because that's not happening."

Mateo's gaze dipped to her stomach. That ghost of a grin curved his lips once more. "I do wonder what the child will be like."

In a flash, Az had the knife at Mateo's throat. "Cut the game, Mateo." A trickle of blood slid down the witch's throat. "Help us or—"

"Or you slice me open? Why use a blade when you can kill me with your hand?"

"Because I don't want you dead. I just want you to bleed." He tossed the knife and shoved Mateo's head over that swirling mirror. Drops of blood fell on the glass. *"Tell me what you see!"*

Clouds formed in the glass. Moving faster. Faster. But Mateo just laughed. "I see you dying at Brandt's hands. His claws tear you apart." He turned his head and met Az's stare. "Because you don't have any fucking brimstone bullets."

That wasn't happening. "I'll do it," Jade said immediately.

Az spun around. "No, Jade—"

"Too late." A faint charge lit the air. A burst of sparks. "There's no going back now."

Her heart thundered in her chest. "Just give us the bullets."

"The deal's made," Mateo said with satisfaction.

"Then unmake it," came Az's furious order, "or *I'll* make sure you're never around to collect on the debt."

"But you're going to try that anyway," Mateo said. "You're going to try and destroy everyone."

No, he was wrong. Az wouldn't do that.

"I've seen the future, Azrael. I know why that witch gave you up to the hunters months ago. I know why the world should fear you." The faint lines around Mateo's eyes deepened even as his tattoos continued to subtly shift. "You were the ruler of the Death Angels, and you're going to bring hell to earth."

# Chapter Fifteen

"No, he's not." Jade's voice was confident and held no fear. "I don't know what you *think* you saw, buddy, but you're wrong. Az has done nothing but help me from the moment we met."

"He's tried to help himself." At Mateo's flat words, Az locked his back teeth. "Stepping into that alley that first night had nothing to do with you and everything to do with Az's need for violence."

Jade shook her head. "You're wrong. He *saved* me—"

"Az likes violence." A pause. "Sex and violence, haven't you noticed? Or maybe he just likes the sex more with you."

"Az has never hurt me!"

The witch was about to push too far. "Create the bullets," Az ordered. Jade had made a mistake in offering a debt to the guy, but Az could take care of that for her. He'd make sure she didn't have to sacrifice anything.

Mateo liked sacrifices too much.

"Once he realized you were human, Az knew he could use you." Mateo's voice was mild. The guy needed to shut up.

Az lunged forward and grabbed Mateo's arm. "The bullets."

Mateo smirked at him. "I'm not afraid of you."

He should be.

"Az isn't using me!" Jade was still defending him. Why did that make him feel so . . . guilty?

"*Sí*, he is. Ask him."

Az shoved the witch away from him. He couldn't kill Mateo, at least, not until he'd gotten the bullets.

A grim smile lifted Mateo's mouth as he studied Az. "After all," he said, "we all know angels can't lie."

"I don't need to ask him!" Jade's green eyes flashed fury as her dark hair tumbled wildly over her shoulders. "What could he possibly be using me for? I'm the one who needs him! He's saving my ass and—"

"And he thought you were his ticket back to heaven."

The witch really did see too much.

"Helping a human, helping one of the favored . . ." Mateo stroked his throat. "That was supposed to fast-pass you back upstairs, right, Azrael?"

"You seem to have all the answers," Az snarled at him. "So why even ask?"

"Because she needs to see you for what you are." Mateo's face twisted with anger. "She's blinded by you. She doesn't get that you are—"

"Enough talk." Jade's voice cut right through his raging words. Az glanced at her, and did a double take. Jade had snatched up the knife from Mateo's table, and she'd just shoved the tip against the witch's side. "We made the deal, now just do your part."

Mateo's mouth slackened in shock.

"It's a magic knife, right?" She muttered. "Hell, isn't everything magic these days? And I'm thinking if it can cut you, maybe it can even kill you, even if you are some super-powered caller." She pushed the blade's tip a bit deeper into Mateo's flesh. "At the very least, I can make you hurt."

Mateo's eyes narrowed. "You don't care what he is." Surprise slipped into his eyes, but vanished almost instantly.

"I want him," she said, "just as he is."

Az rubbed his chest, aware of an ache that rested beneath the skin.

The witch searched her eyes. Then, after a moment, he inclined his head. "Wait outside. I'll give you what you need."

"You'd better." Very slowly, she lowered the knife. "And stop the trash talk about Az, understand? I get it, you're not a fan, but back the hell off."

She was protecting him. Az stepped closer to her. He brushed back a lock of her dark hair. Her head turned toward him. "I don't care, Az. Whatever the reason you came to me, *I don't care.*"

But . . . but there was a flash of pain in her eyes.

*He's using you.*

He wrapped his arm around her shoulders. "Come on." They'd wait downstairs. He'd explain things to her.

"I need your blood, Fallen." Mateo's words stopped him.

And, of course, he did.

"You have to pay, too," Mateo murmured. "So I'll be taking that pound of flesh you offered." A slight pause. "Good thing your kind heals so fast."

But Az didn't want Jade to watch him get sliced open. "You got spells protecting this place?" he asked Mateo.

"Always," was the instant answer.

Exhaling, Az said, "Go downstairs, Jade. I'll be there soon. Give me just a minute."

She nodded and stepped away from him.

But before she left, he wanted her to understand . . . "I'm not going back."

Her body tensed.

"I'm not using you as some trade-off for heaven."

She turned toward him. Her hand lifted and touched the edge of his jaw. If he'd had one, the look in her eyes would have broken his heart.

But angels didn't love.

Angels didn't, but Fallen—

"Good," she told him quietly as her hand slowly fell away, "because a trade with somebody like me—with all the things I've done—hell is more likely what you'd get in return."

Then she was gone. The apartment door shut quietly behind her. Az realized his hands had clenched into fists.

"I guess it's true." Mateo came to stand in front of him. He held a knife loosely in his hands.

Az forced his hands to relax. "What is?"

"That every angel has a temptation."

She wasn't just a temptation.

"Maybe that's the real challenge." Mateo's gaze was hooded. "Can you give her up? If you did, perhaps you'd get what you want."

"You don't know what I want." What he wanted was heading down the stairs. He could hear the soft tread of her footsteps. "So just get to slicing and let's hurry the hell up." He had places to be. An angel to see.

A shifter to kill.

"If that's what you want." Then Mateo started cutting him. Az clenched his teeth, refusing to cry out as the witch carved into him. Mateo caught his blood in a cup, holding it close.

Az didn't make a sound. He didn't want Jade to see him like this, didn't want her to hear his pain.

So he closed his eyes, ignored the hot slice of that knife, and thought of angels . . . and their deadly schemes.

She'd known he was too good to be true. Jade paced the dusty bottom floor of the warehouse, her arms folded over her breasts. That first night—she'd known that fate couldn't be so kind to her.

"Using me," she muttered, and so what? Hadn't she been using him, too?

So why did the knowledge of Az's true intentions make her heart hurt?

*Because you know he doesn't want to stay with you. You know that when this nightmare is over, Az will find a way to get what he wants most.*

And what he wanted most just wasn't her.

Dammit.

The guy wanted to go home.

How could a girl compete with heaven?

She glanced upstairs. She hadn't heard so much as a peep of sound since she'd walked down to the first floor. That was weird, but—

*"Help me . . ."*

Jade tensed at the cry. Faint, drifting on the wind. She hurried to the warehouse door. Putting her ear against it, she listened.

*"Help me . . ."* A woman's voice. Desperate. Louder. *"Please, help me!"*

Jade jerked back. She grabbed the handle of the door. Yanked.

The damn thing didn't open.

The woman screamed, the cry high and full of pain.

Jade yanked harder on the door. It wouldn't open. She ran toward the boarded-up windows. Pressing close, she squinted and could just make out the form of a woman huddled across the street. The woman was holding her stomach, weaving on her feet. And there was a trail of blood in her wake.

Oh, hell. "Az!" Jade yelled for him. "I need you!" Because she couldn't just stand there and watch that woman die. Jade spun around. She needed something, something— *the chair.* She rushed for the old desk and chairs, and her hands closed around the nearest chair.

She dragged it with her and rammed it against the window. The glass shattered. The wood that had been nailed into place groaned.

The woman's cries were getting weaker.

"Az!" Jade shouted again. "Help me!"

The wind howled in the apartment as the magic flared. Mateo was mixing Az's blood and the hellhound claws, pounding them up and re-forming them with his powers.

No furnace was needed to cast these bullets—Mateo used his own firepower to burn and shape them.

The howling sounded like a thousand voices screaming in his head, and even with the fire spinning just feet away, Az felt a chill ice his skin.

Some magic could give even angels pause.

And this . . . the powers that Mateo called, they were damn dark.

Az was glad that Jade was safely downstairs. He didn't want this darkness touching her.

The wood cracked with a groan. Jade heaved the chair once more, and it flew through the shattered beams of wood. Then it was her turn to hurtle through the window. The woman wasn't crying anymore. She'd slumped over on the ground, and she didn't appear to be moving at all.

*Don't be dead. Please don't be dead.*

But Jade could smell the too-sweet scent of flowers, and that was supposed to mean that a Death Angel was close, right?

"Hold on!" Jade cried out as she raced across the street. "You're not alone. It's going to be okay."

She fell to her knees by the woman. The blonde had turned away from her, sagging against the old brick building. Jade reached for her shoulder. "It's going to—"

The illusion fell away. And that's all it was, an illusion, one that couldn't survive touch. Because Jade wasn't clasping an injured woman's shoulder. She was touching the hard strength of a man's arm.

Her gaze lifted slowly, and she found herself caught in the too-bright stare of an angel bent on death.

"Demons aren't the only ones who know how to use the power of glamour." Bastion smiled at her. "Angels hide in plain sight all the time. Why do you think humans never see us?"

She could barely hear him over the mad pounding of her heart. Jade tried to jump to her feet and back away.

Too late. His hand flew out and caught hers. "I can't let you get away," he murmured. "Not this time."

*"Az!"* She screamed his name as loud as she could, but even if he heard her, she knew he'd never make it to her in time.

*Az . . .*

He couldn't hear a thing. Az stalked to the line of windows. The sunlight streamed in, but no warmth filled the room. A puff of chilled air appeared in front of his mouth every time he took a breath. Ice and evil liked to stay close.

He gazed out of the window. All of the nearby buildings were abandoned. His gaze trekked down. Then every muscle in his body locked.

Jade was across the street. She wasn't alone.

Her head turned toward him, and Az saw her lips move in a desperate scream that he couldn't hear.

His name.

He roared and smashed through the glass. Two seconds later, he was on the ground, his knees barely buckling as he lunged forward.

Bastion was smiling. His hands were wrapped around Jade.

"Let her go!" Az bellowed. He didn't know why Jade was out there on the street. Didn't care. All that mattered was getting her back. Keeping her safe and—

And she vanished. Bastion vanished.

*No.*

When the earth stopped spinning, Jade collapsed on the ground. Not the rough asphalt of a paved street, but on soft, grass-covered earth. Nausea roiled in her stomach, and she squeezed her eyes shut as she fought for control.

Then she realized she was still alive. Because if she felt this miserable, she had to be alive.

Her eyes flew open, and she shot upright. That fast movement just made the nausea worse.

"Easy." Bastion frowned down at her. "I'd forgotten . . . humans don't always react so well to magic."

She swallowed rapidly. "Magic? And here I just thought you'd . . . done that angel . . . super speed thing." Second by second, she was getting her control back.

"We needed something stronger this time." One golden brow lifted. "You weren't the only one to visit the witch today."

What? That jerk had totally sold them out!

"Az . . . changed you. Gave you his blood."

Everyone seemed to keep harping on that.

Bastion lifted his hand and stared down at his fingers. "A simple touch from me can't kill you. Az's blood is making your immune from the Death Touch . . . for now."

That was good, right?

Bastion dropped his hand and stared into her eyes. "I don't want you to suffer."

She staggered to her feet and put some precious distance between them. "What a coincidence. I don't really want that, either."

His head cocked as he frowned at her.

"So how about you just go your merry angel way," now she could see the wings bursting from his back. Rather hard to miss them without his extra magic mojo. "And I'll go mine."

Bastion shook his head. "I need you."

"No, you need to get the hell away from me. Once Az gets here . . ." *Get here, Az, get your Fallen butt here.* "You don't want to be around."

"Things have to be set right. Az can't be allowed to change fate."

Oh, no. That sounded very bad. "You-you want to kill me."

"You should already be dead." He gave a short, hard shake of his head. "Instead, the Fallen attacked an innocent. He brutalized Marna, an angel who'd never—"

"Whoa! Hold on there." She was gonna ignore that whole "You should already be dead" part for the moment. "Az hasn't attacked any angel."

Bastion laughed. "Really? Then how'd I get a brimstone bullet in my gut?"

Ah . . .

"I went to take you, and he shot me."

He'd shot another angel to save her? Sweet, but, deadly.

"You're marked for Death, and, once marked, there's no changing what will come." His eyes darkened. "I've seen you die."

Jade licked her lips. "Now when you say that, do you mean—"

"You're on my list. I've seen what will come for you. It's a vicious ending."

Did he have to sound so chirpy about it? Weren't angels who still had those precious wings supposed to be *unemo-tional*?

"As I said, I don't want you to suffer, but other plans are already in place. The Death Touch from me would have been merciful, but now, another end waits."

"Yeah, well . . ." And she dug deep, trying to pull out that new power that she still couldn't even control. "I'm gonna have to take option B on all this and say . . ." She sent a burst of fire out at him. Not a controlled ball of flames, but a swirling, bulging wall of heat. "Screw your plans."

Then she turned and ran, not even bothering to see how Bastion stopped the fire. *Get away.* Fast. That was her priority. Get away. Get to Az. Get—

She hit the dirt. Something hard and strong had slammed into her back, and Jade's feet just flew out from under her.

"Abomination." Gravel crunched as Bastion circled around her. "Humans weren't meant to have such powers."

She tasted blood in her mouth. Jade lifted her head. Nope, the angel wasn't so much as singed. He stood about five feet away, not looking winded, but appearing . . . mildly annoyed.

Well, big damn deal for him. She was feeling pretty annoyed, too.

"You're not going to get away." Bastion's wings fluttered in the breeze. They were doing that neat magic trick again where they seemed to just burst right through his shirt. He crouched so they were more on eye level. "He'll find you soon."

Now why did those words fill her with dread?

*Because he's setting a trap for Az, and I'm his bait.*

Az didn't bother knocking at the witch's door this time. He just blew off the right wall of the place and stormed back inside.

Mateo turned at his approach, holding up the small, black bag that Jade had given him. "Ah, back from your psycho moment, are you? *Bueno,* because I've got your bullets—"

And Az had him. His hands locked onto the witch's shirt, and he yanked Mateo toward him. "You've had another visitor."

Mateo glanced down at the floor. Az was holding him a good foot in the air. "I have many visitors."

"In a moment, you're going to be in many pieces."

Mateo's gaze lifted. "Your eyes have gone black."

"Where. Is. She."

"Some beings are too powerful. When emotions hit them, they lose all control. Power without control can mean—"

"Would you like for me to incinerate you?"

Mateo smiled at him. "I've felt fire before, Fallen. Remember where I came from."

Hell.

Mateo jerked away from him. Wind rushed in the air. "Your friend paid me for a job. The job is done." He tossed Az the bag.

Az caught it and tried to fight the rage surging within him. *Jade. Gone.*

Bastion should have never touched her. *Never.* "Is she dead?" he gritted.

Mateo shook his head.

Az took a breath.

"Now you know better than that . . . there's a price for information."

Az let his power rip from him. In an instant, fire engulfed the building. The remaining walls burned. The windows exploded. Smoke thickened the air.

Mateo's eyes widened.

The flames were less than a foot away from the witch. The fire wasn't touching him, but only because Az didn't want Mateo dead, not yet.

"I think you've confused me with someone else." Az's voice boomed from him, easily louder than the crackling flames. "I'm not Sammael. I'm not here to save your ass and play your games."

With a wave of his hand, he sent the fire to lick across Mateo's arms. Agony twisted the witch's face.

"This isn't hellfire," Az snarled. "You don't control it."

Mateo slapped at the flames, but they just flared higher as he began to scream.

"So the games end now, or you die."

Mateo fell to his knees. The flames closed in.

"The choice is yours."

Jade shoved up to her knees. "Okay, angel, I get it. You're pissed—"

*"Angels feel no emotions."*

Yeah, she'd call bullshit on that one. The guy was a big old vibrating ball of emotion—mostly rage.

"Whatever. So I'm the walking dead, and you want to put me in the ground." She straightened her shoulders. "But here's the deal. Az isn't gonna let you do that, okay?" *He'd better not.* "When he gets here, he'll be freaking furious, and you *don't* want to be in the area when that guy is enraged."

She'd hoped her threat would make the angel back off long enough for her to get a running start. But he was holding his ground.

Then his lips curved a bit. "I never said Azrael was the one coming to find you."

Her heart seemed to freeze.

Bastion pointed to the woods behind him. "Your shifter has found a new base. Just a mile or two over that hill." In the next second, he was at her side. He grabbed her arm, and sliced her flesh with a knife she hadn't even seen.

She didn't give him the satisfaction of screaming. Since when did angels go around knifing people? How was that possibly in their job description?

"Your scent is special to the shifter." Bastion dropped her hand. "He'll follow the blood trail, and he'll find you." He stepped back. His wings began to spread out behind him. She realized then that the jerk was just going to leave her, bleeding, for Brandt to find.

"Order will be restored," Bastion said.

She covered the wound. He'd sliced her deep, a cut that went almost from elbow to wrist. "Why didn't you just drop me on the bastard's doorstep?"

He hesitated.

"Were you scared he'd slice you apart, too?" Her words came fast and she wouldn't let her gaze drift over Bastion's shoulder. *Don't come, Brandt.* "For the record, he's the one who attacked the other angel, not Az. *Brandt.* The guy is some kind of hybrid shifter and angel mix. He attacked her and now—"

Now she definitely had his attention. Bastion stood right in front of her. "Her wings were sliced from her body."

More rage. And the guy thought he didn't feel emotion?

"Yes." Her voice was soft. "We found her in the woods. A doctor is helping her." She left out the little bit about Cody being a demon doctor.

Bastion's brows pulled together. "No, Azrael—"

"He *found* her. Brandt was the one who got off on slicing her apart." She swallowed. *Don't look over the hill.* "Just like he's going to slice me unless we leave here, now."

His gaze held hers.

"I'm telling you the truth. It wasn't Az." She swallowed. "Please, believe me."

"Angels can't lie." His own voice had softened.

She knew what he meant. Angels couldn't lie, but humans could. "Humans can also tell the truth."

He studied her a moment longer, then seemed to . . . be-lieve her? He pulled her against his chest and held tight. His wings were stretching out again as he prepared for flight. In the distance, she could hear snarls.

Brandt had her scent.

They needed to get the hell out of there.

*Now.*

# Chapter Sixteen

Az pulled Mateo from the wreckage. Flames shot high up into the air. Sirens blared as the humans raced toward the burning warehouse.

They'd never arrive in time. By the time the fire trucks pulled up, the building would be ash.

He tossed the witch onto the ground. Mateo had talked. Witches, even half-blood ones, couldn't take the fire.

Az turned away from him.

"S-saw . . . th-this . . ." Mateo's words froze him. "You . . . destroy . . ."

He'd destroy anyone who tried to take Jade. "I let you live." After the witch had deliberately betrayed him. Separating him from Jade had been part of the guy's plan all along. So she'd be vulnerable. Alone. Then Mateo had whipped up the wind in that room so Az couldn't hear her screams.

Not until it was too late.

He glanced into the sky. The flames and smoke had dimmed the sunlight. Yet as he stared, the clouds seemed to thicken. A dark shape emerged.

A shape with the wide, black wings of a Death Angel.

His back teeth ground together. If Bastion was coming back to taunt him, he'd make the angel pay.

And it *was* Bastion. There was no mistaking the angel's form. But—but Bastion wasn't alone.

Bastion touched down just in front of the flames. He held Jade against his chest. One of Bastion's arms circled her stomach, and the angel held a knife to her throat.

"Let her go," Az demanded. The sirens were growing louder. The fire seemed to shriek behind Jade and Bastion.

Bastion's eyes were wide. "You did this?"

Mateo climbed slowly to his feet. Blisters covered his right arm. They'd heal. Mateo was too powerful not to heal now that he was away from the flames. "She's not supposed . . . to be . . . here."

The tip of the knife sliced her throat.

Az couldn't hear the screams of the approaching sirens or the crackle of the flames. Jade's lips were moving but he could discern no sound.

He leapt forward, stopping mere inches from Bastion. "Let her go or die." If he had to use his fists to pound those brimstone bullets into Bastion's head and heart, he would.

No one was hurting Jade.

Fear flashed in Bastion's eyes. Az knew fear when he saw it and smelled it.

"M–Marna . . ." He caught the angel's whisper. "Tell me, did you take her wings?"

"I already told you," Jade muttered, "*he didn't.*"

Az fought the fury inside of him. His gaze held Bastion's. "I did not."

Bastion's wings curled inward.

"Brandt was the one who attacked her," Az told him. "He's more than human. He could see her. And you know what a shifter's claws can do to us."

"Not a weapon of man." Bastion swallowed. The knife lifted. His hands were shaking. "I-I thought you . . ." He pushed Jade toward Az.

He grabbed her, held her close, and smelled her blood.

Az stiffened. Keeping his hand on her, his gaze swept her

body. There was no missing the long gash that had torn open her arm.

"Az," Jade began, with her eyes wide. "Hold on. It was a misunderstand—"

Bastion attacking her wasn't a misunderstanding. Az pushed her behind him. "Do you know what you've done?"

The angel's head hung down. "When I found them, Marna's wings were covered in blood. There was no sign of her in the swamp. I-I thought that you'd—"

"You didn't attack me. You attacked *her*."

The angel wasn't meeting his stare.

"What were you going to do?" Az demanded. The urge to attack, to destroy, was so strong that his body trembled.

Bastion's chin slowly lifted. "I was going to let Brandt have her."

"Bad, bad mistake." He lifted his hand and prepared to beat the hell out of a certain angel.

"Az!" Jade grabbed his hand. "Dammit, we don't have time for this now!"

Sammael would have said there was always time for an ass kicking.

Perhaps he truly was becoming more like his brother. Or maybe he'd always been like him and just hadn't realized it.

"The cops are almost on top of us. We need to get out of here." Fear flickered in her eyes. "There is no way that we want to get caught by human authorities now."

The too-close shrieks of the sirens filled his ears. Jade was right. They had to leave. Vengeance would come second. Protecting her was his first priority.

He took her hand and turned away from Bastion. His gaze swept the scene. Mateo had vanished. No real surprise. But he'd be finding that witch soon.

*Or he will find us.*

Az could see the cop cars and fire trucks circling in now.

He hoisted Jade into his arms. Her hands slipped around his neck and her body . . . *felt so right*. She always seemed to fit against him perfectly. "Hold tight," he told her, pressing a kiss to her forehead.

He lunged forward, but Bastion moved in an instant and blocked him.

"Where is she?" Bastion whispered.

He did not have time for this.

"You know she'll be weak. If a foe comes at her again . . . Marna won't survive another attack so soon after the loss of her wings."

He wanted to tear Bastion apart, but Jade's fingers were lightly stroking the back of his neck and some of the tight fury eased from him. Relenting, but still planning for some vicious payback, Az growled, "At midnight, meet us at Sammael's club."

A fire truck raced onto the street.

"She'll be there," he promised.

Bastion nodded and his wings arched as he rose into the air. The humans wouldn't see the angel.

But the cops and firefighters would sure try to bust him and Jade.

Police cars were swarming the scene now. Az ran forward. He leapt onto the hood of one patrol car, denting the metal, then he propelled forward and up, racing fast, so fast . . .

The humans would never be able to identify him. They'd only see a blur.

Jade held him tighter and the rest of the world faded away.

Sammael didn't need to hear the intruder to know that someone had slipped into his home.

After all, there was very little that went on without his notice.

But the fact that some asshole had come sneaking into his house, while Seline was there, well, that pissed him off.

No one messed with Seline.

"Sam?" Her voice was sleepy, sexy, and it instantly made him hard.

Oh, soon enough for that, but first . . . Sam pressed a kiss to the soft silk of her shoulder. "Sleep, love. I need to tend to some business."

Her brows drew together. She knew all about his business.

He kissed her again and let his fingers skate down her arm. He could hear the faintest tread of footsteps on his stairs. His intruder had gotten past the magical safeguards that he kept in place on his house.

Not a human. But then, humans seemed to instinctively stay the hell away from him.

He climbed from the bed. Waved his hand and instantly had a pair of jeans on his body.

"Want me to call Beelzie?" Seline asked, and he glanced back to see that she was sitting up in bed, her eyes wide and worried.

"No. I've got this one." Because he knew the identity of his visitor. If he didn't have a faint friendship with the guy— even though he'd been on this earth for centuries, he could count his friends on one hand—Sam would have already attacked.

He stalked forward. Yanked open the bedroom door. And found Mateo standing in his hallway.

A rather blistered, ash-covered Mateo.

Sam lifted a brow. "Been visiting hell again, have you?" Shaking his head, he asked, "Why don't you just give up that place and—"

"We have a problem." Mateo's voice was flat and cold. His gaze drifted over Sam's shoulder, probably to find Seline.

The guy had always watched her a bit too much.

Sam shifted his body to block the view. "You're damn right we do. Some bastard caller just busted into my house." Mateo had been the one to put the charms and protections in place. It figured that he'd be the only one who could slip right past them.

Mateo's jaw hardened. "You'll have to stop him. No one else will be strong enough."

He knew Seline could hear every word they said. "Stop who?"

"Azrael."

Fuck. "What's happened?" He didn't let any emotion show on his face. Thanks to his time in heaven, he knew just how to camouflage his feelings.

"It hasn't happened yet. It *will* happen." Mateo exhaled and the scent of smoke deepened around him. "I've seen what's coming. I know what he'll do."

"Yeah? Well then cut through the BS and tell me. Because I never fucking liked riddles." And he didn't like the hard gnawing in his gut, either. Even since his fall, he'd planned to get back at his uptight, rule-following ass of a brother. Then Az had started hunting him. Az the asshole.

Sam had thought he'd have to kill Az during those days.

But since his own fall, his brother had changed. Az had sacrificed. Nearly given his life in order to protect Seline.

So he'd let the guy keep living.

Had that been a mistake?

"His human will die tomorrow, and when she does . . ." Another long sigh from Mateo, only this one carried the scent of death. "He'll break."

Sam found he couldn't speak.

"When Az breaks, he'll go after anyone in his path. He'll kill everyone, do anything."

No, no, this was bullshit.

"She dies tomorrow," Mateo said again, "and that fate

won't change. It can't. So you and I damn well have to figure out a way to stop him."

Az was fond of his human. No, more than fond. Sam had
seen the way his brother looked at the woman.

*The way I look at Seline.*

And he remembered what he'd felt like when he lost his
Seline. Remembered how desperate he'd been.

Desperate enough to take on hell and heaven.

"If you don't stop him," Mateo's gaze searched his, "if you
don't kill him, we'll all suffer."

Sam still didn't speak.

"Will you really just stand back, and let him destroy the
world? All for one lost human life?"

Not just any human though. Not just any life.

A Fallen's mate. Death couldn't take her away, not without one hell of a fight.

"Many have said that Az is the embodiment of all that is
evil."

He'd heard the tales. "They say that about me, too." Some
tales were just stories to frighten children.

"With Az," Mateo continued, "the chains of heaven held
him in check."

Sam knew that was true. Az had always clung so tightly
to his control, because he knew well the beast that waited
inside.

"There are no chains now." Mateo's gaze was stark.
"There is nothing to stop him. The veneer of good will
crack, and the true being that is Azrael will emerge."

Sam glanced back over his shoulder. Seline was safe in the
room, protected.

Seline—his life. "My brother is still chained." Not with
chains forged in heaven, but with a delicate chain that had
been created on earth.

As long as his female lived, Az was bound to Jade.

But when she died . . .

Azrael's dark side would definitely be coming out.

And it might just be one coming out party that the world couldn't survive.

The world didn't stop spinning for Jade. When Az slowed down his super speed, she found herself inside what looked like a bedroom. Gleaming wood surrounding her and—

And Az kissed her and the spinning continued. His tongue pushed into her mouth and his hand skated down her body.

The kiss was hard, almost brutal in its intensity, and she knew it was fueled by rage.

Jade didn't want his rage. She'd had enough rage to last a lifetime. She turned her head away. "Az. *Stop.*"

He instantly stilled.

There was so much to say, and Jade was very much afraid there wasn't enough time to truly say anything. Nothing that mattered, anyway.

Az drew in a deep, shuddering breath and stepped away from her. "I should . . . see about bandaging your arm."

The arm didn't hurt anymore. Actually, the deep wound was closing. Probably thanks to that angel blood still pumping through her body.

"Don't worry about it," she whispered as she lifted a hand to her head. That super speedy bit just didn't work so well for her. "Az, I'm sorry."

He blinked. "You have nothing to be sorry for."

Yes, she did. Jade turned away from him. "Where are we?" She just threw out the question to buy herself more time. If Az had brought her there, then she knew it was a safe place. She trusted him.

He shouldn't trust her.

"It's one of Sam's safe houses in New Orleans."

Ah, Sammael again. The Fallen who liked to be prepared.

"While I was . . . following him a while back, I found this place."

Glancing over her shoulder, Jade lifted a brow. "Following him?" She asked carefully.

"I intended to kill him."

"Not very angel-like of you," she whispered.

His head cocked and his gaze sharpened on her. "But then, I'm not an angel, am I?"

Was she supposed to be afraid of him? "I should never have brought you into this mess." By helping her, he'd lost the one thing he wanted most.

That big trip back upstairs.

"I chose to help you." The wooden floor creaked beneath his feet.

"And I knew the minute I saw you," she stared down at her hands, realizing that she'd clenched them into fists, "that I would use you."

The words fell into the room and were followed by thick silence.

Her heart raced too fast, and she forced herself to lift her chin and face him. "That's why I'm sorry, Azrael. You came to my aid, and I—*selfishly*—knew just how powerful you were. I tried to play on your emotions. I wanted you to be willing to fight for me. To do anything for me . . . because I realized you were the muscle I needed to destroy Brandt." She swallowed. He wasn't talking, and she was just digging one very big hole for herself. "I didn't care what you wanted or what kind of life you might have. I just wanted to use you to kill the nightmare stalking me."

He deserved this truth. They had the bullets now. She could take them and face Brandt on her own. Az could walk away.

Maybe even get his heaven back.

"You played on my emotions?" He repeated, voice quiet. "How?"

Now this was her shame. "By seducing you."

She waited for his rage. Instead, he just laughed.

"Uh, Az?" Did he laugh when he was really pissed?

Slowly, his laughter faded. "I was using you."

That hurt, but the truth often did.

He stalked toward her. "A human. One being hunted. Pursued." His head cocked to the right as he studied her. "Helping you was going to be my first step toward redemption."

"Instead I just led you deeper into hell." What had he called her? His *temptation*.

She wanted to be more, but knew now that would never be. "You need to walk away from me," she told him. "You've already crossed too many lines." Fighting other angels, cheating death. "If you want that redemption, then leave me."

"Is that what you want?"

"I want you to have the chance to get the things you need. I want you to be able to go back home." Jade licked her lips. "I won't let you trade your dreams for my life." That didn't seem like a fair exchange to her.

His gaze dropped to her mouth. "There is no trade. Heaven is gone. I won't be going back."

Her heart ached. "If you had the chance—"

"I'm not leaving you." His mouth took hers. Rough, hard, but without the rage of moments before. Just wild heat and hunger and a passion that burned her from the inside out.

Her hands came up and pressed against his chest. She leaned into his kiss, helpless to back away this time. Desire quickened within her.

*One more time.*

Just once more, before the end game. Once more.

His lips lifted from hers. "I was . . . afraid." The confession was gruff, and the last thing she expected.

Jade could only stare up at him.

"Bastion took you when I should have been protecting you. If you'd died . . ." His gaze seemed to darken. "I'm not sure what I would have done."

The cold whisper of fear chased over her skin again. She kept being told that Az was dangerous. That she shouldn't be with him.

She'd had one monster for a lover. Seen just how wicked he could be. Evil hid so easily behind a handsome face.

When she looked at Az, she saw another handsome face.

Was it one that hid evil?

*No.* The certainty was soul deep. "You don't have to worry. I'm not planning on dying anytime soon."

He wasn't leaving her. She wouldn't leave him. Maybe . . . maybe they could make this work. Hope was small, fragile, but stubborn inside her, growing even when she knew better.

It had been years since she hoped.

But *maybe* . . .

Her fingers slid down his chest. Found the snap of his jeans. He'd given to her. This time, she'd be the one to give to him.

Pleasure.

The snap gave way beneath her fingers. She carefully slid down his zipper. Her eyes were on Az's as she knelt before him.

"Jade?"

She shook her head and wanted to offer him a smile, but the moment was too tense.

He wore no underwear and his cock sprang toward her, thick and full. Her fingers curved over him as her knees hit the floor. She stroked him, pumping him gently from base to tip and Az flexed against her, the sensual move almost helpless.

She didn't want him helpless. Never that. Never him.

Her head bent forward, and she licked the tip of his cock.

The flesh was firm, salty because he was so ready for her, and the head of his erection bobbed eagerly toward her mouth.

Her breath blew lightly over his flesh.

*"Jade."* No question this time. A heated demand.

Her mouth opened over him and she took his flesh inside. She licked him and let his cock slide over her tongue. Her cheeks hollowed as she drew him in deeper, and he thrust into her mouth.

When Jade swallowed, he growled his pleasure.

Her hand curled around the base of his erection so that she could keep the control as she tasted his flesh. Back and forth, his cock slid over her tongue. She sucked him. Licked him. Learned the feel of his cock and grew wet as she savored him.

Her nipples were hard now, aching. Her hips moved restlessly because the need was tightening within her.

His fingers were in her hair, sinking deep and holding her as she held him. But she couldn't seem to get enough of him. His flavor was hot and wild and it was driving her crazy.

She wanted more. She wanted him to come and—

Az pulled away.

Breath panting, she stared up at him. His eyes were blazing with need. His cheeks stained with a surge of hot color.

"In . . . you." That was all he said. In the next second, he had her pinned on the floor. A rug protected her back as he yanked off her jeans and tore away her panties. Then his cock was there, pushing up between her legs. She was slick and ready and in one hard thrust, he'd embedded his length balls-deep within her.

It wasn't enough.

Her heels pressed against his back as she arched up against him. Each downward thrust sent his body sliding against her clit and the sensation had her moaning.

He pushed up, separating their bodies just enough so that he could palm her breast. His fingers plucked the nipple, then his mouth found her.

His tongue licked her even as his hips pounded down against her sex.

*More, more, more.*

The whisper wasn't just in her mind. She was pleading, demanding.

He rolled, repositioning their bodies, and Jade found herself staring down at him. Her hands flattened on his chest as she rose up, then brought her hips back down almost frantically. She just couldn't get enough. The pleasure was close, just out of reach, and she stared into his eyes and his cock filled her, every single inch of her and—

She came on a blast of pleasure that shook her whole body. Az kept thrusting into her, and the deep push of his cock into her just made the pleasure intensify. She wanted to cry out but couldn't catch her breath. Her nails sank into his chest as she rode out the wrenching climax.

His eyes flashed to pure black when his release hit him. His body tightened, turning to steel beneath her touch, and he shoved even deeper into her. When he climaxed, she felt the hot surge in her core, and the pleasure whipped right through her.

Her heartbeat raced too fast. Jade gasped as she stared down at him. There'd never be another lover for her like Az. Never be someone that could make her scream, make her come so hard . . .

Because she'd never love another the way she loved him.

The truth terrified her, but she'd suspected it for some time now.

She'd given her heart to her Fallen. Her head lowered toward his, and she pressed a light kiss to his mouth. Not wild and desperate any longer. Softer, heavy with emotion.

He was so strong beneath her. So powerful.

Her head slowly lifted.

And Jade realized that the darkness hadn't faded from his gaze.

"I would have hunted him down." Az's words were gravel rough.

She held his gaze.

"I'd already gotten a tracking spell from Mateo. I was coming after you." His hands were around her hips, loose, but an unbreakable hold. "Brandt never would have gotten to you. I would have found you, and I would have made sure you were safe."

He was still trying to protect her.

"You can't . . ." He was already firming again in her, and she wanted to lift up her hips and feel the delicious slide of his flesh within her. Wanted to, but . . . "You can't always save the world."

"I'm not interested in the world." He thrust up into her and her sensitive flesh responded with a ripple of pleasure. "Only you."

*Only you.*

The words seemed to bind them, but then, she'd been bound to him from the very first moment she'd seen him.

She just hadn't realized how deeply she'd fallen.

Past heaven. Past hell. Into the arms of an angel who'd burned.

Brandt stared down at the blood drops that stained the earth. Jade's blood.

The panther began clawing up from the inside, maddened with fury.

He'd thought the angel had been protecting Jade. Her lover, her protector.

But the distinctive scent of an angel still drifted in the air around him even as Jade's blood littered the ground.

*Hurt.*

Jade must have been trying to come back to him. She'd sought him out. She must have remembered that he'd used this area for a base once before.

Jade never forgot anything. For a human, her intellect was fascinating.

One of the many reasons she was *his.*

She'd sought him out, been coming to him, but the angel had found her first.

He'd stopped her. Hurt her. Taken her away.

Claws burst from Brandt's fingertips.

He would forgive Jade. She'd be punished, but forgiven because she'd tried to do the right thing. She'd tried to come back to her mate's side.

But the angel . . . there'd be no forgiveness for him. Brandt would slice the skin from his body, one slow strip at a time.

The angel thought he knew of hell? Not yet, he didn't.

But soon . . . *soon.*

And Brandt began to follow the drops of Jade's blood. It was a perfect trail that would lead him back to his mate.

# CHAPTER SEVENTEEN

Midnight. That, of course, meant that Sunrise was packed. The line to get inside the club stretched for several blocks.

Az wasn't exactly the standing-in-line type.

Jade's gaze was on the pack of human and *Other* waiting for eager entrance. "Uh, do the humans even realize what's going on in there?"

Because most of the folks waiting to get in were human. Scantily clad women. Swaggering men.

If they weren't careful, they'd wind up being prey for the *Other* tonight. But perhaps that was what some wanted.

"They think they're getting excitement. They don't realize the guy who'll be waiting at the bar actually *is* a vampire looking for a bite." Humans could find an excuse to explain away just about everything. And for those who saw beneath the masks and into the true hearts of the monsters . . . there were ways to make them forget what they'd seen.

All it took was a little magic.

There was plenty of magic and *Other* things for sale in Sunrise.

"Come on." He caught her hand and threaded his fingers through hers. The bouncer at the door was a demon, one of the demons that Sam usually kept very close. Az knew this particular demon was even considered to be a friend of his brother's.

When Cole saw him coming, he arched a dark brow and snapped his fingers. Instantly, a big, no-neck, bulging muscled mass of a demon took Cole's place at the door.

"I was told you'd be coming by." Cole unhooked the silken rope that blocked the line from rushing up those infamous steps that led to Sunrise. "Right this way."

Az let Jade go in before him. He saw the assessing gaze that Cole slid over her. The demon's eyes lingered a bit too long on her ass.

"Don't." Terse. The only warning he'd give the demon.

Cole smiled. "A guy can look, right? What's the harm in that?" Then he hurried forward and opened the door. The pounding beat of music spilled outside even as they swept into the club. Alcohol. Sex. Perfume. The smells swirled in the air as the bodies danced and gyrated on the small floor.

There were women up in the golden cage that swung lightly from the ceiling. A band screaming on the small stage.

"That way . . ." Cole pointed to the left. "Your . . . um . . . friends have already been shown to a private room."

Good. "The woman was with them?"

Cole laughed with real appreciation then. "Yeah, she was." He leaned toward Az. "Kind of hard to miss a hand-cuffed, pissed-off angel."

Az saw Jade's shoulders relax. "She's alive."

Cole glanced toward her and nodded. "But I doubt those guys with her will be once she breaks loose." He shrugged. "So they'd better hope those cuffs keep holding her in check."

Cole turned to stride back outside, but Az lifted his hand and stopped him. "There will be one more guest for our little private party." He paused. "Be *very* careful around him.

Bastion isn't the kind you want to antagonize. Actually, you don't want to touch him at all."

"Great." Cole sighed and shook his head. "Another Death Angel? Can't any of you assholes just stay in heaven these days?"

"He's not Fallen." Not yet. But if Bastion stayed on the path he seemed to be taking . . . "He's blond, my height, and—"

"And I think I'll be able to figure out which guy's the angel. Not my first ball game." Cole spun away. "Fucking angels," he muttered.

Az waved his hand, and the crowd parted before him. The dancers didn't even realize they were moving back. It was as if a light wind blew right by them, ushering them subtly to the side, but he and Jade could now slide through the crush of bodies without any problem.

They avoided the once-again-bolted metal doors, though Az was sure that the hellhound had been . . . relocated. Instead, they took the winding hallway that led away from the crowd. When he arrived before the reserved room—the room that Sam kept especially for occasions when *Other* needed a private place to meet—Az didn't bother to knock. He waved his hand and the door flew open.

Marna's blue eyes widened with fear when she saw him. She was seated in a wooden chair, with her hands cuffed behind her. Tanner stood on one side of her while Cody paced near the back of the room.

The door slammed against the wall, jerking everyone's attention toward him and Jade.

*"Azrael."* Marna's sharp voice.

"Why is she cuffed?" Jade demanded as she pushed forward. "She should be taking it easy, not—"

"Her wounds have healed," Cody told her as he stepped toward her. Then he stopped and glanced over at Marna. "As much as they can heal."

Marna laughed then. A bitter, tight laugh that Az had never expected to hear from the angel who cared too much. "He means the blood's stopped—but my wings are long gone."

Tears glittered in her eyes, shining like jagged diamonds.

"Uncuff her," Jade snapped.

Tanner's body stiffened. "I'm not real sure that's a good plan, there, Jade." His faint drawl had thickened. "One touch and—"

"She's been hurt enough." Jade strode closer to her. Az made sure he shadowed her moves. "Just let her go," Jade said.

Marna's gaze darted to him. The fear was still there. Fear and fury and . . .

Hope?

"There's some kind of spell on the cuffs," Marna said, her voice soft now, almost broken. "I can't get out of them, no matter what I do."

Jade's attention jumped back to Tanner. "Get the key and get her out."

But Tanner stood his ground. "You really that eager for her to kill you? The wings might be gone, but her powers aren't. One touch, and you aren't coming back."

"The touch doesn't work on me anymore. At least, Bastion said it didn't."

Marna's eyes widened, and Az saw the hope die in her gaze.

He realized that she'd been planning to finish her mission. To kill Jade.

The hell she would.

Az strode forward. He crouched in front of Marna and made sure that their gazes held. "We found you in those woods. The two men behind you—"

"They aren't men!" Her voice was stronger now, more caked with fury than fear. "One's an animal, one's a demon, and they're both linked to the bastard who did this to me!"

"A bastard who's got angel blood." This came from the demon doc who Az knew must have spent hours trying to help Marna. "He's like you, so before you start looking down that perfect nose of yours at us *animals,* remember that. Angels can go bad, too."

She never looked away from Az. "I know that. I've seen bad angels with my own eyes."

He refused to feel shame. "Bastion is looking for you."

Her lashes lowered to conceal her gaze. "He can't take me home."

No, the rules didn't work that way. You had to fly into heaven on your own steam.

"He can take care of you, though. He can help you." Az exhaled. "So can I. You aren't going to be alone down here." He'd make sure of it.

A tear leaked from her eye. "He-he liked hurting me." She took a deep breath. "He was . . . laughing while he cut me."

Tanner backed away from her, fast. Az looked up and realized that the shifter's claws had burst from his skin. Rage drew deep lines on his face, and Az knew that fury was directed right at Brandt.

"We're going to stop him," Jade told her. Her hand lifted, as if she'd touch Marna's shoulder, but she hesitated. "He won't hurt anyone else."

Marna's head rose as she focused on Jade. "If he's really like us . . ." Her gaze swung to Az, "Then how can you kill him?"

The small bag tied to his waist felt too heavy, and so did the gun he'd tucked into the side of his belt. "Even angels can die. He'll go down. Trust me."

She swallowed and Az knew Marna was trying to hold on to her control. Without the magical protection of her wings, she'd be feeling the full brunt of human emotions. The angel probably felt as if she were breaking apart from the inside.

He'd felt that way. Still did.

Jade's hand touched Marna's shoulder. The scent of flowers flooded the room then. Az rose to his feet. He didn't need to glance back to know that Bastion had joined them.

The tears trickled down Marna's cheeks faster now. "Don't . . . look at me." Her stark whisper.

Az knew that she was ashamed for Bastion to see her this way.

In the next moment, Bastion couldn't see her at all. Tanner had stepped in front of Marna, shielding her. "Who the fuck are you?" His gaze slanted to Az. "Don't remember you saying that anyone else would be joining this little party."

No, he hadn't said that. "Bastion is here for Marna."

Tanner glanced over his shoulder at the sobbing angel. "Maybe Marna doesn't want to go with him." His claws were still out, but Az noticed the shifter carefully kept them from Marna's line of sight.

"I can't go!" Marna bit out the words. "Bastion, it's too late."

In a flash, Bastion was standing toe-to-toe with Tanner. "You don't want to come between us," he told the shifter. His wings brushed the top of the room. He was letting all of them see him—just as he was.

But Tanner didn't look particularly intimidated. "I know how this works," Tanner said as he barred his sharp canines. "Unless my name turned up in that fancy book upstairs that used to belong to Azrael here, you can't touch me." He smiled. "Unless you're looking to see those wings of yours burn right off. 'Cause killing someone not marked for death, that's a falling offense, right?"

"It was for me," Sam said from the doorway, his voice lazy but lethal.

Bastion stiffened. "Sammael."

"Long time no see huh, Bastion?"

Jade's gaze swept the room. "Well, isn't this just the big old angelic reunion." She shoved Tanner. Her elbow caught him off guard and made the shifter stagger. Or maybe he wasn't caught off guard. Maybe that blood was still making her stronger than she should be. "Give me the keys to the cuffs."

Tanner's eyes narrowed on her. "Don't have them."

"I do." Cody lifted a small, golden ring from his pocket. "But I want her promise first." It wasn't surprising that the demon would be the less trusting one. "No one dies by her touch tonight."

Sam strolled forward. "Seems like a fair enough trade for your freedom, Marna."

Bastion didn't speak.

"I-I promise," Marna spoke softly.

Tanner turned. Cody tossed him the key. Az thought the shifter's eyes softened when he glanced back at Marna. A mistake, that. Marna might seem weak now, but she wouldn't be that way for long.

Tanner reached behind her and a moment later, Az heard the soft snick as the cuff was released.

Just that fast, Marna was up, out of the chair—and she had her right hand punched into Cody's chest as she slammed him into the nearest wall.

"I thought we had a deal!" Tanner shouted as he lunged forward to help his brother.

"We do." Marna didn't spare him a glance. "I'm not killing him. I never said anything about not *hurting* him." A pause. "Or you." Her smile held a cruel edge.

*An eye for an eye.* Angels were too acquainted with the old ways.

"They helped you," Jade reminded her. "They're the reason you're not still lying in a pool of your own blood in the woods. And by the way, Brandt was hunting out in those woods. If he'd found you—instead of them—what do you think would have happened?"

Marna frowned and took a step away from Cody. That small movement was all Tanner needed. He grabbed her hand, twisted her, and then trapped Marna within his embrace.

She screamed.

"Easy," he said, holding her carefully. "I'm not gonna hurt you, but that's the brother I actually like."

She shuddered in his arms.

Az grabbed Bastion's hand when the angel tried to step by him. "You don't want to do that." Az glanced deliberately at Bastion's dark wings. "Killing a shifter will cost you too much."

Bastion managed a nod, and Az could see him trying to pull his control back. Az didn't move, though, not until he was sure no one in that room was about to die.

It took them all a few moments to calm back down. Az did think it was interesting, though, that Marna didn't once try to use her Death Touch on the shifter. Seemed like a good sign. She bit him, she scratched him, but she didn't kill him.

Sam shut the door and secured them all in the room.

"Looks like the team's all here," Jade murmured. "Well, most of the team. Where's Seline?"

"Somewhere safe, with a hellhound making sure she stays away from Sunrise." Sam's answer was instant. His gaze cut to Bastion. "I wasn't about to let a Death Angel near her."

Bastion's gaze narrowed.

"And I can't help but wonder . . ." Sam sauntered closer to them. Knowing his brother, Az suspected that Cole was now standing guard outside of the closed door. "Just how many angels does it take in order to stop one hybrid shifter?"

"It only takes one," Az said, meeting his brother's gaze. "Because this fight is mine."

"It never hurts to have backup."

And it never hurt to protect the man you'd wronged too many times before. "Brandt is mine. I know how to take him down."

The others weren't speaking. It was Jade who cleared her throat. "I just . . . need to know." She looked at Tanner—who was still holding tight to Marna—and Cody. "How'd he wind up being the son of an angel?"

Cody's lips tightened, then he said, "Our father wanted an unstoppable son. The bastard liked to experiment."

"No," Tanner cut through his words, "he liked to think he was God."

The silence beat heavily in the room.

"What kind of angel was she?" Sam finally asked as his head tilted to the left. Ah . . . Sam *would* be the one to ask that question. Since Seline had been a hybrid, too, one with a powerful angel side, it made sense that Sam would want to know about the angel type that had created Brandt.

He understood just how dangerous a hybrid like Brandt could be.

"I don't know," Tanner said, meeting Sam's eyes with a level stare. "Brandt is my half-brother. His mother . . . she died before I was born."

"Killed by father's tender hands—and claws," Cody added.

"Huh." Sam cast his assessing gaze toward Az. "I'm guessing their father's on the hit list, too?"

"The father's dead," Bastion spoke without looking away from Marna. "He was dispatched years ago."

"By my hand," Jade told them, voice flat.

"Interesting." Sam nodded, and Az saw the spark of admiration flare in his eyes. "Some humans can be surprisingly strong."

"And some angels can be surprisingly weak." It was Bastion who spoke. "And Lailyn was weak." He offered his hand to Marna. "We need to leave here. You're not strong enough for the battle that's coming."

Tanner's arms tightened around her.

"Lailyn?" Az repeated the name. It was familiar. An image of a small, dark-haired, fair-skinned angel flashed through his mind. He hadn't seen her too much, because she'd been a . . . guardian.

"She was sent to watch over Vincent Dupre. To help guide and protect him." Bastion's lips twisted in what would have been disgust, if he'd been human. If he'd been plagued by emotions.

Of course, he wasn't. So the angel pretended.

"She traded heaven for a chance to redeem him. Lailyn thought she could save him, by staying by his side and offering him a life with her."

"But some people just can't be saved." Az spoke the truth that all the angels should already know. Even those blinded by the human emotions. Guardians were the ones tempted the most by those emotions. They were around the humans so much, it was easy for them to be tempted . . . to want what was right in front of them.

So close, but so far from what they were meant to have.

"I saw what he did," Bastion said. "When he drove his claws into her chest and cut out her heart, I was there, watching, and I could do nothing to help her." His gaze fell to Tanner's hands, no, to Tanner's sharp claws. "All animals know is violence and pain."

Slowly, Tanner's arms fell away from Marna. His claws didn't recede. But they also didn't so much as scratch her delicate skin.

Bastion took Marna's hand. "I'll keep you safe," he promised her. "Until this is over . . . then we'll figure something out."

She nodded, but Az wondered if Bastion could see the

doubt in her eyes. But in the next moment, Bastion pulled her close against his chest. His wings began to wrap around her.

"I'm not like him." The words seemed torn from Tanner.

Marna glanced back at him. Her lips trembled.

Then she and Bastion vanished.

Brandt stared at the line of humans waiting to gain entrance into the club. They were so stupid. Sheep, offering themselves to the monsters who were hungry for a bite.

He'd assembled his pack. A dozen strong shifters waited behind him, ready to attack on his order.

Jade was in that building. In that club with the desperate, avid humans. He could still smell her blood. Her wound hadn't closed completely, not yet.

*You should never have hurt her.*

Whenever Brandt closed his eyes, he saw the image of his claws sinking into her chest, again and again. It was an image that haunted him.

*Because I saw the old bastard do the same thing to my mother.*

He'd been three, and she'd smiled at him even as the blood trickled from her lips.

*I love you.* Her last words.

And his mother had died. Left him. Left him all alone with the sick fuck of a father who liked to torture him.

He'd been seven when his father had first used his claws to strip the skin from his back.

Not even old enough to shift, much less to heal from the wounds.

*"You'll be strong, boy, you'll be stronger than them all. Take the pain. Don't fuckin' cry, don't ever fuckin' cry."*

He hadn't. Not since his mother's eyes had closed. He'd cried then.

The torment from his father had been never-ending. The alpha had ruled the pack with an iron fist, and Brandt—he'd been like a whipped dog. Too afraid to move, to strike back in any way.

*But Jade struck for me.*

She'd killed the alpha. Given Brandt freedom.

Now Brandt wanted to give her everything. Why, *why* wouldn't she let him?

He'd never meant to hurt her. Those chest wounds had been the angel's fault, too. He hadn't realized it in the heat of the moment, but Brandt was now sure that Azrael had deliberately used Jade as a shield to protect himself.

The angel had sacrificed her.

Now he'd hurt her again.

Azrael deserved hell, and Brandt would be the one to give it to him.

But first, he'd have to kill a few humans.

Because they were in his way.

"Someone has been visiting Mateo," Sam murmured as he gazed at the spot where Bastion had been moments before. "I'd recognize that get-me-the-fuck-out-of-here spell anywhere."

Az grunted. "Mateo sold me out to Bastion when we paid the witch a visit today. Mateo *gave* Jade to him. And she nearly died." The thought still had his gut clenching in remembered fear and fury.

"Really?" Sam sounded mildly curious. "Mateo doesn't usually work with angels. He finds them . . . annoyingly dull."

"I guess if the price is right, he'll work with anyone." Az pulled out his gun and began to load in the bullets. The gold veneer on the bullets seemed to shine. From magic? Or hellfire?

Tanner whistled as he came closer for a better look at the bullets. "You actually got them."

"Was there any doubt?" Jade asked as her brows rose.

Az almost smiled at her. Instead, he glanced at the shifter

and said, "Guaranteed to stop an angel," *even an earthbound one,* "in his tracks." He closed the chamber with a snap of his wrist.

"And what if he . . . changes?" Sam asked, and Az glanced at him, struck by the odd note in his brother's voice. But Sam's face was perfectly blank as he said, "Seline's a hybrid, too, and when her human body died, the angels just took her to work upstairs."

Az knew that had been the moment Sam's real hell began.

He spared a glance for Jade and saw worry flicker in her emerald gaze. *Can't have that. I don't want her to worry.*

"If that happens, I guess I'll just chase his winged ass down and make sure he stays dead." The gun was a light weight he barely felt in his hand. "But something tells me after all the crap he's pulled, heaven isn't going to be real eager to welcome him past those grand gates."

"They'd better not be," Cody muttered.

"So what's the plan?" Tanner wanted to know. The shifter's body seemed to vibrate with barely leashed energy. "You want me to go out and track the bastard?"

Screams trickled through the shut door. Shouts. Pounding footsteps.

"I don't think that tracking will be necessary," Sam said as he strode toward that door. His fingers curled around the doorknob as he yanked the door open. The screams spilled into the room then. "Something tells me our boy has found us."

Jade's eyes widened as she stepped toward the door. Az blocked her. "No way." If Brandt thought he was getting his hands on her, the guy could think again. The hybrid shifter would have to go through him first. His gaze flew to Tanner and Cody. "You two stay here with her. Make sure no one but me comes back in that door."

One entrance. One exit. Two powerful *Other.* They'd keep her safe.

Or he'd make them wish for death.

He glanced over his shoulder. Sam was already gone. The guy had disappeared into the screams and the chaos.

Jade grabbed his arm. "So that's it? I just stay here while you run out and risk your life?"

That was the general plan, yes.

"Let me help you."

Az shook his head. "I won't risk you again. Brandt almost killed you before. He won't have you tonight."

He could hear animalistic snarls now. Brandt and his men had shifted to attack. With humans there? They really were crazy.

Bending, he kissed her. A fast, hard press of his lips. "It'll be over soon."

She didn't speak, but just watched him with worried eyes.

Then it was Az's turn to follow the screams. He raced outside of the private room and saw the stampeding mass. He'd been wrong—Brandt's men hadn't shifted, not all the way, but they were using their claws to slice apart anyone who got in their way. Slicing, laughing, and snarling like panthers as the blood flowed.

Sam was already running toward them. One touch, and the laughing asshole to the right of Sam went down.

His brother was fast.

Az was faster.

Another shifter cut a redhead, slicing her right across the stomach. Az jumped forward and ripped her away from the guy. He pushed her behind him even as he shoved his hand against the shifter's chest. Before that panther hit the ground, his body was stone hard and his eyes—wide, horrified— stared at nothing.

Two down. The rest of the pack to go.

Az smiled in anticipation.

\* \* \*

No way. Jade watched Az's powerful form rush from the room. She wasn't just going to stand back, to *hide*, while Az went out there and faced her nightmare.

The guy had forgotten, she wasn't just a human anymore. As the adrenaline pumped through her, Jade's body began to heat up with a charge she'd felt before. *Burn, baby, burn.*

If she had to, she could burn her way right through that pack.

*I won't let you take all the risk, Az.*

The guy needed to think again.

She strode forward. Tanner's fast grip on her arm jerked her right back. "Just where do you think you're goin' now, ma'am?"

Jade narrowed her eyes. "I think I'm going into the fight."

*Snick.*

She glanced down at her wrist. The gleaming, gold cuff that he'd taken off Marna now locked around her wrist.

*Snick.*

The other cuff circled his thick wrist.

Son of a bitch. She really hadn't seen that one coming. Sneaky shifter.

"Don't think so," Tanner said softly. "You see, despite what you may think, I don't have a death wish, and I don't want that Fallen lover of yours coming to send my ass to hell."

She yanked on the cuff.

His brows lowered. "Settle down. Once we hear the shots, and we know it's all clear . . ." He glanced over at Cody. The demon had taken up a position blocking the now closed and barred door. "Then we'll go out and you can take as many swings at me as you want."

And she would. *Settle down, my ass.*

But then she heard a groan. A long, shuddering groan that seemed to be shaking the building itself.

"Fuck," Tanner spat and whirled toward the right wall.

A long crevice was sliding down the white surface. Breaking it open, breaking—

An explosion rocked right through the wall. Bricks and boards flew into the air, fire roared, and Jade and Tanner both slammed backwards before they hit the hard floor.

The explosion froze Az. Two shifters surrounded him, each using human females as shields, and when the thundering reverberation rocked through the club, they started to laugh.

*"Too late now,"* one said, and he tossed the sobbing blond female at Az.

Az grabbed her, barely stopping her from crashing into the ground. She clung to him, desperate. Hysterical.

"Should've left the humans to rot," the other shifter muttered as he sliced his claws down the brunette's face.

She shrieked in pain and fury.

Az shook off the blonde and jumped forward, but the shifter had already jerked back and tossed aside his prey like a piece of trash.

*All* of the shifters were pulling back now.

They dumped the wounded humans on the floor and laughed at their pain.

Az's heart thudded in his ears. The shifters were in his way. Deliberately lining up so that they stood between him and the winding hallway that led back to Jade.

*The explosion had come from that side of the building.*

"Divide and fucking conquer," Sam snarled as he maneuvered to Az's side. "The animals are smarter than we thought."

"Yeah," the shifter in the front said. His green eyes almost glowed and his fangs glinted as he grinned. "We are." Then the guy yanked open his jacket and pulled out a thin, white vial.

What the hell—

"Oh, shit," Sam snarled as he shoved at Az.

But that guy wasn't the only one with a vial. Two other shifters also pulled them out. They tossed the bottles at Az. At Sam. The glass shattered, and white powder spilled around them.

More vials hit him from the back. Other shifters who'd closed in. Others who'd been armed.

Ready. Too ready. He wasn't the only one who'd come packing a magical weapon.

He tried to step forward and found himself trapped. No big surprise.

Because he knew by the scent that it wasn't just powder that those bastards had tossed at him.

It was Angel Dust.

The one weapon powerful enough to hold a Fallen trapped in place—because it was a weapon forged from the wings of an angel.

"I guess the bitch's wings didn't go to waste after all." The green-eyed shifter smirked. "Brandt was right. You grind 'em up, and they really are as good as gold."

Az's hands slammed into an invisible wall.

"Now . . ." The shifter's fangs sharpened even more as he glanced around. "Let's torch this place."

# CHAPTER EIGHTEEN

Tanner's body slumped on top of hers. Choking on smoke, Jade shoved up, trying to push the guy to the side.

But in the next instant, Tanner was tossed away from her—well, tossed as far as he could go with those cuffs locking them. She tumbled after him, but was brought up short by the iron-hard grip on her waist.

She'd know that too-hard grip anywhere. Especially in her nightmares.

"Hello, Jade."

The flames were flickering around her. She choked down the ash and forced herself to look up and into Brandt's bright eyes. "H-how did you—"

"Plain, old-fashioned explosives." His rather boyish grin widened. "Humans do come up with some good inventions, you know."

Tanner groaned.

Brandt's smile vanished. He stared at the cuffs, then reached down and tried to yank them apart.

His shifter strength would have shredded normal cuffs, but in this case . . .

"N-not gonna work," Tanner managed as he shoved what looked like a dislocated shoulder back into place. "You're not . . . gettin' her away . . . from me."

Brandt's eyes narrowed. "Wanna bet, brother?"

*Az—where are you?* He must have heard the explosion. He'd be rushing in, any minute, with gun literally blazing. He'd better be. She just had to stall Brandt long enough for her angel to arrive.

"Th-they're *Other* proof," she whispered to Brandt. "You have to find the key to unlock them." She tried to look weak and defenseless. While he searched for the keys, Az could have more time to burst in and—

Brandt just laughed. "I don't have time for a fucking key." Claws burst from his fingertips. "I'll just cut off his damn hand."

He lifted up his claws and sliced down.

*"No!"* Jade screamed as she dove for Tanner. She slammed into him, and they rolled across the floor.

Rolled, until they came up against the still form of Cody.

The demon's neck was twisted. His eyes closed.

And the sickeningly sweet scent of flowers hung in the air around him.

Jade sucked in a fast breath. "Az!" She screamed his name as loud as she could. "Get that angel ass of yours in here!" *Hurry!*

Brandt's fingers sank into her hair, and he wrenched her head up. "The angel's not coming."

Her blood chilled. The screams from outside had nearly died away now. She hoped that meant all of the humans had gotten out.

As for Az . . .

"Did I ever tell you," Brandt asked as he tilted up her head and forced her to meet his gaze. "Just how my father killed my mother?"

She didn't want to know this story.

"He cut off her wings."

Like Brandt had cut off Marna's wings?

"Then he ground them up until they were the finest dust. It felt like silk on my fingers."

She swallowed the bile in her throat. He'd *touched* that dust?

His expression tightened as he stared at her. "I learned then that wings are full of magic. Full of power."

She did not like where this was going.

"When I saw the pretty little angel coming for you in the swamp," he said, "I knew I had to get her wings. I just couldn't let that power go to waste."

It felt like he was about to rip her hair right out of her head. "Let me go," she managed.

But he didn't. Not even when Tanner lunged up at him. Brandt just drove his fist into Tanner's jaw and the shifter fell back.

"That fine powder . . . some call it Angel Dust. It can kill demons, and it can trap angels."

*No.*

His lips kicked up in a grin, and she knew that Brandt was enjoying her fear.

"If you surround them with the dust, angels can't move. They're trapped in a prison, one made of their own power." His grin slipped away and shadows chased into his eyes. "My father trapped my mother in the dust. Then he used his claws to cut out her heart." He leaned toward her and pressed a kiss to her cheek. "Just like I'll cut out your Fallen's heart."

Fear was choking her. *Not Az.*

"Unless you come with me now." He eased away from her. "Come with me, and I won't take his heart tonight."

He could be bluffing. Totally bullshitting about the Angel Dust.

But his eyes told her he wasn't. And if Az had been free, he would have been in that room by now. He would have come to help her.

"D-don't . . ." She made sure her voice held a weak, trembly edge. Brandt always felt stronger when she was weak. She wanted the guy to think he was in control. Right until the moment she ripped that control away from him. "Don't hurt Az."

She caught the faint hardening of his eyes and knew she'd made a mistake. He always hurt those she cared about.

Jade reached over Tanner's body and fumbled in his pockets. He groaned beneath her, and his eyes began to open. "Jade?"

Her fingers curled around the key.

"Stay down," she whispered, but she knew Brandt would hear. With his shifter ears, there'd be no way for him to miss her order.

She pulled back. Her hands were shaking as she unlocked the cuff on her wrist. She dropped the key onto the floor.

Brandt caught her arm and yanked her away from Tanner. His gaze darted between them.

"Don't," Jade said, voice hardening despite her efforts to play weak.

But Brandt just smiled. "Death should have come for him long before." His claws sliced down as Jade yelled and grabbed at his arms.

Tanner lunged up in the same instant. His hands caught Brandt's wrists, and he held those razor-sharp claws away from his face.

Fury beat at Jade. Brandt had taken so much from her. Too much. "No more," she gritted and the fire seemed to burn beneath her skin. Burn, *burn* . . . Her fingers heated where she touched Brandt.

He slowly turned his head to look at her.

She lifted her hands and stumbled back. They were so hot they burned. *I'm burning.* "No. More!" She yelled and a ball of fire shot from her fingers—and flew right at Brandt. The fire slammed into his chest and the scent of burning flesh stung her nose.

He fell down, flames eating at his flesh, screaming.

She grabbed for Tanner and hauled him to his feet. "Get Cody!" That demon had better be alive. He'd saved her before, and now they'd damn well save him.

Tanner nodded and hurried toward his brother. The cuff banged against his wrist as he lifted Cody and rushed for the door.

Jade followed on their heels, moving as quickly as she could—

"No," Brandt's growl. His fingers, blistered, singed, curled around her wrist, and she felt the lick of heat scorch her from his touch. "You're not getting away from me that easily."

Body tensing, Tanner glanced back at her.

"Get him out of here!" She yelled at Tanner. She could summon more fire. She could attack Brandt again. Dammit, she wouldn't be afraid.

Not anymore.

Tanner slipped away with Cody.

*At least they're safe.*

Brandt yanked her against his chest. The fire had melted away his shirt and the flames had charred his flesh.

But—but that flesh was healing before her eyes.

"Aren't you full of surprises?" he murmured as he bent his head toward hers. His breath, carrying the scent of ash, blew lightly over her face. "Since when can my human play so well with fire?"

"Since someone was willing to risk his life for me. Since he *gave* me life." And didn't just try to destroy everything she had.

The faint lines around Brandt's eyes tightened. "You think he's so damn special, don't you? But I know what he's done. I followed the blood. He's *hurt* you."

"No." Her chin lifted. "Never him. He wouldn't. Az isn't like—"

He yanked her up against him, and her toes left the floor. "Me?" Brandt finished, the word a savage snarl.

She nodded.

"So *I'm* the fucking bastard?"

Yeah, he was.

Brandt shook his head as if denying something to himself. To her? "You loved me once."

This was it. The moment that she'd known would come. Jade stared him in the eyes, refused to let the fear take her, and said the words she knew would break him. "And now I love him."

She expected an eruption of rage. An attack. Jade would take the pain. It would buy Tanner and Cody the time to flee. Buy Az time to get out of that Angel Dust trap.

But Brandt didn't erupt. He pressed his forehead against hers. "That's a mistake." His lips feathered over hers. Gentleness that she knew cloaked a killing rage. She could feel his fury, feel it even as—

He slammed her head into the nearest wall.

"You can't love a dead man." His whisper followed her into the darkness.

Flames danced around Az. Bright, dark, gold, and red. The fire was so hot that it scorched his skin.

"I can't believe this is happening again," Sam snarled from the trap just beside Az. "This is it—my next club will damn well be fireproof, no matter how many witches I have to hire to enchant the place."

The sprinklers installed in the ceiling of Sunrise had shot on moments before, but they couldn't stop the blaze. Especially since the fire just flared higher and higher because the shifters were pouring liquor everywhere. Soaking the place and growling in triumph when the flames burned brighter.

Those flames were rushing across the wooden floor toward Az now.

So close, but not close enough. Not yet.

*Come closer.*

Through the smoke and fire, he caught sight of Tanner's tall form. The shifter was carrying something—someone? Someone who wasn't moving.

"Jade!" Her name burst from his lips, but Tanner didn't slow down. The shifter swiped out at two attackers who lunged for him, and then he raced outside, away from the flames.

"I'm sorry, Azrael." Bastion's voice came from beside him and barely rose over the crackle of the fire.

"Don't be sorry," Az snapped right back at him. This wasn't the end for him. "Just get ready to collect all the souls I'm about to send your way."

Then he saw her. Brandt walked right through the fire, and he had Jade held tightly in his arms. Brandt's gaze met Az's.

*No.* For an instant, it seemed that even the flames stilled.

"I have to do it," Bastion's voice was tense. "You know there's no choice."

Az's fist slammed into the magical trap. "Get me out of here, Bastion!"

Sam was dead quiet next to him.

The flames burned higher.

Brandt stalked toward him. Jade's eyes were closed, and her head sagged against his chest.

*Bastard. I will rip you apart.*

Brandt lifted Jade and positioned her so that she hung over his right shoulder. "I had wanted her to watch . . ." The shifter began.

"And I want you to beg for death." *Death's ready for you.*

"But I guess we don't always get what we want." Brandt's claws burst from his fingertips. He lifted his hand.

And slammed right against the invisible wall of the cage that had been forged by Angel Dust.

"Dumb asshole," Sam's voice called out. "You're angel, too. It keeps us in, and you can't cross it, not unless you break the line."

Brandt's gaze dropped to the fine line of dust on the floor. When he looked back up, Az had the gun in his hand. He aimed it right at Brandt's face. "I'm betting these bullets can get out though," Az said. He bet they could get out and kill Brandt where he stood.

Brandt didn't hesitate. In a flash, he hauled Jade in front of him.

Her eyes opened slowly, and, with growing fear, she stared down the barrel of the gun that Az had pointed right at her.

"Go ahead," Brandt taunted him. "Kill me, but kill her, too."

Bastion had vanished. The other panther shifters raced for the door. The flames just grew bigger and hotter with every moment that passed.

"Az . . ." He saw her lips move but no sound slipped from Jade's mouth. Her gaze held his. So deep, so intense.

He lowered the gun.

Brandt hauled her back. The grip he had around her throat had his claws just an inch from her flesh.

"Don't hurt her," Az ordered, voice booming.

But Brandt didn't answer.

"Dammit, *don't hurt her*!"

"I wasn't just using you, Az." Jade's words were being swallowed by the flames. He had to fight to hear her as she said, "I was loving you . . ."

Then the flames flared higher. Brandt took her away.

"I am sorry," Bastion's whisper filled his ears as the angel appeared once more.

Now Az knew just why the angel was apologizing.

"*No!*" Az clawed at the invisible wall, but it wouldn't give. The magic was too strong. The fire burned.

And Jade was gone.

★　★　★

The shifters had split, running away into the darkness as soon as they escaped the growing inferno that was Sunrise.

Brandt moved quickly with Jade and her body bounced and ached with each step since she was tossed over his shoulder like a damn sack. Snarling, Jade kicked out at him. Her nails dug into his back.

He didn't slow down.

They rounded the corner. Sirens wailed in the distance. Those fire trucks damn well needed to hurry.

"Fire won't . . . kill him," she managed to grit out. Her hair dangled over her face as all the blood rushed to her head. "He'll come after you." Flames wouldn't stop Az for long.

"I'm rather counting on that."

Cocky bastard.

Another turn. This time, she recognized the street. Hard not to recognize Bourbon Street. Partygoers strolled around, laughing, and beads crunched beneath Brandt's boots as he stalked forward.

"Help me!" Jade screamed through the fall of her hair.

She managed to temporarily shove that hair out of her way and saw two men glance her way. Oh, come on, even during Mardi Gras, it wasn't cool to just let some asshole run away with a struggling woman over his shoulder.

The guys realized that. She heard the thud of their footsteps running toward.

"Hey, man, let her go—"

Brandt growled at them, a deep, inhuman growl. "Stay away or die." She had no doubt that he was flashing fangs.

But the guys didn't back away.

"Look, freak," one snarled right back, "let that lady—"

Brandt tossed him away with one hand.

The other guy's feet beat a hasty retreat.

Brandt dropped her to the ground. As she scrambled to

her knees, he stared down at her with eyes that glowed with his fury—and with the power of the beast inside him. "Call for help again, and I'll cut the head off the first dumb ass-hole who comes to your rescue."

He would.

Brandt grabbed her arm. "Let's go, baby."

The flames licked their way across the floor, slowly destroying everything in their path. Too slowly.

Sam alternately snarled and swore as the heat and smoke thickened in the room.

Az didn't move. Not now. He just waited. The flames only had to come a bit closer.

Just a bit.

The fire crackled over the edges of the Angel Dust. The dust ignited, flaring in a blue-white flame.

And the prison was broken.

Az lunged from the trap and shoved out his hands. The flames lanced his skin, but he ignored the fire and pushed out with his own power. A bitter wind swept through Sunrise, howling like a wolf, and the flames died in an instant.

Slowly, his head turned to the right. Toward the door that Brandt had used when he took Jade away.

Bastion was gone. The angel had better not be near her.

Az took a step forward.

"Uh, yeah, *brother,*" Sam's voice stopped him. "Before you head out to kick ass and save the day, do you think you can do me a favor and *get me the hell out of here?*"

He glanced back. Sam stood with his arms crossed over his chest and managed to look both pissed and bored.

Az shook his head. "You'll just try to stop me."

Sam's jaw dropped. "What?"

"It's my fight." He took a breath. Tasted ash and death. His eyes closed. "Good-bye, Sam."

His brother screamed his name, but it was too late. Az used his enhanced speed to rush out of the bar and to whip right past the dazed-looking firefighters who stared up at the smoldering scene.

He raced forward two blocks and only stopped when he was sure no humans were around. *"Bastion!"* The angel had better heed his summons. "Get down here, *now*!" Az might have been kicked out of heaven, but he still possessed plenty of power.

He'd ruled the Death Angels, and even those still dwelling in heaven knew to fear him.

Wind blew lightly against his face. Not wind—air stirred by wings. Bastion's form appeared before him. No expression was on the angel's face.

"Where is she?" Az demanded.

Bastion gazed silently back at him.

"If she's in the damn book of death . . ." His book—once, he'd been the one to note the names and the passages of lives. But those names hadn't mattered to him. Collecting souls had been his duty. *Jade* mattered. "If Jade's in that book, then that means someone is keeping track of her pretty much twenty-four seven."

The angel didn't deny or confirm that.

Az grabbed Bastion and shoved him against the alley's brick wall. He yanked out his weapon and put the gun to Bastion's heart. "It's loaded with brimstone. I won't shoot your stomach this time. I'll shoot you right in the heart."

Bastion swallowed. "No, you won't. You won't shoot at all."

Testing him? The guy should know better.

"You . . . of all the angels . . . you understand duty." Bastion didn't struggle in his hold. Just stood there as the barrel of the gun dug into his chest. "You know what must be done."

Az's finger tightened on the trigger. "Tell me where she is or get ready to say good-bye to heaven."

Bastion shook his head and held his ground. "It's . . . you I'm protecting. You need to let her go."

Gravel crunched behind them. "I've got his scent," Tanner said. "Forget the angel, I can lead you to Brandt."

Az tensed. "What about Cody?" He knew the form that Tanner had carried out of Sunrise must have been the demon doctor.

"He'll make it." Though Tanner didn't sound so confident. "Demons can heal from just about anything."

Az stared into Bastion's gaze. "If I let you go, you'll try to take her."

"No." Bastion shook his head. "My touch doesn't work on her anymore, remember? I won't be the angel who takes her life. The one who loves her will be."

What? He frowned at the angel, lost. Then understanding sank in, understanding and horror.

He spun away. "Get me to her, *now*," he barked at Tanner.

Tanner, fangs bared, nodded.

As they rushed away, Az could feel his control ripping. He had to get to Jade before it was too late.

*I was loving you.*

And he . . . had he been loving her?

*Hold on, Jade. Hold. On.*

Brandt took her to the cemetery. The rest of his shifters appeared from behind the heavy, white tombs, coming out like ghosts as they surrounded her.

The broken tomb that Az had fallen on so long before lay in pieces just feet from them all.

"This is where he dies," Brandt said. "Heather told me about this place . . . how he fell." His lips curled as he glanced up at the starlit sky. "It seems only fitting that I send him to hell at this spot."

She rubbed her arms. A chill was in the air, beating down on her. "He's stronger than you are."

Brandt's smirk said that he doubted that. "I kicked his ass once before."

"Only because he didn't know what you *were* then." Az hadn't been prepared for Brandt's strength.

Brandt's gaze cut to her. "And just what am I?"

*Evil.* If only she'd seen it from the beginning. "Half angel, half beast."

The others were transforming around them. Changing with the pop and snap of bones as the moon shone down on them.

Brandt held up his hand and stared at the claws that burst from his fingertips. "I always thought it was a curse, having her blood in me."

She edged away from him.

"My father said it made me weak. Made me too soft-hearted on our prey."

"Yeah, well, your father was a dick." She needed to find a weapon. Her gaze darted around the area. Those panthers would be done with their shift soon. She needed to attack before then. They were always at their weakest during those moments of transformation.

*There.*

One of the tombs had been separated from the others by an old-fashioned, wrought-iron fence.

"My father was the most vicious shifter I've ever seen." Brandt rolled his shoulders. "But you put him in the ground for me."

She stumbled toward the fence, deliberately tripping so that her hands had to fly out and catch onto the iron for support. Slowly, she turned toward him. Her hands locked around one of the posts. "I didn't do that for you. He was trying to rape me. I killed him *for me*."

"Fair enough." A pause. Brandt's head tilted to the right as he studied her. "I killed your parents *for me*."

Bile rose in her throat and her hand tightened around the fence post. Jade kept her eyes on Brandt even as she pulled on that post. She thought she heard the iron groan, and it seemed to bend in her hand.

*Oh, please, angel blood, don't fail me now.* Because that blood seemed to be giving her the strength she needed to get this makeshift weapon.

"I knew you'd go back to them eventually. Once you realized what I was . . ." He lifted his hands, and the moonlight glinted off his claws. "You'd run away like a scared little human."

Because she had been a scared little human. What was so wrong with that? A seventeen-year-old, scared girl.

"I had to make sure you had no one to run to. So I killed them." He shrugged. "I made it quick, though, if that makes you feel better."

Sick freak. "You're as crazy as your father was!"

He lunged at her and wrapped his hands around her throat. "No," his voice was lethally soft. "I'm not."

She didn't speak. Mostly because she couldn't. Brandt was crushing her windpipe.

He leaned his forehead against hers. He'd done that move often in the old days, back when they'd first started dating. Pressed his forehead against hers. A gentle, almost affectionate gesture. Only back then, he hadn't been choking her when he leaned in so close.

"I don't want to be like this," Brandt whispered so softly she almost didn't hear him. "But I just can't stop myself." He sounded . . . lost.

And, for one instant, he was the boy she'd met. The boy

with the sad eyes and wistful smile. The boy who watched her like he was watching a rainbow.

The boy she'd loved.

Not the monster she feared.

Except the boy was strangling her. Jade's left hand pulled away from the fence, and she clawed at his hold on her throat.

Brandt blinked and the past faded from his eyes even as his hands fell away from her. "We're going to start fresh. Get the hell away from the South and do things right."

She sucked in a couple of deep gulps of air. "It's . . . too late for that." Surely he knew that. "I don't love you, Brandt."

He stiffened.

Part of the fence gave way but she didn't lift it up. Not yet.

"You think you love him?" Disgust tightened his face.

"Yes." She just wished that she'd told Az sooner. She'd been afraid to trust anyone else after Brandt. After being so blind, Jade had been terrified she'd make another mistake with a man.

But Az wasn't just any man. He wasn't a man, period.

Her Fallen. Her lover.

*Hers.*

"How will you love him when he's dead?"

She shook her head. "He's not dying." A smile curved her lips. She'd been waiting for this moment ever since she'd stood over her parents' graves. "You are." She swung up with the chunk of broken iron and slammed it into the side of his head. There was a loud thud, and he went down.

She raised the iron over her head. She'd broken off the top of the fence, so the sharp point would be perfect for driving right into his heart. "Tell your dad I said hi—"

The panthers were snarling.

Jade froze, then looked up.

Oh, hell. They'd finished their shift from men to beasts.

The panther pack leapt into the air and attacked.

# CHAPTER NINETEEN

Before the panthers' claws could tear into her skin, he was there.

Az appeared right in front of her, in front of them, and he wrapped his arms around her. "Close your eyes," he told her.

She did, but she felt the force of the heat on her skin and knew that Az had used his power to burn and destroy.

The whimpers of the panthers filled her ears—whimpers from the beasts and screams from the men as they transformed.

Her feet left the earth and when they touched down again, she was a good ten feet away from the flames sputtering on the ground. The shifters were still alive, but out of commission.

And Brandt—

Where was he?

"Are you okay?" Az's hold on her arms was too tight. "Did he hurt you?"

She still had the iron in her hands. "No." Not any pain worth mentioning. Her throat would heal. Az had arrived just in time.

She was so glad to see him that tears wanted to fill her eyes.

The injured shifters began to edge away. "Brandt." She licked her lips and blinked away the tears. Now wasn't the time to get weak. "He was just here!"

"My bastard brother ran as soon as the fire started." Jade jerked towards the sound of Tanner's voice. He'd just grabbed a fleeing shifter and knocked him back on the ground. "Don't worry, I got his stench." He pointed toward a small space between the tombs on the right. "That way."

Az nodded. "Stay here." In the next second, before she could even get the breath to argue, he was gone, racing away after Brandt's trail.

And leaving her behind.

Rage pumped inside of Az as he streaked through the cemetery. That bastard had dared to touch Jade again. And he'd let his pack of sadistic shifters get killing close to her.

No more.

Az pushed ahead even faster. A few quick shots from his gun, and this would all be over. Jade would be free. She wouldn't have to spend her days looking over her shoulder and wondering when her psycho ex would pounce.

She could have a life again.

*A life with me.*

Because if she'd have him, he wanted to spend all of his days with her. Heaven could wait. He'd found something he wanted more.

Jade.

To him, she was . . . everything.

He'd make her happy. Get her to laugh. To smile not just with her beautiful mouth, but with her eyes.

She'd live again.

He paused at the heavy stone wall that marked the edge of the cemetery. Had Brandt left the cemetery? Run back into the city? Where had he—

"There's something you need to see."

Az spun at the voice and came face-to-face with Mateo. Not exactly the asshole he'd wanted to see. "Out of my way," he growled. The witch had betrayed him once already.

He didn't intend to give the guy a second chance to screw him over.

"I can show you the way," Mateo said, eyes dark. "You just have to trust me."

He wouldn't trust that guy any day.

Mateo pointed to the right. "Come here, and see . . ."

Hell. Az could smell blood. He surged forward, heading down the path Mateo indicated.

He didn't look back, and he didn't see Mateo's slow smile.

Jade sucked in deep gulps of air and stared after Az. Really? He wanted her to just . . . *stay there?*

It sucked being human. Or, half human—or whatever the hell she was these days. Dammit, she—

Tanner took off toward the left, running as fast as he could. Jade blinked. The left? Now why would he run that way?

*I got his stench.* Those had been Tanner's words, and Tanner had sent Az running into the opposite direction.

Why?

*Because Tanner wants to be the one to take out his brother.*

Oh, hell. She raced to the left and followed him. Tanner was overmatched in this fight. He couldn't defeat Brandt, not when the guy had the strength of an angel on his side.

The graves whipped by her. Or rather, she whipped by them. Thick and white, the tombs seemed to reek of the dead. A few candles flickered near the ground, silent offerings to the spirits, promises to a long-gone voodoo queen.

*"You son of a bitch!"*

Jade rushed toward that yell. A turn to the left. To the right. The graveyard was a twisted maze and—

And Tanner had Brandt pinned against a tomb.

"It ends tonight," Tanner growled at him. "You don't get to hurt anyone else."

But Brandt just laughed. And he drove his claws into Tanner's stomach. "You never could stop me."

*"Tanner!"* The horrified cry burst from her.

"W-watch me . . ." Tanner managed and he sliced his own claws right across Brandt's throat. Brandt's blood flew out, soaking him, and Brandt didn't even have a chance to scream.

Brandt's gaze turned to her. His eyes widened. He smiled.

Tanner yanked away from him, and Brandt's claws slid from his chest with a wet slosh of sound.

Brandt fell face-first onto the ground.

Jade stared down at him, stunned, as her breath heaved out.

Slowly, Tanner turned toward her. "I d-did . . . i-it . . ." His shirt was soaked with blood. His skin ashen. His whole body was shaking.

Jade rushed to him. She grabbed Tanner as his knees buckled and eased him to the ground. "You have to shift," she told him, voice desperate. Her gaze flew over his wounds. They were bad. Brandt had ripped right through him. Ripped things *out* of him. "Shift *now*." Jade forced steel into her order.

His lips were paler than the moon. A ripple shook his body and fur burst out on his arms, only to vanish a moment later.

She realized that Tanner wasn't strong enough to shift. And if he wasn't strong enough, he'd die in her arms.

She ignored the scent of flowers. The scent was deepening around her. The scent . . . it wasn't from an Angel of Death. Just flowers from the graves. Nothing more.

Nothing . . .

Tanner's claws retracted.

"You don't get to die like this!" She snapped and slammed her palm into his chest. "You don't get to—"

Hands grabbed her from behind. Strong hands. Hands that knew too well how to hurt.

Brandt wasn't done yet. Or maybe the devil just hadn't wanted him. "Tanner never was as strong as me," he whispered into her ear.

Her breath choked out as horror and fear swamped her.

"No." Az's voice. Cool and lethal and cutting right through the night. Cutting through her fear and giving her hope. "But I am," Az promised.

Jade's head whipped up. Az stood before them, just inside the gateway of tombs.

Damn that man looked sexy. Strong. Determined. Pissed. He lifted his gun. "Let her go."

*Brimstone bullets, asshole. Choke on them.* If she hadn't been trapped against said asshole, she would have smiled.

"You're not going to shoot her." Brandt was mocking now. Something wet slipped down her shoulder, and she was pretty sure that it was his blood.

Jade twisted and turned to look at Brandt. Only the thinnest cut remained from the torn hole that had been his throat. *Damn—that was some fast healing.* But his clothes were soaked red and now so were hers.

Brandt met her gaze. His eyes were glowing with his rage. "You did this," he told her. "You should've just been happy with me."

"And you should have left my parents alone, you sick freak." Her head whipped forward. She stared right at Az. "Shoot."

Brandt laughed. "He won't—"

"This is the best chance we have, Az. *Shoot!*" She yelled.

But Az wasn't firing. She could see the struggle on his face. He didn't want to hurt her, but she was all for taking a bullet or two if it meant they could get Brandt out of commission. "Kill him, just kill—"

*Snap.*

She didn't feel any pain, but, suddenly, Jade's body was

falling. She slammed into the earth. She didn't feel that either. She couldn't get her fingers to move. Her legs were numb and her heart . . .

Thunder rumbled. Once. Twice. Someone was screaming. Yelling.

Wait, that wasn't thunder. *Gunshots.* Az had fired. He'd fired—and Brandt's body crashed onto the ground beside her. His face was inches away. Blood trickled from his mouth. Brandt's eyes were wide open—and empty.

Dead.

Jade wanted to turn away from that empty stare, but she couldn't move. And why was she so cold?

*"Jade!"* Her name was a roar. But panthers roared, not angels, and that was Az's voice, wasn't it? "Don't do this!"

Do what? She'd just fallen. She'd be fine in a few minutes. Brandt was dead. They'd all be fine now. Better than fine. She could live again.

*"Don't!"*

Strange. That word had been choked and so full of pain. She didn't want Az in pain. Had he been hurt? Had Brandt managed to attack him before Az fired his gun?

She tried once more to turn her head and look at him, but couldn't move. Everything was getting dark. Perhaps the moon had gone behind some rain clouds.

The light would come back soon. She'd figure out what was happening in a few moments.

Her heartbeat seemed so weak in her ears.

*The light would come back soon.*

But then the whole world vanished.

The bastard had broken Jade's neck. One hard snap of his hands, and Brandt had taken her life away.

Brandt's chest was full of brimstone, and he lay dead on the ground, but *he'd taken her away.*

Bones snapped and popped behind him. Tanner. Az didn't glance at the shifter. He couldn't.

He bent his head toward Jade's. Her eyes were open. "Sweetheart, it's going to be—"

*Empty.* Her eyes were empty.

Az grabbed her and yanked Jade up into his arms. He held her body against his chest. How could she already feel so cold? Jade should be warm. Her silken skin should singe him with a touch.

Not ice. Not her. She'd only been cold once before, when death had come too close to taking her.

Her head hung limply, and his heart stopped. "Jade, dammit, come back!" A desperate order. A painful plea.

She wasn't moving.

He bit into his wrist. Forced his blood into her mouth. His blood had helped her once. It would help again. She'd be okay, she'd be—

"You know it doesn't work like that." Sam's voice. Quiet. Sad. He didn't even know how Sam had gotten there, and he didn't care.

There was only one thing he cared about. One person. *Her.* "Tell me how to bring Jade back." His hand smoothed over her dark hair. Had he ever told her how beautiful her hair was? Had he ever told her that she was beautiful?

*You are, Jade. The most beautiful thing I've ever seen. Better than even the golden streets in heaven.*

"I . . . don't know how to bring her back."

"Then get me someone who fucking does!" Rage beat at him. A constant scream echoed in his head. She'd been looking at him when she fell. When that asshole had snapped her neck, she'd been looking right at him and begging him to shoot.

He hadn't. "I didn't want to hurt her." Az's lips feathered over Jade's cold cheek.

"I know." Sam's hand closed around his shoulder. "She's not hurting anymore."

Az stiffened. "Bring her back." A demand. His control was splintering. He could feel it inside. A darkness opening up, yawning, swallowing everything.

Sam didn't move his hand. "I can't. I don't have that kind of power."

He couldn't take his eyes off her. His Jade. Had he ever told her that he'd been . . . happy . . . when she was near? That he'd started to dream when he slept. He'd never dreamed before. Until her.

All of his dreams were of her.

His hands were shaking. "Seline came back to you. She died." He knew. He'd been there. "You got her back."

"Seline was half-angel." Sam's voice was soft, still with that sad, sympathetic edge that was tearing into Az. "Your Jade . . . she isn't built to come back. Even with the blood you gave her, she's human at heart."

His blood had smeared on her cheek. "Summon Mateo." The witch was close by. He wouldn't have been able to flee this quickly.

Sam's fingers tightened. "He can't help you."

"Someone had better." He wasn't letting her go. Az rose, holding her close in his arms. She was so still. *"Fucking. Summon. Mateo!"* He roared the words, and the tombs around him cracked. Skeletons fell onto the ground as the earth buckled beneath him. "Witch, get back here!"

He turned and found Tanner standing, weak, pale, but alive. Why was he alive, when Jade wasn't? He hadn't seen a Death Angel, would have fought the bastard if he had, but he'd seen *no* signs of dark wings.

She shouldn't be dead. *There'd been no Death Angel.*

But Jade was still and quiet in his arms. Her heart didn't beat. No air swept into her lungs.

Had the angel just come and claimed her too swiftly? Had

he been so blinded by his grief that he'd missed that desperate moment? The scent of flowers was so strong in this wretched place. So many angels had been there. *Were still there?*

Tanner was alive. Az's rage focused on the shifter who'd sent him on the wrong path. Why did Tanner still live? *Why?*

Why was anyone alive? If Jade couldn't live . . .

Deep crevices opened beneath his feet. More tombs shattered.

"You had her for a little while. That will have to be enough," Sam said as he backed away a few steps. His face was tight, his eyes staring at Az with—fear?

*He should be afraid. Everyone should.* Az wasn't going to let her be taken from him.

The rage and grief tore through him. *Brandt had broken her beautiful neck. In one, fast, brutal instant, Brandt took her from me.* Az swallowed and tasted hate. "Is the time you have with Seline . . . *enough*?"

His brother flinched. "No."

"Then get me that crossroads spirit." The fury was breaking through. Fire burst beside him, racing right over the graves and scorching the ground. He tilted back his head and glared up at the starlight sky. *"Bastion!"*

"You can't call back the dead." This came from Tanner. Az pinned him with a scathing stare. The shifter swallowed and straightened his shoulders. "Even you aren't that strong. It hurts, I know, but you have to let her go."

He didn't want to let her go. "I . . . need her." She was so slight in his arms.

Why were his cheeks wet?

His gaze fell to her once more. "I-I love her." Love. A human emotion. But a human had slipped into his heart. Now that human was breaking his heart.

Was this his true punishment? For all the sins he had committed, was this the end he'd been fated to receive?

*Don't take her. Please.*

She should live. Be happy. Be free.

*You aren't that strong.* Tanner's words echoed in his ears. The shifter was right. He wasn't strong. Without Jade, he was weak.

The angels should have known that. They should have taken better care . . .

Wind whipped against his cheeks. The scent of flowers teased his nose. The angel had heeded his call. Az kept his eyes on Seline and simply said, "Give her back."

"I tried to tell you what was coming." No emotion shadowed Bastion's voice. "I am sorry, Azrael. But this was meant to be."

The words drifted in and out of his head. Jade's face had bleached of color and raindrops began to fall on her face. Rain, from a cloudless sky. But thunder was rumbling. Lightning flashing across the heavens.

Power leaked from him. Holding her with one arm, he raised his gun and aimed it at Bastion. He still had two bullets left in the chamber. "Bring her back or see what it's like to die." His head pounded and the scream echoing in his mind just wouldn't end. That scream—it was Jade's voice. Jade calling his name, over and over. She wanted him to help her.

Jade.

Flashes flew through his mind, images of her.

*Jade . . . smiling at him.*

*Kissing him.*

*I . . . wasn't using you, Az. I was loving you.*

And he'd been loving her, but he'd just been too blind and foolish to realize it sooner.

"I can't," Bastion said, almost sounding regretful. "It's too late. She's gone—"

The screams in his mind grew louder. *Jade is calling me.* Az fired. The bullet burned right through Bastion's chest. "If she's dead, then so are you."

A howling filled his ears, blending with the chaos of the screams. The fires around him flared higher, hotter, destroying everything in sight.

*"Azrael!"* Sam's horrified yell tore through the blaze. "What have you done?"

Smoke drifted from the hole in Bastion's chest. "He took her." Az knew he had. Bastion had been close the whole time. And when Jade's neck had broken . . . "He took her from me—took her, when I'd just found her!" A woman who could love the darkest of the angels.

Gone.

Sam stood behind the line of blazing fire. "You're out of control. You need to—"

Az aimed the gun at him. "I told you to summon the witch." Angels couldn't help him. Rule followers. But the witch . . . Mateo followed no one's rules. He'd cheat death.

For the right price.

Sam frowned at the gun. "So now you'd shoot me?"

No. Yes. He couldn't think. His heart was gone. Ripped from his chest. Jade's scent—*strawberries*—surrounded him and the fire's heat told him that only hell waited for him. He wouldn't see Jade again when he left this earth. He'd never see her again.

"The world doesn't go on without her," he gritted out. Tanner screamed as the fire caught him and burned his flesh. *"It doesn't."*

Swearing, Sam leapt through the flames. He grabbed for the gun.

Az tried to yank the weapon back. He wasn't letting go of it. He wasn't letting go of Jade.

*Never let go.*

The gun fired. He was staring straight into Sam's eyes. He saw the shock in his brother's gaze. The flash of pain.

Then he saw the whisper of life leaving as Sam's spirit was pulled from his body.

Sam fell to the ground, dead at his feet.

*One brother, killing another . . .*

The ground split around him. No longer small crevices, but deep, giant fissures that seemed to stretch all the way to hell.

A prophecy had been made once. *When one brother kills another . . . hell comes.*

Jade's scent faded until he could only smell brimstone. And the screams in his mind had finally stopped. Now he could hear laughter. Whispers.

*Hell comes.*

He dropped the gun. Held her cold body even tighter. *"Mateo!"* The witch would appear. The witch would save her.

Or . . . at least . . . *kill me.*

Because the chains that had always held him in check were broken and only fury raged within him.

*"Mateo!"*

Jade was dead. He'd destroyed his brother, and if Mateo couldn't kill him . . . Az was afraid he'd destroy the world. *"Mateo!"*

"I'm right here," the witch said as he shook Az. "Look at me, Fallen. *Look.*"

Az realized he was kneeling on the ground. His whole body shook, and sweat soaked his skin. He glanced up, and found Mateo staring down at him.

"Bring her back," he whispered, his voice broken.

Mateo sighed. "She's not gone yet."

In an instant, Az was on his feet. But he stumbled, his knees weak, and he shoved his hand out—

And touched blood.

He turned his head slowly and stared at the wall of the crypt beside him. The blood looked black in the moonlight, but he knew what it was. Blood covered the side of the crypt, twisting and turning in a series of ancient symbols.

A broken mirror lay shattered at his feet, and his heart was still trying to jump out of his chest.

"It's always been thought that a Fallen Angel would be the one to open the gateway to hell. At least, that's what my sources downstairs told me." Mateo's voice was carefully emotionless.

Az swallowed and tasted ash. "Where is Jade?"

"Right this second? She's racing through the cemetery on the far left side, running after Tanner and Brandt."

What? "She's . . . not dead?"

"Not yet."

Az turned away.

"Did you learn anything?" Mateo's sharp voice stopped him. "Or do you not even realize what the hell just happened here?"

*I lost everything.*

"I gave you a very special gift, Fallen. I used my own blood and my own power to show you what *could* be if you chose wrong tonight."

What could be . . . Jade dying. Tanner burning. Him killing Sam.

"You need her. I get that." And the witch was suddenly before him. "But everybody else needs you to fucking hold it together. Don't let that rage eating through your gut break free." Mateo's eyes glittered. "Make the right choice. Change fate. Do you hear me, Fallen?"

*Fate can't be changed.* All angels knew that.

And he realized he'd just whispered the words by rote.

"Then I guess the angels are wrong. Or maybe those precious rules have changed." Mateo glanced up at the sky. "Maybe someone wants them to change." His gaze fell back on Az. "What do you want?"

Jade. Alive. Happy.

"I let you into her mind with that vision. You know what she wants."

She'd begged him to shoot. But he'd been too afraid of hurting her.

"You know what *you* desire." Mateo sighed. "Now let's see just what happens . . ."

Az still had the gun. Still had the chance to save her.

To save them all.

"I'm not a monster," he whispered. No matter what he'd seen or . . . *done* in those dark images. He wasn't . . .

"Prove it."

He would. Or he'd die trying.

*I am not a monster.* And he wouldn't let the darkness in him break free. He wouldn't hurt those he loved.

He'd sacrifice himself first.

# CHAPTER TWENTY

Az raced around the graves. He turned to the left. His body shook and his heart seemed to burst through his chest.

He pushed forward with a furious blast of speed and saw them. Brandt—with his hands wrapped around Jade's struggling body. The bastard's claws were out. Killing close.

But it hadn't been the claws that killed her in Az's vision.

Tanner was on the ground, covered in blood, and not moving. But the shifter wasn't dead. Not yet.

No one was.

*Not. Yet.*

Az froze and stared at Jade. So beautiful. His frantic heartbeat began to slow. The shaking left his hands.

The center of his focus narrowed just to her. Brandt had his mouth close to Jade's ear and Az heard him growl, "He never was as powerful as me."

*My cue.* Az took a deep breath. *She won't die.* "No," Az said quietly, and Jade's desperate gaze flew to his. "But I am." He looked away from Jade and held Brandt's blazing stare.

*You're dying tonight.*

Az lifted the gun and pointed it at Brandt. "Let her go."

Brandt's eyes narrowed, and he made no move to free Jade. "You're not going to shoot her." Brandt's voice mocked him as Jade twisted and shoved against her captor.

Such a fighter. She was the strongest woman he'd met. Human or *Other*. She made him want to be stronger.

To be better.

*I will be.* He wouldn't be the monster from the vision. He'd be the man that she needed him to be.

Brandt held her easily in his grasp. "You did this," he told her, voice snarling. "You should've just been happy with me."

*Never would have happened, bastard.*

Jade strained against him. "And you should have left my parents alone, you sick freak." Her head turned back to Az. Her eyes held his. So many emotions shone in her stare. Determination. Love. Fury. No fear as she said, "Shoot."

Brandt laughed. "He won't—"

Because Az didn't want to hurt her. He wanted to protect her. To keep her safe and keep her happy.

But he'd watched this scene before, and he was damn well getting a different ending. "I love you," he told her, the words halting.

Her lips parted in surprise. "Wh—"

He would try to hurt her as little as possible. With his angel blood in her, he wasn't sure what the bullet would do to her. *I'm sorry, Jade.*

Aiming carefully, Az fired. The bullet tore through Jade's shoulder, ripping past flesh and muscle. She didn't cry out, just watched him with eyes that saw straight into his soul.

The bullet drove through her—and sank into Brandt's chest. Brandt staggered back, releasing Jade.

She fell to her knees. "Thank you," she whispered as blood and a sliver of smoke spilled from her wound.

Brandt hadn't fallen to the ground. He was still on his feet and staring in shock at Az.

*Guess I missed his heart.* But he hadn't wanted to risk aiming at any other location on Jade. If Brandt had moved her, had so much as jerked her a few inches . . .

*My shot would have killed her.*

Brandt's bones began to pop and crack as he started his shift. The guy thought he'd heal. That he'd attack and get stronger.

*Not happening.*

Az leapt forward. He pressed the gun right against Brandt's heart. "I'm not losing her, and I'm not fucking losing my sanity either."

Brandt grabbed for the gun. Az had seen this scene before, too. Only he hadn't been struggling with Brandt. He'd been battling Sam.

*Change fate.* He would do it.

Another bullet exploded from the gun. Brandt's eyes widened, and he stumbled back. This time, he hit the ground.

Brandt's claws retracted. His fangs turned back into a man's teeth. And his blood thickened on the earth.

"Jade?" Brandt whispered her name. "I'm . . . I'm sorry . . ." He broke off, gasping, and stared up at the sky.

Smoke rose from his chest. The brimstone bullets were burning him, from the inside out.

"Wanted . . . different . . ." Az could barely hear Brandt's words now. He felt a touch on his arm and found Jade standing beside him. She stared down at Brandt, her body stiff, but her lips trembling.

"Guess . . ." Brandt's breath wheezed out. "Can't change . . ."

Sometimes, you could.

Brandt stilled.

Az didn't move. What if this were just another vision? What if Mateo was jerking him around?

*Be real.* Because he didn't want to live in a world without her. That truly would be hell.

Jade wrapped her left arm around him. "It's over." Her breath blew lightly on his neck. Her scent—sweet strawberries—filled his nose. She was warm against him. Soft, silken, *alive.*

He pulled her close. Held her as tight as he could. He'd been given something special tonight. A second chance he would have gladly traded his soul for.

Over her shoulder, he saw Sam walk out from behind a crypt. His brother stared down at Brandt's unmoving body, then he waved his hand. Flames engulfed Brandt, a white-hot fire that would destroy all traces of the shifter.

Brandt wouldn't be able to withstand the fire now—he was already gone. Only the empty shell of his body remained. He wouldn't hurt anyone.

Not ever again.

Az pressed a kiss to Jade's temple.

"I told him you could handle things," Sam said with a nod. "I knew Mateo was just being a paranoid asshole." His brother sauntered past the fire.

*His brother.*

"Ouch," Jade said as she pulled back a bit. His fingers had accidentally brushed her wounded shoulder. "You need to ease up a bit there, Fallen." She offered him a half-smile that made his heart ache. The smile lit her eyes and made her dimple wink. "I'm wounded."

He brushed back a lock of her dark hair. "I'm sorry."

She pushed her hand over the wound. "Hey, I'm the one who told you to shoot. We had to take him out. Who knows what would have happened if—"

Az kissed her. Not a hot, wild kiss, though he knew that would come later. It had to. No, this kiss was soft. As gentle as he could be. He kissed her with tenderness and with love.

Because he knew *exactly* what would have happened.

He'd be seeing those images for years to come. Every time he closed his eyes, he'd see her die in his nightmares.

And he'd see his own destruction.

*We can change.*

Slowly, his lips left hers. She tasted sweet. Fresh. Like life. Paradise.

Her lashes slowly lifted. "You saved me."

Az shook his head. That hadn't happened. Not at all. "Wrong, sweetheart. You were the one who saved me." She'd stopped him from losing everything.

She was the bravest woman he knew. The one who'd reached right into his dark soul and made him need, made him want.

More than just death.

More than heaven.

Jade was everything.

The fire had died away. Faint ashes drifted up toward the sky.

Carefully, he inspected her shoulder. The brimstone bullet had gone right through her. "I want to get you to a doctor."

Bones began to crunch behind him. He turned, keeping his hold on Jade—Az didn't think he'd be able to let her go anytime soon—and saw Tanner fighting to shift on the ground. Fur rippled across his skin. His face elongated. His eyes widened. His legs shortened, reshaped, and the hands that grabbed at the earth became claws.

It was a slow shift, and one of the most savage that Az had ever seen. But shifts were meant to be savage, and powerful. After a time, Tanner's human body was gone. In its place stood a trembling, black panther. The panther parted its jaws to roar, but fell to the ground. The beast's form melted away until only the man remained.

Tanner hadn't held the shift long, but it appeared the brief shift had done the trick for him. His wounds were closing.

They'd all survive. All live to face another day.

"I'll take care of the cat," Sam said as he stalked toward Tanner. "You hold tight to your lady."

He already was. Az lifted Jade into his arms. Her head fell against his shoulder and her light scent drifted around him.

He swallowed.

"We need to get out of here"—Sam continued as he bent over Tanner—"before the humans come to find out why fire has been lighting this place up."

With Brandt's body gone, only the ash and scorched earth remained to mark his passing. The nearby tombs had been smashed, and rubble littered the area.

When the humans arrived, Az knew they'd invent some explanation for what had happened this night. They always did. Leave it to the humans to be the ones who actually covered their tracks.

This cemetery already had a reputation. When the mortals discovered the wreckage, they'd blame it on the ghosts that were said to slip from these graves. Or perhaps the scorched earth had come from a voodoo ritual gone wrong. Either way, no one would ever think of angels.

They never did.

Yes, the humans would tell stories to explain this night away. And more tourists would come to see the destruction left in his wake.

Sam slung Tanner over his shoulder. Tanner growled and Sam just laughed. "Yeah, you can thank me later," he said.

Az strode from the rubble. He passed an old, faded statue of an angel. She was looking down at the graves. Sorrow was etched onto her face.

Angels weren't supposed to feel sorrow.

But they did. They could even regret the loss of a killer's life.

*Can't . . . change.*

Things could have been different for Brandt.

*Things will be different for me.*

He heard voices then. Excited, high-pitched voices that he knew belonged to humans. The other shifters had long since run away. If they wanted to keep living, they'd keep running.

His gaze met Sam's, and he nodded. Together, they lunged straight up and over the high stone wall that surrounded the cemetery. When Az's feet touched down, his knees didn't buckle. Sam landed beside him a bare second later.

Then they rushed forward together, moving fast into the night. Human eyes couldn't track them any longer.

And only ash was left in their wake.

From his perch atop his family's crypt, Mateo watched Azrael and Sam vanish into the darkness.

The Fallen had done it. Stopped the promised prophecy of destruction. Saved the damsel. Let the world live to face another day.

Mateo glanced down at the gun he held in his hand. He opened the chamber, and two bullets fell into his palm. Brimstone bullets. He'd made them at his apartment, made them when Azrael had been too distracted by Jade to notice his movements.

If necessary, he'd planned to use those bullets. He and Sam were . . . friends, of a sort, but if Sam had gotten between him and Azrael, one of those bullets would have been for him.

The other would have been sent right into Azrael's heart.

Mateo knew too much of hell. He didn't want it slipping into this realm. He wanted the humans—and even the so-called monsters who dwelled on this earth—to keep living as they were.

Hell didn't belong here.

Azrael had possessed enough darkness in his heart that he could have bridged the gap between the worlds. A dangerous foe. A dangerous ally.

But Azrael had fought the darkness. For a human. The vision of what *could* have been—that vision had been enough to strike fear into the Fallen's heart. Az had changed fate, because he hadn't been willing to let his human die.

Humans.

Most *Other* thought humans were weak. Prey. Little more than food . . . or toys to play with when boredom struck.

They were wrong. Humans were the strongest beings to walk this earth.

After all, they were the ones who could break angels, and one human woman—*just one*—had brought a Fallen to his knees.

He tucked the bullets into his pockets. He would keep them close, because Azrael and Sam weren't the only Fallen with darkness in them. So many more . . .

Angels were falling more often these days. Giving in to temptation.

Was a war really coming? He didn't know, but, just in case, he'd be ready.

And he'd make sure hell kept waiting.

Dawn came. The faint light slipped through the blinds and spilled onto Jade's bed. She stretched slowly but then her body stiffened as she realized—

*I'm in my bed.*

She really was back in her own bed. She didn't have to be scared anymore. Didn't have to keep running. Keep glancing over her shoulder.

It was over.

Jade looked down at her shoulder. Only a thin, red line remained to show where she'd been shot. The bullet had burned like fire—maybe it had been—but her shoulder didn't even ache now.

Her head turned to the right. Az lay beside her. He was fully clothed while she was naked. She was under the covers. He was on top.

She frowned at that. Hardly acceptable behavior.

Jade pushed up to better see him. His lashes cast deep shadows beneath his eyes. She could actually see his eyes moving behind his closed lids. Moving quickly.

What was her Fallen dreaming about?

A smile lifted her mouth as she leaned toward him. She'd kiss him and find out—

"*No!*" The snarl burst from him and froze her. "*Jade, no!*" His hands fisted in the bedcovers and deep lines suddenly bracketed his mouth. "Don't leave me . . ." A lost whisper.

Oh, no. This wouldn't do. Jade put her hands on either side of his face. "Az, wake up."

He tried to pull away from her.

"Az, it's okay." She raised her voice even as she leaned closer to him. "I'm right here." Her lips feathered over his. "Everything's okay."

He gasped beneath her mouth, and in the next instant, his hands were curling tight around her. His tongue pushed inside her mouth, and he kissed her with a wild desperation that made her heart race in her chest.

Her legs straddled his hips, and there was no missing the growing arousal pressing against her.

When her head lifted from his, her breath was ragged and her sex was wet. "Bad . . . ah . . . bad dream?" Jade managed to ask in a voice gone husky with need.

His eyes glittered at her. "The worst thing I can imagine."

Her right hand slid down his chest and pressed over his heart. "Want me to help you forget it?"

"I won't ever forget it."

She frowned at him. "Az?"

His gaze searched hers. "Did you mean it?"

Her knees tightened around him. "Um . . . I'm not sure that I'm following you."

"You said you loved me. Back at Sunrise. I heard you."

Right. That. She straightened her shoulders. Hard to look

dignified when you were sitting astride an angel. "You said you loved me, too." Maybe it had been the adrenaline talking. They'd been in a life-or-death situation. Maybe . . .

*Please love me.* Her lips pressed together so that she wouldn't let the words escape.

"I did." His voice was deep, rumbling.

"And did you mean it?" Wait. Why was she trying to push this back on him? *Pull up those big girl panties.* "No, just . . ." She exhaled. "Yes. I meant what I said. I love you, Az." She'd told two men that she loved them in her life.

One had burned and was probably in hell.

As for the other—she wanted Az to stay with her. Forever.

"Can you have a life with me?" She didn't know how this worked. Hadn't ever even thought this far ahead. She'd tumbled fast and hard for him, and now he was all that she could see when she imagined her future.

But an angel . . . and her?

"I can't have a life without you." His quiet words seemed to sink right into her heart. "You are what makes me whole in this world." His fingers curled around her hips. "When I'm with you, I want to be more than a monster that others fear."

"You aren't a monster." She'd kick the ass of anyone who said so. "You're strong. Brave."

But sadness had slipped over his face. "One day," he said quietly, "I'll prove I'm good enough for you."

No, he didn't understand. "You don't have to prove a thing to me." She loved him just as he was.

The sadness didn't leave his eyes. She didn't want him to look that way. It was time for him to be happy. The guy deserved some happiness.

"Do you love me, Az?" Jade asked him.

"I didn't know what love was until I found you."

Oh. Okay. That was—great. Jade blinked quickly because her eyes had just gotten all misty on her.

"It ripped into me," he said as he stared deeply into her misty eyes. "Tore me apart on the inside."

Um, not sounding so great. Her brows lifted.

"It destroyed who I was." Az's face was solemn.

Again . . . what he was saying definitely fell into the *not so great* category.

"And I'm glad," he said, voice rough. "Because I don't want to be *him* anymore. I want to be someone who can love. Who can be happy. With you."

Now that was what she wanted to hear.

"I'll give you everything that I have." His promise.

She smiled at him. "I know."

"And I will love you long past this life."

He was seriously going to make those tears start. Ah, hell. Who was she kidding? They'd already started. She was past the misting stage.

Leaning forward, Jade pressed her lips to his. This kiss wasn't as desperate as the one before, but the need still flowed between them. She could taste the salt of her own tears in the kiss.

As she kissed him, her fingers slid down between their bodies. She found the bottom of his shirt and yanked it up. Their mouths parted only long enough for her to toss the shirt to the floor.

"I love you," he whispered before their lips met again.

*I love you.*

Her hand pressed over the thick bulge of his erection. He'd always made her want, far more than any other man.

But then, he wasn't just a man.

She unsnapped his jeans and lowered the zipper. His cock sprang forward. Heavy and full, right into her hands.

One day, she'd love to have his child. A child with his bright eyes and slow smile.

But maybe his smile wouldn't always be so slow. Perhaps one day, happiness would come easily to him. And to her.

One day.

She didn't want long foreplay then. Didn't want anything but his mouth on hers, kissing her so softly but deeply, and his cock filling her body.

Az positioned his shaft at the entrance to her body. She was more than ready for him.

With one smooth thrust, he slid deep into her sex. She gasped into his mouth because the fullness felt so good. Everything with him felt good.

Right.

She rose slowly and stared down at him. His cock stretched her inside—a wicked good pressure—as he grew even bigger. She tightened her inner muscles around him. Held even tighter.

The nightmares were over for them.

Life was finally beginning.

His fingers closed around her hips, and he lifted her up. The length of his flesh stroked right along her clit, and she smiled at the surge of pleasure.

Then she pushed down on him, and he filled her even better than before.

She didn't look away as she rose and fell on him. His eyes burned up at her, but he didn't take control of the pleasure.

Neither did she.

This time, they were equal. Giving. Taking.

Her breath panted faster as her heart thundered in her chest. His pupils widened, seeming to make his eyes go pitch black.

*More.*

Her knees pushed into the bed. He picked up the tempo with her as his hips plunged harder.

Jade's fingers stroked over his chest. Found his tight nipples and stroked them. His cock jerked within her in eager response.

The need built. The tension tightened. The pleasure waited just out of her reach.

She leaned toward him and her hair slipped over his skin. Jade had to kiss him. Had to feel his lips on hers when the pleasure swept over them both.

Her lips touched his. His tongue slid into her mouth, skimming right over her lower lip.

Then he was rising up, holding her tight, even as he kept his lips on hers and his cock in her. He sat on the bed, his legs balancing her so that they faced each other.

The position drove his cock even deeper into her. *I like that—like it a whole lot.*

Her hands curled around his shoulders, and she kept kissing him. Rising, falling, taking him inside as far as he could go.

Jade's fingers slid along his back. Traced the heavy scars that had made him into the being that he was. Az shuddered beneath her touch, and his thrusts became rougher.

She'd told him before that she wouldn't break.

Jade stroked him again. Again and again and knew that later, she'd kiss those scars on his back. But for now . . .

The climax slammed into her. It blinded her with a wave of pleasure so intense that her heart seemed to stop.

And Az was with her. As he came inside her, Az held her even tighter.

Her lips lifted from his, and she stared just over his shoulder at the shadow of his wings. Wings that she couldn't touch, not really, but wings that marked him as what he was.

Fallen.

An angel cast out.

An angel that she loved.

The pleasure slid away so slowly. She shivered as her sex contracted in a little aftershock around him.

There were more questions that she needed to ask. More

truths that she wasn't sure if she really wanted to hear. But for now, she had him.

He loved her.

And that was all she needed.

They went to Sunrise that night. The club was closed. Marked off with yellow police tape. No thick line of eager humans waited to slip inside and dance with danger.

Az figured they'd be back. Sooner or later, they always came back.

He and Jade eased under the tape. A hard shove of his hand had the club's front door opening. The inside of Sunrise was hollowed out and blackened from the fire. He stared at the floor, remembering what it was like to be trapped while Jade was dragged away.

*Never again.*

His fingers intertwined with hers.

"Well, well . . ." Sam's voice boomed as he strode down the hall. "Here to help me torch the rest of this place?"

Sam's Seline was by his side, but her face didn't have the same mask of unconcern that Sam wore. No, when she looked at Sam, there was worry in her eyes.

Az shook his head. "We're here to help you rebuild."

Sam blinked. "You? You're into destruction and death, not into putting some two-bit bar back together."

But the bar mattered to Sam. He could see it.

"It's time to move on," Sam said with a shrug. "More places to see in this world. More things to—"

"This is home." Their new home. "And we can rebuild." He offered his brother a smile and both Sam and Seline stared at him in shock.

"Uh, Az, did that hybrid shifter hit you on the head?" Seline wanted to know.

Jade laughed lightly at that. He loved her laugh. To him, that was the sound of pure—

*Happiness.*

"I realize that I owe you a debt," Az said, "and I'm here to start repaying." Because he *would* be the man that Jade deserved. She said that she loved him as he was. Well, she'd love him more once he atoned. Once the darkness was gone from his soul.

He'd make her happy every day of her life, and he'd see to it that she never feared again.

He blinked and found Sam in front of him. "What's happening here?" Sam demanded as he studied Az with eyes that seemed to see too much. "What did I miss in that cemetery?"

Some stories weren't meant to be told. Az offered him a faint smile. "Everyone always said we'd kill each other one day."

Sam wasn't smiling back. "No, they said if we did, the end of the world would come."

Jade sucked in a sharp breath at that hard truth.

Seline strode toward them. *"Sam . . ."* A warning note entered her voice.

Finally, Sam's lips twisted into his usual hard grin. "But I don't see the end of the world."

*Hopefully, you won't ever.* "Fate can change."

Now his brother stepped back in surprise. That too-sharp gaze of his widened.

"It can change," Az said again, and that was all that his brother needed to know.

Slowly, Sam inclined his head.

"Now why don't we get started cleaning up this place?" Jade asked, and Az saw her nose wrinkle. "Because, no offense, but it really smells like piss in here."

Piss. Ash. Hell. Whatever.

Seline laughed a bit as she agreed with Jade. She came closer, and Jade lifted her eyes to the ceiling as she said, "While we're doing the cleaning, tell me we get to ditch that cage . . ."

The cage, though blackened with soot, still swung from the ceiling.

Seline looped her arm with Jade's. "Oh, no," she told her as they walked away. "I'm rather fond of it." She glanced back and winked at Sam.

Sam's face softened as he gazed after her. But when he turned back to Az, tension spread lines near his mouth and eyes. "Fate . . ." He sighed. "You should know better than to think that it can be totally changed." His voice was pitched low so that the women wouldn't overhear his words.

Yet fate *had* changed.

"Jade was meant to die last night." Sam jerked a hand through his hair. "How long do you think you're going to be able to keep her by your side?"

Forever. Az's stare darted to the left. Found Jade. "I told you, fate changed." He paused and turned his focus back to Sam. "*I* changed."

Sam studied him in silence. What was he seeing? The shell Az had been before? Or the man he was becoming?

Then his brother nodded and offered his hand.

Az stared at Sam's extended palm. He'd been the one who sat in judgment when Sam had been banished from heaven. He'd watched as his brother fell, and he'd fought not to show any emotion.

"You were always stronger than me," Az confessed.

Sam frowned. His hand began to lower.

Az didn't take the hand. He grabbed his brother and held tight. The brother he'd lost centuries ago. The brother he'd found again. "I'm sorry."

He should have fought for Sam that long-ago day. He'd make damn sure he always fought for him now.

The wall he'd kept around his heart was gone. Battered away by Jade. Now he felt—so much.

But Sam had frozen against him. Az stepped back. Stared

right into eyes so like his own. Sam had been his only family. The one closest to him, until that bitter day that had burned a divide between them. Burned as surely as Sammael's wings had burned away.

"You were the better angel," Sam said slowly, softly. "I could never follow the rules."

No, he hadn't followed those rules. And nearly a whole army had been killed by his fury.

But . . .

"Some of those rules are shit," Az admitted.

Sam laughed, a sputter of surprise, and so did Az. He laughed and felt . . . free.

Strange. An angel without wings had finally found his happiness, and it was with a family standing in a burned-out club on one of the wildest streets in New Orleans.

Jade glanced over at him. He couldn't miss the love in her eyes.

He realized then just how lucky he was. Once, Sam had told him that angels weren't always pushed out of heaven because they'd done something wrong. Sometimes, they lost heaven as a reward.

Because they were offered something . . . more.

He saw that *more* in Jade's eyes.

*Thank you.* He sent the silent thought out and knew that it would be heard by the one that mattered.

All he'd needed to do was experience a little fall in order to find his paradise.

As the last streaks of darkness slid from the sky, Az walked out onto Jade's balcony. The sun would be up soon. He could already see the faint streaks of red—like blood—sliding across the horizon.

He stared at the darkness and quietly called, "Bastion."

Az knew the angel would come. He'd caught Bastion's scent several times that night.

A rustle of wings, then Bastion appeared beside him. The angel was frowning. Ah . . . Bastion had better be careful. He was showing more and more emotions lately.

Soon he might find himself walking with humans.

"I have an offer for you," Bastion said with a dramatic air.

At that, Az lifted a brow. Maybe it was too late already. The guy almost *sounded* human.

Az glanced toward the open balcony door. The white curtains billowed in the breeze. "What kind of offer?"

"You can come back."

His hands tightened around the railing. "Says who?"

"The angels in charge."

But they weren't really in charge.

"I've earned redemption?" Az knew he sounded doubtful. "How?"

"You . . . ah . . . haven't earned redemption."

He frowned. *Right, thought so.*

"But some think you might be perfect for a new position that is becoming available." Bastion paused and cleared his throat. "The punishment angels need a leader. After the way you dispatched Brandt—a being tainted by evil who possessed our own powers—you seem the first choice for the job."

Az didn't speak.

"You'll get your wings back. Your full powers. You'll even have an army of angels at your beck and call again."

His gaze returned to that open balcony door. "What happens to Jade?" Az asked quietly.

"Ah . . . well . . ." Bastion exhaled. "Nothing."

Az looked at him and waited for more.

"She's off the books. Your Jade isn't slated to meet her end for a *very* long time." Bastion shrugged. "Seems someone gave her a direct dose of angel blood," his lips curved lightly, "so she has a very *un*-human-like life expectancy now."

The tightness in Az's chest eased.

"You can come home tonight. Ditch this world and be free again."

He had his freedom.

"I only wish Marna could come, too." Bastion's gaze turned toward the empty street below them. "But she is lost."

Perhaps.

Perhaps not.

Bastion's wings stretched behind him. "Let's leave so that we can—"

"No."

Bastion's wings froze. "Uh, I'm offering you a chance to return through the gates. For power, for—"

"I'm not leaving." He wasn't even tempted.

He could see Bastion struggling to understand. "For . . . her?"

Az nodded and stared silently back at the angel.

"You'd trade all that heaven can give, for a human?" Bastion seemed both shocked and horrified.

Az still didn't speak. What was there to say? Heaven had given him his human. He needed nothing more.

A muscle flexed along Bastion's jaw. "Fine. But know that the offer won't be made again. You'll be chained here, forever."

Promises, promises.

Bastion turned away.

"You should be careful," Az had to tell him. He felt it was only right to offer the warning. After all, he'd almost killed the guy. Amends had to be made some way.

Bastion hesitated and spared him a fuming glance.

*Ah, there it was again.* "When you let the emotions get to you too much, the lure of the earth will become too strong."

"I *won't* fall."

How many angels had said that? *He'd* said that. "We all have temptations."

"I know my duty. I won't—"

"You're already weakened, and you don't even realize it." How could the angel be so blind? *He's blind, just like I was.* "The rage got to me first," Az admitted. "The fury about things I couldn't control."

Like Sam falling.

Innocents dying.

The guilty sliding away from the punishment angels.

Fury had been his weakness. It was also Bastion's. "You're enraged over Marna. That rage is burning in your gut right now."

"You know *nothing!*" Bastion snapped at him.

"I know the sound of emotions when I hear them." He'd warned the angel. The rest would be up to Bastion. "Be careful."

"I don't need care. I don't need—"

"I once told Sam that it was the fire that would make him scream the loudest when he fell." The fire that burned away an angel's wings and stole so much of his magic.

Fear flickered in Bastion's eyes. He rose into the air. "I won't fall." His wings carried him higher. "I *won't.*"

He was already on the path to a fall. The angel just didn't realize it yet.

"Watch out for the burn," Az whispered. Because he could see it coming. "It'll make you scream."

The angel vanished.

Az didn't leave his post on the balcony. He waited for Jade to come and join him. He'd known she was there all along. No way to miss that sweet scent.

The curtains rustled once more.

"You . . . you can call him back." Jade's voice was hushed.

"Why would I do that?"

"So *you* can get home." She came toward him with the softest whisper of sound as her bare feet slid across the balcony. "So you can get your wings back. So you can—"

He turned and caught her hands. "Spend the rest of my life missing you?"

Her gaze searched his.

"No. I'm where I want to be." Jazz music drifted up the street. "Where I'm *meant* to be." With her.

The world wasn't a safe place. It was brutal and hard and filled with evil . . . and good.

Angels weren't just needed in heaven. They needed to be here. Protecting the ones that they loved. Fighting to hold a balance between good and evil on earth.

"I'm glad to hear that," Jade said and her full lips tilted into a smile, a smile that was echoed in her eyes. "Because following your butt into heaven wouldn't have been easy."

His own eyes widened. Would she have truly—

*Yes.* He could see the answer in her gaze. Jade would have gone with him anywhere.

Fair enough. He would gladly follow her even through the gates of hell.

"Now I can stop worrying about trying to grow my own wings," she teased as her arms wrapped around him. "That was not going to be an easy job, let me tell you . . ."

The sun was rising. The darkness gone at last.

"You don't need wings." Az pulled her closer.

"Damn right I don't." She licked her lips and rose onto her toes. "And neither do you. I want you, I love you, just the way you are."

As he bent his head toward her, Az realized that if he had to do it all over again . . .

He'd fall, in an instant.

Just to be with her.

Some things in this world were worth dying for, but there were far more—*far more*—things that were actually worth living for.

He'd always live for Jade.

He kissed her and knew that he was home.

Did you miss the first two books in Cynthia's FALLEN series?

*Angel of Darkness*

*He Fell for Her*

Nicole St. James was a nice woman. An innocent, pretty, twentysomething schoolteacher with her life ahead of her. But as the angel of death, it's Keenan's job to take that life away. So when a vampire attacks Nicole, Keenan is not supposed to snap and take out the vampire instead. It cost him his wings—but she's worth it.

Except when Keenan catches up to his pretty schoolteacher, she's not so innocent anymore. Hot red lipstick, tight black shorts, and long white fangs—she's ready to kick the asses of anyone who helped turn her into a damn bloodsucker. Unless that ass is unusually shapely and attached to a certain fallen angel. Even with all of heaven and half of hell after them, someone will have to teach Keenan about the fun kinds of sin. . . .

*Angel Betrayed*

## A Little Bit of Angel Lust

Sammael—call him Sam—was an angel once. An angel of Death. But the dispassionate, watch-from-above thing just wasn't working for him when it meant watching evil torture innocent souls day in and day out. It might have cost him his wings, but these days he gets to apply the direct method on the bad guys. Problem is, what's making his life difficult is a bad girl.

Seline O'Shaw needs protection, and with the hounds of hell on her tail, she's not going to quibble too hard about where she gets it. Sam's virtue is questionable, but he's smoking hot, massively powerful, and owes her a favor. So what if she's getting a little case of angel lust? There are some damn deadly sins after her hide. . . .